PRAISE FOR HEIDI MCLAUGHLIN

Before I'm Gone

"*Before I'm Gone* is a heartbreakingly beautiful love story about finding your soulmate against all odds."

—*USA Today* bestselling author Ashley Cade

"A heartbreakingly beautiful story about love, friendship, perseverance, and learning to live life to the fullest."

—Samantha Baca, author of *Just in Time*

"This book is absolutely gut wrenching and broke my heart into a million pieces, but the story hit me in such a beautiful way."

—Vanessa Valencia, Goodreads

"Beautiful and emotional—I cried buckets."

—*AC Book Blog*

"I am not okay. And that's okay. Damn, this book wrecked me with all the feels. Such a cathartic cry I hadn't realized I needed."

—Courtney, Goodreads

Cape Harbor

"I love a good second-chance romance, and Heidi McLaughlin did NOT disappoint."

—*New York Times* bestselling author L. P. Dover

"This is a story that will stay

odreads

"A beautifully written story that will pull you in and tug at your heartstrings."

—Nikki, *Crazy Cajun Book Addicts*

"The reader will instantly fall in love with Cape Harbor."

—Nicki, *The Overflowing Bookcase*

"McLaughlin knows how to put a person in touch with their emotions."

—Isha Coleman, Hopeless Romantic

The Beaumont Series

"If you want to read a book that is all heart—full of characters you will instantly connect with and love from the first page to the last—then *Forever My Girl* is the book for you."

—Jenny, *Totally Booked Blog*

"*Forever My Girl* is a sweet, loving, all-around adorable read. If you, like me, have a thing for musicians and reconnections, then this read is for you."

—*Jacqueline's Reads*

"This is an utterly moving story of second chances in life, of redemption, remorse, forgiveness, of loves lost and found again, of trust regained. Through alternating points of view, we feel both Liam's and Josie's emotions, fears, and sorrow. These are well-developed characters whose love for each other survives time and distance."

—*Natasha Is a Book Junkie*, on *Forever My Girl*

"*My Unexpected Forever* completely outdid my expectations and blew *Forever My Girl* out of the water. *My Unexpected Forever* is without a doubt a book that I would recommend, and Harrison is officially my new book boyfriend!"

—Holly's Hot Reads

The Beaumont Series: Next Generation

"Heidi McLaughlin delivers a breathtaking addition to the Beaumont series. *Holding Onto Forever* is everything you want it to be and so much more. I fell in love all over again."

—*USA Today* bestselling author K. L. Grayson

"A roller coaster of emotions. McLaughlin takes you on a journey of two hearts that are destined to be together."

—*New York Times* bestselling author Kaylee Ryan

"Heidi McLaughlin delivers yet another heartfelt, emotional, engaging read! I loved every second of *Fighting for Our Forever*! You will too!"

—*USA Today* bestselling author M. Never

The Archer Brothers

"I *loved* everything about this book. It is an emotional story that will have you begging for more. Even after I finished reading, I can't stop thinking about it. A *must* read!"

—Jamie Rae, author of *Call Sign Karma*

"McLaughlin will have you frantically turning pages and make your heart beat faster because each page has something more surprising than the one before it. You'll be dying to see what happens next!"

—*New York Times* bestselling author Jay Crownover

"I needed this book. I didn't even realize how much until I read it!"

—*USA Today* bestselling author Adriana Locke

The Boys of Summer

"Heidi McLaughlin has done it again! Sexy, sweet, and full of heart, *Third Base* is a winner!"

—Melissa Brown, author of *Wife Number Seven*

"*Third Base* hits the reading sweet spot. A must read for any baseball and romance fans."

—Carey Heywood, author of *Him*

"*Third Base* is sexy and witty and pulls you in from the first page. You'll get lost in Ethan and Daisy and never want their story to end."

—S. Moose, author of *Offbeat*

"McLaughlin knocks it out of the park with her second sports contemporary . . . This novel goes above and beyond the typical sports romance with a hot, complex hero and a gutsy, multidimensional heroine. McLaughlin keeps the pace lively throughout, and just when readers think they have the finale figured out, she throws them a few curveballs. This novel will appeal to McLaughlin's fans and will win her many more."

—*Publishers Weekly* (starred review), on *Home Run*

"Heidi McLaughlin never fails to pull me in with her storytelling, and I assure you she'll do the same to you! *Home Run* is a home run, in my book."

—*New York Times* bestselling author Jen McLaughlin

"Top Pick! Four and a half stars! McLaughlin has hit the mark with her third Boys of Summer novel. There's more than one great storyline to capture the imagination."

—RT Book Reviews

Heartbreak Hill

Other Titles by Heidi McLaughlin

THE BEAUMONT SERIES

Forever My Girl

My Everything

My Unexpected Forever

Finding My Forever

Finding My Way

12 Days of Forever

My Kind of Forever

Forever Our Boys

Forever Mason

The Beaumont boxed set #1

THE BEAUMONT SERIES: NEXT GENERATION

Holding Onto Forever

My Unexpected Love

Chasing My Forever

Peyton & Noah

Fighting for Our Forever

A Beaumont Family Christmas

Give Me Forever

Everything for Love

The Beginning of Forever

THE PORTLAND PIONEERS: A BEAUMONT SERIES NEXT-GENERATION SPIN-OFF

Fourth Down

Fair Catch

False Start

THE SEAPORT SERIES

The Lobster Trap

The Love in Sunsets

CAPE HARBOR SERIES

After All

Until Then

THE ARCHER BROTHERS

Here with Me

Choose Me

Save Me

Here with Us

Choose Us

The Archer Brothers boxed set

NASHVILLE NIGHTS

Sangria

LOST IN YOU SERIES

Lost in You

Lost in Us

THE BOYS OF SUMMER

Third Base

Home Run

Grand Slam

Hawk

NORTHPORT U SERIES

Line Change

THE REALITY DUET

Blind Reality

Twisted Reality

SOCIETY X

Dark Room

Viewing Room

Play Room

THE CLUTCH SERIES

Roman

STAND-ALONE NOVELS

Before I'm Gone

Stripped Bare

Blow

Sexcation

HOLIDAY NOVELS

Santa's Secret

It's a Wonderful Holiday

Stranded with the One

Love in Print

THE DATING SERIES

A Date for Midnight

A Date with an Admirer

A Date for Good Luck

A Date for the Hunt

A Date for the Derby

A Date to Play Fore

A Date with a Foodie

A Date for the Fair

A Date for the Regatta

A Date for the Masquerade

A Date with a Turkey

A Date with an Elf

Heartbreak Hill

a Novel

HEIDI MCLAUGHLIN

This is a work of fiction. Names, characters, organizations, places, events, and incidents are either products of the author's imagination or are used fictitiously. Otherwise, any resemblance to actual persons, living or dead, is purely coincidental.

Published by Montlake, Seattle

www.apub.com

ISBN-13: 9781662521430 (paperback)
ISBN-13: 9781662521423 (digital)

Cover design by Caroline Teagle Johnson
Cover image: © Magdalena Wasicek / ArcAngel; © Katsumi Murouchi / Getty

Printed in the United States of America

To my supportive, loving husb . . . Bubby Dog

ONE

GRAYSON

At six foot six, Grayson Caballero likened himself to a basketball god, as if the world needed another Michael Jordan, LeBron James, or Larry Bird.

The only problem was, he wasn't nearly as good as his favorite players, hadn't been allowed to play in college, and had no aspirations of trying out for the G League, or the "baby NBA," as all his friends called it. However, he was a powerhouse in the local recreation league that met every Sunday during the winter.

Before every season, other team managers would reach out to him, begging him to be on their team. Teams hated playing against him. He could post up, slam the ball down, and drain the three-point shot from anywhere just past the half-court line. Everyone wanted him on their team because they'd win if he played for them, and no one could really guard him. Although Grayson let them until he'd "turned it on," so to speak.

Grayson watched as the play developed. He flashed across the key, keeping his hands high for a pass. When it didn't come, he dropped down the block and posted up. Finally, someone passed to him. He palmed the leather basketball and held it out of reach from his opponent—who jumped, swatted, and tried to climb Grayson to get to it.

"Get off." Grayson gave the man behind him a little push and laughed at the *umph* sound he made.

"Foul!" the man from the other team yelled as he fell to the ground. Grayson used this to his advantage and spun to the hoop, jumped, and slammed it through the rim. Unfortunately for the guy on the ground, the ball landed in the spot no man ever wants to get hit.

He rolled over and groaned. Grayson laughed. He didn't have sympathy for his opponent, mostly because the men in the league liked to play dirty, and besides, Grayson had caught the man talking to Reid.

Reid Sullivan. The love of Grayson's life.

"You pinched me," Grayson pointed out as he bent to pick up the ball, keeping his eyes on Reid. He stood there with the ball on his hip, watching the woman he was deeply in love with as she smiled and chatted animatedly with some guy Grayson hadn't seen before.

"Ball!" someone yelled from behind Grayson. He flicked the ball off in the direction of the other team and then headed down the court to play defense. It didn't matter what team he was on; they always played a zone defense, with Grayson in the middle. This setup forced the other teams to shoot from outside, unless they had someone who could match up with Grayson's height.

When the horn sounded for halftime, Grayson looked up at the scoreboard. They were up by twenty. Not nearly the cushion he wanted. They had another twenty minutes to increase their lead.

Grayson made his way to the wooden bleachers, where Reid sat, watching him play. When he wasn't in the game, she'd read on her tablet. She didn't have a real interest in basketball. Every weekend he asked her to come with him, and every weekend she said yes.

She smiled as he approached. To him, she was "Sully," because in his mind that kept her in the friend zone, where he needed her to stay. It was safer for them this way, especially for her.

They'd met at work, during their first day of orientation at the Wold Collective, where he was a project manager specializing in custom boardroom tables, and she was in Human Resources. They'd hit it off, their palpable attraction to each other soon increasing tenfold with the amount of time they spent together. They became fast friends. Best friends, even. They told each other everything and could finish each other's sentences. They spent countless hours together, which had only worsened Grayson's attraction to her.

Then one night, everything changed.

Grayson didn't regret spending the night with her. He knew she was the one for him and bemoaned not being able to give her the life she wanted from him. He'd told her the best he could offer her was best friend status. A friendship with all the benefits, minus the romantic entanglements of broken hearts and feelings he wouldn't be able to show her.

It wasn't that he didn't like her. He did, more than he'd ever admit to her, or anyone, for that matter. It was that he couldn't.

Sully reached into her weekend bag and pulled out a bottle of water for him. While she reached for it, he tugged the ends of her auburn hair, winked, and sat down one row in front of her, stretched his legs, and leaned against the bench behind her.

"Thanks, Sully."

This was one of the times he hated being so tall. Had he sat next to her, he'd have to slouch to see her. Sitting like this, all he had to do was tilt his head, and he could see her clearly.

She looked down at him and smiled.

"Don't mention it."

He would. Repeatedly. It was the only way he could show or tell her how much he appreciated her.

Before twisting the cap off and chugging the water down, he caught her gaze for a moment longer than he should. Her eyes were a warm brown, two shades lighter than his. If he wasn't careful, he'd find himself staring into them. Staring could easily lead to leaning, which could lead to kissing.

Nope.

There wasn't anything he didn't like or even love about Sully. She was compassionate, patient, and fiercely loyal to her friends and family. Even after he'd tried to distance himself from her, she'd remained a steadfast presence in his life.

He absolutely despised any man she talked to, hence the dude he'd elbowed before the half, and he felt murderous rage whenever she went on a date. None of them were ever good enough for her, in his opinion, and his opinion was the only one that mattered. She took his word, valued his opinion, and shared her deepest, darkest secrets with him, despite him hating her stories about the men she dated. At her request, he'd done the same—most of it lies so she wouldn't think something was up. Sure, he'd gone on some dates, but those were set-ups by his best friend, Pearce Carey, who was also his coworker and the male counterpart to Reid in Grayson's life, and who also had no idea how he felt about her.

"What's his name?" Grayson nodded toward the other team's bench, but not specifically at the guy who'd taken one to the groin after Grayson had slammed the ball down.

"Dunno," Sully said as she handed Grayson a peeled orange.

"I saw you talking to him."

"No," she said with a sigh. "You saw him talking to me. I listened while he went on about how he has a boat and could see me on it."

"Was that his pickup line?"

Sully shrugged. "Seemed to be."

"Well, I'm glad you didn't fall for the cheese," he said.

"Why's that?" Her eyebrows rose in a challenge to him.

He had to think fast. He couldn't very well come clean that he was jealous. "He pinched me." To prove his point, Grayson lifted his shirt. Reid looked and shook her head.

"I don't see anything."

"Are you defending him?" Grayson acted hurt, but he knew she would never take anyone's side but his.

"Nope, just pointing out the obvious."

"Thanks, Captain Sul—"

"Don't say it." If Reid hated the nickname he'd given her, she never said anything. Except when he called her Captain Sully, after the famed airline pilot who'd landed a plane on the Hudson. She hated that reference.

Pearce placed his bag on the bleachers and pulled at his tie. "I'm sorry I'm late."

"Where have you been?" Reid asked.

"Lunch date with Emelia's father."

Grayson's and Reid's eyes widened. "Are you asking her to marry you?" Reid asked before Grayson could.

"Nah, and that's the problem. Her father asked me to lunch to discuss the future. We've been together for a year, we don't live together, and he wants to know what my plans are for his daughter."

"What did you say?" Grayson asked.

"Not much. There wasn't much to say. I stammered my way through some bullshit about how we're happy, in love, and taking things one day at a time."

"Do you think she asked her dad to say something?" Reid asked.

Pearce hung his head. "I don't know. I don't want to think she did, but come on. The invite was unexpected and more of a demand than a 'Hey, let's meet for lunch' thing. And this was the first time he's ever reached out to me. Sure, we've golfed, but Emelia set that up, and we were together." He dropped his pants to the ground, apparently not caring who saw his boxers.

Grayson laughed as Reid rolled her eyes. He nudged her leg and winked at her, only for her to shake her head.

"Give me a slice," she said as she pointed to his orange. He handed her two, knowing she'd ask for more.

"Anyway," Pearce said as he sat down to tie his shoes. "Emelia has been calling and texting since I left the restaurant. I'm afraid to look or listen to what she has to say."

Grayson started humming the wedding march, which caused Pearce to scowl.

"I'm not ready," he said. "Not even thinking about moving in with her. How could she do this to me?" he groaned.

"Good luck," Reid said. Grayson choked, and she patted him on the back.

"Rude," Pearce replied to her.

The horn sounded, signaling that halftime was over. Grayson handed Reid the rest of his orange slices, finished his water, and then went back onto the court. He paused midway and placed his hand over his chest. The twinge was familiar but not something he'd felt for some time. He tried to place the memory; it had been well over ten years, if not longer.

He felt a hand on his shoulder as he closed his eyes, hoping to alleviate the pressure he felt. Grayson took a deep breath, and then another.

"Hey, man, we don't have time for the Pledge—" Pearce stopped and moved to shroud Grayson from onlookers. "Are you okay?"

"Yeah, I'm good." Grayson walked away from Pearce without looking at him. He didn't want or need his pity or his questions. Pearce followed, but Grayson held up his hand. "I said I'm good."

He walked to the middle of the key, spread his arms wide to show everyone his impressive wingspan and to prove to anyone who watched him that he was, in fact, okay, and then rested his hands on his knees. He figured no one would question him if he stood like this. Most athletes do when they're tired. Except he wasn't tired. He was suddenly exhausted. "Let's go!" He clapped his hands loudly, hoping the others took notice.

Throughout the game, he spotted not only the guy from earlier chatting with Reid, but two others as well. The last one sat next to her and took all her attention away from Grayson, which he didn't like. When he should've been focused on the game, he was distracted by what he saw going on in the bleachers.

When the final horn sounded, Grayson looked up at the scoreboard and tried to smile. They had won, but the margin of victory wasn't what he'd come to expect. He changed his shoes, put his sweatpants on, and waited for Reid to join him.

"Who is that?" he asked for a second time today.

"Alaric."

"What kind of name is Alaric?" There was no hiding the sarcastic tone emanating from him.

"The kind his parents gave him. What's your issue?" Reid stopped walking.

Grayson turned to face her, waiting for the others to move on past them. "I don't like men talking to you. Hitting on you."

"Then do something about it," she dared him as she crossed her arms over her chest and smirked.

He shook his head slowly. He knew better than to go down this road with her.

"Look, Grayson . . ." The door behind them opened, and Pearce walked out.

"You guys heading home or to the Green Turtle?"

"Turtle," Grayson said without making eye contact. "We'll meet you there."

Pearce looked at them and nodded. As soon as he exited, Grayson looked down at Reid. He wasn't sure what to say, and he wasn't sure he wanted her to finish her tirade.

"I'm going to start dating," she blurted out. "And I'm not going to listen to you complain about the men I go on these dates with. Someone out there is the right guy for me." Her eyes bore into his.

"The dating pool sucks."

"Yeah, well . . ." She walked past him, paused, and turned around. "If you're not going to date me, then I'm going to go on dates. There are things I want out of life, and one of them is to fall in love, get married, and have a family. You don't want that, at least not with me, so I need to move on and close the door on these feelings I have for you."

Grayson couldn't find the words to tell her she wasn't going on any dates. He shook his head and started to speak, but his words caught in his throat just as his heart seized. He placed his hand over his heart and leaned against the clothing rack for some stability. Grayson gasped.

"Knock it off," Reid seethed. "You don't get to pretend like you're hurt," she told him. "Every day, I wake up wondering if this is going to be the day when you start dating someone else or when you finally tell me that you're in love with me, which I know you are, but you're too chicken to say the words to me."

Grayson's eyes watered as he gasped for air. "Help."

"Help, what? Help you with your broken heart? No, I won't. You can't do this to me."

He fell to his knees and somehow managed to mutter, "Nine one one."

Those three numbers caught Reid's attention. She was by his side and guided him to the floor instantly. "What's wrong?"

He could only pat his chest.

"HELP! SOMEONE HELP!"

Two

Reid

Her screams had been answered when a janitor came running toward her with his phone pressed to his ear. He'd asked Reid questions about Grayson, which she'd answered. It was scary how much she knew about him. Her best friend, Melanie Scott, often told Reid she was far too intrusive into the life of a man who didn't want to be with her. Reid knew Melanie meant well, but it still always felt like a slap in the face.

Now, her knowledge of Grayson's life would come in handy.

After the ambulance arrived, the medics quickly took over. Grayson's eyes stared off into space, and his head lolled from side to side. Reid tried to stay in his line of vision, hoping to show him that she was still there. They loaded him onto a stretcher, and Reid followed them out of the recreation center.

"Can I go with him?" she asked as she walked briskly next to Grayson, holding his hand.

"Aren't you his wife?"

The question gave her pause. Reid wanted to be. Ever since they'd met. She'd fallen head over heels for him. The one night they'd spent together after their holiday party had only made her feelings for Grayson worse. She'd thought they'd start the new year off as a couple; instead they were still friends. Grayson kept Reid at arm's length when it came to romance and treated her like the best friend he couldn't live without.

Reid couldn't or wouldn't live without him, either, and had resigned herself to thinking and feeling that he was worth it in some roundabout way. Besides, relationships were messy. Especially with your best friend. At least that's what she told herself.

If lying meant she could stay with him, then so be it. She nodded quickly.

The ambulance ride was undoubtedly the longest, loudest, bumpiest, and scariest ride of her life. Reid held on to Grayson's hand and spoke to him, letting him know everything would be okay, even though she was certain her expression didn't match her words. She didn't want to think about how she'd thought he'd been faking what the medic called a "myocardial infarction" when he spoke into his radio. She knew that meant "heart attack," but Grayson was young and fit. He worked out all the time; only people with poor health had heart attacks. Not men like him. Not someone in his midthirties with his entire life ahead of him.

"We're almost there," she told him, even though she had no idea where they were going. There were multiple hospitals in the DC region, and she hadn't a clue which one they were closest to. "Everything's going to be okay."

Grayson blinked. He lay with his shirt cut up the middle. It was one of his favorite ones, and he was going to be pissed when he found out it was now a tattered rag. Those sticky electrode patches were stuck to his chest and arms, with wires leading to a machine, and he wore an oxygen mask.

Reid smiled and gripped his hand tighter as she looked into his eyes. Eyes that lacked life and vibrancy. *What is wrong with him?*

"Everything's going to be okay," she said again, more for herself than him. Her words were just that, words. She had no doubt that fear filled Grayson. She had to be the strong one, the one he looked to for comfort. Once she was alone, she'd have her breakdown. Until then, she'd smile and run her free hand through his hair.

"When we get to the hospital, I'm going to call your mom. I'm sure by the time she gets there, you'll be ready to go home." Even as she spoke the words, she didn't believe them. "I bet she'll take you out for ice cream, because at the end of the day, you're still her baby boy."

Reid loved Sydney and thought of her as a mother. Having lost her own mother before she'd turned three, she didn't know what it was like to have one. Her father, Luther, had never remarried and very rarely dated. She recalled one time her dad had dated a woman for about a year, but then one day she was gone. Reid didn't even remember her name.

"We're here, ma'am," the medic said.

"Did you hear that? The doctors are going to take care of you, and then we'll be on our way."

The back doors of the ambulance opened, and within a flash, Grayson was out of the back and the medics were running him through the door. Reid could barely keep up. She tried to follow him through the double doors, but a nurse with a pinched face and blue scrubs stopped her.

"That's my friend," Reid said, looking over the nurse's shoulder toward the double doors, which read **Emergency Room**. "I need to be with him."

The woman placed her hand on Reid's back and guided her toward the waiting area. Reid stumbled, unable to take her eyes off the doors. "I understand your concern, but it's best to let the doctors work on him. Wait here, and someone will be out to speak with you when they know something."

"But—" Reid sat and continued to stare at the space where, around the corner, the doors to the ER would have been.

"Is there someone we can call for you?"

Reid shook her head. "Um . . . no, but I'll call his mom."

The nurse nodded and left Reid sitting there. She glanced around at the others, each there for some reason or another. Some were probably sick and waiting to be seen, while others waited for news of their loved ones.

She stood and stepped into the hall, away from people, and dialed Sydney's number. Her call went to voicemail. She hung up and dialed again.

"Hello?"

"Hi, Sydney, it's Reid."

"Heavens, dear. What's wrong?"

"It's, uh—" Reid looked over her shoulder when she heard someone wailing.

"Reid, what's wrong? What happened to Grayson?"

Was this mother's intuition, or did Sydney know because of Reid's incoherence? She swallowed hard. "Grayson possibly had a heart attack. That's what the medic said in the ambulance. We're at . . ." Reid had no idea where they were. She looked around for a sign, anything that would tell her. She walked frantically down the hall until she could see one. "MedStar," she told Sydney. "They took him back and won't let me see him."

"We're on our way," Sydney said and hung up.

It took Reid a solid minute to shake the fog from her mind and return to the waiting area. Only she couldn't sit. So she paced. Only there wasn't a place to pace without causing a disturbance to the others waiting, or to the staff.

She sat and her leg shook, annoying the person sitting three seats away from her. "Sorry," she muttered when the man huffed out a sigh.

Reid tapped the screen on her phone and contemplated texting Pearce. He'd want to know, and she believed Grayson would want his best friend there if . . . no, there wasn't anything wrong. She repeated her earlier thoughts: Grayson was a young, strong, and healthy man. People like him didn't have heart attacks. She texted Pearce to let him know what had happened, where they were, and that she would keep him updated when she knew more.

When her leg started bouncing again, she stood and tried pacing again. She didn't have a choice, and neither did the people in the waiting room. She *had* to do something because sitting there made her mind wander to places it shouldn't.

Every time the doors opened, Reid waited to hear "Grayson Caballero's family," but those words didn't come. The staff looked for others, with mixed news. Families either went back with the doctor or they broke down.

"Reid."

She scanned the room for whoever had called her name and felt an insurmountable wave of comfort, like a blanket of relief, when she saw Sydney coming toward her. Reid fell into Sydney's outstretched arms and cried. She should be comforting Grayson's mother, not the other way around.

Sydney Haney was the type of woman who took life by the horns and led it down the path she created. When she found out she was pregnant at seventeen, she'd chosen to become a mom. The first time Reid met her, she was awestruck by her beauty and jealous of her long, luscious, dark curly hair and captivating brown eyes. Sydney had been given up for adoption and raised outside Annapolis and had never bothered to look for her birth parents. Grayson favored her, with the same dark hair and olive skin tone, except he towered over his mother. His father was out of the picture and had been long before Grayson was born. As far as Reid knew, Grayson had never met his father.

Strong hands guided the women back to the chairs. The smell of Polo cologne filtered through her senses, relaxing her. There were only two smells that could do that—Polo and Old Spice—which was what her father wore.

Reid wiped her eyes and tried to smile at Gilbert, Grayson's stepfather. He gripped her hand tightly and offered a kind but sad grin. "Did you call your dad?"

Gilbert Haney was as handsome as they came. He exuded charm and charisma and could turn a dreary situation into a lighthearted moment. He'd met Sydney when Grayson was ten and took the role of stepfather to a whole new level. Grayson loved Gilbert and never introduced him as his stepdad. With his salt-and-pepper hair and brown eyes that matched Grayson's, Gilbert was almost as tall as his son.

She shook her head. Why hadn't she thought to call him?

"I'll take care of it. Stay with Sydney." He leaned down and whispered through Sydney's hair before he left them to talk.

"Tell me what happened."

"I don't even know," she started. "On Sundays, Grayson has his basketball league. We're at the rec center and everything is fine. After the game, we got into an argument. He didn't like these guys chatting with me, and I became defensive. I told him there are things in life that I want and I'm no longer going to sit by and wait, that I'm going to start dating." Reid swallowed hard. "He placed his hand over his chest, and I thought he was joking, acting like I was breaking his heart or something, and I told him to knock it off. Only it wasn't a joke, and he couldn't speak. I yelled for help. There was a janitor there, and he called for an ambulance. On the way here, the medic guy said he showed signs of having a heart attack, which doesn't make any sense because he's only thirty-five, and people his age who are fit and healthy don't have heart attacks."

"Breathe," Sydney said as she wiped Reid's tears away, despite her own wetting her cheeks. "Breathe, honey."

Reid hiccuped and shuddered. "I'm so sorry, I should be consoling you, and here you are, telling me to breathe."

"It's a mom thing," Sydney told her. She sat back in the chair and put her arm around Reid. "Gilbert went to see what he can find out, and he's going to call your dad. He should be here."

"Yes and no. I mean, he's pretty upset with Grayson because he thinks he's leading me on."

Sydney nodded. "I understand, but you'll want him here."

It took a moment for those words to sink in. She raised her head and looked at Sydney. "Why?"

Sydney only shook her head and brought Reid back to her shoulder.

When Gilbert returned, he told them that Grayson was in surgery and that it could be a while. He sat next to his wife and held her hand, while she held Reid.

The television aired the news, but the sound had been muted. People had come and gone. There were more tears and some elation. The sounds of the doors whooshing, the sirens wailing, and the constant beeping began to grate on Reid's nerves.

She'd stood and had begun to pace again when her father came in, straight from work. He rushed over to her and wrapped his big, beefy arms around her. She nuzzled into his work jacket. The smell of Old Spice, oil, and nature soothed her.

Luther Sullivan was a hardworking man and had done everything he could to provide Reid with the best life he could. He was six feet, with a head of dark-auburn hair, matching Reid's. He was what she called a rugged man and preferred to be outdoors unless it was football season and his beloved Ravens were on, and then you'd find him in front of the tube. He didn't care for many other sports, unless it was something Reid wanted to watch. When her mother died, he'd taken the role of sole provider to heart and vowed to never let her down.

"I'm so glad you're here."

"I'm here for you." Reid didn't miss the undertone. She also didn't blame him.

Luther led Reid back to where Sydney and Gilbert sat. He shook Gilbert's hand and offered a kind smile to Sydney.

"What do we know?" he asked as he sat down.

"We're waiting." Sydney wiped at her tears. Neither she nor Reid had been able to stop crying.

"Well, no news is good news. Have you eaten?" Luther asked.

Reid and Sydney said they weren't hungry.

"Coffee it is." Luther stood, with Gilbert following.

Reid stood and began pacing again. Sydney begged her to sit down, but she couldn't. There was a level of unease festering beneath the surface, and Reid knew if they didn't hear something soon, she was going to lose her shit.

"It's taking too long," she said to Sydney. "Whatever this is . . . something's wrong." Reid walked toward the nurses' station, paused, and then walked back. She did this until her father and Gilbert returned with paper cups filled with stale coffee. She didn't care because she needed something to keep her wits about her.

"This tastes horrible," she said as she brought the cup to her lips again.

"The worse it tastes, the more kick you'll get." Her father laughed and drank. "Come on, come sit. Pacing isn't going to help any of us right now."

She let her father lead her back to the pleather and fabric chairs. As she stared around the room, she thought it wasn't only the waiting game that made people restless; it was the fact that the seats in the waiting room were the most uncomfortable things possible. Others slouched, their bodies contorted in unnatural positions, and one sat on the floor and used the seat as a pillow.

"You'd think the hospital could provide a better place for people who have to sit here and wait to find out if their loved one is okay," Reid said in disgust. "Imagine how much money the CEO or whatever makes. Whoever they are is probably living in the lap of luxury in Georgetown or Potomac."

"You know they are," Gilbert agreed.

Reid stood and had started toward the coffee station to refill her cup when a doctor strode toward the waiting area. She froze, thinking this was it—this was the news they'd waited hours for. The man stood on the cusp of the room and looked at the file in his hand. Reid's eyes studied Sydney.

"I'm looking for Grayson Caballero's family."

"That's me," Sydney said as she stood up. "That's us." Gilbert followed and Reid stepped forward. She wasn't his family, at least not in the sense of the meaning according to the hospital.

"I'm Dr. Wynn, the cardiologist on staff. You must be Sydney?"

She nodded.

"If you'll follow me."

Everyone took a step forward, but the doctor shook his head. "Family only."

Reid opened her mouth to protest but quickly shut it.

"She's family," Sydney said. "Everyone here is."

The doctor nodded and motioned for them to follow him. They went down the hall to the bank of elevators, stepped in, and rode to the intensive care unit. When they stepped off, the mood was vastly different from what they'd experienced downstairs. It was quiet, subdued. Reid had the need to whisper and tiptoe along the white linoleum floor. The doctor showed them to the waiting room, which held a bit more appeal than the one in the emergency room. The wood floor had a tiled pattern, and the couches looked big enough for someone to lie down on. Still, it was the quiet that unnerved Reid. She wanted noise and action. She wanted to see that nurses and doctors were working. On this floor, it was anyone's guess.

They went into a small room that had an equally small round table with three chairs around it. Sydney and Gilbert sat, as expected. Reid leaned against the wall, while her father stayed in the doorway.

"Let me start by saying Grayson's alive and in intensive care. When he came in earlier this afternoon, we evaluated him and determined he had unstable angina. We began treatment and conducted an echocardiogram. It was then we saw a tiny hole in the wall that separates the two upper chambers of his heart. Immediately, we took him in for surgery. It was at that time I made the diagnosis that Grayson suffers from a sinus venosus defect, which is a rare type of atrial septal defect. This was likely present at birth and can often go undiagnosed unless the patient presents with some symptoms. This abnormality is considered a congenital heart defect, which, left untreated, brings us to right now. Unfortunately, when I went to repair the hole, I discovered his heart is very weak. I've done what I can at the moment. Grayson is on extracorporeal membrane oxygenation—ECMO is the term we use. It's a bridge until Grayson can receive a heart transplant."

The collective gasp echoed in the room. Followed by a gut-wrenching sob from Sydney. Tears that Reid thought had dried up were back in a rush. Her father was by her side as the first sob took over. They embraced until Reid went to Sydney and hugged her tightly. The two stayed like that until Gilbert asked, "Can we see him?"

"You can. We have a two-person limit in his room. You'll need to wear a protective gown while you're there. He's heavily sedated and may slip in and out of consciousness, but it's unlikely he'll be coherent. This is for his safety and well-being. The charge nurse will come in and give you more information on how the ICU works here and where other family members can wait."

"What's next?" Gilbert asked as he held on to Sydney, who wept quietly.

"From this point, it's a waiting game. My staff is working now to move him up the list. That's the best we can do at the moment. I am consulting with my peers on possible treatments, but short of a miracle, Grayson needs a new heart." Dr. Wynn closed his folder. "I wish I had better news for you." He stood, put his hand on Sydney's shoulder for a brief moment, and left without another word.

No one knew what to say. Should Reid comfort Sydney? Tell her how sorry she was? Was there protocol for something like this? Knowing she might never speak to Grayson again felt like she had a wheelbarrow full of bricks on her chest. Reid was afraid to breathe out of fear the weight would become even more unbearable.

When the nurse came, Sydney and Gilbert followed her out of the room. Reid and her father sat in empty seats and said nothing until Reid said she needed to call Pearce. Texting him wouldn't suffice. When he answered, she recounted what Dr. Wynn had told them as best she could. By the time she'd hung up, another wave of tears streamed down her face. She made another call to her best friend, Melanie.

"I'm on my way."

"You don't have to come," Reid told her.

"I want to be there for you."

Reid smiled. "I appreciate you. I'm okay for right now. Pretty numb, actually."

After some more back-and-forth, Melanie said she'd wait for Reid to let her know when it would be a good time to visit.

The next call went to Grayson's boss, who seemed a bit put off by the whole thing and had the audacity to ask if he'd be in on Monday. Reid hung up on him and figured she'd deal with him when she returned to the office.

"Reid."

She turned at the sound of Gilbert's voice. He wore a yellow gown and looked ready for surgery.

"Would you like to go in and see Grayson?"

She stood and rushed forward. Gilbert stepped out of the doorway and pointed down the hall. Reid remembered her kindergarten teacher reminding her to not run in halls. She ignored the voice in the back of her head and sprinted toward the double wooden doors. She pressed the button and anxiously waited for someone to answer.

"I'm here to see Grayson Caballero. I'm Reid Sullivan."

"One moment."

A minute or so later, the doors clicked open and a nurse greeted her. "Follow me." She took Reid into a room, instructed her to wash her hands, and then helped her put a gown on over her clothes. She then took Reid down another hall and to Grayson's room.

All the rooms faced the nurses' station, and each room had its blinds pulled. Reid was thankful she couldn't see anyone because she wasn't sure she'd be able to handle it.

She took a deep breath and rounded the corner. Her hand covered her mouth in a failed attempt to stifle the gasp she let out. Grayson . . .

her Grayson lay on the bed, lifeless. The machine at his side, taking and filtering his blood back into his body, did all the work for him.

"Reid." Sydney said her name softly. "I have to know—was Grayson taking his meds?"

"What meds?"

"Grayson was born with congenital heart disease."

Reid absorbed the words and shook her head slightly. "I had no idea," she said in a whisper.

Three

Rafe

Rafe Karlsson woke seconds before his alarm sounded. He shut it off, rolled over to where Nadia slept, and kissed her on her cheek.

"Let me sleep," she mumbled into the darkness.

"You can sleep while I shower." He slipped out of bed and walked into the en suite bathroom, which the former owner had put in as an addition along with a nice walk-in closet.

He turned on the water for his shower, went to the bathroom, and then stepped into the navy blue and white mosaic tiled stand-up he and his father had built a few years after Rafe and Nadia bought the craftsman-style home. They'd kept most of the old charm and character of the home and changed only the kitchen, modernizing it with brand-new appliances, granite countertops, and white subway tiles. Rafe and Nadia had fallen in love with the exposed ceiling beams, the extensive built-ins, the large windows, and the spacious porch with its thick, tapered columns.

Rafe stood under the hot spray and worked the muscles in his shoulder while he imagined the road course he'd run many times prior to this morning. This year, he was going to win. None of this coming in second or third shit. This was his year.

The Commonwealth Cup started a hundred years ago, when two townies got into an argument over the location of Heartbreak Hill. According to the map and every Bostonian, the famed hill was in the town of Newton. Some of the questionable folks who didn't know their heads from their . . . said it was "on the outskirts" of the city. No such thing when it comes to Boston. You're either within city limits or you're not.

Newton was not.

Instead of a good ole fistfight, they decided to race each other uphill for a half mile. When they both crossed the made-up finish line, they kept going, running along Commonwealth Avenue, past Boston University, and across the bridge, then continuing along the Charles River until they reached Harvard Square, where they both collapsed from exhaustion. Neither man declared victory, and both vowed to race again, after they'd had a year of training. Thus, the Commonwealth Cup was born. Over the decades, the course had been altered to create a ten-mile road race from Newton to Harvard.

At some point, the race had stopped being about two townies. It was about two communities coming together and raising funds to aid in the development of parks and recreational activities for the youth. It was about police officers earning bragging rights over their counterparts. It was about a father pushing his wheelchair-bound son across the finish line.

Rafe didn't have an objective, other than winning. He loved running, but mostly he loved seeing his family along the route, cheering for him. Even if he didn't cross the finish line first, he'd have his daughters, Gemma and Lynnea, there at the end, telling him how proud they were of him.

Still, he wanted to win. He wanted the Cup to sit proudly on his desk and to have his new clients ask him about it. Doing so would give him an opportunity to encourage them to not only invest their money with his firm but also give back to their community.

He got out of the shower, dried off, and dressed in a pair of running shorts with compression shorts built in, a long-sleeve moisture-wicking shirt and socks, and his favorite brand of running shoes, which were fairly new and perfectly broken in.

When he came out of the bathroom, he found their bed empty but could hear laughter coming from downstairs. As soon as he entered the hallway, he smelled bacon, eggs, and coffee. His stomach growled.

On most mornings when he'd come downstairs to greet his daughters, he'd find chaos. Mornings were hectic, with him trying to get to work and Nadia trying to wrangle two rambunctious girls out the door for school before she headed off to work. When he could, he'd go in an hour late so he could stay and help his wife.

Rafe entered the kitchen and made his way to the breakfast nook, which had a built-in bench that offered them prime sitting space, where he found his youngest dressed in last year's Halloween pirate costume, complete with eye patch. He just stared, unsure of how to proceed. He and Nadia encouraged Lynnea's creative process: her "individuality," as the pediatrician had called it. This was a phase she'd grow out of; at least that was what they were told. He kissed the top of her head and then made his way over to Gemma and did the same.

At eight and six, respectively, they were as opposite as they came. Gemma was cool, calm, nurturing, and wise beyond her years, while Lynnea was the hurricane in their household. She had a sassy mouth, loved to watch horror films (even though they were strictly forbidden), and pushed her mother's buttons often. Lynnea went from zero to one hundred and stayed there until the crash happened, which thankfully came around eight at night, like clockwork. Lynnea exhausted them most days, but Rafe and Nadia wouldn't have had it any other way.

"Daddy," Gemma said, getting his attention. "You know the father-daughter dance is coming up at school. Do you want to go?"

"I don't know. Can you dance?"

Gemma nodded and stood up from the table. She began moving back and forth and waving her arms in some fancy motion she'd undoubtedly seen on a video. Rafe reached for her hand and told her to put her feet on his. She did, and then he waltzed them around the room, with him dipping her at the end.

"Do we have to dance like that?" Gemma asked.

Rafe shrugged. "Maybe, maybe not. I can dance like this." He started flailing his arms around and contorting his body. Lynnea loved it. Gemma not so much.

"Mommy, make him stop."

Nadia refused and laughed right along with Lynnea.

"Daddy!" Gemma moaned. Rafe stopped and pulled her into his arms. "I'd absolutely love to go to the dance with you, Gemma. Tell Mommy the date, and she'll put it in my calendar."

"Can I get a new dress?"

Rafe glanced at Nadia, who shrugged. "Only if you make sure to buy me a matching tie."

Gemma smiled brightly. "We can do that, right?" She looked at her mom.

"Of course. We have time. I think the dance is in May."

"Loads of time," Rafe said.

"What about me?" Lynnea asked.

"Yours will start next year," Nadia told her. "Then Daddy will take you."

"Do I have to wear a dress?"

"Nope," Rafe said. "You can wear whatever you want." He'd probably regret those words later.

Rafe helped Nadia finish preparing breakfast. He made toast and his oatmeal, while she plated eggs and bacon for herself and the girls, and then he carried everything over. Before he sat, he noticed Gemma's and Nadia's shirts: **RAFE KARLSSON IS #1 IN MY HEART**.

His eyes misted.

"I love your shirts," he said as he pulled his chair out, sat down at the table, and reached for the orange juice and a banana from the basket of fruit on the table. He held it up to Lynnea, silently asking her if she wanted some. She nodded.

He peeled a banana, gave the top half to Lynnea, and added pieces of the rest to his oatmeal, along with a dollop of peanut butter. This was his normal go-to breakfast. Nadia handed him two slices of toast, also with peanut butter. For the past couple of months, while training for this road race, he'd changed his diet.

Rafe's phone chimed. He glanced at the screen and groaned.

"What's wrong?" Nadia asked.

"Kiran," Rafe said with a sigh. "He's not running today." Kiran Dunlap had been Rafe's best friend since their freshman year in college, when they'd met on the rowing team. This would've been Kiran's first time running in the Commonwealth Cup. Rafe had asked him, in hopes they'd be able to convince more coworkers to join them next year and enter as a team.

"How come?"

Rafe shook his head. It didn't matter what excuse Kiran came up with; Rafe would run regardless. He turned his attention back to Nadia and the girls. "I can't wait for tonight."

"Why, what's tonight?" Nadia asked.

"Nachos," he said with a wink. "I don't even care where we go out to eat, as long as there are nachos."

"Can we go with you?" Gemma asked.

Rafe nodded. "Big family dinner. Grandma and Grandpa will join us."

"Yay," Lynnea said with a mouth full of banana.

They ate breakfast and washed up, and Nadia somehow convinced Lynnea that pirates weren't allowed at the race. She reluctantly changed, donning the same shirt her mother and sister wore, and begrudgingly made her way downstairs.

Rafe stood at the bottom of the stairs. When she was three steps from him, she launched herself into his arms.

"Are you going to win?" She placed her hands on his cheek and scratched her nails against his scruff.

"No," he told her, despite wanting to. He figured if he won, she'd be over-the-moon happy for him. And if he didn't, she'd still be proud, and he wouldn't have let her down. "There are way better runners than me."

"Next year," she said. "You can practice more better."

Rafe didn't bother correcting her, even though he knew he should. He pulled his youngest closer and held her to his chest, kissed her forehead, and then moved her to his hip. He'd carry her as long as she'd let him.

Rafe couldn't have scripted his morning any better.

Rafe drove them to the staging area, not far from the starting line. Nadia got out of the car and moved over to the passenger side. She reached for her husband.

"Today is going to be great. I'll see you at the finish line," she told him. Rafe kissed her, much to the annoyance of their daughters, who heckled them from the back seat.

"Thank you."

"I'm so proud of you."

"I haven't raced yet," he reminded her.

"Doesn't matter. When you first raced, three years ago, you said you'd better your time each year. Now you have a chance to win."

His smile beamed at her compliment.

"You wanted something and worked to achieve it. That's exactly the kind of work ethic we're working to instill in our children. You're a very good role model, Rafe Karlsson."

Rafe thanked her again and stepped aside to open the back door. He leaned in. "I'll see you girls at the finish line."

"Good luck, Daddy," the girls said in unison before he shut the door.

He gave Nadia one last kiss. “Run fast,” she told him.

Rafe laughed. “It shouldn’t take me more than an hour.”

“I’ll be waiting.”

Rafe kissed Nadia again. He waited for her to get back into the car and leave before he left the parking lot. He let a couple of cars pass by and then made his way over to the tent where he needed to check in. After he gave the young woman at the table his name, she gave him a bib to pin to his shirt and directed him to the starting line.

He stepped off to the side and looked at his bib numbers, 777. Rafe was far from superstitious but would take this as a sign. “Lucky sevens,” he muttered to himself. On his way home, he’d buy a lotto ticket.

“Everyone line up, please,” someone with a loudspeaker said. Casually, everyone moved toward the starting line. Rafe looked around. Last year, they’d had thirteen hundred runners, and if he had to guess, the amount was the same this year.

Rafe had a plan—keep pace with whoever jumped out front; then he’d turn on his boosters, as Lynnea called them, and beat them to the finish line.

The firing gun sounded, and everyone took off. He wove in and out of groups of people and found himself a nice groove rather quickly. Rafe liked running alone. He enjoyed the solitude but also the freedom he felt. After passing a couple more runners, he counted five people ahead of him. The woman to his right wore those over-the-ear headphones and had established a good pace. He matched it easily. In two or three blocks, he’d surge ahead to the next person, and then again until he had a mile to go. Unless the leader had bigger boosters than him.

Along the route, people cheered. They had signs, miniature megaphones, and other artificial noisemakers. He heard cowbells, lots of clapping, and a car horn. The latter seemed odd, until he saw the group of people blocking the street scramble out of the way.

In a split second, he saw the car careening toward him and the other runners. It was like time had stopped, and nothing existed except the car and the muddled sound of its horn. In a flash, the runner he had passed, the one with the headphones, zipped by.

Rafe saw it all unfold. He rushed toward her and pushed her out of the way. She turned and looked at him with horror etched across her face. She yelled, but he couldn't hear her over the screaming and the horn. Why wasn't she grateful he'd moved them out of the way?

Four

Nadia

Nadia sped through the side streets, getting as close to Harvard Square as she could. They had planned poorly. Rafe should've taken the car, while she and the girls should've taken the T. Parking was hard to find any day of the week, but add in an annual road race and it became nonexistent. Panic grew as she navigated the narrow streets of Cambridge. She shot down one side street and then another, finally choosing to turn in to one of the parking lots at Harvard. If she got a parking ticket, oh well. They weren't going to be there for very long.

After gathering the girls (and against angry protests from both), she all but dragged them to Harvard Square, where the finish line was. Thankfully, her in-laws were already there, holding a spot for them.

"We didn't think you'd make it," Cleo, her mother-in-law, said. Her tone had a bite to it, which Nadia didn't appreciate. Over the past year, Cleo's attitude toward Nadia had iced, for unknown reasons. Nadia had mentioned it a few times to Rafe, who had witnessed a couple of encounters of his own. He, too, didn't understand the change in demeanor. Nor had Otto, Rafe's father.

"We wouldn't miss it," Nadia said as she fought against rolling her eyes. She moved the girls to the front and then stood next to Otto, apologizing to the people behind him.

"How was our boy this morning?" Otto asked. Rafe was their only boy. He was the older brother of Freya. Uncle to Leif and Astrid. Brother-in-law to Lars.

"He was good. Ready to have fun. He said he'd finish in under an hour." Nadia looked at the time on her phone. "Which should be soon." She pressed the button for her video camera and told the girls to start watching for their dad.

Nadia leaned forward but didn't see any runners coming toward her. She wondered if the race had started late, which was possible. Rarely did anything start on time these days.

A medical alert tone sounded. Nadia glanced across the street at the medical tent, which had been set up at the finish line to aid runners if they needed attention. She watched as medical personnel grabbed their bags. Two medics ran up the street, while another few jumped into one of those utility vehicles known as side-by-sides. Her eyes followed them up the middle of the race route, where spectators scrambled.

Then she heard it.

The screaming.

The sirens.

"Something's wrong," she said to Otto, Cleo, to whoever heard her. "Someone's hurt."

Lynnea went to Nadia, with her hands covering her ears. Otto picked her up. "Grandpa will hold you," he said to her.

Very few people moved away from the finish line, and those who stayed watched with rapt attention, waiting for some news. An uncomfortable silence fell over the crowd.

"Where's Rafe?" Cleo asked.

Nadia pulled her phone from her pocket and looked at his location. He was near where the ambulance was blocking the street. Her husband was up there, likely helping whoever needed aid.

"I'll be right back," she told her in-laws. She made her way through the crowd, periodically looking at her phone and where she was going. When she saw an opening into the street, she took it and briskly walked toward the commotion. Halfway there, she pressed Rafe's name and held her phone to her ear.

No answer.

"Hey, babe. It's me. Just checking to see where you are. We know something happened on the course. Call me." She hung up after leaving the voicemail and called him back. Again, no answer.

The closer she came to the commotion, the more anxious she felt. A police officer stopped her from coming any closer to the ambulance. "I'm sorry, but you can't go this way."

"My husband . . . ," she started to say and then stopped. Nadia tapped her phone and pulled up Rafe's location. "This says he's in there, somewhere. I need to find him."

The officer shook his head. "I'm sorry, but you can't go in there. All the runners have been sent back toward the starting line."

Nadia looked at her phone again. "But he's there."

Instead of repeating himself, he directed her toward the sidewalk, where a horde of people had gathered. She pushed her way through the crowd until she could get to the sidewalk. If Rafe would just answer his damn phone, she could stop worrying about him.

"Rafe." She said his name loudly. "Rafe Karlsson." This time her voice was a little louder. She continued to call his name until she saw the car, which wasn't supposed to be there. The front end was pushed against the street, its front caved in. The windows had been shattered and the driver's side door left open.

Medics and fire personnel gathered around it; some chatted, while others picked up pieces of the mangled car. "Oh God," she said aloud.

"I know. It's so sad. I don't think he'll survive," a lady next to Nadia said.

Nadia looked at the woman and asked, "The driver?"

She shook her head. "No, the runner. He saved that woman's life." She pointed to another runner, who sat on the road, visibly shaken. She cried while talking to the police and pointing.

The ambulance doors slammed, and the siren roared to life, causing Nadia to shudder. The piercing sound grated her nerves and sent chills down her spine. Tapping the screen on her phone, she tracked Rafe's location. He was on the move. She looked in the direction he was heading and didn't see him but could tell he was moving with some speed. Was he running toward her?

No, there was no way. Not when he turned down the side street nearest her. Rafe moved in the wrong direction to get to her. She rose on her tiptoes, but all she could see was the ambulance. No one was there.

"The runner, the one the ambulance just took away, you said it was a man?"

The woman nodded and tried to leave, but Nadia placed her hands on her shoulders and held her there.

"What was he wearing?"

"Oh, I don't know. There was so much blood it was hard to tell. If I had to guess, something dark."

"Like navy blue?"

The woman shrugged and stepped out of Nadia's grasp. Nadia looked back at her phone, and her heart sank as she watched Rafe's photo move farther and farther away from her.

Nadia spun around, looking in every direction she could for help. She stepped off the curb and made her way toward the woman, the one who sat on the road speaking to the officer.

"Excuse me, but is this the man who helped you?" she asked as she showed a photo of Rafe to her.

"Ma'am, please step back." Two hands forcibly kept Nadia in place while she held her phone out.

"Look at this, please," she said to the woman as she fought back the anger and tears threatening to take over. "Please, is this the man?"

"Ma'am, please." The officer stepped in front of her. "You need to step back."

She held her phone up. "I'm looking for him, and according to his location, he's moving faster than he runs. Does he look familiar?"

The officer glanced at her phone and frowned. He then motioned for another officer to come over. The two spoke in private.

"Come with me," the other officer said. "What's your name?"

"Nadia Karlsson."

"I'm Officer Luca DeMarco. You can call me Luca."

"Where are you taking me, Luca?"

"We transported a dozen or so runners to the hospital for treatment," he said as he opened the passenger side of his cruiser for her. Before he shut it, he said, "I'm taking you to Mass Gen."

Nadia had never been in a police car. She'd never sped through the streets of Boston with sirens blaring and had never seen cars move so slowly to get out of the way until now. Her phone rang, and without looking, she answered.

"Rafe?"

"No, it's Otto. Isn't he with you?"

Her heart sank as she closed her eyes. "No, I'm having trouble locating him. I'm on my way to the hospital now. There was an accident on the course, and some of the runners had to be transported. Go back to our house, and I'll call you once I find him."

"Okay, we're going to go get some lunch. Just give me a call."

"I will, Otto. Kiss my girls for me."

"Will do." They hung up, and she stared out the window at the passing Charles River. A crew team of eight glided down the river. In six months, the largest three-day regatta in the world would come to town, bringing thousands of people with it. The event was fun, and something she and Rafe looked forward to attending every year, and every year, she'd told her husband she wanted to learn how to row. He'd been a rower in college and often joked that he and his best friend, Kiran, were going to put a team together and compete in the "old man" bracket. Maybe this year they would.

Officer DeMarco pulled into the emergency part of the hospital and turned off his siren, but he left his lights flashing. He helped Nadia from the car and guided her into the hospital, where chaos reigned. The waiting room was wall to wall with people, talking over each other, some crying, others pacing. Everyone wanted or needed help.

DeMarco spoke briefly to a woman in flower-printed scrubs, and then the double doors opened. Behind those doors, the bedlam had peaked. Beeping came from all directions, with staff moving and colliding with others. People barked out orders, while some ran with machines toward rooms.

He directed Nadia to the nurses' lounge. Luca poured her a cup of coffee and handed it to her, but she shook her head.

"Where's my husband?"

"The nurse I spoke with when we came in, she's locating him."

Nadia paced in front of the door, hoping to catch a glimpse of Rafe. She looked at his location and noticed he was, in fact, in the hospital. She tried calling him, but his phone went to voicemail again. A doctor walked in, and Nadia froze. Officer DeMarco stood and introduced himself and Nadia.

"Hi, I'm Dr. Costa. May I see a picture of your husband?"

Nadia switched screens on her phone and showed him the most recent photo of Rafe. Dr. Costa looked quickly. Far too quickly for Nadia's liking.

"Please, come with me."

She followed him out of the room and looked over her shoulder at Luca. For some odd reason, she wanted him with her. He took up the rear, almost as if he knew he'd have to catch her.

"How's Rafe?"

"Rafe," Dr. Costa muttered. "Do you have family in the waiting room?" She shook her head as he led her down the hall and into a small room that fit no more than three or four people.

Before he had a chance to say anything, she knew.

"He's hurt badly, isn't he?"

There wasn't a nod or a shake of his head, but the answer was in his eyes.

"How badly?"

Dr. Costa closed the door behind them and motioned for her to take a seat. She refused.

"I don't know everything that happened earlier; what I do know is Rafe suffered severe trauma to his head and neck. Despite the quick efforts of bystanders and the paramedics, we were unable to save him."

Nadia didn't hear him correctly.

Surely, he hadn't . . .

But he had.

"Wh-what?"

"I'm very sorry to tell you, but your husband is brain dead."

Nadia shook her head. "No. No. He was running and . . ." She paced the small room. "He's healthy and he's running." Tears streamed down her cheeks, wetting her shirt. "He's not . . ." She couldn't bring herself to say the word. She refused.

He saved that woman's life.

"I'm very sorry for your loss." Dr. Costa reached out and touched her elbow.

"But how?"

"We won't know until the crash report comes in. Someone will be by to talk to you about this shortly. Without the details, I can only assume from the damage to Rafe's body . . . his legs are shattered, which is where he took the brunt of the impact. According to the paramedics who brought him in, Rafe flew a distance and landed on his head. Right now, he's on life support," he told her. "The machines are breathing for him until we could find his next of kin. Would you like me to take you to your husband?"

The finality of his words sank into her mind. Her husband, her best friend, her lover, her partner, was gone.

Nadia fell to her knees, caught by Luca before she crumpled to the ground. "I've got you, Mrs. Karlsson," he said as he helped her stand.

She could barely walk and leaned heavily onto Luca for support. They followed Dr. Costa to Rafe's room. He held the door while Luca guided Nadia to her husband's side.

"Rafe." His name came out of her mouth in a wail. She covered his body with hers and cried at the sound and feel of his heart beating. It didn't matter to her that a machine was keeping him alive; to her, he was there. Sound, mind and body.

His beautiful face, the one she'd loved from the second she'd met him, was marred with road rash. She touched him gently, needing to feel him under the pads of her fingers. "Open your eyes, baby," she said to him, knowing deep down he'd never leave her.

Nothing.

Nadia took him in. He was stock still, with a tube coming from his mouth. His arms—stilled at his side—sat atop the white blanket. She cupped his face, pressing kisses on his dry lips.

"Come back," she whispered. "Come back to me, Rafe. Don't leave me." She had watched enough medical drama shows to know talking to patients always made them miraculously wake up, but deep in her bones, she knew they wouldn't get a miracle. Not today.

"Is there someone we can call for you?"

Nadia shook her head. She'd have to be the one to make the calls. Even though she didn't want to say the words out loud, the news about Rafe needed to come from her.

"What are our options?" she asked Dr. Costa. "Surgery?"

"No, I'm sorry. There isn't anything more we can do for him."

"Nothing at all?"

He shook his head slowly. "Again, I'm sorry for your loss."

None of this made sense. How could her husband, someone who was running with hundreds of other people, get hit by a car?

She looked from Dr. Costa back to her husband. "He'll wake up."

Dr. Costa walked toward one of the machines. "This one is monitoring his heart. It shows rhythm because the machine is keeping him alive. This one here"—he pointed to another one, which had a continuous straight line going across the screen—"this is his brain activity. The brain isn't like the heart, where we can restart it. The trauma he suffered, it's irreparable."

Her husband was gone.

A nurse brought her a chair, along with a pitcher of water and a cup. "There's a bathroom through that door if you need to use the restroom," she told Nadia. "If you need anything, please press this button, and I'll come running. What's your name?"

"Nadia Karlsson," she told her.

"And your husband's?"

Nadia knew the nurse asked because they needed his name for their records. He would become someone to them now, and not just "Patient X" or the standard "John Doe."

"Rafe Karlsson," Nadia said through a haggard breath.

The nurse (Nadia couldn't remember if she'd given her a name or not) laid a hand on her shoulder. "I'm so very sorry for your loss. If you need anything, please press the button."

If she pressed the button, would her husband come back to her?

Nadia said nothing.

The words, while likely genuine, felt empty.

She didn't know how long she sat there, staring at him. In her mind, he was in pain and sharing in her grief. Nadia put off calling his parents because any minute now, her husband was going to wake up. He would open his eyes and attempt a weak smile when he saw her.

Any minute now.

Her phone vibrated. Otto's photo showed on her screen. It was one Nadia had taken weeks ago, with him and the girls. She stared at it for a moment before answering.

"Hi, Otto."

"Did you find him?" The eagerness in Otto's voice was evident.

"Yeah, we're at Mass Gen. You should come now. But, uh . . . can you ask Hazel to watch the girls?" Hazel Pittman was Nadia's best friend from college and had bought a house a block away from her and Rafe. Hazel's daughter, Hayden, was Lynnea's best friend.

"Nadia, what's wrong?"

"Just come. You and Cleo."

Nadia hung up and pressed the contact icon for her mom. "Did he win? We've been looking for results, but nothing has been put online. I don't understand why they take forever or why they didn't stream the race. Don't they know people from out of town want to watch?" Lorraine Bolton prattled on without taking a breath.

"Mommy," Nadia said quietly.

"Nadia, what's wrong?"

She choked on a sob.

"Warren, we need to go now," she yelled. "Nadia needs us, something happened. Where are you?" she asked her daughter.

"Mass Gen," she told her mom. "He's dead, Mom." Nadia wailed uncontrollably on the phone to her mom. She'd heard the words from the doctor, but they hadn't registered until she said them to her mother. Strong arms wrapped around her. Without looking, she knew it was the nurse from earlier, the one who'd said she would be there if Nadia needed anything.

She took the phone from Nadia and spoke. "Hello, this is Geri, I'm the nurse assigned to Rafe. I'm sorry to have to tell you over the phone, but he's passed away from injuries sustained in an accident earlier this morning. Yes, ma'am, we'll see you then."

Geri went back to Nadia and held her. "Your parents are on their way. Come on, I've got you."

Nadia cried while Geri held her. She gripped her arms and wailed, asking repeatedly, Why Rafe. Why her? Why her girls. They were good people and didn't deserve this. None of them did. He just wanted to win the race and have nachos with his family later.

Now he was gone.

"The police need to speak with you when you're ready," Geri told her after Nadia had calmed down a bit.

"How much time do I have with him?"

Geri smiled kindly and rested her hand on Nadia's arm. "As long as you want. There's a team that will want to speak with you about organ donation when and if you're ready."

"Oh."

"It's a decision you should make as a family," Geri said. "Rafe was young, fit, and by all accounts healthy. He could help others. But organ donation isn't for everyone, and no one says you have to do it."

"I don't want to decide just yet. I need time."

Geri soothed Nadia. "Then time is what we'll give you." Nadia generally didn't like strangers touching her, but Geri was different. She had a motherly quality about her, which Nadia found relaxing.

Geri stayed in the room with Nadia, asking questions about Rafe and the girls. There was a knock on the door; another nurse pushed it open and let Rafe's parents in. When Cleo screamed and threw herself onto her son's body, Nadia quietly excused herself to give his parents the time they needed with their son.

FIVE

NADIA

Nadia slept in Rafe's room. The sound of the machines keeping him alive oddly kept her calm. They made her feel like he was still there with her, even though he wasn't. Geri, the nurse, offered Nadia a cot, but she refused. She wanted to hold him. Lie next to him one last time. She hadn't come to terms with what had happened and honestly expected to never understand why her husband had to die. Nadia also hadn't watched the news and had stopped listening to Otto after he'd said "freak accident." Accident or not, Rafe had lost his life doing something he loved, but not enough to be ripped away from his family.

While Otto and Cleo had their time with Rafe, Nadia had met with the police. Although the crash investigation was still in its preliminary stages, they told her the car that hit Rafe had lost its brakes. The driver, who they didn't name, had honked and tried to alert people. Most were able to move out of the way. Even Rafe.

Except the woman he saved. She didn't hear the car, and he pushed her out of the way, but he was unable to get himself to safety before the car hit him.

Rafe was being touted as a hero.

Nadia wanted to puke. She didn't want him to be a hero to anyone but her and the girls.

When Hazel had brought the girls to the hospital, Nadia had done her best. She hugged them tightly and told them what had happened, and how their daddy was no longer with them. Gemma cried instantly, while Lynnea had questions. Each one started with "Why."

Why did this happen?

Why Daddy?

Why will Daddy not wake up?

Why can't the doctors help him?

Why?

Why?

Why?

Nadia had the same questions. The girls had said their goodbyes, given their dad one last kiss, and then gone home with Hazel, who promised to shield them from the television. As much as Nadia wanted her girls with her, they were best off with Hazel for the time being. Nadia needed to be a wife to Rafe in his last moments.

Later, when everyone seemed exhausted and no one knew what they were supposed to do, Nadia, Otto, and Cleo met with staff about Rafe becoming an organ donor. They gave the family brochures for something called the United Network for Organ Sharing, or UNOS.

Cleo was vehemently against it, saying she didn't want her baby boy chopped up like some science experiment gone wrong, while Otto had concerns about who would get Rafe's organs. He didn't want someone who didn't deserve his organs to get them over someone who did.

Nadia was numb. She may have been present in the room, hearing the staff talk about what a final gift organ donation would be for Rafe, but she wasn't listening. Her mind and soul were in the room with him. Willing him to defy every odd there was and wake up. Because she knew she would never see him smile again, hear his voice, or feel his touch, she wasn't in any hurry to unplug him.

Still, a decision had to be made, and she was the one to make it. Unless Cleo found a way to stop her.

They had fought in the hallway. Cleo told Nadia that she was Rafe's mother and should be the one to decide what happened to him. Nadia let her say her piece. She had to. His mother grieved, and Nadia imagined she'd feel the same way if it was one of the girls in there and she and her husband had to make this choice. It wasn't easy, and yet it seemed so simple. Rafe had organs that would help others live longer, better lives. Why shouldn't his memory live on in this way?

Would he have wanted this?

Nadia struggled with that question. Organ donation wasn't something they'd ever discussed, and it wasn't listed on their driver's licenses. It wasn't something she'd ever thought about because this—the situation they were in—wasn't supposed to happen to them. They were good people who loved their children, their jobs, their community. They gave back and volunteered. They donated clothes, books, and toys all year long, not just over the holidays. God was supposed to look out for them.

She looked at her husband, peaceful and resting. With Geri's help, they'd cleaned his face and hands. He no longer looked like someone who'd been hit by a car but a man who slept deeply. Oh, how she wished she could wake him.

The door to his room opened, and her parents, Warren and Lorraine Bolton, walked in. They had driven to Boston from Washington, DC, stopping along the way to pick up Nadia's brother, Reuben, and older sister, Sienna.

Nadia rose and fell into her mother's open arms. Sobs racked her body, and tears that she thought had long dried up streamed down her cheeks. Her father wrapped them both into his strong arms and soothed her. Normally, his touch would calm her, but not today. Probably not ever again.

"What am I going to do?"

Nadia didn't expect them to answer. There wasn't one to give. No one knew how to cope after something like this. Her healthy husband had run in an annual road race and was now dead because someone's brakes had failed. Was it the driver's fault? In a sense, yes. What were they doing going down the street at a high rate of speed to begin with? Why didn't they downshift? Apply the emergency brake? How does someone not listen to their car when it needs new brakes? How could someone be so irresponsible?

Now, Nadia sounded like Lynnea with all her questions.

"We'll figure it out as we go," Lorraine Bolton told her daughter. "Dad and I aren't going anywhere until you're ready."

"What if I'm never ready?" Nadia stepped back and watched their expressions.

"Then I guess we're moving to Boston," Warren said. "Wherever you need us, we'll be there."

Nadia stepped aside and gave her parents a moment with Rafe. Her parents sobbed at the sight of their son-in-law. Warren and Rafe, along with Reuben, were golfing buddies and had traveled to Georgia to attend the Masters last year. This year, the plan was for everyone to take a cruise, and while the guys golfed on some tropical island, the women would shop. Lorraine had arranged for Hazel's younger sister to come so there would be a babysitter for Nadia's two girls and her sister's two boys.

"How are Cleo and Otto?" Lorraine asked.

"Otto's okay, but Cleo . . ." Nadia took a deep breath and shook her head. "Rafe's organs are viable for donation. His heart, lungs, kidneys, and liver, and the doctor said something about tissue." Nadia wiped her hand across her face. "Cleo doesn't want him cut open and says it's her choice as his mother, but I'm his wife, and it's my decision. Yet I don't know what to do. Like, this shouldn't be my husband lying there."

Nadia cried. Her mom came to her and pulled her into her arms. "We were supposed to grow old together, and now he won't watch our girls graduate or get married. They probably won't even remember him in ten or fifteen years. And I know I'm going to forget the way his laugh sounds or his voice, the way he smells. Even now, I try to hear his voice in my head, and I can't. It's fuzzy and garbled, like he's underwater."

"Once the shock wears off, everything you love about him will be fresh in your mind."

Nadia didn't believe her mother.

"I don't know what he would want. We never talked about this or what songs would play at our funerals. He's only forty! He's not supposed to be dead, Mom." Nadia looked at her mom and began crying again. "Look at my husband." She pointed at Rafe's body. "He can't even hold me one last time."

Warren came over and wrapped his arms around Nadia, while Lorraine stepped away to dry her eyes. She excused herself from the room, leaving them alone.

"It's not fair, sweetheart."

"All he wanted to do was run, Daddy. And now look at him. He's gone. I've lost my husband, and my girls have lost their father. How is this fair?"

"It's not," Warren said. "It was an accident, honey. Rafe saved a woman."

But not himself.

He saved a woman.

"Are you saying I should donate his organs?"

Warren led his daughter to some chairs, and they sat. He held her hand in his. "I think Rafe would want to help people, as long as they're people that are going to use the gift of life to their advantage."

"Otto said the same thing. He told the doctors he didn't want someone who's mistreated their body to get a second chance over someone who can't help but need a transplant or whatever."

"If you decide to do this, will Cleo be a problem?"

Nadia shrugged. "I don't know. She lost her son. Her pride and joy. She may not be thinking clearly. Hell, I'm not thinking clearly. Last night I asked the nurse if I could take him home because I think he'd want to die there, where he's comfortable, but he doesn't know. He's not even alive right now. The machine is breathing for him until I give them the okay to unplug him."

"Is there a chance—"

Nadia shook her head. "I had thought the same thing. I honestly expected a miracle once he heard my voice. The doctors showed me an x-ray or whatever it was of where he sustained most of the trauma." Nadia covered her face with her hands. "He's just gone, Daddy."

Warren sniffled and rested his head on his daughter's shoulder. "I'm so sorry, baby girl."

"It's just not fair. We weren't done living. He wasn't done being a father."

"No, he definitely wasn't," her dad said. "Whatever you and the girls need from me, I'll be there."

The knock on the door had Nadia and Warren sitting upright. The nurse, Geri, stepped in and smiled softly. She had taken Rafe as her patient during her shift, even though doing so wasn't normal. Staff rotated patients to avoid getting too close to them.

"Hi, Nadia," Geri said when she entered. She went over and checked the machines, which Nadia imagined hadn't changed. She had studied the monitors for a long time, and every line held steady.

"Any signs of a miracle heading our way?" Warren gave a little chuckle at the end of his question, hoping to lighten the mood. Nadia squeezed his hand in appreciation. She would need laughter, love, and whatever else her friends and family could provide her moving forward.

Geri smiled grimly. "Each time I come in, I wish I could give you a little hope." She shook her head slightly and sighed. "As is, I'm the bearer of bad news. Rafe's sister and her children are in the waiting room and want some private time with him."

Nadia fought hard not to roll her eyes. "Those children don't need to see their uncle like this."

This time, Warren squeezed her hand.

Nadia sighed. "What else?"

"The doctors want to meet with you again regarding organ donation."

Nadia covered her face with her hands and groaned. Warren wrapped his arm around her shoulders and leaned in. "Come on, let's give Freya time with her brother."

She nodded, but she still had no idea what the right thing to do was. Rafe was a selfless man who would do anything for anyone, so it made sense to her that he'd want to help as many people as possible. On the other hand, the idea of doctors chopping up her husband for pieces unnerved her. Even if she knew that wasn't how things worked.

With a deep inhale, she nodded. "You can let my sister-in-law in and tell the doctors I'm ready to make a decision."

Warren kissed the side of her head. "I'm proud of you, no matter which way you decide."

"Thanks."

Moments later, Freya Andersen walked in with her son, Leif, and her daughter, Astrid. Leif was three years older than Gemma, and Astrid was a year younger than Lynnea. Behind the kids, Freya's husband, Lars, took up most of the doorway.

Nadia hugged Freya and the kids, and then Lars. He and Rafe had been close, and she imagined he probably wanted his own time with his brother-in-law.

"I'll give you guys some time with him."

"Auntie Nadia." Astrid's small voice stopped Nadia in her tracks. "Will you still be my auntie after Uncle Rafe goes to heaven?"

Nadia crouched to her niece's level and pushed her pin-straight blonde hair away from her crystal-blue eyes. "I'll always be your auntie, Astrid. Always and forever." She kissed the child's forehead and fought back a sob. If adults couldn't understand death, how could children? Nadia left the room, closing the door behind her, and made her way toward the waiting room, where most of her family sat.

When she rounded the corner, strong arms wrapped around her waist in surprise. "Hey, what are you guys doing here?" she asked of her twelve- and ten-year-old nephews, Lincoln and Jaxon.

"Hey, Nadia." Adam, her former brother-in-law, came up behind her. "Sienna called and asked me to bring the boys up." Nadia hugged Adam. She had always liked him and was sad when he and her sister divorced.

"Thank you, Adam. I'm glad you're here. After Freya's done, you can go say your goodbyes."

"We appreciate that," he said as he gripped Lincoln's shoulder.

Nadia led her nephews into the waiting room, where her brother Reuben sat, along with their sister.

"When's the last time you ate?" Sienna asked Nadia.

"I don't even know." She shook her head. "Maybe I'll walk down to the cafeteria."

Sienna shot Adam a look. He cleared his throat. "How about I grab you something?"

"I'm okay, I could use a break. I think." Nadia rose and came face to face with Cleo; her anguish was clear on her face. Nadia couldn't begin to fathom how Cleo felt, and she didn't ever want to think of herself in the same situation. Children are supposed to outlive their parents. She went to her mother-in-law and hugged her tightly. The two women began to sob and were cocooned by the others. No one needed to see their grief.

When they parted, Cleo cupped Nadia's face. She opened her mouth to speak, but there were no words. Nadia nodded. She understood. Warren pulled Nadia into his strong arms and held her. Nadia needed her parents. And Rafe's.

"I'm going to get us some coffee," Adam said, giving them a small reprieve from the sorrow-filled room.

"Adam." Sienna said his name quietly. "Maybe order from the nearest Dunkin'. I think everyone deserves something fresh and not that watered-down crap from the basement."

"Good idea." He pulled his phone out of his pocket and typed as Warren directed Nadia to a chair.

"Why aren't you in there with Rafe?" Otto asked.

"Freya, Lars, and the kids are in there now. I wanted them to spend time alone with Rafe."

"I'm going to go see them," Cleo said and then walked off. Again, Nadia fought against rolling her eyes. Her thoughts on Cleo were topsy-turvy at best. She was an amazing grandmother, but a meddler as a parent. Freya and Rafe couldn't do anything without Cleo expecting some sort of consultation. When women joke that mothers and sons need to cut the cord—well, it wasn't much of a joke when it came to Cleo and Rafe. Nadia had thrown him a cord-cutting party the first time he'd told his mother no. Once he'd said it the first time, he said it more often.

Just never to Nadia.

By the time the coffee arrived, Freya and her brood had come out of Rafe's room, red eyed and with tearstained cheeks. The others exchanged greetings. Freya sat next to Sienna, while Adam and Lars stood, and the kids sat on the floor. The kids didn't need to be there, but they weren't hers, and there wasn't much she could do about it.

The voice of her nephew Lincoln rang out. "Aunt Nadia." She looked at him. "Do you think it's okay if we go in and say goodbye to Uncle Rafe now?"

Tears fell from her eyes as she nodded. "Of course it is."

Sienna kissed her sister on her cheek as she passed by and took her boys and Adam toward Rafe's room. Nadia watched them until they'd disappeared.

"I should probably call the funeral home," Cleo said to the rest of them.

"Please don't," Nadia stated quietly.

"You have enough on your plate," Cleo replied.

Nadia shook her head slightly and sighed. "I want to organize my husband's funeral. It's something . . ." She paused, closed her eyes, and let the tears stream down her cheeks.

"It's something Nadia needs to do," Warren said for his daughter. "As much as we all want to help, I think our efforts are going to be best used where the girls are concerned, on the household, and helping Nadia where she needs."

Cleo said nothing.

Nadia couldn't be with her at the moment and stood. "I'm going . . ." She pointed toward the hall. "I need a moment."

She walked down the hall, past the wooden doors leading to intensive care, past the small room where a doctor had shattered her world, and around a corner, where she found a solarium, lit up by the sun. She'd had no idea they were on the top floor of the hospital until she opened the door and stepped in.

Inside the solarium were a couch and a couple of chairs, with a fountain in one corner and a flower garden in another. This could easily be a place for prayer or a sanctuary away from the madness down the hall. It made sense for this room to be near the roof, closer to where people believed heaven was.

The sun enveloped her in warmth. She closed her eyes and absorbed the energy, wishing she could turn back the clock to Saturday morning and ask him not to run. They could drive out to Cape Cod instead and let the girls play in the sand and surf.

Nadia had long given up on wiping her tears away. She let them flow down her cheeks, onto the shirt her mother had brought from the house, and even onto her arms.

She lay down on the couch and stared through the glass ceiling at the blue, cloudless sky. If they were home, the girls would be outside and Rafe would be on their deck, turning the grill on for burgers and dogs, while Nadia sat on their swing with a book in her lap, secretly admiring her husband. She choked on a sob and didn't bother trying to stop it. She was the only one in the room, so no one was there to judge her.

Crying was supposed to be cathartic. It wasn't. She feared nothing would ever ease the pain she felt. Her husband had been gone for a day, and she missed him something fierce. She had to accept that once the machines were turned off, she'd never feel his heart beating against her hand or the warmth of his touch. Once he was sealed into a coffin, she'd never see him again.

"Rafe, please tell me what I'm supposed to do here."

A whooshing sound and a shadow appeared overhead. She caught the tail end of a helicopter flying by. Nadia stood and walked to the corner of the room and watched it land on the helipad. Once the blades had slowed, two people carrying a cooler ran toward the helicopter and got on. Then it was airborne again. She knew from her many shows that the cooler contained an organ destined to go and save someone's life.

Nadia had never been one to believe in signs until now. With a deep breath, she left the room and walked back to where her family waited, feeling a newfound purpose. When she reached the edge of the waiting room, she cleared her throat.

"I've decided to donate Rafe's organs. It's what he would want." She looked directly at Rafe's parents and sister. Otto nodded, while Freya sent daggers her way and comforted her mother.

To her own parents, she said, "Please have Hazel bring the girls. I want them here." She then left to go find the doctor.

An hour later, Nadia, Gemma, and Lynnea held hands and followed Rafe's bed into the elevator. When they reached the surgical floor, the doors opened to strangers lining both sides of the hall: nurses, orderlies, doctors, and other hospital staff, and the police officer who had helped her yesterday, along with other police officers, firefighters, and medics. At the end of the hall was their family. As Rafe passed by, everyone took their turn saying goodbye.

Before the doctor pressed the button to open the doors and take her husband and her children's father away, she told the girls to say their last goodbye.

"Dance with me in heaven, Daddy," Gemma said as she kissed her dad.

"I love you, Daddy," Lynnea cried as she said goodbye.

Nadia gripped Rafe's warm hand. "I will love you forever," she told him as she pushed her fingers through his hair. "Thank you for loving me, Rafe Karlsson."

She nodded to the surgeon and stepped back from his bed. She stared at the ground, unable to watch him disappear behind the doors.

Six

Reid

As much as she hated to admit it, Reid despised being at home or work without Grayson. It didn't help that they lived in the same apartment complex, a little fact they'd figured out the first day they'd met. Since then, they had fallen into an easy routine. Each morning, she'd text him she was leaving, and he'd meet her at the elevator. They'd walk to the train station, stopping to get coffee on the way. They had a work-life balance that worked for them. Reid liked routine, and right now, hers was off.

Almost a month had passed, with no end in sight. Reid kept her phone by her side, with the ringer full volume, in case Sydney called. Every day after work, Reid went to the hospital and sat by Grayson's side, reading to him, while Sydney went home and showered and saw her husband before coming back to sleep next to her son. Sydney was an optimist, and each day she said to Reid, "Today's the day, I can feel it."

Reid also detested hearing her say those words because it meant someone would need to lose a loved one for Grayson to live. In this day and age, science should've figured things out by now and created some way for people to live without a heart. As soon as she thought about it, she realized how ridiculous it would be. Science and technology were keeping Grayson alive for the time being.

During the day, when her thoughts ran wild, she spent far too much time on the web, looking up Grayson's illness and prognosis. The first night, she'd gone right to his place and rummaged through his drawers and cabinets until she'd found the pills Sydney had asked about. They were under his bathroom sink, hiding in the back. He'd refilled the bottle over six months earlier but hadn't taken any of the pills. She counted them. More than once. And each time, she'd grown angrier with him because all this was preventable. Reid pictured herself waking him up and shaking the ever-loving shit out of him for what he'd done to his mom and her.

Reid had read that heart transplant patients might experience some changes after the fact. Like going from loving something to hating it. She hoped Grayson wouldn't start hating basketball. He loved the game and loved playing it. That wasn't it, though. What if, after the transplant, he no longer wanted to be her friend? She felt guilty about him being there. Maybe if she hadn't brought up dating, he'd be at work right now. No, she knew this wasn't true. Grayson was lucky she was there when he had the heart attack.

Her phone rang, startling her. The screen showed Melanie's photo. After her heart went back to a normal rhythm, she put her earbud in and answered. "Hey."

"You busy?"

"Nah, just sort of going through the motions. I pretend I'm busy, though, so they don't fire me."

"Would they?"

"I hope not. Honestly, being here sucks."

"I get it. You're probably spending all your time reading obituaries."

Reid said nothing.

"Don't tell me you are! I was kidding."

"No, I'm not. I hadn't thought about doing that. I think it would be weird to know someone died and then Grayson's awake."

"Awkward."

Reid groaned. "What are you doing? Why aren't you working?" Melanie sold high-end real estate in Baltimore. She'd graduated from American with a degree in business and had fallen into the real estate market shortly after graduation.

"Waiting for my next showing."

"What football player are you selling a mega-house to now?"

Melanie laughed. "Nothing like that. I was thinking I'd come up after my showing, though. Spend the weekend."

As much as she wanted to see her best friend, she didn't want to miss time with Grayson. "I . . . uh."

"I know, you want to sit in the hospital with Grayson. I'm good with that, but we'll also hang with Pearce, get something to eat, sit on your couch, and eat Dibs. I'm not taking no for an answer."

Reid sighed as she gave in. "Fine."

"And because I love you so much, I'll come right to the hospital. Make sure I'm on Grayson's list."

"I will. Call me when you get there."

"Love you." Melanie disconnected the call.

Reid took her earbud out, then picked up the receiver of her desk phone and dialed Pearce's extension. "Can you come to my office?" she asked when he picked up.

"Am I coming to HR because I'm in trouble, or is this a social visit?"

"Social," she told him. Anytime HR had to talk to Grayson or Pearce, Reid made sure it was one of the other staffers. She never wanted to give any employees an excuse to accuse her of favoritism.

Moments later, Pearce strolled into the office, which had a large receptionist's desk and four cubicles, one for each staffer. Only the director had a private, behind-closed-doors office.

"Hey, just here to see Reid," she heard Pearce say. She leaned over her chair, her head hanging past her partition.

"Hey," she said when he came into view.

"What's up?" Pearce sat in the extra chair in her office. Both he and Grayson sat there often when they came to "shoot the shit" with her. Part of her hated that they treated her like one of the guys, but if they didn't, she wouldn't spend nearly as much time with Grayson. Maybe that was her problem—she was one of the guys, when she wanted to be the only woman in Grayson's life. Aside from his mom.

"Mel's coming to town tonight. She wants to hang out this weekend. Do you have plans tomorrow?"

Pearce waggled his eyebrows.

Reid swatted his legs. "Uh, did you forget you're getting married?"

His face scrunched. "Yeah, about that."

"What?"

"Remember when I went to lunch with Emelia's father?"

The day Grayson had his heart attack.

Reid would rather not remember that day. She nodded.

"Well, lunch was a test, and I failed. Emelia wants a ring, wants to buy a house and have three children, all two years apart, unless she has twins on the first try." Pearce covered his face with his hands and groaned. "Here's the kicker—I don't need to buy the house or even impregnate her, but I do need to be her husband because she's not getting any younger and the clock is ticking."

"Wait," Reid said. "I thought she was twenty-five?"

"She is."

Reid's mouth made an O, and then she quickly shut it. "I'm sorry, Pearce."

"Me too. I suppose there are more fish out there."

"There is. Once you stop thinking about us women being fish. We're not fish."

Pearce's cheeks flushed. "You're right. Anyway, I'm down for hanging out. What are we doing?"

"Mel's going to meet me at the hospital later. She said dinner, eating ice cream, that sort of thing. I know she's trying to keep my mind off Grayson."

"Are we hanging at the hospital?"

Reid shook her head. "No, I'll stay until Sydney comes back. Then Mel and I will head to my place. Tomorrow, Gilbert will be around, so I don't necessarily need to go to the hospital."

"You will, though."

Pearce wasn't wrong.

"You're very kind to do that for him, all things considered."

Pearce didn't have to elaborate. Reid knew. Her feelings toward Grayson were obvious to anyone in their path. Most people who saw them together thought they were a couple.

"I don't do it for him," Reid said. "I do it for Sydney."

Pearce nodded. Reid didn't care if he believed her or not. If Reid didn't volunteer to stay with Grayson a few hours each day, Sydney would never leave. That wasn't healthy. Gilbert did his part on the weekends, but with Sydney taking a leave of absence from work, he couldn't be there every day. The way Reid saw it, Grayson was her best friend—despite her being in love with him. After he made it through this, she'd start to ease herself out of his life. No matter how badly it hurt.

"He loves you. You know that, right?"

Reid inhaled quickly, the statement catching her off guard. She didn't know anything. Not when it came to Grayson.

"The wheels are turning, Reid. I can see them. Look, I don't know why he lied about this thing with his heart or why he wasn't taking his meds. I've known for a while, but he said everything was under control. Guys don't hound each other about this kind of shit. I wish I had, though. Six months ago, he mentioned being a better person. This was something I did push him on, and he said he wanted to pursue a relationship. Another push and he finally admitted it was you he wanted to be with. Saying he was in love with you but feared he'd ruined everything. Whatever that meant."

Reid absorbed Pearce's words, unsure what she should believe, him or Grayson's actions, because actions often spoke louder than words.

Over the past six months, Grayson had not shown her he was interested at any given time. Unless she hadn't been paying attention.

"Anyway." Pearce stood and stretched. "I'm in for this weekend. Call me with the details."

"I will. See you later."

Later, she found herself sitting in a chair next to Grayson's bed while she waited for Melanie to arrive. Reid flipped through the most recent issue of her favorite magazine. She took the love quiz and found out the strong, manly type with a soft side was the type of man she was destined for. Scoffing, she glanced over at Grayson. He was the strong, manly type for sure, and he had a soft side, but he rarely showed it to anyone. On occasion, when they were alone watching a movie, he'd do something like hold her hand or rub her feet, but then he'd make some wisecrack comment about how they smelled or how she needed a pedicure, and the moment would be ruined. The more she thought, the more their life together replayed in her mind. They'd had a lot of moments together, too many to count, but each time they got close or she had the "dreamy eyes," as Grayson would say, he'd do a one-eighty.

Reid stood and leaned against his bed. She studied him for a long moment, jealous of how long his eyelashes were and envious because if she ever wanted hers that long, she needed a special mascara or falsies.

"Grayson Caballero, I am mad at you. The doctors say this could've been prevented, but your stubborn ass hasn't been taking your meds. And now look at ya. To make things more complicated, Pearce tells me that you love me. Do you?" She waited for a response that wouldn't come. "You know how I feel about you. I've been in love with you since the day we met." Reid chuckled slightly. "Okay, yeah. We know that's not true. Instant attraction for sure, but the feelings were there rather quickly. At least for me."

Reid held Grayson's hand. It was warm, thanks to the machines keeping him alive. "And then we . . ." She couldn't bring herself to say the words as her body heated from the memory of the night they had spent together.

◆ ◆ ◆

The Wold Collective holiday party was one for the record books. Dinner, dancing, and an endless flow of champagne and an open bar. The owners really knew how to treat their employees. Music thumped, the DJ in the corner playing all the top hits, mixing it up occasionally with some holiday jingles.

Reid's red dress was tight fitting, accentuating every curve she had and pushing her girls up for attention. She only wanted Grayson's attention. After months and months of flirting and innuendoes, it was the right time for her to do something about it. She finished off the last bit of champagne in her flute.

"It's now or never," Reid said to herself.

She sauntered over to him, making sure to move her hips seductively. Grayson leaned against the bar, talking to Pearce and some new guy who'd recently started. Reid couldn't recall his name. None of that mattered. She was solely focused on Grayson.

"Sexy" was not a word she used to describe herself. "Plain," "average," "run-of-the-mill" were more her speed. The champagne gave her courage to loosen up, to be sexier. When she approached, Grayson angled himself to greet her. His smirk told her he liked what he saw.

Reid trailed her finger up his black tie, then wrapped her hands around it and tugged him forward. "Welp, guys, duty calls," she heard him say as he followed her. Grayson closed the distance between them and brought her hips flush against his groin. She could feel him, pressing into her backside.

She took him to the dance floor. To her surprise, he laced his fingers with hers and gave her a twirl. She laughed, loving the feeling of this new flirtatiousness. Reid stepped away from Grayson and started moving her hips to the music. It was a fast song, and she had regrets about making her move then instead of during a slow one.

Grayson wasn't having it. He linked his arm around her back and pulled her close to him. She gasped and slowly looked into his eyes. Later, she'd wonder how long she'd stared into his brown orbs before she realized the song was over and they were leaving.

Outside, Grayson hailed a cab and held her close in the back seat. They never took their eyes off each other, and she never stopped his hand from sliding up her dress. Reid wanted him.

The moment they stepped into his apartment, he had Reid pressed against the wall. His lips were on hers. They were all hands, tongues, and need. He gathered her dress in his hands and hiked it over her hips, and then he picked her up. Her legs wrapped around his waist, her fingers fumbling with his tie and the buttons on his shirt when she felt him tease her. Reid lifted herself slightly and then pushed down on him.

Grayson groaned.

"I need you out of this dress," he said when his knees hit the edge of his bed. He set her down, stepped back, and began ripping his shirt off. Reid watched, lost in the moment. They'd waited so long to get to this part of their relationship, and it was finally happening. After Grayson undid his belt and the button on his slacks, he pulled the zipper down slowly, showing her his bulge.

Reid swallowed hard and licked her lips in anticipation. She got onto her knees and slowly bunched her dress up until she'd pulled it over her head. She was there, naked except for the black lace thong she wore. Reid couldn't look at him. She didn't want to see his expression.

"Look at me," he said as he slowly lifted her chin with his finger. "You're so fucking beautiful. Don't hide from me."

Reid did what he asked and saw nothing but adoration and yearning.

He pushed his pants and boxers to the ground. His cock sprung free, slapping against his stomach. Reid wanted to see him, all of him, every part of him, and didn't know where to look. Instead, she watched him as he opened his bedside table to get a condom.

Reid moved toward him, their height difference working to her advantage. She peppered his chest with open-mouthed kisses until she'd reached his lips. He smiled down at her, his eyes glittering with keenness and desire. His fingertips traced the outline of her lips, causing her heart to flutter wildly in her chest.

The smell of him, a heady mix of familiar musk and the comforting scent of his cologne, stirred something deep within her. She traced the curve of his lips with hers, the sweetness of their connection blooming into an intoxicating warmth. Being there with him, naked and vulnerable, knowing they were about to cross a line, was overwhelming yet comfortingly real.

His hands gripped her waist, pulling her closer until their bodies were melded together. The air between them sizzled with electricity, the tension palpable. His breath hitched as their bare skin met.

"I want you, Reid," he whispered against her lips.

"You have no idea—"

Grayson didn't wait for her to finish her statement. He plunged his tongue into her mouth and slipped his finger under her thong and between her folds. Grayson swallowed her wanton cry and deftly pushed his hand in an upward motion. If she hadn't been kneeling, she would've crumpled to the floor. Being touched by him felt like no man had ever touched her before.

She called his name when his thumb grazed her sensitive bud. He smiled against her lips and slowly maneuvered Reid onto her back. Grayson removed his fingers and sat back on his knees, kissing a path along her thigh until he'd reached her core. He nuzzled her and kissed her lace panties before taking them off.

"You don't know how long I've wanted to do this, Reid," Grayson said against her skin, his scruff tickling her. She ran her fingers through his hair, tugging on the ends.

"Hopefully as long as I have."

Grayson ripped open the condom and settled between her legs. He leaned forward, hovering over her, and then lowered his mouth to hers. She felt him there, at her entrance. Her hips bucked in an attempt to guide him where she wanted him. Where she needed him.

He smiled and let out a small chuckle. "Eager?"

"God, yes," she said between breaths. "And horny."

"Me too," he said as he kissed his way down her neck until he'd reached her breast, taking her taut nipple into his mouth.

"Shit," she muttered as her body squirmed.

Grayson chuckled again. "Ah, she likes this. Duly noted." He paid attention to her other breast and then worked his way back up her body. "Look at me, Reid. I want to see you when . . ."

She met his gaze, and he didn't need to finish his sentence.

Reid wiped an errant tear from her cheek. She'd thought that was going to be their turning point. She looked back at Grayson. "I thought things were going to be different for us, and they sort of were. You were always there, but never close enough. You let me in, and you keep me there, but always on the edge. I feel like you're always waiting for the next shoe to drop, and I guess it has. This was the shoe. It's finally dropped, and there isn't anything either of us can do about it unless you get a new heart. And if you don't . . ." Reid trailed off.

She was in love with Grayson, but she was ready to settle down and start a family. Reid wanted kids, a house, a husband to love her. At this point, she wanted a boyfriend. Someone to adore her, worship her, make her feel like no one else mattered in their world.

Grayson wouldn't give her what she needed, and it was foolish to think she could have everything she desired with him as her friend. Anyone looking at them would assume they were a couple or at least messing around with each other. Their closeness went way beyond friendship. No one would believe her if she told them they were just friends.

Friends were all they'd ever be unless . . .

Thinking about the alternative made her stomach twist into knots. She didn't want her last conversation with Grayson to be about her dating. They'd argued, and she'd accused him of faking the heart attack. It was like him to prank her. He'd pulled silly little jokes on her before. This time, there was a hint of panic in his voice that had made her go to him.

Reid sighed and went back to her chair. She was out of things to talk to him about. The spring weather only went so far in conversation, and she had no idea what was happening in his department at work. Pearce would have to fill him in there.

She reached for the blanket Sydney kept at the end of the bed and wrapped herself in it. Reid nestled into the chair, getting as comfortable as she could before closing her eyes. She'd grown accustomed to the beeping and whooshing from the machines and oddly found it pacifying. As much as she hated what those noises stood for, she'd learned to accept them. Grayson would recover. He had to. Reid wasn't ready for him to leave her. She refused to give up on loving him or him loving her. If what Pearce said was true, then maybe Grayson and Reid had a future together. Of course, once he was out of the hospital. He needed a miracle, and she was confident one would come.

When she woke, it was dark out. She combed through her purse, looking for her phone. Melanie should be in town, and Sydney should've been back by now. Reid stood, stretched, and glanced at Grayson, and while he hadn't moved a muscle, she secretly hoped he'd be awake. She was about to head to the door when Sydney burst into the room, startling Reid. The two women looked at each other, eyes wide and hearts beating fast.

"There's a heart, and it's a match."

SEVEN

REID

"What?" Reid was certain she hadn't heard Sydney correctly.

"We have a heart, and it's a match," Sydney repeated. "We got the call right when we pulled into the parking lot." Gilbert leaned around and waved at Reid, bringing a tiny bit of humor to a very delicate situation.

"He's going to be okay?" Reid asked as she burst into tears. She stood and went to Sydney, hugging her tightly. "He's going to be okay," she said again, but this time it was more for Grayson's mom than anything else, even though Reid needed the reassurance as well.

As happy as they were that Grayson would get a second chance at life, someone had died. A family, somewhere out there, was going through the unthinkable. They had lost someone they loved and would move forward with their lives without them, while Sydney, Gilbert, and Reid would have endless days with the one they loved.

Reid expected the surgery to be first thing in the morning and was shocked when the staff came in moments later and started prepping Grayson for surgery. They moved like well-trained robots, and within seconds, they were pushing Grayson's hospital bed out of the room before Reid could blink.

"What just happened?"

"They're taking him to surgery," Gilbert told her. "The heart is in transport."

"Just like that?" Reid shook her head. "The doctors drop everything?"

Sydney nodded. "Time is of the essence."

Reid blinked and cleared the fuzziness away. She'd been napping when Sydney startled her with the most amazing yet heartbreaking news. Thoughts of the latter wouldn't do any of them any good, so she pushed them out of her mind. Unsure of what to do, she gathered her things, folded the throw blanket she'd taken from Grayson's bed, and went to put it back, only to see it was gone. She sat in the chair and sighed. "Wow."

"I know, it's a lot to wrap my mind around as well," Sydney said. "Come on, let's go to the atrium. The restaurant there is twenty-four hours. We can at least drink some coffee and eat something while we wait. It's going to be a while."

Reid nodded and stood. She followed Sydney out, with Gilbert trailing behind them. "I just don't understand how doctors are alert at this hour to do surgery."

"They'll be fine," Gilbert said as they stepped into the elevator. "They wouldn't risk anyone's life."

She hoped he was right.

Upon entering the restaurant, they placed an order for food and coffee and found a booth near the window, which Reid was thankful for. Her body welcomed the cushioned bench with a sigh. Finally feeling more relaxed, she pulled out her phone and texted Pearce to give him an update. She expected him to return to the hospital, knowing he'd want to be there, and then she sent one to her dad. Lastly, she sent one to Melanie, letting her know what was going on.

Their food came: pasta for her, and an assortment of cookies and pastries for Sydney and Gilbert.

"You're so calm," Reid said to them both. "How can you eat, knowing your son is . . ." Reid couldn't finish her question.

"Idle hands means idle minds," Gilbert told her. "If I'm not doing something, I'm going to sit here and think about what they're doing in the operating room. I'd rather not right now."

Sydney nodded and rested her head on her husband's arm. "I like to think we're having dinner and dessert with a friend." She smiled at Reid, who appreciated Sydney's optimism.

They ate, made idle chitchat, and watched the clock. Time was on their side. The doctors had given Sydney a three-to-five-hour window for surgery—Gilbert guessed it would take four. But everything on the internet told Reid they might end up waiting up to eight hours. That was how long it took for the complicated surgeries—the ones that needed more time—and her gut told her Grayson would need all the time the doctors could muster.

By the time Pearce and Luther arrived an hour after she'd texted, the three of them had been picking at their food for a couple of hours. Melanie had opted to go to Reid's apartment and wait. Reid tried to keep from looking at the clock every ten minutes. Instead, she looked every eleven, fifteen, or twenty minutes.

Luther brought over more coffee and pulled a chair up to the end of the table. Pearce sat next to Reid.

"Should we be doing something?" Pearce asked.

"Like what?" Reid asked.

Pearce looked at each of them and shrugged. "I feel like Grayson would want us playing cards or something."

Reid chuckled. "Playing cards?"

Pearce picked up the wrapper from his straw, rolled it into a ball, and then unraveled it. "My go-to is basketball, but it's too dark," he said. "Besides, I want to be here and there isn't a court, and I don't really want to deal with anyone from work right now."

"Grayson will be happy when he can go back to work," Sydney added.

"Do you know when that'll be?" Pearce asked.

"At least six months," she said. "Unless he can work from home; then he can go back after three. Gilbert and I liquidated some assets to make sure Grayson's rent is paid."

"You did?" Reid asked.

"Yeah, we don't really know his financial situation or how much sick time he has at work," Sydney said.

"We all donated to his sick time," Pearce said before Reid could answer. It was against company policy for her to do or say anything about Grayson's sick time. However, Pearce had taken it upon himself to send out a company-wide email asking people to contribute a day to Grayson's leave.

"He has enough time until medical leave kicks in," Pearce said as he looked at Reid for confirmation. She nodded.

"I've already submitted the paperwork," she told Sydney. "Grayson should be all set until he can return to work."

"That's such a relief." She smiled kindly at Pearce and Reid.

Luther cleared his throat. "Anything I can do to help, you'll let me know?" He directed his question at the group of them.

"Of course," Gilbert said. "This is definitely going to be one of those village moments where we all pitch in."

"We can work out his physical therapy schedule as well," Reid added. "There's a site near our office—if we can book him there, Pearce and I can help out most days. We'll just have to get him there." It dawned on her that none of them had cars, except for the parents in the group. Living in the city, everything they needed was either within walking distance or could be accessed by train. She could get any big purchases delivered.

"I can borrow my sister's car, if need be," Pearce told the group. "She runs an at-home day care and doesn't leave during the day. I don't think she'll mind, as long as I give it a good wash every now and again. Plus, it's one of those minivans, so super easy to get in and out of."

Sydney put her hand over her heart and closed her eyes for a moment. "Grayson truly has the best friends and support system."

Reid thought the same, even though she had a barrage of questions for Grayson. As much as she loved him, she was angry with him for hiding this situation from her. She would've made sure he took his meds and watched his diet. Was that why he never told her?

She could've been more prepared when he collapsed, instead of thinking he was faking it. What would've happened if she'd walked away from him? Would he have died? Surely, someone would've stepped up and aided him, but then what? Where would she be now? Riddled with guilt.

The more she thought about the situation, the angrier she became. So much of what was happening now could've easily been avoided if Grayson had been honest.

Reid moved her empty cup of coffee back and forth in her hands and stared at the carpet until her vision blurred. Rampant thoughts filtered through her mind, about Grayson, her, and the two of them together. Every day she worked to remind herself they were friends—the best of friends—despite their mutual attraction to each other. He could tell her until he was blue in the face that he didn't feel anything for her, but she knew that wasn't true. His feelings for her were evident in how he acted around her, especially when other men were interested. "Machismo" didn't even scratch the surface of his personality when other men entered the picture.

With her thoughts taking her in a direction she didn't want to go, she tried to focus on the conversation going on around her. Pearce filled everyone in about how one of their coworkers had suggested that people either plan a dinner for him or donate to a fund to buy groceries.

"That's really nice of them," Reid said and wondered why she hadn't heard of it. Although it wasn't uncommon for the people at the Wold Collective to leave Human Resources out of things. The company employees often looked at HR as the gatekeepers—and people didn't appreciate that.

Reid looked at the time on the clock and sighed. "Three hours in," she said to the group.

Sydney tapped the screen on her phone. "They're going to call when he's out of surgery. They'll take him to recovery and begin weaning him off the anesthesia."

"Will he regain consciousness?" Pearce asked.

"Yes, if all goes as planned, Grayson will be coherent by the afternoon," Gilbert said.

"Great," Pearce said with a half chuckle. "He's going to be pissed he missed March Madness."

Reid and Gilbert groaned.

"Let's not tell him right away," Gilbert suggested.

"Makes me appreciate the lack of television in the ICU," Reid added.

Luther chuckled. "He's going to be pissed off, that's for sure, but he's neither a UConn nor San Diego State fan, so maybe he won't be that mad."

"That's what we'll say when he figures out that he's missed some time," Gilbert said. "We'll play it off like the game wasn't worth watching."

"I like the way you think," Pearce added.

They sat there another hour, watching the clock and Sydney's phone. When the screen finally lit up, she waited for a couple of rings, the fear of not knowing clear in her wide brown eyes. With a shaky hand, she picked up the phone and answered. Everyone at the table waited with bated breath for her to show some sort of recognition on her face. When she hung up, she had four sets of eyes studying her.

"Well?" Gilbert said before Sydney could open her mouth.

"Surgery was successful."

Everyone exhaled in relief.

"The new heart started beating as soon as the arteries and veins joined. It was like this heart was meant for Grayson." Sydney sobbed at the end, and Gilbert brought his wife into his arms. He held her and shed his own tears.

Reid, Pearce, and Luther found that they were crying as well. Reid would never admit this to anyone, but there was a time when she thought this day would never come, or it would be too late. The longer Grayson needed the machines to stay alive, the more his body deteriorated.

They cleaned their space, thanked the overnight workers for accommodating them for hours, and headed toward the ICU. Once Grayson was out of recovery and back in his room, Sydney and Gilbert would stay with him until he woke; then Reid and Pearce could go in. Luther said his goodbyes, kissed his daughter, and headed home to get a nap in before he had to go to work. He told them he expected a text later, letting him know Grayson had woken up, and said he'd happily share the March Madness news when the time was right.

Now, they waited.

Back on the floor, they sat in the waiting room, with the television muted and next to other family members who were waiting for visiting hours to start. There was an unwritten rule that you didn't ask about others in the unit, but after being there for so long, it was nice to talk to people. Reid had learned about a couple of the others staying on the floor. One woman had had a kidney transplant. Her daughter, who didn't have a great relationship with her mother, was the donor. Reid thought the situation was a bit odd but kept her thoughts to herself. Another woman had severe pneumonia and needed constant monitoring.

When Sydney and Gilbert finally got the call, they were out of there like their asses were on fire, leaving Pearce and Reid to wait. Anxious, she ran her hands over her pants and told Pearce she couldn't sit there any longer.

He followed her out of the room and directed her to the coffee station, even though they'd drunk enough through the night and really didn't need any more. Pearce guided her to the end of the hallway, where a large picture window and bench were. They sat and stared out the window.

Clouds covered the sky and blocked the sun from shining through as it rose. Reid focused on the orange ball of fire and tried to recall the last time she'd watched the sunrise. She needed the sun, and wanted to feel its warmth on her face. Reid leaned forward and cast her eyes upward, in hopes of seeing a ray or two.

Nothing.

Resigned, she rested against the wall and sipped the stale coffee. "You know, someone should man the coffee station."

"I'm sure they have someone who's supposed to do it, when they aren't covering a million other things," Pearce said as he leaned against the glass. "Freaking clouds," he muttered.

"At least it'll be somewhat warm out."

"As much as I'm ready for summer, I'm not ready for the humidity."

"Nope," Reid agreed. "Not to mention, summer's going to look a lot different this year. Grayson won't be able to go to the lake. I mean, I guess he can go to the lake, but he won't be able to go out on the boat or in the water."

"I'll probably stay in town during vacation this year," Pearce said.

"He won't want you to."

"I know, but it's the right thing to do."

Reid nodded. She, too, would change her plans to stay with Grayson. "Can I ask you something?"

"Sure."

"You said earlier that he was in love with—"

Before she could finish her question, Pearce began nodding.

"If he is, why not say something? Why does he keep me at arm's length?"

Pearce looked from her, out the window, and then at the ground. "I don't know, Reid. I do know he's in love with you. He's said as much. Each time I'd ask why you guys weren't together, he'd brush me off. For the longest time, I thought it was because you didn't want to date a coworker, but I know that's not true."

"That's what I thought about him," she said. "It's not a policy. I mean, they definitely don't like it, but there isn't anything enforceable in our handbook."

"You could always ask him."

Reid shook her head. "Doesn't change anything," she told him. "I still want to date and find the one I'm supposed to be with. I used to think that was Grayson, but he's made it clear over the years we're nothing more than friends."

"With benefits," Pearce pointed out.

She opened her mouth and then closed it quickly. "Absolutely not. We've been together one time," she told him. "And the next day, he told me it would never happen again."

Pearce's mouth dropped open. "Yeah, he's led us all to believe you're in a benefits situation."

"What an asshole," she muttered. "You know he said that so no one would pursue me."

Pearce nodded. "Without a doubt. Damn. I know there's a handful of guys who would've asked you out."

Reid rolled her eyes. "Jerk. I have half a mind to tell him I'm seeing someone since he's been out of it for so long."

Pearce laughed. "Can you imagine? I think you should totally play it up. Do the whole 'I didn't know if you'd make it' thing. He'd crap himself."

Reid grimaced. "I told him I was going to start dating—that's how we ended up here." She ran her hand over her face. "I'm so stupid."

"You're not," he told her. "I think we've all been there at one point in our lives. You just gotta move forward with your life and let him do his thing. He'll realize he messed up sooner or later."

"Yeah, maybe." She felt guilty about wanting to date and Grayson's reaction, even though she knew she wasn't at fault.

Gilbert found them at the end of the hall. He had a beaming smile on his face. "Reid, if you want, you can go in. Grayson's asking for you."

"He is?" She stood and took a shaky step toward Gilbert, who nodded.

"After he asked what happened, he asked where you were."

Reid glanced at Pearce. "I told you."

Okay, so maybe Grayson was in love with her, and it had taken this colossal moment for him to realize it.

"Wow, okay." Reid had tunnel vision. She dumped her coffee cup in the nearest trash can and walked briskly toward the double doors. Once she was in, the nurse helped her scrub her hands and put on a gown, which would be necessary until the sutures healed.

Reid paused at the door. Grayson was awake, and gone were the machines that kept him alive. He still had oxygen, but now the tubes rested along his cheeks and pushed air through his nostrils. She cleared her throat, and Sydney looked over. She smiled.

"Grayson, Reid's here now."

"Yeah?" His eyes opened slightly, and he smiled. "Hey," he said as he tried to lift his hand toward her. Reid rushed to his side and gripped his hand in hers. Tears she thought had long dried up streamed down her face.

"Hey," she said.

"I'm going to give you guys a few minutes." Sydney left the room.

"I've never been so happy to see those brown eyes of yours." She brushed her hand through his hair, like she had done many times during his stay.

"I'm sorry," he said quietly.

"Don't be," she told him. "Everything's good now."

"Yeah," he said as he started to fall back to sleep.

Reid sat next to him and refused to let go of his hand.

"I should've told her that I love her," he said softly.

"Told who?" Reid asked. She waited for him to respond. When he said nothing, she prodded. "Who do you love, Grayson?"

"Sully."

Eight

Nadia

Nadia woke, startled, heart racing, beads of sweat dripping from her forehead. Her eyes came in and out of focus. Colored shadows danced on the wall and voices spoke softly, their words muddled and unfamiliar. She blinked, and her eyes darted around the room, absorbing the familiarity of her bedroom. Nadia exhaled and rolled onto her back. It was a nightmare. That's all. The sound of crushing metal, the agonizing and scared screams of the injured—she made it all up. She wasn't there. Her girls weren't there. She reached for Rafe.

He's not here.

Where was he?

She sat up quickly, scrambled out of bed, and rushed to the bathroom.

Empty.

His clothes hung in the closet. He had to be in the house.

She opened her bedroom door. More voices. More unfamiliar sounds.

"Rafe?" she called out as she inched her way down the hall toward the noise. "Rafe?"

Nadia crept down the stairs and into the catchall room. Rafe sat at their shared desk with his head bent. "Rafe?"

He looked up with the blackest eyes possible. She took a step back. "Rafe?"

He stood and came toward her. Arms outstretched, waiting for her.

Her heart thumped wildly in her chest. A voice told her to run, and to run fast. But she couldn't make her legs move.

"Rafe?" she said, her voice quivering. He stopped and turned. The side of his head was caved in, and she could see into the depths of his skull. His neck contorted in angles it shouldn't. Bugs, snakes, and worms crawled out.

Nadia screamed.

"Wake up, Nadia."

She felt pressure on her shoulders and fought whoever tried to hold her down.

"Nadia, wake up!"

Her eyes darted open at the sound of her father's voice. He hovered over her, fear etched across his face. An instant wave of emotion took over, and realization weighed heavily on her as her senses returned. The dream hadn't been a nightmare but her reality. She sobbed as her father pulled her to his chest.

"It's okay. I got you," he said as his hand moved up and down her back. The side of the bed dipped where Rafe should've been, and she smelled the familiar scent of strawberries-and-cream shampoo. Small arms wrapped around her midsection, and her body sighed, almost as if it needed her children.

Nadia let go of her father and brought her babies to her, holding and caressing them as best she could. Gemma was tall for her age, but not Lynnea. Not the baby of the family. She curled into her mother's side, stuck her thumb in her mouth, and wept quietly. Gemma maneuvered her body so she was on the other side of her sister and rested her head on her mom's chest. She, too, cried.

When Nadia woke again, she had no awareness of the time or even the day. For all she knew it had been weeks since her world had been upended. When she glanced at the TV, she was reminded abruptly that days had passed.

Over a sleeping Lynnea, Nadia reached for the remote and shut the television off. She vaguely remembered turning it on hours ago and falling asleep to *Rudy*, Rafe's favorite movie, with her girls snuggled next to her.

Nadia looked at Lynnea, with her thumb in her mouth. A habit they'd broken when she was three. Nadia left her thumb there and would deal with it later. She turned to Gemma, who stared back at her with the same soulful brown eyes as hers.

"Hi," she said quietly so as to not wake Lynnea.

"Hi," Gemma replied. "I don't want to go to school today." Tears pooled in her eyes.

"You don't have to," Nadia told her. "You can stay home for the rest of the week."

Gemma nodded slightly. Nadia kissed her forehead. If she had her choice, her girls wouldn't ever leave her sight.

"And Lynnea."

Nadia shook her head. "Nope. And me neither." She didn't want to return to work. In her mind, it would be one thing if her husband had passed away, but to be killed while saving another woman during an annual road race all because someone's brakes had failed—someone who shouldn't have been driving down the road to begin with—put Nadia's situation front and center. Everyone knew how Rafe had died. It'd been on the news and continued to air while an investigation took place. The news channels interviewed people who'd been there, reminding Nadia repeatedly that people had witnessed her husband dying.

"Does Daddy get a funeral?" It was after they had returned home from the hospital that Nadia explained to the girls what the doctors were doing to Rafe. Lynnea didn't like it, and Gemma said she was proud of her dad and how he was going to save someone's life. Those words only sparked Lynnea's outburst as she questioned why someone couldn't save her daddy's life. Nadia had the same thoughts.

"Yeah, he does."

"Do I have to go?"

Nadia pondered her question and nodded. "If you don't go, you might regret it later, and it's not something you can change."

"But I don't want to see Daddy in the coffin."

"I understand. You can sit in the pew, next to me. You don't have to see him if you don't want to."

"Okay." Her voice was small, nothing like the outgoing child she was a few days ago. Nadia pictured her and Rafe, dancing in the kitchen, and him telling her to put her feet on top of his. He'd twirled her around like a princess.

"I'm so sorry, Gemma," Nadia found herself saying. "I know I'm hurting, but I can't even imagine how you and Lynnea feel."

"Lynnea's angry. She was throwing stuff in her room."

"That's okay too," Nadia told Gemma. "I'm angry. Sad. Hurt. My heart is broken for you, your sister, Daddy, and me. Daddy didn't want this."

"The person who did this needs to die."

As angry as Nadia was, she didn't want that. Deep down, she knew this was an accident, an avoidable one. The person who hit Rafe would have to live the rest of their life knowing they'd killed someone.

"Then their mommy would be very sad. We don't wish death on anyone, no matter how badly they hurt us."

Gemma's lower lip quivered. "Okay," she said in a broken voice. Nadia pulled Gemma to herself and did her best to cradle her daughter without disturbing Lynnea. Nadia wept with her oldest and wondered how they were going to get through the next stage of their lives.

They lay there, waiting for Lynnea to wake up. Tragedy had struck their family, but Nadia and Gemma both knew waking Lynnea before she was ready was never a good thing. Instead, Nadia turned the television back on, chose a movie on one of the streaming platforms, and hunkered down in bed with Gemma.

Gemma laughed at the funny parts, which made Nadia happy, despite the heaviness she felt weighing on her chest. Sooner than she wanted, she would have to start making plans for Rafe's funeral and figure out how to manage the household on one income. They had life insurance policies for each other, which Nadia never thought either of them would have to use. That paperwork could all go away until tomorrow or the next day. She didn't want to take any time away from her babies.

When Lynnea finally woke, she complained about being hungry. Nadia could've sent her girls downstairs, where her parents would've taken care of them. Had she done that, her mother would've come upstairs and lectured her on how the girls needed their mother.

With a herculean effort, Nadia got out of bed. She started toward her bathroom, saw Rafe's clothes, and immediately turned back into her room. Gemma and Lynnea watched her every move. Nadia would have to eventually walk through the closet to her bathroom—today wasn't that day.

"Come on, let's go downstairs." She didn't have to tell Lynnea twice. Gemma, on the other hand, eyed her mother warily. After she stopped to use the bathroom in the hallway, Nadia stood at the top of the stairs, questioning why she was out of bed. There were so many voices coming from the living room and kitchen. Mixing and mingling with each other. Dishware clanked against counters, chairs scraped against the hardwood floors, and the TV blared with the news.

"Are you staying up there?" Gemma asked from the bottom of the stairs.

Nadia shook her head and slowly made her way down. Gemma gripped her hand and led her mother into the madhouse that was the kitchen.

"Oh, honey. It's good to see you up." Her mother wore an apron Nadia didn't remember owning. Nadia's sister and Rafe's sister sat in the breakfast nook where Nadia and the girls had shared their last meal with Rafe.

"Where's Dad?"

"The men are in the other room, watching the news," Sienna said. "Cleo's in there as well."

"I don't want that on when the girls are in the room," Nadia said to everyone there.

"Why?" Freya asked.

Nadia stared incredulously at her sister-in-law. Freya had to be kidding, right? Nadia looked from Freya to Gemma and Lynnea, and then shook her head.

"I don't feel well. I'm going back upstairs."

"Nadia, honey," her mom started, but Nadia was already headed to the stairs. She felt Gemma staring at her each step she took, but she never turned around. Nadia didn't need to see the disappointment on her daughter's face.

No one prepares you for death. At least an unexpected death. Sure, if your loved one has a terminal illness, you can go to a support group or read a book about how to prepare. But there isn't a manual on how to handle your grief, and the grief of others, when someone unexpectedly passes away.

No one prepares you for life after death. The things someone must do before they can properly grieve. The phone calls, paperwork, meetings—it's a never-ending list of *We need this, Give me that*—all while you're trying to come to terms with losing your husband, lover, father of your children . . . your best friend.

Rafe was gone, and to Nadia nothing would ever be the same. Not the way she slept, showered, dressed, or got ready in the morning. Her once shiny and vibrant hair, the color her husband loved so much, was dull and lifeless. Her once naturally rosy cheeks looked pale.

Nadia stared at herself in the mirror of the guest bathroom. Whatever she had to do today, she could do tomorrow or the next day. What would the morgue do with Rafe's body if she didn't make arrangements right away? Throw him away? The doctors had already cut a massive Y in his torso to remove his heart, lungs, liver, kidneys, and whatever else they wanted. They piecemealed his body parts, spread them across the country to others. People who needed an organ to live, to restart their lives. The one Rafe needed couldn't exist without its natural host.

She gripped the edge of the counter and swayed. She wasn't ready and probably never would be. What was the rush in burying her husband? There wasn't one. At least not for her. Nadia could go on and pretend Rafe was away on a business trip or gone for the weekend with his friends. The weekend would just never end, and she'd be okay with that.

Nine

Grayson

"Good morning," an unfamiliar voice called out.

"Hi," he said hoarsely. "Where am I?"

"MedStar," the voice said. "How are you feeling?"

"Tired. Sore."

"Grayson!" His mom sprang out of the oversize chair and was in his face. He closed his eyes at the way her hand felt in his hair.

"What happened?"

"You're in the hospital. Do you remember me telling you this the other day?"

The other day?

"No," he mumbled as he tried to adjust himself in the bed. "Why does my throat hurt?" Grayson looked at his mom and frowned. He had never seen her look . . . old before. She had always been young for her age, and people often mistook her for his sister. One time someone had asked if she was his girlfriend, which made Grayson want to punch the guy. Not because he was insulted but because the man insinuated that his mom had done something untoward to him.

Sydney had raised Grayson on her own when her boyfriend abandoned her after he'd gotten her pregnant. Young (still in high school) and with no place to live, she'd worked and continued her education.

She always put Grayson first and hadn't abandoned him when the doctors told her he was sick. Sydney worked harder to give him a good life.

Now, her features made her look older than she was. Grayson was concerned.

He reached over, closed his eyes when stretching hurt, and rubbed his thumb under her eyes.

"What's wrong, Mom?"

"Not a thing, my sweet boy."

"Then why have you been crying? And why does it look like you haven't slept in days?"

"I'm okay. I promise." She ran her hand through his hair and inhaled deeply. "You collapsed after one of your men's league games."

"I did?"

Sydney nodded, and tears fell from her eyes. "Yes, and you were brought here by ambulance."

"Oh."

"That's not all," she told her son. "Your heart condition—" She paused and made eye contact with him. Grayson saw the look in his mother's eyes and knew a lecture was forthcoming. He hadn't taken his meds in a while, and when he had taken them, it had been sporadic at best. For whatever reason, he lived by his machismo attitude: nothing could bring him down. He was climbing the corporate ladder at the Wold Collective, he had an amazing group of friends, and for some reason the woman he was in love with gave him the time of day, even though he didn't deserve it. Grayson didn't need pills to make himself feel better because he felt great. Besides, he was healthy and happy. Those bottles, hidden in his bathroom, reminded him he was weak, and he didn't like how they made him feel.

And then he remembered when he didn't feel so well or when his chest hurt, and he'd ignored it. He looked away from his mom before she could see any type of realization in his gaze.

"Everything's good now?" he asked in a shallow voice.

Sydney hesitated and then offered a weak smile. "You have a long recovery ahead of you, Grayson."

"For a heart attack?" he asked. "That seems extreme."

"Honey." Sydney sat on the side of his bed and held his hand in hers. "Your heart . . ." She paused as her breathing hitched. She cleared her throat. "Your heart was too damaged to repair. You were put in a medically induced coma due to several things, but mainly to keep you stationary and allow your body to get stronger."

"My heart's damaged?"

Sydney shook her head. "Not anymore. Now it's healthy."

"How?"

She inhaled deeply and smiled. "Because you received a transplant."

Grayson let the words sink in. They sank. And continued to do so until they were fuzzy and not making any sense. He looked around the room. Sterile. Plain. He was by himself, aside from his mother and a barrage of machines. Grayson followed the lines to under the blanket that covered him, and then he saw the tubes with pink-tinged liquid traveling through the casing.

"Mom," he said in a panic. "What is that?"

Sydney leaned over him and saw where he pointed. "Drainage tube."

"I have a tube in me?"

She placed her hand on him. "It's best you remain calm. Do you want me to get the doctor?"

Grayson shook his head quickly. "No, but what the fuck is going on?" As soon as his breathing deepened, the monitors began beeping. He looked at them in panic and felt his blood pressure rise.

The door to his room slid open. "Hey, Grayson," the nurse said as she came in. She pressed some buttons, and the beeping stopped. "I'm Jillian. How are you feeling?"

"Scared."

"That's normal. I'm going to take a look at your incision."

"My what?"

Jillian lifted his blanket and pulled back the bandage that covered his chest. He watched every movement and questioned how he hadn't known he had a massive piece of gauze covering his torso.

"It might be best if you don't look," Sydney told him as she pulled his face toward hers.

"But—"

"Later. You can look later, once you've processed everything."

He nodded and kept his focus on his mom. She was beautiful and the most important person in his life, aside from Reid. Although she didn't know it. Grayson had wanted to tell her how he felt, but he couldn't. At least not then.

When the nurse finished, she told him she'd be back in a few.

"Mom." Grayson looked to her for answers.

"I know it's a lot to take in, honey. You're going to be fine."

"With someone else's heart?"

She nodded.

"Whose?"

"We don't know, honey. Donations are anonymous."

"But someone died to give me a heart?"

"It doesn't work that way, Grayson. Someone passed away, and you were a match."

"And they just cut me open?"

Sydney didn't say anything. Grayson wanted to be alone but didn't have the nerve to ask his mom to leave him. Not that he excepted she would, under the circumstances. He also couldn't roll over, because looking at the machines that were doing who knew what wasn't an option either. Grayson tried to lift his head to look at his blanket-covered body, but the strain was too much. He was weak—something he had never been, and had promised himself he would never be.

A tear dripped from the corner of his eye. He lacked the effort to wipe it away or even care it was there. So much went through his mind as he stared at the ceiling. Would his new heart love Reid? His mother?

His stepdad? Would he still be able to play basketball? Did he even love basketball anymore?

What about his job? How was he going to pay rent or for health care if he couldn't work? How long would he be out of work?

And then the ultimate, soul-crushing question popped into his mind—did he even want this heart?

He wanted to live, but not at the expense of someone else. Was there someone more worthy than him who could've used a new ticker? Grayson was certain there was.

"Do you want to see Reid?" Sydney asked.

Did he? He waited for the excitement that normally came when he thought of her. Was the extra thump he felt his new heart's way of saying he still felt the same?

"Grayson?" Sydney said his name softly. "I know it's a lot to take in. We're all here for you, though. Reid has been here every day since you came in. Gilbert comes every night after work. I stay here. Pearce comes every other day after work. We all love you so much."

"How long have I been in the hospital?"

"A little over a month," she said quietly.

"A month?" He could barely get the question out.

"Yes," she said.

"Jesus. I lost thirty days of my life?"

"We don't look at it that way," she told him. "Your body needed rest in preparation for your new heart."

"It's not mine," he told her.

"It is," she countered.

"No, it belongs to some dead person." Until now, he had never thought about organ donation. He always assumed that when his time was up, it was up. That's why he kept Reid at arm's length, because he wasn't supposed to be here. Had his mom just messed with the natural order of things?

"I'm going to get Reid for you." Sydney rose and left Grayson alone in his room. Well, as alone as he could be with the machines chiming next to him. The tube running from his chest sloshed, and he was thankful he was smart enough not to look.

Grayson could smell Reid before he saw her. She gripped his hand and then came into view. God, she was damn stunning, with her auburn-colored hair and expressive eyes the color of milk chocolate. He waited for his new heart to react, to be on the same page as his brain. He was relieved when he felt a surge of love wash over him as she trailed her fingers down the side of his face.

"Hey," she said melodiously. "I'm so happy to see those beautiful eyes of yours."

"Is that all?" he asked, cracking his first joke.

Reid smiled and chuckled. "You just had major surgery, and you're already joking?"

Grayson would've shrugged, but he had a hard time moving. "What can I say? You bring it out in me."

She ran her fingers through his hair. He closed his eyes and waited . . . anticipating his body would push her away, reject her. His mind knew he loved her, but did the rest of him?

Yes, he decided, it did.

"Will you answer some questions for me?"

Reid nodded. "As best as I can."

"Why does my throat hurt so badly?"

She smiled. "You had a breathing tube in until yesterday."

"I don't remember."

"No, I suppose you wouldn't. They put it in when they took you for surgery the first time."

"The first time?"

"Yeah, they rushed you into surgery when we first got here. That's how we found out you needed a transplant."

"Oh."

"How come you didn't tell me you were sick?" she asked.

Grayson closed his eyes. "I didn't want you to judge me or mother me about things."

"I wouldn't have."

He eyed her questioningly, and she shrugged. "Okay, fine. I would've. But only because I care about you so much. This really scared me, Grayson. I thought I was going to lose you, and the last thing you would've remembered me saying was for you to stop faking."

"Faking?"

"I thought when you asked for help that you were faking things because I told you I was going to start dating."

"Oh." His heart sank, and he knew this new one would love her the same because *he* loved her. Grayson didn't need some blood-pumping organ to tell him how to feel. "Are you dating?"

She shook her head, much to his relief. "No."

"Are you going to?"

"Maybe? I don't really know right now, Grayson. There are things I want out of life."

Tell her how you feel!

He squeezed her hand. While he might not know what those things were at the moment, he surmised he could probably give her something she needed or wanted. "When I get out of here, do you want to go on a date?"

"Of course. I'll come over and make you a low-fat meal, and then eventually we'll be back to doing trivia night at the Green Turtle."

"Gross."

She smiled. "Lots has to change, Grayson. You're going to have to live a whole different lifestyle. I'm sure the doctors will fill you in before you're discharged. I've already cleaned out the garbage from your apartment."

He should've been mad, but he didn't have it in him to be angry at her. He did, however, want an answer to his question. "So, about that date?"

"What are you talking about, Grayson? I'm with you all the time."

Grayson tried to adjust but felt something pull and thought better of moving. Instead, he angled his head, hoping like hell he was flirting with her. "I want to take you on a real date," he said. "Not out to dinner after work, but the two of us, where we get somewhat dressed up, go dancing, and have a nice meal."

"Sure, but let's get you mended first," she said, a little less enthusiastically than he'd hoped.

Grayson lifted his hand toward her face. It hurt to move his arm, and thankfully Reid recognized this and came closer. When she was close enough, he cupped the back of her head and pulled her closer. "Reid," he said before his lips pressed to hers.

She didn't gasp the way he thought she would. Not how he imagined she would when they finally kissed again. Not how she had when they'd spent the one night together.

He hated that his lips were rough against her soft ones. Gently, he moved his lips with hers. Lightly caressing them as if she were the fragile one at the moment. The thump in his new heart felt stronger, sounded louder, affirming that he was, in fact, still very much in love with her.

Grayson went to deepen the kiss, but Reid pulled back abruptly. She tasted sweet like cinnamon apples, which reminded him of last fall, when they'd gone apple picking and then made a pie in her kitchen. He tossed flour on her, they flirted, and while he wanted to kiss her then, his life was so complicated.

A new heart removed the complication between them. He had a new lease on life. A second chance. And something deep in the recesses of his mind told him not to squander it.

She covered her lips with her fingers, and then it was like a veil had descended over her. The moment shifted.

"You should rest," she told him. "You need to heal."

He deserved the cold shoulder, the brush-off. If he were in her shoes, he'd act the same way.

There was a knock on the door, and then three doctors came in. They introduced themselves, and Reid said she'd be back in a minute. As soon as she was gone, the medical team began detailing his recovery, the need for physical therapy, and the strict diet he'd have to follow.

That third item had Grayson rolling his eyes. He wasn't some old man and shouldn't have to eat like one.

"We also suggest therapy," one of the doctors said. "You'll need help coping with the changes your body is going through and accepting the magnitude of what you went through. Most of our patients know beforehand about their transplant and meet with a therapist prior to surgery. You didn't get the opportunity to do that."

Grayson didn't say much. Everything the doctors said was a reason why he didn't take his meds, never watched what he ate, and enjoyed drinking beer every night after work. He wanted to live on his terms, not the terms of some medical association telling him what to do.

But now he had a second chance at life after being reckless with his first one. He'd kissed Reid and told her he liked her, or at least hinted in that direction, although he wasn't entirely sure she'd believed him. He'd have to show her he meant it. There was no way he could let her down now. She'd never forgive him.

So he nodded and listened to what the doctors told him. Grayson would go to therapy, both physical and mental. He'd eat better, because his mom and Reid would make sure of it. He'd follow the rules and guidelines and make it to all his follow-up appointments. Grayson would be better for his mom. For Reid. And for the person who had died in order for him to have a new lease on life.

That was heavy. Having thoughts about a person who had died. He placed his hand over his heart, and everything hurt.

Except it didn't.

Grayson's mind was playing tricks on him. The drugs kept him pain-free. Anything he felt was a figment of his imagination. Sure, they'd cut his chest open, removed his second-most-vital organ, and put a new one in, so to his mind, his body should hurt. He should feel the pain from the incision, from them breaking his ribs and then sewing him back together.

He felt longing. Desire. Love.

Reid came back into the room after the doctors left and sat next to him. They held hands and looked at each other.

"I'm alive," he told her.

"You are, and I'm so damn happy because of it."

"I'm sorry I scared you."

"It's okay," she told him. "You're fine now, and that's all that matters."

Grayson asked her about his job, and she filled him in. Everyone at work was happy he'd made it through surgery. They had donated sick days to cover what he lacked until his medical leave kicked in. Pearce had a countdown going to when they could get back on the court, and the women had started a calendar of meals they planned to make him.

It all sounded good, except for the fact that he'd have to spend his days by himself. One of the aspects of his job that he loved so much was the fact that he worked with Reid every day. He was about to ask her again about the date when his mom and stepdad walked in. More alone time with Reid would have to wait.

TEN

NADIA

Nadia lay in bed, mindlessly watching television and then aimlessly flipping the channel each time a commercial came on. She regretted the last channel change immediately when a local late-morning news show showed a picture of Rafe on the screen. Her heart sank at the sight of her husband, smiling and perfect. She should've kept scrolling, but she couldn't tear her eyes away from the screen. And then she heard the words: *The City of Boston plans to honor hero Rafe Karlsson, and the Commonwealth Cup is considering changing its name.*

Nadia sat up. No one had called and asked her if she wanted this. If her children wanted this. She had a hard enough time grappling with Rafe being labeled a "hero," and now he was going to be honored. With what, the key to the city? The last thing she wanted was to be reminded every year by the media that her husband had died. She didn't want the girls growing up, year after year, hearing about how their father had died while running a road race. Nor did Nadia want Rafe to be the face of the annual event. She wanted to forget and go back to the last morning they'd spent in bed together and beg him not to go.

The thoughts made her sick to her stomach. She barely made it to the bathroom before she lost what little her stomach held. Her mother came in with her and held her hair back. Nadia sat on the floor and cried. There wasn't anything anyone could do or say to change things, not now. Not ever.

"You need to eat," Lorraine told her daughter. "You have to be strong for the girls, Nadia."

"I don't want to," she sobbed. "I want my husband back."

"I know, sweetie. Believe me, I know."

But did she? Lorraine Bolton had married her high school sweetheart. They were happy with their three children and four grandchildren. They were doing exactly what Rafe and Nadia had planned—growing old together.

"You don't know what it feels like." She looked at her mom and put her fist over her heart. "It hurts so bad, and it feels like I can't breathe." To prove her point, her body shuddered and gasped for air. "He's gone and . . ." She couldn't finish her sentence. Her husband was just gone.

Lorraine shook her head and cried with her daughter. "I know, honey. I'm so sorry."

She finally let her mother help her off the floor. They went into the kitchen and then the formal dining room, where everyone was gathered at the table. Her and Rafe's family were crammed next to one another, while the six kids sat at the kiddie table they used for Thanksgiving. As Nadia took in each one of them, her thoughts drifted to why all these people were in her house and where she was supposed to sit. The only open seat was where Rafe had sat last year, when they'd bought this monstrosity of a table so they could host both families at Thanksgiving. As a family, the four of them rarely ate dinner in the dining room, always opting for the dinette set in the kitchen. It was informal and yet had a feeling of intimacy because they were always so close.

"Hi, Mommy," Lynnea said as she came over. Nadia picked her youngest up and held her. She spotted Gemma, in between her nephews. When Lincoln, the oldest, glanced in his aunt's direction, the look on his face told her not to worry about her daughter. He would take care of her.

"She's sucking her thumb again," Cleo said as she patted her granddaughter on her back.

"Yep, and I'm going to let her do it. It brings her comfort." Nadia hadn't meant to come off angry at Cleo, but the last thing she needed or wanted was for someone to point out the obvious to her.

"I know, I was just—" Cleo shook her head and went to check on the other grandkids.

"She's only trying to help," Warren said as he walked by his daughter. "Come on, come sit. Have some pizza."

He held a chair out for Nadia. She sat, moving Lynnea around to cradle her. She brushed her daughter's hair out of her face and held her to her chest. "Did you eat?" Nadia asked her.

Lynnea shook her head.

"Here, let's eat this together." They shared a slice of pizza. It was all Nadia could stomach. When Cleo brought out a tray of brownies, Lynnea perked up. Nadia gave her one.

"These are yummy, Grandma," Lynnea said as she stuffed the square into her mouth. Cleo's eyes watered. Nadia stared and wondered what was going on in her mother-in-law's mind. She'd lost her son, and as of late, her relationship with Nadia had been on rocky ground. They didn't always see eye to eye on parenting, and Cleo often sided with Freya on things.

Last year, when Rafe and Nadia had wanted to host Thanksgiving, Freya had had issues with everything. The menu was an issue, even though it was the same thing Cleo always cooked at her house. The time they ate, which was an hour later than the year prior. But the one that sent Nadia over the edge was Freya's insistence that her children sit at the main table with the adults and not at the kids' table with the rest of the children. Rafe told his sister to grow up, but Cleo defended her daughter, saying Leif and Astrid didn't know Lincoln and Jaxon that well and they'd be uncomfortable. Rafe suggested his sister stay home or go to Lars's family for the holidays, and ever since, she'd noticed a strain among them. Cleo blamed Nadia, even though she wouldn't come out and admit it.

She looked across the table and caught Freya staring at her. Nadia held her gaze for a moment and then returned her attention to her daughter. In the blink of an eye, everything had changed. If she'd thought the holidays were strained before, now they'd forever be altered. She could see Cleo and Otto coming over for the girls' birthdays, but that was about it. Cleo or Freya would host Thanksgiving and Christmas, and Nadia wouldn't be there. Neither would her girls. Their family would be even more fractured than it was before.

A knock on the door sounded. Otto went to answer and cheerfully welcomed Kiran Dunlap into the house. Nadia had mixed feelings when they made eye contact. He was Rafe's best friend and should've been given the opportunity to say goodbye to him. Nadia had failed him and her husband. Kiran came toward her as tears filled her eyes. She choked on a sob and slid out from under Lynnea's lap and moved hastily into the kitchen.

Nadia gripped the edge of the counter, heaving in deep breaths in an attempt to push the impending panic attack away.

"Nadia." Kiran's voice was soft and soothing when it shouldn't have been. She didn't deserve his kindness. Not now, and probably not ever. His hand touched her shoulder, and her knees buckled. Kiran caught her before she crumpled to the ground. She buried her face in his jacket, inhaling his clean, fresh scent. Nothing like Rafe's spicy, musky cologne she loved so much.

Kiran wrapped his strong arms around Nadia and held her. His heart beat rapidly in his chest, vibrating against hers.

"I'm so sorry," she muttered into his clothing. She repeated her sentiment until another wave of tears washed over her.

"Nadia," he said softly. "I understand."

Nadia took another big breath and then stepped out of his grasp, hiding her face from him as she wiped at the wetness on her cheeks. She was tired of crying. Tired of feeling shattered. Tired of it all.

"You shouldn't," she said as she looked out the kitchen window. "I should've called. Someone should've called you. You had a right to be there. To say goodbye to him. I took that away, and I don't even have a valid excuse as to why."

"I'm not angry, Nadia."

"You should be."

Their gazes met. "Why? So I could say words to him that he wouldn't hear? So I could tell him how I should've been there, with him, but bailed at the last minute because I didn't want to run? I have a lot of guilt right now, Nadia. I can't help but think that if I was there, maybe it'd be me you'd be mourning and not him. That his girls"—Kiran paused and pointed to the other room—"wouldn't be missing their daddy."

"Why do you say that?"

"I have nothing to lose," he told her. "I don't have a wife waiting for me or two little girls who need me. Bachelor life here," he said as he pointed to his chest. "If I hadn't gone out the night before, I wouldn't have been hungover, and I would've been there."

"Kiran—"

He held his hand up. "It's my guilt, and I need to live with it. Whatever guilt you have about not calling me, let it go. I honestly didn't deserve to be there."

"Don't say that. He would've wanted you there."

"I appreciate you saying that, and maybe someday I will believe it. Right now . . ." He shook his head.

"Kiran," she said softly. "You shouldn't have guilt over something you couldn't have prevented. Rafe did what Rafe always did." Even as Nadia spoke, the word "hero" popped into her mind. As much as she didn't want it to be true, Rafe was a hero. This still didn't mean she wanted his efforts broadcasted or brought up again next year. Or the year after. She and her family needed to heal. They needed to find some semblance of normal, and that wouldn't exist if they had a constant reminder of the man they'd lost.

"Mommy?" Lynnea came into the kitchen, interrupting Kiran and Nadia. Lynnea beckoned her mother to come to her level. Nadia knelt and then found herself smiling at what Lynnea said to her.

Nadia remained crouching. "You can ask him."

Lynnea leaned into her mother and rested her head on her shoulder, almost knocking Nadia over. "Do you want a brownie?" she asked Kiran.

He squatted, bringing himself to eye level with Lynnea. He reached out and touched the hem of her shirt. Kiran had uncle status in the house but had yet to develop a close bond with Lynnea. He was closer to Gemma, being that she was older and would often go places with Rafe when Kiran was around.

"Did you make them?"

Lynnea shook her head.

"No? Who did?"

"Grandma Cleo," she said after taking her thumb out of her mouth, and then it went right back in. Nadia frowned at the sight, knowing it wasn't going to be an easy habit to break. Nor tackle. If sucking her thumb brought her daughter comfort, she'd leave it for the time being. Besides, she had more pressing issues to deal with, like planning a funeral, which could wait until tomorrow.

"You know, I think I'd like one."

Lynnea ground her face into Nadia's neck and then pushed away from her mother. Lynnea took Kiran's hand and led him out of the kitchen. He turned, gave Nadia one last look, and smiled softly at her.

Nadia leaned against the cupboard and slid the rest of the way down until she sat on the cold, hard floor. She listened to her family, their chatter and laughter, in the other room and wondered when she'd laugh again. Not a chuckle here or there, but a full-on belly laugh that brought happy tears and side aches. The kind of laugh you told your friends about. The kind you shared with someone special.

Her someone special was gone. Her rock. The person she counted on the most. Never in her wildest dreams did she think at thirty-five she'd be a widow with two small children, having to learn to live without a partner.

ELEVEN

NADIA

It had been a week and one day since Nadia had last heard Rafe's voice. Since he'd last told her he loved her, kissed her, held her in his arms. She'd gone through a barrage of emotions. Sadness, loneliness, longing, and anger. This one, along with complete and utter heartbreak, was at the forefront of her feelings. Not a second had gone by when she hadn't thought of her husband. Alive and vivacious to cold and dead. Every time she pictured the love of her life, she saw him as she last had, in a bed with wires and machines keeping him alive. All she saw was the double doors that had swallowed him as she stood there, watching as the doctors wheeled him away to harvest his organs.

Now, she and her family were being asked to attend a memorial and to meet with the driver, who wanted to express her sincere remorse for the accident. Not accepting fault for not keeping her car properly maintained. Deep in her mind, she knew it had been an accident. It was, however, avoidable, and she couldn't help but think the person should be held accountable. Nadia hadn't even buried her husband yet, and the city wanted to unite and show the citizens how the people of Boston were strong and would recover. How Rafe's legacy would unite a community. How the organizers would learn from the tragedy and move on.

Nadia would not recover. There was nothing for her to rebuild. Her husband was gone. The life they'd planned out for themselves, blown to bits. Shattered.

She didn't want to be there, but her parents had insisted. This tribute was supposed to be cathartic. It would help her begin her healing process. She thought it was a waste of time. The last thing she wanted to do was see where her husband had died. Yet there they were, sitting in black folding chairs, under a tent, listening to the mayor talk about the city Rafe had loved so much. Aside from family, she didn't know anyone sitting behind her. Maybe they were the other people, the ones who had been hurt when the car broke through the crowd.

Lynnea whined and tugged on Nadia's arm. She picked her youngest up and held her. In a week, Lynnea had gone from a sassy spitfire who tested her mother's every nerve to a child who didn't want to speak to anyone, who whined more than she had as a toddler, who was a shell of herself. And then there was Gemma—their formerly loving, vivacious daughter who'd wanted to dance and sing and always had a smile on her face but now spit venom, hit her sister, and insisted on slamming her door repeatedly while screaming at the top of her lungs.

As a family, they needed counseling. Nadia knew this. They would not survive without it. Her family had told her the girls were mourning in their own way, which Nadia understood to an extent, but they needed help coming to terms with what had happened to them. All she had to do was pick up the phone. And yet, she couldn't bring herself to do it.

Maybe next week or next month.

The women in her family had planned Rafe's funeral. Nadia had expected resistance from Cleo when she told her mother-in-law she intended to have Rafe cremated, but Cleo said it was the right thing to do. The wake, however, would be open casket. Nadia wanted to give

Rafe's friends, coworkers, and extended family a chance to say goodbye, despite the pain she felt.

Nadia arrived an hour early to the funeral home, alone. Her father drove her, walked her in, and then left her there. It was where she wanted to be, with her husband, one last time. Just them. She sat in a chair and stared at the dark wooden casket. The company that made it had donated it to Nadia for Rafe. This was one of the many things gifted to them since Rafe's death. Aside from food and flowers, they'd received gifts of memberships to gymnastics, dance, and theater classes for the girls, clothes for the three of them, a year's supply of this or that. The list grew daily. She was grateful but wanted to know what would happen at the end of the year, when the free memberships ran out—who would pay for those gifts then? Her dual-income home now had a single income, and she wasn't even sure she could afford to live on her income alone in the home she and her husband had purchased to raise their family in.

She sighed, wiped away her tears, and rose. Each painful step led her to her husband. She'd dressed him in his favorite black suit, the one he wore for special occasions, and the tie the girls had bought him the previous Christmas. As soon as he'd opened it, he'd proudly said it was his favorite and wore it to work twice a week. Her sister had brought Rafe's cologne to the funeral home the day prior, and as Nadia leaned closer, she inhaled. He smelled like the man she was in love with, and not death. Rafe wore his wedding ring, but tomorrow, it would be given to her in a pouch, along with his watch. She would keep these things and pass them on to their children or grandchildren.

Her fingers ran along the smooth, polished wood, and then the satin lining. The casket was beautiful, if one could be beautiful. Quantifying death and beauty wasn't something Nadia could do very well.

She knelt and rested her chin on her hands. Despite death, Rafe was still handsome. She ran her fingers through his hair, not caring about the gel and hair spray the mortician had used to keep it in place. It was never coiffed perfectly, and it didn't make sense for it to be now. Besides, no one would remember that Rafe Karlsson had had messy hair in his casket. She would, however, remember what her husband looked like before the funeral director closed the casket.

"Would you look at you," she said, trying to find some humor in the moment. "I've never seen you look so still in all the years I've known you. I hope you're doing anything but being still wherever you are, my love. Just please, no more running." She didn't wipe her tears this time. She needed to cry, needed to feel the tightness in her throat, in her chest. She needed the pain to remind her she was still alive and had two tiny humans depending on her.

"God, I miss you so fucking much." She choked on a sob. "I don't understand why you were taken from me. From us. What did we do to deserve this?"

There would never be a satisfactory answer.

Nothing would ever make sense to her.

"I want to wake up from this nightmare and find you lying next to me in bed, loving me. I want to look into your eyes and see that you love me, to hear your voice again telling me everything's going to be okay, and to feel your arms wrapped around me while we sway to the music in our heads. Those are the things I want right now. Tomorrow they'll be the same, except I won't get to say them to you because your body will be gone." Nadia slumped against the casket. "This is the last time I get to see your handsome face, get to touch your strong hands, get to run my fingers through your hair. They're going to take you from me again, and there isn't anything I can do to stop them.

"I love you, Rafe," she said to him. "And I'm failing without you by my side. I don't know how to be me without you. I don't know how to be a single parent and raise our girls the way we discussed raising them. They're hurting, baby. Our strong babies are in so much pain. We all are. We just want you back."

"Mrs. Karlsson." Mr. Mahar, the funeral director, cleared his throat and waited. When she didn't answer him, he continued. "The rest of the family are here."

Nadia nodded and waited for him to leave. She trailed her fingers down Rafe's face and then did what she never thought she'd do—she leaned forward and kissed him. "I love you," she told him again before she stepped away.

She found Mr. Mahar in the hallway, waiting for her. "You can let them in. I need to freshen up." She made her way to the bathroom and looked at herself in the mirror. The woman who looked back wasn't the Nadia she knew. No, that woman was long gone and was unlikely to return.

With a steady breath, she returned to the parlor, where her family members were saying goodbye to Rafe. She sought out her girls and went to them, taking each one by the hand. They would go last, before the public came in.

"Mommy, there are a lot of people outside for Daddy," Gemma told her. Nadia leaned forward to look out the window and saw a line of people.

"Daddy will appreciate that they came to say goodbye."

Gemma nodded, while Lynnea clung to Nadia's side. She tugged on her mother's skirt. "I want to go home."

"I know, sweetie." No one wanted to be there. "All of this is almost over." And then they would have to find a way to heal.

When it was the girls' turn to say goodbye, they climbed the small steps in front of the casket. At first, Lynnea was adamant she didn't want to see him, but Nadia taught her about remorse, and how if she didn't take the opportunity, she might regret it later. After the wake, she wouldn't have another chance, unless she looked at his photos.

Somehow, Nadia held it together while the girls said their goodbyes. They moved to the side, with Nadia at the front of the receiving line, Gemma next to her, and then Lynnea. Reuben stood behind his nieces, ready to whisk them away when they were tired of shaking hands and hugging strangers. Otto and Cleo stood next to Lynnea, followed by Freya, Lars, and their children. The Boltons stood in the back of the room, ready to greet the people they knew.

"Mrs. Karlsson, are you ready?"

Nadia shook her head. "Unfortunately."

Kiran came in first, making eye contact with Nadia before turning toward the casket. When he got to the receiving line, he pulled her into his arms and wept. Nadia gasped. Kiran hadn't done this the other night when they were at the house, when he'd held her. He'd been strong for her, and now she felt as if she needed to be strong for him.

Kiran had lost Rafe too. The hug was bone crushing and necessary. They wept together.

"Thank you for coming," she said into his suit jacket.

"I'm where I need to be, Nadia."

Kiran crouched in front of Gemma and Lynnea. "If you or your mom need anything, you call me. Got it?"

The girls nodded.

"I'm still your uncle, no matter what." He pulled them into his arms and hugged them. Nadia couldn't watch, not without losing it.

She wouldn't cry. Not today, and not in front of people she didn't know.

Today, she'd be the strong wife of Rafe Karlsson.

Nadia watched Kiran make his way through the line and then mingle with her parents. He caught her staring and smiled. Somehow, amid the heartache, she found the strength to smile back.

Her best friend, Hazel Pittman, came with her daughter, Hayden, who was the same age as Lynnea. The girls were close. Besties, according to Lynnea. When Aida McGee, Gemma's best friend, came in, the "oh my Gods" made Nadia's eyes roll. Eight-year-old girls didn't always know how to express themselves very well and often mimicked others, especially those from the television shows they watched.

After coworkers and friends had made it through, Nadia saw nothing but a sea of blue. The police, fire, and ambulance departments had come to honor Rafe. She knew they'd be there tomorrow, leading the procession, but had no idea they would be at the wake. When Luca

DeMarco, the officer who'd helped and stayed with her on that fateful day, stepped in front of Nadia, he said the standard "I'm sorry for your loss." She surprised not only him but herself when she hugged him. She would be forever grateful to him for being there for her when she needed someone.

"Thank you."

Strangers came to pay their respects to a man they didn't know but had felt something for. Each person shook her hand and told her how sorry they were. A few said they had run with Rafe during previous races or rowed with him on the Charles.

After the last person had left, Nadia once again sat in the room with Rafe. This time, candles burned around her, the sky had darkened, and she was physically exhausted. She knelt on the steps and rested her chin on her hands. Rafe would've hated the attention he'd received today and would've said something about how he didn't deserve it. But he had. He was loved by many, and that was evident in the volume of people who'd come to pay their respects.

For the last time until she saw him again, she ran her fingers through his hair. In her mind, it would be forever messy. She leaned forward and kissed him. "I love you."

A throat clearing had her looking over her shoulder. The funeral director stood there, poised with his hands clasped in front of him.

"Would you like his ring and watch now?" he asked her.

Nadia nodded. She reached for Rafe's hand and slipped his wedding ring off, unable to recall a time he had ever not worn it since the day she'd set it on his finger. Next, she unclasped his watch and slipped it over her wrist. They would've given them to her tomorrow, but now was better.

"I'll see you in the morning," the director told her. "The limo will pick you up and bring you here, and we'll start the procession from here."

"Thank you."

Tomorrow, the family limo would follow a police detail as they made their way through the city to the Cathedral of the Holy Cross, where her husband would be honored.

Six pallbearers would carry an empty casket to the front of the church, where Rafe's family and friends would stand in front of pews filled with people, some he'd known and some there in honor of him and in support of his wife and children. Speeches would be read, telling everyone who wanted to listen about the man who'd been taken from them.

When the service concluded, Nadia would walk down the aisle, with a daughter on each side, while her husband's empty casket left the church.

And then, she'd start over.

If she could figure out how.

TWELVE

GRAYSON

Grayson sat on the edge of the bed in the doctor's office. While he waited for the cardiologist to come in, he played on his phone. More so, he thought this was the time to look random things up on his phone, like if the bed he sat on was really called a "space saver cabinet treatment table." The next search was something he'd put off, thinking he was suave enough to figure it out on his own, but had failed miserably at, and that was romancing Reid. He'd been naive enough to think that asking her out on a date—which hadn't happened yet—would be enough to show her he was interested. Of course, he understood her hesitation. Hell, if the roles were reversed, he'd keep the cement wall up between them and throw away any tools she had for a possible teardown. Grayson had to find a way to let her know he was serious about the date and dating, because his subtle hints had continued to fall flat.

The doctor came in, followed by a nurse. Grayson tossed his phone onto the chair where he had left his shirt. He hated looking at his chest. The scar wasn't as gnarly as it had been, but it was still red in spots and sometimes itched like a bitch. Reid had bought him a cream to put on it, which seemed to work. Except she made him apply the cream instead of doing it herself. He didn't like that.

"Hello, Grayson. How are we feeling?" Dr. Wynn stood at the computer cart and clicked the mouse what felt like a million times. Grayson almost leaned over so the doctor would look at him but thought better of it. While he asked questions, his nurse took Grayson's temperature, checked his pulse and blood pressure, and asked him to stand on the scale. She relayed the numbers to the cardiologist.

"Good."

"How's the pain?"

Grayson shrugged. "Meh. Comes and goes. It's more like a shock or stabbing."

"That's going to be normal. How are the ribs?"

"They're good, I think. It's not like I do anything physical."

"What are you doing for exercise?"

"A lot of walking," Grayson told him. Between his mom and Reid, all they did was walk.

"Are you getting outside and enjoying the weather?"

Grayson nodded, even though the doctor wasn't looking at him. He also didn't seem to care, because he didn't ask him to repeat his answer. He came over and smiled at Grayson.

"Scar looks like it's healing nicely."

"Thanks. Reid gave me some cream she found. Seems to do the trick."

Dr. Wynn set his stethoscope to Grayson's chest. "Let's have a listen."

For the first two months after Grayson had received his new heart, he'd had to come to the doctor's every week for a biopsy to make sure his body wasn't rejecting his new heart. Knowing his body could quit his heart at any time had put the fear of God into him. He was determined to do right by the gift he'd been given. Even though he hated his new healthy eating, Reid had joined him on the change, and they ate dinner together every night. Grayson liked that it wasn't just him eating the bland diet; they were doing it as a couple . . . well, a soon-to-be couple, if he had anything to say about it.

Dr. Wynn smiled as he moved the stethoscope around. "I love what I'm hearing."

"Thanks."

"Everything sounds as it should, but we're still going to follow up with an x-ray. I don't want to take any chances."

"Me neither, Doc."

Dr. Wynn sat down on his medical stool. "Any questions for me?"

Grayson nodded. "I'm curious about sex."

"Ah yes. Probably the most common question I get, and rarely covered during discharge. Generally speaking, twelve weeks is the standard, as long as you feel up to it. If you're not experiencing shortness of breath or fatigue, I'd say you're probably okay to engage in sexual activity."

For a moment, Grayson thought about asking his doctor if he could write that down, but then figured there was no point, at least not yet. He couldn't even get Reid to sit next to him on the couch like she used to—she was probably afraid she'd hurt him or something. Tonight, that would change. The old Grayson would emerge, the playful, fun-loving one Reid was used to.

And he'd tell her he was interested in her.

Somehow.

After he left, he went down to the lab to have his blood drawn, which he was tired of, and then went to radiology to have the x-rays done. Then, finished with his appointments, he texted his mom for a ride home and counted down the days to when he wouldn't need a babysitter. They'd given him the okay to do things on his own at six weeks, but his mother had insisted, and he didn't have the heart to tell her no.

Grayson sat outside on the bench and people-watched. Summer was in full bloom, and by the looks of things, it was surely going to be an amazing one. With a new lease on life, Grayson planned to embrace everything he could. Picnics in the park, romantic strolls, and anything else with Reid were at the top of his list.

When she came into view, he smiled. "What are you doing here?"

"Your mom had some errands to run, and it's too nice to be at work."

For the first six weeks after his surgery, she'd been there every night with him. Reid had told Sydney it was easier for her to stay at Grayson's, since they lived in the same building, and besides, Sydney hadn't slept in her own bed in a long time.

When Grayson found out his mom had spent every night in his hospital room, he'd had mixed emotions. He loved his mother more than life itself, and he knew she would do anything for him and him her, but he hated knowing she'd slept on a cot or in an uncomfortable chair because of him. As soon as he was able, he'd asked Reid to buy his mom a weeklong getaway for her and Gilbert—a gift they hadn't yet taken advantage of.

On the Reid front, Grayson knew she'd also taken a lot of time off from work to be with him and had spent every evening in his room while Sydney ran home to eat and shower. After the way he'd treated her, in the sense of rebuffing her advances, Grayson knew he didn't deserve someone like Reid. Yet he wanted to change and prove to her that he did, or that he could be worthy of her love and affection, as a couple. The wall between them needed to crumble, and it would once he found a way to do it.

"Well, this is a beautiful surprise," he said as he reached for her hand. She gave it willingly for a second or two and then pulled away. Grayson stood, stretched, and slung his arm around her shoulders. This move wasn't out of the question for him, so the likelihood of her shrugging him off was slim.

"How was your appointment?"

"Great," he said enthusiastically. "Did the usual blood work and x-rays. The new ticker is doing its job. Doc says it sounds good, and I gotta tell you, Sully, I like the way it makes me feel."

"Sully" was the nickname he'd given her when they'd first met, and each time he called her "Sully," her cheeks turned a lovely shade of pink, and she batted her eyelashes in response. Grayson was fairly sure she had no idea the latter happened, and he wasn't about to tell her.

"That's good," she said. "Anything else? Blood pressure good?"

"Perfect," he said. "Healthy as a horse."

"That's really great news, Grayson."

He stopped in the middle of the sidewalk. She stepped back and pulled him closer to her to clear the path for others. "What's wrong?" she asked him.

"Nothing at all, Sully." He pushed her hair off her shoulder and smiled. "Remember when I was in the hospital, and I asked if you wanted to go on a date?"

She gave him a noncommittal nod.

"I'm serious, Reid. That is, unless you don't want to explore this with me, which I'd totally understand."

"Grayson . . ." She paused and bit her lower lip. "I don't think this is the place to have this conversation."

He looked up and down the street, and then across it. "Then we'll have it at the park or on the subway or at my apartment. It doesn't matter where, but we're having it unless you tell me you're not interested, because I'd get it if you weren't. I was a dick, and while I had my personal reasons for being such, that doesn't negate that I hurt you, and I want to fix things. Or make it up to you."

"Make it up to me or date me?"

"Both. One and then the other or at the same time. Whatever you'll allow."

Reid huffed and leaned against the wall with her arms crossed. "Why now?"

"Because someone's given me the gift of life, a second chance at doing this the right way, and I don't want to waste a single second of it. And in all those seconds, I want them to be filled with you by my side. Not only as my best friend, but as a lover and partner as well."

She eyed him warily. He accepted the scrutiny. He deserved it and more. But he'd give her time, because he now had it in spades. As long as he maintained a healthy lifestyle, his new heart would give him another twenty years, and by then, advancements in medicine would afford him another twenty or so. Grayson wasn't worried.

They started walking again. At the street corner, when it was time for them to walk, he placed his hand in the middle of her back. He wanted to hold her hand but feared rejection. This was as good as it was going to get for the time being. If they were going to date or even have a relationship, he'd have to move at Reid's pace and not his. His pace of jumping right back into the sack wasn't going to work. They'd already been there, and his recollection of the night was nothing short of magical. He was the one who'd pumped the brakes on anything developing. Even a friends-with-benefits-type relationship. Those never turned out the way the parties thought they would. It was inevitable that someone would end up hurt.

Now all he had to do was not mess things up.

For the first time since his surgery, Grayson swiped his Metro card and boarded the subway. His healed incision allowed him more exposure to the elements and society. They found a two-seater and sat down. Normally, he would sit on the aisle. It was the right thing to do, but Reid insisted he sit near the window.

"There's always a chance someone comes by with a large bag or something and bumps you."

"My eyes still work," he told her jokingly.

She rolled hers for effect. "Humor me."

Grayson did, but not without some exaggeration.

For his part, he wouldn't have to change the way he approached her. He would still open the door for her, compliment her, and tease her, all the while turning on the romantic charm he'd kept hidden. He was ready to unleash the beast. To prove his point in a bold move, he reached for her hand and brought it to his lips, kissing the back of hers. Despite the rumble of the train, there was no mistaking her intake of breath when his lips touched her skin.

"Don't do that," she told him.

"Do what?"

"Act like we were on our way to being this couple before you had surgery. We weren't." She didn't need to remind him. "There are things I want, Grayson. Things I need as a woman. I'm sorry, but you're going to have to do a lot better than telling me you want to date, that you want to be my partner, and kissing the back of my hand, for me to be all in."

He lifted his eyebrow, challenging her. "Okay."

"'Okay'? That's the best you can come up with?" Reid rolled her eyes.

She was right. His response was lacking. He needed to shift his way of thinking. This wasn't Reid, his best friend. This was Reid, a woman he wanted to date. Grayson needed to approach the situation as if nothing had ever happened between them before. He was going to have to romance her. Wine and dine her.

Grayson was going to have to work. He nodded. "I see you, Reid Sullivan."

She shook her head and rolled her eyes again.

After transferring trains, and a few stops on the one that would take them to their apartment complex, they were out and walking up the street. Since his release, he hadn't walked much outside, mostly in the courtyard of the complex or from the car to the doctor's office.

Grayson kept his gait slow, savoring nature, the beauty of the city in which they lived, and being with Reid. An idea struck, and he stopped walking. She turned, and a look of horror washed over her.

"No, I'm okay," he told her before she could ask. "I just had an idea."

"And you couldn't say that before abruptly stopping and making me think something's wrong?"

"You're right, I'm sorry." Grayson cleared his throat. "What are you doing tonight?"

"Uh, making you dinner?"

Really? That's what her life had become—taking care of him? He had to change this because she didn't need to live like this. And neither did he.

"Tonight, we're going out," he told her, much to her surprise. Grayson took her hand in his. "Reid, would you like to go out with me tonight?"

She nodded. "Nothing crazy, though, okay?"

"I promise. Nothing outlandish." She'd kill him if he took her to a dance club. Not to mention, he wasn't sure his new heart was ready to get its groove on.

They climbed the stairs to their complex, and he held the door for her. Inside the elevator, he selected her floor, but not his, hoping she wouldn't question him. When they reached her floor, he walked her to her door. "I'll see you later."

"What time?"

He looked at his wrist, fully aware he didn't have a watch on, but he did so in hopes she'd call him out for being goofy. She didn't.

"I'll pick you up at five," he told her.

"We live in the same building," she reminded him. "I can come to your place."

He shook his head. "Absolutely not. This is a date. I'll pick you up." Grayson winked and strode toward the elevator. "Nothing fancy, Sully, but we'll have a good time."

At least he hoped.

In his apartment, he showered. Even though he'd done it before heading to the doctor, now he did it with a purpose. Tepid water splashed onto his scalp, wetting his dark hair and matting the ends to his face, and then it dripped down his back, buttocks, and legs and finally circled the drain.

Grayson watched the water swirl around the silver drain cap. He likened the motion to his life. His recycle phase. The ultimate second chance.

The water turned colder than he preferred, and Grayson adjusted the dial. He could easily spend all day in the water, something he'd learned to love during his teen years of being a lifeguard at the rec center near his childhood home. Being paid to swim whenever he wanted, flirt with all the good-looking girls, and blow his whistle when kids became too rowdy added up to the perfect summer job for him. Thankfully, he never had to use the lifesaving skills the organization had taught him.

Grayson washed and rinsed before shutting off the water. One of the dates he would plan with Reid would be a trip to the beach. She deserved a getaway. She'd gone way above what a friend or even best friend did for another person. Grayson needed to thank her in ways only he could do.

He shook his head, spraying water droplets onto the already damp walls. Only after he'd slid the door back did he realize he hadn't grabbed a towel—he was left with the choice of walking naked and wet to his linen closet or using the hand towel Reid insisted he keep in his bathroom.

"Hand towel it is," he muttered as he reached for the monogrammed cloth. He had a set of towels that matched—a gift from Reid last Christmas—but they weren't for everyday use, according to her. Household decorations were out of his realm. He didn't understand the need to put something in his apartment that he couldn't use. Reid and his mom had made his life hell when they'd shown up at his place with bags from HomeGoods.

Grayson rehung the dank towel on the towel bar, thought better of it, and took it, along with his clothes, to his hamper. If Reid used it to dry her hands after he'd used it to dry under . . . *Nope.* He had far too much respect for her to allow that to happen.

In his bedroom, he stood in front of his closet, looking at his clothes. He'd lost a few pounds since his surgery, and most of his clothes were a bit baggy. Nothing a belt couldn't fix. He pulled a pair of jeans from the top shelf, reached for a white button-down, and set them on his unmade bed. He groaned at the sight of it.

Grayson pulled his sheet and comforter up. That was the best he'd do when it came to making his bed. At least for now. As much as he wanted Reid in his bed, he was going to have to move slowly on building this relationship, and rightly so.

He dressed in sweats while he made plans for the night. They'd start off with dinner at the new salad place that had opened up not far from their apartment. This would appease Reid in the quest to keep him healthy, and then they'd go to the movies. He thought that keeping it low key was the best way to start. Of course, he'd invite her over for another movie or just to chill on the couch. Whether she came in or not, he still planned to walk her to her door, and if the vibe was there, he'd kiss her good night. Just a peck. One that lingered. And possibly showed her some promise.

Thirteen

Nadia

Nadia rolled onto her side and stared at the empty space next to her. The girls slept with her off and on, but last night she'd wanted to be alone. It was Rafe's birthday. The first of many to come without him, and it would be a day of mourning, remembering, and crying. Not a day had passed since his death when she hadn't cried. There was always something to bring on the emotion, and it was usually something as trivial as a sock on the closet floor that he'd left there the morning of the marathon, or the folded pile of his clothes on top of the dryer. This morning it was because of his birthday and the fact that his pillow no longer smelled like him. In fact, very little did, unless she opened his bottle of cologne and inhaled. His scent had long since dissipated from their bedroom.

Over the past few months, she'd waited for life to return to normal like everyone told her it would. She'd taken a leave of absence from work and had barely made the girls go to school. If they didn't want to, she didn't force it. On those days, they stayed huddled in their house, on the couch under a blanket, watching movies. She knew she needed to be a stronger parent and force her children to go to school, but she couldn't bring herself to do it. If she wasn't going to work because of how she felt, why should the girls be subjected to the same thing.

Nadia brought Rafe's pillow to her face and screamed into it. She let the anger flow. Her sounds were muffled by the place her husband used to lay his head at night. Life was unfair, and she didn't know if she would survive the pain she felt in her chest. Nothing would ever be the same, no matter how hard she tried.

If she wanted life to get back to normal, she would need to *try*. Nadia would have to put in the effort to be the mother the girls had had before and deserved. She removed the pillow and then hugged it before setting it back in its place. She got out of bed and made her way down the hall, only to find the girls' rooms empty. When she got to the staircase, she heard them giggling downstairs.

Nadia sat down on the top step and rested her head against the newel post. She listened to their laughter. It had been months since she'd heard them laugh, and she found herself smiling. They needed her to be a better mother, or none of them would endure the days and months ahead.

She took the stairs slowly, so as to not interrupt whatever Gemma and Lynnea were doing with her mom. Nadia paused in the doorway to the kitchen and set her hand on the wall to steady herself. They were making a birthday cake, even though their dad wouldn't be there to eat it. With a deep inhale and a fake smile, she rounded the corner and greeted her girls.

"Mommy!" Lynnea squealed and got down from the chair, covered in flour. Nadia scooped her up, not caring about her child's dirty hands. "We're making Daddy's birthday cake."

"I see that." She set Lynnea down and went over to Gemma, rubbing her hand down her hair. "Good morning, Gemma."

"Morning." Gemma knelt on the chair but didn't look too engaged in the cake making. Nadia kissed the top of her hair and inhaled the clean coconut scent.

"Morning, Mom."

"Hi, sweetie."

Lorraine Bolton had all but moved in with Nadia and the girls, and when she wasn't here, Sienna was. Both had put their lives on hold to be there for Nadia. She was grateful, and part of her wanted them to leave her alone, but if they did that, she had no idea where she would be.

The last thing she wanted to do was make Rafe a cake. She had no idea how the day would go, but it seemed pointless to celebrate. What were they going to do, sit around and sing "Happy Birthday" to him as if he sat at the head of the table?

Still, she went to the pantry and took her apron off the hook and slipped the strap over her head. As she walked back to the makeshift baking station, she tied the back. She would try and be present for the girls on this day because it was important to them.

"What can I do to help?" It took great effort to ask when all she wanted to do was curl up in bed and watch their wedding video on repeat. She was incredibly thankful she'd insisted on having a videographer at their wedding. When she wanted to hear him say "I love you," all she had to do was turn it on.

"The batter is almost done," Lorraine said. "How about you start on the frosting? I put a couple of bags of powdered sugar in the pantry, and the softened butter is on the table. I told the girls they could pick the colors."

Nadia's attempt at a smile fell short. Her mother saw and offered her a kind one in return. She was thankful her mom didn't coat her with words of sympathy like *I know what you're going through* or *It's going to get easier*. Neither was true. Lorraine had lost her parents, but that's expected when people age. And nothing was going to get easier. Nadia was alone and raising two small children without the help of her partner. She'd rather be divorced than have to deal with life this way.

Over the years, Nadia and the girls had made a million cakes. Lorraine had taught her how to make them from scratch. "They always taste better," she would tell Nadia and Sienna. Frosting, too, would always be homemade, and in vibrant colors and flavors. None of the store-bought stuff. Besides, those containers you bought in the store were never enough to fully cover a cake or cupcakes and were just a waste of money.

Gemma came over to help her mom. She poured milk after Nadia measured, and she slowly moved the mixer around while the ingredients bound together.

"What colors are we doing for Daddy's cake?" The words barely came out without her choking on them.

"Blue and red," Gemma said.

Nadia nodded. "He also liked green."

Rafe was a die-hard Boston sports fan, and he always wore whatever team gear he had during the season.

"How about we do a little bit of color for each team Daddy loved?" Nadia asked Gemma. "This way we get them all in there."

Gemma nodded and wiped at her eyes. She tried to quiet her sob with a cough, but to no avail. Nadia pulled her oldest into her side and held her.

"It's okay to cry," she told her. "We all miss him."

"I just want him back," she said into her mother's side. "He was going to take me to the daddy-daughter dance."

Nadia had forgotten about the dance. It had come and gone, and she'd paid it no mind. Her father or Reuben would've taken Gemma, or even Otto or Lars. She could've easily called Kiran to take her. There were plenty of men in Gemma's life who would've stepped up and filled Rafe's space—not his shoes, because no one would ever be able to do that—but they'd be there if Gemma or Lynnea needed a male figure for anything.

"Next year," Nadia told her as she looked into her eyes. "Uncle Reuben or Uncle Lars, or one of your grandpas, can take you. You won't miss it again." She kissed the tip of her nose and turned her attention back to the frosting, setting out a bowl for each color with a heaping spoonful of frosting.

"Do you want to do the coloring?" she asked Gemma, who shook her head. "Okay, I'll do it, and you mix so we get the right color."

"Do you think Daddy will see his cake in heaven?"

"Yeah, baby girl, he will."

Nadia dropped blue food coloring into one of the bowls and handed it to Gemma with a spoon. She held it while Gemma mixed the coloring into the white concoction.

"It's not dark enough."

"We can fix that." With a few more drops of blue food coloring and some more stirring, the frosting was almost the right color. Nothing would ever be perfect in Nadia's mind. After blue, they did red, green, and gold. All New England team colors. Lynnea sat in front of the oven, with the oven light on, and watched the batter rise to form a cake. If this made her happy and kept her thumb out of her mouth, then Nadia would leave her alone.

Gemma found the piping bags and brought them to the table. She and Nadia filled each one with frosting and then made another batch, "just in case," according to Gemma, who promptly took a spoonful and stuck it in her mouth. She smiled up at her mom, a toothy grin that Nadia hadn't seen in months. Nadia put a dollop of frosting on Gemma's nose and delighted in her laughter. As sad as the day was, hearing her daughter giggle made her heart swell.

"Can I have some?" Lynnea left her perch in front of the oven and came over to her mom and sister. Nadia gave her a spoonful of frosting and put a dollop of it on her nose as well. Another laugh and another pang in Nadia's heart. Happiness, sorrow, and regret. She longed for Rafe to be with them and hated that he and the girls were missing out on so much of each other.

After the cake had finished baking and cooled, the girls frosted it in the assorted colors while Nadia and Lorraine sat back. The girls were messy and having fun. Gemma bossed her little sister around, but that was to be expected.

"You used to do the same thing to Reuben, and Sienna would tell you both what to do."

"She still does," Nadia quipped. Her sister wasn't there to defend herself. Not like there was much she could say. Sienna had always been the leader of the pack. The take-charge type of person. She was the reason Rafe's funeral had gone off without any issues, and why Nadia had had a proper goodbye. Sienna had demanded it. Nadia had never been more appreciative of her sister than she had been during that time.

"We're all done, Mommy," Gemma said as she and Lynnea slid out of their chairs. Nadia approached the breakfast table with an open mind. As soon as she saw Rafe's birthday cake, a cake she'd had zero intention of making, her heart filled with pride, joy, and an insurmountable love for her daughters. Before her, the small sheet cake had been decorated in squares, each one a distinct color representing Rafe. The girls had done an impeccable job, for their age, at creating the perfect cake.

"Wow, this is beautiful."

"Now you just have to add the words, Mommy," Lynnea said. She pointed to each square. "This one is for baseball." She went on to each one, showing Nadia which team went where, along with basketball, football, and hockey.

"Girls, this cake is perfect," Lorraine said when Nadia couldn't find her voice. "Your dad is going to love it. Let's clear the space so your mom can add the words."

The girls moved quickly. Gemma cleaned her chair off, and then held it for Nadia to sit.

"Here you go, Mommy," Gemma said as she handed Nadia the first piping bag. Nadia cleared her throat and pushed the thoughts of Rafe to the back of her mind. She needed to do this for her children, to make them happy, despite the pain it caused her. If she had her way, she'd still be in bed.

Nadia decorated the edges of the cake and then wrote "Happy Birthday" in the middle. She sat back and studied her work. Years ago, on a whim, she and her friend Hazel had taken a cake-decorating class because they were tired of paying bakery prices. It had panned out for any home project and caused anxiety anytime the school needed something. Everyone always assumed Nadia and Hazel would do it for free. Of course, it didn't help that they never spoke up about wanting to be compensated for their talents.

"Wow!" Lynnea exclaimed. "It's so beautiful."

"Daddy would love his cake," Gemma said as she clapped and hugged her mom.

"He would," Nadia agreed. The question at the forefront of her mind was, What next? Did they add candles? Sing "Happy Birthday"? Celebrate as if he were there?

"Okay, girls, run upstairs and change. I'll box this up," Lorraine said. As soon as their thundering footsteps reached the landing upstairs, Nadia gripped her mother's arm as she reached for the cake.

"What's going on?"

"The girls want to go to the cemetery and celebrate. I know you probably don't want to, but they do, and it's important to them," Lorraine said pointedly. Nadia opened her mouth to say something but then shut it. "Go get dressed," Lorraine told her daughter. "We're leaving in ten minutes."

Lorraine packed the cake into a box and set a bag on top of it. If Nadia had to guess, it was paper plates. They were going to have a celebration whether she wanted to or not.

Slowly, she made her way upstairs and paused at the bathroom, where the girls were. She listened to them talking about how Daddy would love his cake and how he'd see them from heaven when they were at the cemetery. Nadia had no choice.

In her closet, with her back to Rafe's clothes, she chose his favorite dress and cried every second it took for her to put it on. She went without makeup and ran a brush through her hair before slipping a hair tie around it to keep it out of her face. She slipped into a pair of sandals and, on her way out of her room, paused. The silver picture frame she kept on her nightstand that held a photo of Rafe danced in the sunlight. Nadia picked it up and ran her fingers over the glass cover, tracing the outline of his face. "God, I miss you," she said to his image. Instead of putting it down, she held it to her chest and carried it with her.

Half Rafe's remains were at the cemetery, in a niche of a columbarium. The other half were at home, on Nadia's dresser, in a steel gray marble box. At any given time, she could open it and remove his ashes, but she had yet to do that. She figured eventually, they would find a place to spread his ashes, but until then, the box sat there.

When they arrived, Lorraine set a blanket out near Rafe's niche and carefully unboxed the cake. Gemma and Lynnea sat down, while Nadia placed a bouquet of roses in the metal vase adhered to the columbarium. As she looked around at the other flowers, she saw notes taped to the front of some and wondered if writing a letter to her husband would be therapeutic. But then, she wouldn't want a stranger to read her thoughts.

Nadia hesitated when she turned toward her mom and daughters. "Sit between the girls," Lorraine told her. Nadia did before her mother caused a scene.

In the center of the cake, underneath "Happy Birthday," Lorraine placed a single candle. *Is it to mark Rafe's first birthday in heaven?* Nadia wondered.

"Okay," Lorraine said as she sat back on her heels. She began singing, and the rest of them joined in. They sang softly, saying either "Daddy" or "Rafe" when the song prompted. By the time they'd finished, everyone had tears on their cheeks.

Lorraine kept the celebration going, despite the somber mood, and cut into the cake. She handed a piece to Gemma, Lynnea, and then Nadia before taking her own. They each took a forkful and savored the homemade cake.

"This is yummy, Grandma," Gemma said with a mouthful of cake, and also a very colorful mouth thanks to the frosting. Nadia couldn't help but smile. She didn't want to be there but was thankful her mother had pushed her to be.

"This is a really great cake, Mom."

"And me," Lynnea said. "I helped."

"You did, and it's perfect," Nadia said.

"It really is, if I do say so myself." Lorraine patted herself on the back, and everyone laughed.

"Can I say something to Daddy?" Gemma asked.

Nadia's breath caught in her throat as she nodded. "Of course."

Gemma stood and looked at Rafe's niche. "Hi, Daddy." As soon as she started, Nadia couldn't hold back her emotions. "I'm sorry you're not here for your birthday. We made you the bestest cake, though, and I hope you can see it from heaven. I miss you so much." Gemma choked on her words. Nadia began to stand, but Lorraine set a hand on her and shook her head slightly.

"The girls need this. Let her do it."

All Nadia wanted to do was comfort her children. To take their pain away. She nodded and bit her bottom lip in an attempt to keep her emotions in check.

"Happy birthday, Daddy," Gemma continued. "I love you." She kissed her fingers and set them to the glass.

Lynnea went next, and it took everything in Nadia to not stand and pull her youngest into her arms and run away. She'd failed as a mother when she couldn't protect them from this shattering heartbreak. She wished this on no one.

Lynnea's words were the same as Gemma's, only quieter. She stretched on her tiptoes to put her fingers to the glass, and then sat down to finish her cake. Children were resilient. Adults, not so much. Nadia's heart was in her throat, burning with anger, resentment, and longing.

They stayed for an hour and then packed up. Lorraine took the girls to the car, while Nadia stayed back. She needed a moment. Once they were out of sight, she traced Rafe's name with her fingertips.

"Today, like every day since you left us, has been unfathomable. Time doesn't heal wounds," she said out loud. "My wounds are gaping. My heart and soul fractured." Nadia took a deep breath. "You're somewhere, while we're here, trying to survive. Trying to figure out how we live without you being the constant in our lives. Nothing is the same and never will be. My love for you is immeasurable, Rafe Karlsson. Happy birthday, my love."

Nadia stepped back and turned, only to find a woman holding a bouquet, staring at her. She knew, without confirmation, who this woman was.

"Your husband saved me." The woman said the words slowly. "I know that me saying those words won't mean anything to you, at least not today, or even next year. I don't pretend to understand the sacrifice your family has made for mine. There isn't a day that goes by that I don't think about you and your children."

At one point, Nadia had so many things to say to the woman before her, but words failed her. This woman lived with survivor's guilt, which was probably enough to cripple her being.

"Are those for Rafe?" Nadia asked of the flowers.

"They are. I got his birthday from his obituary. I hope this is okay."

She nodded. "Rafe would like that you visited him."

Nadia turned and walked away. When she came to the end of the column, she turned back and saw the woman staring at Rafe's niche. "I hope you're doing something magnificent with your life. Rafe would want that."

"I will," she said. "To honor him for what he's done for me."

Nadia smiled and walked away.

Fourteen

Reid

When the knock sounded, Reid smiled and hung up her call with Melanie. She went to the door and, thinking she was funny, asked, "Who is it?"

Grayson laughed on the other side. "Your . . ." He paused. Reid frowned as she waited. "It's Grayson." She suspected he was going to say something cute and possibly romantic but didn't. Why? Was it because she'd put the thoughts into his head that she didn't want to be with him? That was the furthest thing from the truth. She wanted him more than anything, but not at the expense of her heart.

Reid opened the door. She wore a rosy, thin-strapped summer dress with a pair of white sandals. In comparison to Grayson's white shirt and darker skin complexion, they'd look good together. She made a mental note to take pictures together, wanting to capture the night.

He leaned against the doorjamb, turning on the charm. His hands were in his pockets, and the sleeves of his button-down were rolled partway up his arms. Grayson smiled, his lips turning up in a half grin.

Cocky, she thought.

Mine also popped into her mind. She quickly cleared the thought away.

"Are you ready, Sully?"

"I am." She grabbed her cardigan and small clutch and then met him in the hallway. He took her hand, set it on his arm, and then put his hand back into his pocket. Cocky and self-assured. She was in for a whole new side of Grayson.

They walked a few blocks to a new eatery in town that specialized in salads. Reid knew this wasn't what Grayson had in mind for dinner, but the fact that he was sticking to his diet on their first date meant a lot. His health was important to her. Witnessing what she had—she never wanted to go through that again.

During their dinner, Grayson picked at his salad, moving the copious amount of vegetables and lean meat around.

"Are you okay?"

"I am." He looked up at her and smiled.

"Then what's wrong?"

"Just thinking about how I should've done this earlier." Grayson sat back in his seat. "This isn't a great first date place." He looked around. "I mean, I guess it is like the very first date, but we've known each other for years. Do you remember when we went to the Inn at Little Washington for your birthday last year?"

Reid nodded.

"Those are the types of places our first official date should be at. Not this place."

Reid reached for his hand and held it. "If we didn't know each other, would you bring me here?"

He looked around and shook his head. "Honestly, no. It's because of this." He pointed to his chest. "That's why we're here."

"Grayson." She said his name softly. "We can go to all those places and still eat healthy. It's all in what you order. No one's saying you can't have a nice meal; you just have to watch things more carefully. Would you like to go someplace else?"

He pushed his salad forward and nodded. "Yes, but first, we have tickets to the movies. The Heritage Palace is showing *The Notebook*. It's been twenty years now."

A wave of excitement coursed through Reid. She smiled brightly. "And you bought us tickets?"

Grayson blushed and nodded. "I knew it was your favorite."

She tapped her feet on the floor and let out a squeal. "After the movie, we'll go get dessert."

"Aren't you hungry?" he asked her.

"Yes, but let's get popcorn."

Finally, the smile Reid loved so much was back. Grayson cleaned away the disposable cartons and then held the door for her. Once they were outside, she put her hand back where he had placed it, and she realized then that they were almost like a scene out of her favorite movie. Only she and Grayson wouldn't let seven years pass between them. He wanted to change things now.

The Heritage was one of the oldest theaters in DC, and luckily for Reid and Grayson, it was within walking distance of their complex. They often showed foreign and indie films. They didn't have new releases or any of the box office hits. Reid and Melanie often went when she was in town, but this would be Reid's first time with Grayson.

The circular ticket booth with a brass-framed window sat under a large marquee displaying the names and times of the two movies that were playing. Red carpet, and at one time probably velvet, greeted patrons before they went through two double doors to the lobby. The concession stand smelled of freshly popped popcorn.

Reid guided Grayson to the counter, where they ordered a large popcorn with butter, a box of hard-shelled candies, and two sodas. Reid carried the popcorn and handed the usher their tickets.

"Theater one," he said as he ripped the tickets in half and gave the stubs to Reid. Because Grayson carried their drinks, Reid opened the door for them. He stuck his foot out, jamming it against the door.

"Ladies first."

Reid beamed, and it was silly to do so. Grayson wasn't the type of guy not to hold the door for her or carry things for her, but tonight was different. He wanted tonight to feel different. Reid chose the top row, in the middle. This was normal for them, anytime they went to the movies. Grayson was tall, and Reid always felt bad for anyone who got stuck behind him.

The seats were worn and uncomfortable. They weren't there for comfort but nostalgia. Grayson set their drinks down on the floor and put his arm around Reid, tickling her shoulder. The problem with older theaters was that while they had upgraded their screens, they hadn't upgraded the seats, and the pesky armrest was there. Last year, they'd gone out with Pearce and his then girlfriend to a newly remodeled theater where you could sit in a love seat or in an oversize recliner. Reid had fallen asleep after getting too comfortable.

After she'd handed Grayson the popcorn to hold, she opened the candies and dumped them in. "Give it a shake," she told him.

"I forgot you like to do this," he said as he carefully tossed the popcorn, creating a sweet-and-salty mixture.

"It's been a bit since we've gone to the movies."

"I don't even remember the last one we saw."

Reid gave it a thought for a moment and then shook her head. "Nope, me neither." She brought her legs up, tucking them under her and to the side, which forced her to lean closer to Grayson. He placed the popcorn bucket in the pocket she'd created and relaxed a bit. When the previews came on the screen, he picked up a piece of popcorn and fed it to her. A first for them. And something she wouldn't forget.

Halfway through the movie, Reid rested her head on Grayson's shoulder. He angled his body the best he could to be somewhat closer to her and tried to drape his hand more over her shoulder. Every so often he would feed her popcorn, and when she found one of the candies, she'd give it to him.

When the last three minutes of the movie aired and tears started to fall, Grayson handed her a napkin and tried to hold her as best he could to console her. She glanced at him and, with the illumination coming from the screen, saw he had tears in his eyes.

They sat there until the lights came on, needing the small reprieve to get their emotions in check.

"Every time," Reid said.

"I don't think I've watched it since the first couple of times you made me. I certainly never cried before."

No, he hadn't. He'd been a tough guy, saying movies didn't make him cry. She looked quickly at his chest and then to him, refusing to say what was on her mind. Had his new heart changed his feelings on sappy movies? Reid had read up on transplant patients, specifically with the heart. There was a strong chance Grayson would love new things and dismiss things he used to love. She was fine with that, as long as it wasn't her.

They made their way back to their complex. It was a nice night out. Reid was able to ward off the chill in the air with her cardigan, and oddly enough, she felt warmth coming from Grayson.

They walked past an Italian restaurant. The windows were open, and they could hear the jazz music playing from inside. Instead of going in, Grayson took Reid's hand and twirled her out in front of him. She giggled as he pulled her to his chest. Her hand rested over his heart, feeling it thump rapidly against her palm.

Slowly, she looked up at him and found him staring down at her. "I'm afraid."

"I know," he said as he began swaying them to the music. "You have every right to question my motives and intentions, Sully."

She looked away, feeling her heart tug in a direction she wasn't familiar with. Grayson caressed her face and then brought her chin toward him so he could look into her eyes.

"I want you to know," he softly began, his voice barely louder than the low melodies from the jazz bar filtering through the night air, "I'm not here to play games or hurt you, Sully. I'm all in. Whatever you want."

"There are things I want."

"Give me the honey-do list." Despite the seriousness of their conversation, he tried to make the situation lighthearted. She appreciated his efforts.

"Marriage," she said, skipping the dating part. They'd spent enough time together. There wasn't anything, at least not anymore, that they didn't know about each other.

Grayson smiled. "Okay."

"Kids."

"Tell me when, and I'm there," he said, smiling.

His words gave her pause. She looked into his eyes, seeking answers to questions she was afraid to ask. If she didn't, though, Reid would always wonder. "Why now, Grayson?"

A glimmer of realization washed over his face. It was as if he'd waited for her to ask those two words, needing an explanation. He looked away briefly and then back at her.

"You know, I don't remember much from the day I collapsed, but I remember some guy talking to you, and I was angry. At him. At you. When the only person I could be angry at was me. I made the decision to keep you at arm's length because I thought I was protecting you. Protecting myself, in a way. It's been the worst decision of my life. All it did was make me miserable, living each day worrying that it could be my last. Our last. Wondering when you'd come to me, telling me you've met someone, that you were finally done with my shit and leaving Wold or moving away.

"Everything you want, the house, the kids, I want that, too, and I want it with you. I hate being in the friend zone, but I did it because I didn't want you to see me as broken and I didn't want you to feel like you had to take care of me or have our relationship be about my care." Grayson looked away for a moment and shook his head. "Reid, I'm probably not the brightest guy on the planet for what I've done, and you have every right to kick my ass to the curb, but I'm asking for one chance to show you, to prove to you that I'm in."

Reid inhaled deeply and nodded. "No more back-and-forth," she told him. "I can't do the friends thing with you anymore."

His gaze was gentle, understanding, and filled with a raw honesty that made her breath hitch. She felt an undeniable pull toward him that she couldn't ignore. His fingers remained under her chin, delicately holding her as if she were the most precious thing in the world.

"If you want me, want us, then I'm here." He delicately brushed a strand of hair away from her face, tucking it behind her ear. Each second she spent in his presence felt like a warm embrace, making her nerve endings tingle. She watched as his eyes traced over her features and the grin that came when their eyes met. Reid had wanted him for a long time, and now that he was here, in front of her, all she had to do was take a leap.

They continued to sway to the music, under the moonlight. This was by far the most romantic thing she'd ever done, and she was elated to experience it with Grayson.

Grayson moved closer, pressing his forehead against hers while maintaining eye contact, their height difference be damned. His thumb traced circles on her cheek soothingly as she swallowed hard, contemplating a decision that could change their lives forever. Butterflies fluttered wildly within her stomach. His lips were inches away from hers now, creating an electric tension between them that could only be broken by a kiss.

"I am here, where I belong and where I've wanted to be from the jump. You're the only one who invades my thoughts, who my heart beats for," he continued quietly with a slight smirk playing on his lips as he glanced down at her mouth for a brief moment before meeting her gaze again. "Because I'm willing to risk everything for the possibility of having something real with you. If you're willing to do the same. We can take it as slow as you want. Just knowing you want to try is enough for me right now."

Reid's heart pounded so hard against her chest that it mirrored the rhythm of the jazz music coming from the club. Fast and intense.

Overwhelmed with emotion, she leaned into him, closing the gap between their bodies and hearts.

She looked up at him one more time before whispering in a tender tone, “I’m willing to take that risk with you too.” A small smile played on Grayson’s lips as he tilted his head slightly.

Their lips met in a sweet kiss under the moonlit sky. Their first date was the start of something beautiful and terrifying. Reid had everything to lose if Grayson changed his mind, and everything to gain if he didn’t. Without a doubt in her mind, body and soul, he was the man for her.

FIFTEEN

NADIA

Summer slowly faded away. Lorraine and Sienna had returned to their lives. As had Reuben. Cleo and Otto had kept their distance, which bothered Nadia. They still had two other grandchildren, and she needed their help. Warren came to visit every other weekend, taking the train from DC to Boston. His visits were short and mostly came from a need to make sure the house didn't require repairs and the lawn stayed mowed. Everything in Nadia's life continued to evolve and change, but none of it was for the better. People who'd cared and expressed grief over Rafe's passing, or brought food for them in the days after, no longer called or stopped by. They had all forgotten, while Nadia and the girls continued to live with the crippling grief.

When Nadia returned to her classroom for the first time since Rafe's passing, it wasn't the same. The substitute had taken down all Nadia's decorations, boxed up the pictures of her girls and Rafe, and made her classroom unwelcoming. The wall dedicated to the American Revolution and the history of Boston was blank, the bookshelves bare. The books had been piled in stacks, in a disorderly fashion. She felt out of place, like she didn't belong in the room that had been hers for years, and she definitely didn't want to be there. Not yet at least. She spent most of the first week putting things back where she wanted them. A task that should've taken her hours took her five days. Nothing was as it was, and she couldn't make it the same, no matter how hard she tried.

It was just like her life.

By the time staff meetings rolled around, she had found some kind of groove. It wasn't the one she was used to, though. Gone was bubbly Nadia who loved life. In her place was a sad, sullen woman who had trouble getting out of bed in the morning and found every excuse to stay home.

Nadia dreaded the first day of school, a day she used to look forward to. She used to love meeting new faces and seeing returning students who took her advanced class. Teaching history was her thing, and she'd thought living in a place that had done everything to preserve it was something people should embrace. The annual field trip they took, walking the Freedom Trail, had always been a highlight of her year. So had been stopping at Boston Common to ride the carousel, weaving their way through history, knowing that the men and women who'd forged our country had battled in the same spots they walked; then they'd eat lunch at Quincy Market. Their field trips led them to Marshall Street, where they would visit the Green Dragon Tavern, which dated back to 1654. It was where Paul Revere penned his memoirs about his clandestine meetings with Samuel Adams, John Adams, and others. It was where they sat and eavesdropped on British troops who openly discussed war plans.

She needed to find a way to get back to the Nadia of old, which was easier said than done when she felt so empty on the inside.

The first day of school also meant they'd each embark on a new school year with a change none of them had expected. Their morning routine would be different. Rafe wouldn't be there to wrangle an overly excited Lynnea or calm Gemma's nerves. He wouldn't kiss them goodbye and wish them the best first day ever or tell Nadia to teach history in a way the students would never forget. He wouldn't share in their first-day-of-school breakfast or be waiting for them when they came home, eager to hear the tales of new teachers, friends, and the smelly boy who pulled Gemma's hair.

Nadia would be the one to fill out the paperwork, pack lunches, and make sure the girls were presentable for school. She'd look over their homework, help with their bath time, and tuck them in at night, all while grading papers, making dinner, starting laundry, and picking up after them. The help she'd had with her family coming and going since the accident was gone. They wanted her to be independent, which she understood. The problem was, she had never done parenting by herself. She and Rafe had been a team, from the onset.

At night, she talked to his photo, telling him her fears and how she felt inadequate as a mother because she had trouble coping. This was her form of therapy. She didn't need a head shrink telling her she was a shitty mother or hung up on the death of her husband. Nadia had that one figured out for herself. For fifty bucks an hour, she could tell you everything that was wrong with herself, the girls, and herself as a mother—she'd lost her husband and the girls their father to a freak accident that had been preventable. You don't move on from that in days, weeks, or even months. You don't cope and move on because society doesn't allow it.

If Nadia intended to get through the school year, she would need help. As it was, she couldn't afford a part-time babysitter on her salary alone, and the life insurance policy hadn't come in yet. If it hadn't been for the city, donations, and their parents, Rafe's funeral would've been held in their backyard. People had come through for them, and she needed one more to do the same.

She picked up her phone and pressed Cleo's number and waited for her mother-in-law to pick up. In the past five months, since Rafe's funeral, Nadia hadn't seen much of her in-laws. They came around, but nothing like they used to. That needed to change.

"Hello," Cleo said in her singsong voice, which for some reason made Nadia mad. She shouldn't be cheery.

"Hi, Cleo," Nadia said and then took a deep breath. Asking for help wasn't something she was comfortable with.

"Are the girls okay?"

Only the girls? Not me?

"They're the reason I'm calling. School starts tomorrow, and they finish their classes before I do. I was hoping you or Otto could pick them up for me, and stay at the house until I get home?"

"Every day?"

Don't sound so enthused to spend time with your grandchildren.

"Until I can find someone part time who isn't working every day until five."

"I didn't know you were looking for someone?"

How would she? It wasn't like she called, stopped by, or stopped blaming Nadia for donating her son's organs. Nadia sat there, unable to come up with something to say. She wanted to scream and tell her Rafe wouldn't appreciate the way she acted, but he would've expected this from his mother.

"It's fine, Cleo. I'll figure something out." Nadia hung up before her mother-in-law could say something. She didn't need her or Otto, even though she loved Otto dearly. Her next call was to Hazel.

"She hates me," Nadia said when Hazel answered. "And she's taking it out on the girls."

"I think you knew this was going to happen. She isn't like your mother. I have no idea how she raised someone like Rafe."

"Me neither." Nadia paused. "I'm in a bind, Hazel. I don't know what to do."

"What's wrong?"

"I don't have anyone to pick the girls up or stay with them until I get home. Any after-school activities don't start for another couple of weeks."

"I'll get them," she said without hesitation.

"How? You have to work."

"I can work from home in the afternoons," she told Nadia. "I wasn't going to because Lord knows I'll never get any work done with Hayden yammering in my ear, but I can do this for you."

"Are you sure?"

"Without a doubt. I'll stop by in the morning and pick up your extra key. I'm assuming you're taking them to school?"

"Yeah, as much as I don't want to. I have to. It's going to be hard."

"We'll go together. A team effort. Besides, Hayden misses Lynnea, and it'll be good for the girls to be together."

"You're right. Thank you."

"You'd do the same for me," Hazel said.

"I pray you never have to go through what I'm going through."

Hazel didn't respond. She didn't need to. Nadia knew what her friend would say—*Me too.*

"I'll see you in the morning. Try to get some sleep, Nadia. You're teaching middle schoolers tomorrow, and you need to be quick on your toes."

After they hung up, Nadia felt a smidge better. She still didn't want to go to work, leave the house every day, or have the kids out of her sight. She welcomed the day when she'd be better, when missing Rafe was easier and her life made sense again.

The next morning, she woke up well before Gemma and Lynnea had to be out of bed, determined to start fresh. She showered, dressed, and avoided everything in her room that reminded her of her husband. In the kitchen, she fixed the batter for pancakes, poured orange juice into cups, and set the table. Nadia hummed a song she'd heard but wasn't sure of the words or the title. She wasn't even sure where she'd heard it.

Nadia piled three pancakes on her spatula and turned. The girls weren't at the table, nor could she hear them upstairs. The pancakes fell to the floor, and tears welled behind her eyes. She had forgotten to wake them up, and judging by the numbers on the stove clock, they'd be late.

Everything in her screamed to go back to bed, to call out sick, to keep the girls home because they weren't ready to return. How would she survive if she couldn't get them up on time?

She wouldn't, unless she tried. Trying was as hard as living these days.

Leaving the pancakes on the floor, she made her way upstairs, working to clear her thoughts and feelings on the already chaotic morning. Tonight, she'd order Gemma an alarm clock and ask her to please help her with Lynnea. It was the best Nadia could do.

"Gemma," Nadia said as she went into her room. She turned her light on and found her daughter awake and staring at her. "How long have you been up?"

She shrugged. "A while."

Anger surged inside of Nadia, rising to an instant headache. She knew she shouldn't be upset. Gemma was only eight, but irritation baited her, causing her to feel emotions she never wanted to.

"Get out of bed and help me with your sister. We're going to be late." She left Gemma's room and went into Lynnea's, pushing the door open abruptly. Lynnea startled and rubbed her eyes.

"You need to get up. We're late." Nadia looked for the clothes she'd laid out the night before, remembering specifically that she'd left them on the chair. "Where are your clothes?"

"I don't like them."

"I don't care, Lynnea. Where are they?"

Lynnea said nothing and started to cry.

Gemma was her morning girl. The one who woke up with a smile on her face and was ready to take on the world. Lynnea, not so much. She was a grumpy sunshine who wanted to be held and needed time to wake up before the demands of the day took their turn.

Nadia knew this and had failed.

At the first sight of Lynnea's tears, Nadia walked out of the room. She couldn't comfort the first grader. Not in the way she needed. Nadia went into her bedroom, into the bathroom, locked the door, and turned on the shower. With the water blasting, Nadia screamed. The guttural sound coming from her body shocked her. She held on to the counter for support. She caught her reflection in the mirror. Her shoulders heaved and her chest grunted as she continued to emanate air. The exhaustion of the past five months had finally caught up with her, and it was as if she was only noticing now. Her eyes had sunken in, surrounded by deep dark bags. The natural auburn hair Rafe loved so much was lackluster, at best. On closer inspection, split ends covered the bottom three or four inches, but that was nothing compared to the wrinkles around her mouth and eyes and along her forehead. She had aged fifty years since her husband had passed.

Nadia needed to get her shit together or she wouldn't survive. She had two children to think about. They needed to come first.

After shutting off the water, she left her room, walked to Lynnea's room, and found her sitting on her bed, still in her pajamas. Nadia felt the anger boil and ignored it. "I'm sorry for yelling," she told her. "Mommy's frustrated and angry, and I took it out on you. Come on, let's get dressed. You can wear whatever you want. Meet me downstairs for breakfast, but hurry because we're already late." She kissed the tip of Lynnea's nose and ignored the thumb in her mouth.

Gemma's room was empty, but she'd made her bed, which made Nadia smile. She found her oldest downstairs, sitting at the table. The pancakes weren't on the floor anymore, and the griddle had been turned off. Guilt washed over Nadia. Gemma was eight, turning nine in December, and more of an adult than Nadia at this point.

"I'm sorry I yelled." She ran her hand down Gemma's hair and kissed the top of her head.

"I miss him, too, Mommy."

Nadia nodded, unable to find her voice. She moved toward the griddle and turned it back on to make more pancakes.

"Maybe we need help."

Nadia looked out the kitchen window, staring at the bird on her neighbor's fence. How could a child be wiser than the parent?

"You're right, Gemma. I'll call someone today."

By the time they'd made it out of the house, Nadia was late for work. She called into school and said she would be there shortly and offered no other explanation.

Lynnea opened the front door and said, "What the heck."

"Lynnea, please don't say that in school." Nadia came toward the door and froze. Kiran paused as he came toward the house. He held flowers in one hand and bottles of chocolate milk in the other. Rafe had bought the girls flowers and chocolate milk on their first day of school each year. Nadia swallowed the lump in her throat.

He smiled, but it wasn't the one she was used to. Today was different. The wide, bright, cheerful smile showed happiness, excitement.

"What are you doing here, Kiran?"

"Well," he said as he looked at his hands. "I was hoping to catch you at home before you lovely ladies left for the day." He took the steps and stopped in front of Lynnea, handing her a bottle of chocolate milk and one of the bouquets in his hand, and then did the same for Gemma. "I know it's not the same when it doesn't come from your dad, but I wouldn't be doing my job as his best friend if I didn't have these for you today."

"Thank you," both girls said for their gerbera daisies.

"Why don't you take your flowers into the house. Gemma can get you a vase, Lynnea." Nadia watched the girls until they'd disappeared from her sight.

She turned back to Kiran. "You didn't have to do that."

"I did," he said, nodding. "It's not fair, what you and the girls are going through, and if something as simple as showing up on the first day of school makes them smile . . . makes you smile, then I know I've done the right thing."

"Thank you."

He extended his hand and gave her the last bouquet. Hers had white roses and carnations, along with lavender lilies, accented with baby's breath and greenery. This wasn't a bouquet you bought at the grocery for under ten dollars next to the checkout. This was an arrangement someone had put some thought into. After she inhaled the roses, she glanced at Kiran. He looked embarrassed.

"Thank you, Kiran," she said. Nadia inhaled again, but only to hide her smile. She didn't want him to see her grin.

"It's my pleasure, Nadia." He nodded and turned around. She watched him walk down the path to his car. When he got to the driver's side, he stared back at her for a long moment, and then he ducked inside to drive away.

SIXTEEN

REID

The text from Grayson read: Be ready by 6!

Reid had lost count of how many times she'd looked at it or any of his previous ones. The shift in their relationship was definitely playing out in the way he texted her as well. Long gone were the ridiculous memes, although he still sent a few on occasion, and in their place were hearts and googly eyes. Each text brought a smile to her face.

She'd finally gotten her man.

Melanie, Reid's best friend, had told her that if Grayson didn't want to be with her, a minor thing like having his heart replaced wasn't going to change his mind. Of course, there wasn't anything minor about a heart transplant, and Melanie knew this. It was her way of proving to her friend that her errant thoughts were just that: wayward. Ever since Grayson had come home from the hospital and Melanie had seen them together, she could see for herself how in love he was with Reid, and Mel made a point of telling her friend that every chance she could.

Reid closed her phone and tried to work, but the words blurred on her computer screen. Three months ago, Grayson had told her he was all in, that she was the one he wanted to be with. While Reid accepted this, she'd made him wait until she was ready to jump back into bed with him again. She had to protect herself, and while she was madly in love with him, giving herself to him that way again was something she took very seriously.

Grayson took this as a challenge and showered her with gifts such as flowers as well as random visits to the office (which he was eager to return to), candlelight dinners that he'd prepared, and picnics on the weekends. They'd gone to the beach for Labor Day with their friends and were dressing up for Pearce's Halloween party in a few days as Ariel and Prince Eric, which was Reid's idea because she already had red hair like Ariel. Not to mention, she considered Grayson her prince. He had wanted them to go as Forrest Gump and Jenny. Mostly because he liked exaggerating the name in his Forrest accent.

She picked up her phone. Her fingers hovered over the buttons, ready and willing to type a message to Grayson. She'd only responded to his text with an "okay" and a winky face, hoping he'd elaborate. He hadn't, and that left her reeling with curiosity.

Reid had never thought of Grayson as the romantic type. The one time they'd hooked up before his transplant, they'd been at a party, and while they weren't drunk, they were tipsy, and she'd flirted, and he'd reciprocated. Unfortunately for her, that one night hadn't led to many more, like she had hoped, even after she'd told him she was madly in love with him.

He'd said he didn't love her back.

She now knew why.

Hearing those words from him had hurt. She had tried to distance herself from him, chalk the night up to one giant mistake, but he'd refused to fade into the night. Grayson was there, acting like nothing had happened, like he hadn't broken her heart into a million little pieces, each one more jagged than the next. It was like he'd taken those shards and continued to stab her, until she stopped feeling and just enjoyed being in his presence. The only saving grace was that he didn't date. He wasn't bringing other women around or telling her about someone he'd met at the bar. Grayson and Reid spent as much time together as a couple would, without the benefits of being a couple.

And now her life with Grayson was different. With his new lease on life, he embraced what she'd known all along: they were meant for each other. They could finish each other's sentences and sensed when the other was ready to leave a friend's house, and he never pressured her to take the next step in their relationship. Reid wanted to. She longed to be with him again.

The Human Resources office at the Wold Collective was set up similarly to the other offices, and it had an open concept with cubicles. The problem this layout created was that staff were unable to have private conversations with employees, and they always had to book a conference room. The setup also gave no one any privacy. So, if you were having a bad day or an emotional moment and needed some time for yourself, you didn't have a place to take a break. That was a drawback for Reid. While she loved working for Wold, ever since Grayson had made it known they were a couple, she'd been bombarded with nosy Nellies prying into her personal life. Of course, dating a coworker probably wasn't the smartest thing to do.

Reid heard her name and peeked around the end of her cubicle. Her office space was in the back, toward the wall, with one office in front of her and then the open desk area where applicants waited for their interviews. The receptionist, who'd started earlier in the week and whose name Reid couldn't remember, stood at the counter with a massive bouquet of red roses.

"Reid?" she called out. "You have another delivery."

Her coworkers stood up to watch the receptionist bring the bouquet toward her cubicle. She couldn't tell if they were jealous or if, as she suspected, some of them had their own crushes on Grayson. The bouquet of roses was undoubtedly the largest she'd ever received, and over the past few months or so, Grayson had either brought flowers to her or had had them delivered. In fact, she still had a vase on her desk from last week's delivery.

"You know, none of us need to ask about your relationship if he keeps this up," Lily, one of her coworkers, said with a laugh. She wasn't wrong. Grayson wasn't being shy about his affection for her. Deep down, Reid appreciated every gesture, basked in them, really, and even marked them on her calendar.

She leaned forward and sniffed one of the fragrant blooms. "Heavenly."

"Who's the lucky guy?" the new receptionist asked.

"His name's Grayson. You'll meet him soon. He works here and has been out on leave."

"Can't wait," she said cheerily as she gave a finger wave and left.

Reid grasped the weighty glass vase and positioned it on her desk. The arrangement took up most of her free working space, and she spent the next ten minutes cleaning off the top of her filing cabinet to make room for the roses.

"Thank you for putting them up there," Lily said. "Now we can all enjoy them."

"Are you being facetious, Lily?"

"Absolutely not. I want my husband to spend a week in here and see how Grayson's treating you—then maybe my lump will get a clue. I think the last time he gave me flowers . . ." She trailed off. "Yep, it's been so long I don't even remember." Lily had fifteen years on Reid. She was a mom of three and had been married since she was eighteen. Reid liked her a lot and often went to her for motherly advice. She knew everything about Reid and how she felt about Grayson: the fear she had while he was in a coma, and the way he made her feel now.

"I'm sorry, Lily. In all fairness, until Grayson, no one has ever bought me flowers, other than my dad." Reid wasn't counting the customary corsage her prom dates brought her. Mostly everyone knew the moms were the ones to order those, not the boys.

"Whoa, is it Valentine's Day or something?" Rosalyn said as she came into the office. She walked right to Reid's station and sighed. "Damn. That man is wining and dining you big time." Her fingers shot out, as if they were fireworks.

"He has a lot of making up to do, if you ask me," Lily yelled from her cubicle. "That man should kiss the ground you walk on, Reid. And other things."

Grayson had done a stand-up job of showing her how much he loved her over the past handful of months.

She decided to share with her coworkers. "He has something special planned tonight. He won't give me any hints, though, so I'm a bit nervous."

"Maybe he's going to ask you to move in with him." Lily came over to Reid's cubicle and leaned on the half-wall divider. Reid studied her for a moment. She was average height and kept her hair long with natural curls that Reid envied. She'd pay good money to have texture, body, and some life to her hair that didn't require her to add product and curl it every day. Devorah had deep-blue eyes and wore very little makeup, saying that with three kids she barely had any time for herself in the morning. Not that she needed it; her skin was flawless.

"Doubtful," Reid said. "I think if anything he'd move into mine. I have better furniture," she added, laughing.

"Then that's what he's doing," Rosalyn said as she stood up and leaned her elbows on her half wall. "He's going to ask you if he can move in with you." Rosalyn was on the taller side, almost matching Grayson's dominating height. With her long blonde hair and ocean-blue eyes, men flocked to her. She'd been unlucky in love too many times to count. She was the ultimate "fall in love with everyone" type and planned all her future weddings within days of meeting the next great love of her life. At one time, she'd had a major crush on Grayson and had asked Reid if they were a couple. Reid had given her permission to pursue Grayson and was secretly happy when he'd rebuffed her.

Reid could easily picture Grayson living with her, and honestly it would make things so much easier. She wouldn't have to ask every day if he'd taken his meds or if he had them with him when he came to her place. The last thing she wanted to do was harp on him about the medication, but he literally needed it to live. One of Reid's biggest fears was that his new heart would reject his body and they'd be back at square one.

"I'd let him," she told her coworkers with a shrug. "We spend so much time with each other now, it only makes sense." Even if they hadn't slept together yet. She already knew they had chemistry between the sheets.

Rosalyn sighed and tilted her head back. "Color me green because I'm officially jealous."

"He's high maintenance," Reid joked. "Be thankful."

Rosalyn waved her hand in the air. "It doesn't matter," she told Reid and Devorah. "I remember when I first started. I was hot for him." She fanned herself. "The rejection hurt."

Tell me about it.

"Anyway, I'm happy for you, Reid."

"Thanks," she told her friend. "I feel like whatever he has planned for tonight, I'm going to love it."

"Gah, how can you not," Rosalyn said.

"Back to work, ladies. We'll chat about the date tomorrow," Lily said. "Because Reid *will* give us all the details."

Reid could've rolled her eyes and balked, but Lily was right. She'd spill everything in the morning over coffee and doughnuts.

Be ready by 6!

Reid had given in and texted Grayson about what his text meant, only to receive the shrugging emoticon in return. The only information he gave her was for her to wear something casual, but not "going for a run" casual.

She'd left work early, afraid one of the trains she took home would be delayed or there'd be some incident that would put her behind schedule. Being late for whatever Grayson had planned wasn't an option, at least not in her mind. Besides, she prided herself on being as punctual as possible, and even fifteen minutes early was late in her opinion.

After showering the grime of work and the subway off, she stood in front of her closet and pushed each hanger to the side. Grayson's mention of "not going for a run" casual meant he didn't want to see her in her comfortable yoga pants or one of his sweatshirts that was so big on her it could double as a dress.

Reid reached for a pair of black slacks but thought better of dressing like she was about to go to the office, and she pulled out a simple shift dress. The late surge of summer still hung in the air, despite Halloween being on the horizon. She paired her dress with strappy sandals with a modest heel, thankful that she and Melanie had spent last weekend having a spa day. Freshly painted and pedicured toenails and manicured fingernails went a long way in helping a woman feel pretty. Plus, the massage and facial Reid had gotten was divine. She'd fallen asleep and ended up snoring.

Reid dabbed on the French perfume Grayson had bought her for Christmas and curled her hair, making sure to fix the pieces that had fallen. She concentrated mostly in the front due to her inability to not run her fingers through her hair during the day. It was a bad habit, and she did it mostly when she was bored or spending too much time wondering what her boyfriend was up to. She applied natural makeup, dabbed some red-hued lip gloss on, and called it good. If she went to Grayson's too dressed up and he wasn't, one of them would feel the need to change, and she didn't want that. He had something planned, and she wanted to make sure it went off without a hitch.

It would be faster for Reid to take the stairs. She could be at Grayson's door in under two minutes. Doing so would increase the rate of her already pounding heart. She opted for the elevator and would use the time it took to calm her nerves. For all she knew, she had no reason to be nervous. It wasn't like Grayson hadn't spent the past few months planning every single date he took her on. He'd ask her if there was something she wanted to do, but most of the time he had everything planned for them by the time she came home from work. This was something she appreciated without knowing it was something she wanted. With her prior boyfriends, it was always the classic "What do you want to do?" followed by endless hours of back-and-forth as they tried to figure out what they should do before giving up and calling it a night.

With Grayson, if Reid mentioned a movie she wanted to see, he'd buy the tickets and tell her days in advance, not hours. When she brought up a festival, he booked a car for them because the train wouldn't go as far out as they needed. Since they'd begun dating, he'd been fully attentive, which showed her what kind of man he could be. She hated that he'd hidden his true self from her due to his heart condition.

Reid understood, though. She was young when her mother passed away, but she remembered certain parts of growing up when she saw her father long for his wife. There were times, even so many years later, when Reid would get flashes of memories with her mom. They would dance in front of the Christmas tree or sing carols. Her father would don a Santa hat and hand out presents, each one coming from Santa. The first Christmas without her mother was quiet. They'd had a tree, but Luther hadn't gotten around to decorating it. He barely lit the fire, or played music, and he definitely didn't put the hat on again. The morning of, he sat on the couch and told Reid she could sit by the tree and open the few presents he had managed to buy. The following year was better, as were the subsequent years, but they were never the same as they were when her mother was alive.

Her parents had the kind of love Reid wanted, and when she'd first met Grayson, she knew he was the one. Every day, she was thankful she hadn't given up on him.

The elevator dinged and brought her out of her reverie. She stepped in, smiled at the others who were in there, and pressed the button for Grayson's floor. They made a stop on the second, and then the doors were opening for her to step out. Normally, Grayson would open his door to peek out when he knew she was on her way to his place, but his door remained shut. Her mind had the ability to think of every possible scenario, from *Is he hurt?* to *Is he home?*

She stood in front of his door, raised her hand to knock, and then thought how ridiculous that would be. They hadn't knocked on each other's doors in years, unless they were locked. She knew Grayson's door would be unlocked because he expected her.

Reid opened the door, and her breathing hitched. From the front, rose petals lined the hallway. She stepped in and followed the trail, even though she could see the man of her dreams, near the sliding glass door, on bended knee.

SEVENTEEN

REID

Reid covered her mouth as soon as her eyes found Grayson there on bended knee. All around his apartment candles burned, and vases of roses covered almost every visible space. In the background, soft music played, and near the sliding glass door that led to a small balcony was Grayson, patiently waiting for her to take a few more steps closer so he could ask her a very important question.

Was she ready for this?

The hopeless romantic in her wanted to scream *Yes!* before the words had even come out of his mouth. The hopeful romantic felt their relationship was too new for this type of declaration. They'd jokingly said they loved each other, but neither had come out and made the avowal. Sure, she loved him—and, she sometimes suspected, more than he loved her, but that could also be because she'd loved him so long and he had a lot of catching up to do. Then there was the part about intimacy. He'd made advances early on, but she'd shut the door on anything between the sheets. Reid couldn't afford to get her heart broken again. Grayson hadn't brought it up. He never asked why she didn't want to have sex with him. This sort of bothered her. Shouldn't he want to be with her in every way? Was he afraid, just as she was?

As frightened of the future as she was, she confidently stepped toward him. Their eyes met, and both smiled widely at each other. Happy tears welled in her eyes as Grayson held his hand up higher.

"I had this entire speech planned . . ." Grayson shook his head and cleared his throat. "I know this seems out of the blue, but I woke up last week from a dream and you weren't there, or I wasn't in your life anymore, and I thought I was going to die, and I knew I had to change things before I lost you for real." He looked at the ring in his hand and then at her.

"I'm in love with you, Sully. I have been this entire time but was afraid to let you in because of my issues. I didn't know how to exist as the man I was, the one who was slowly dying, and being the man you deserved. I do now. I know what I want, and that is you, in my life. In a life we build together. Reid, will you marry me?"

With zero hesitation, she nodded and wiped at the tears spilling over. "Yes," she said as she stepped forward. Reid bent to his level; avoiding the ring, she cupped his face and kissed him hard. When they parted, he stood and slipped the ring onto her finger, and then he kissed her again.

Afterward, he picked her up and spun her around. "Holy shit, I was afraid you'd say no."

He set her down. "Why would I say no?"

He shrugged. "I know a few things are missing from our relationship. Well, not missing, just not—"

"Are you talking about sex?"

Grayson blushed a deep crimson. He opened his mouth to say something and then quickly closed it. Reid laughed.

"It's not like we haven't had sex before," she pointed out.

"I know, but . . . Shit, why is this so hard?"

Reid wanted to have some fun with him. She placed her hand over his crotch and gave him a squeeze. He started. "Not yet, but we can work on it."

"Sully!"

"Oh, don't 'Sully' me." She laughed. "I'm the one who's pumped the brakes on sex this time. I needed time, and then when I reached the pinnacle of time, I didn't know how to bring it up," she told him.

"Oh, simple," he told her. "You say, 'Grayson, take your shorts off because I need sex,'" he scoffed.

Reid rolled her eyes. "Always the romantic."

"Reid, listen closely to what I'm about to say: ever since the night we spent together and I foolishly pushed you away, I haven't been with another woman."

Her mouth dropped open in shock. "Wait, what?"

Grayson shook his head slowly. "No one, Sully. Not a single one since you."

"What about all those times Pearce set you up with someone?"

"Do you mean all the times I'd end up at your apartment afterward?"

She nodded.

"Do you really think I had sex with someone and then came over to your place?"

Now she was the one who was embarrassed. Yes, that's what she'd thought, and she'd often cried herself to sleep after he'd left. "I—I . . ." She stopped talking.

"Jesus, Reid." Grayson ran his hand through his hair. "Hell no. I came here after those dates because you were the one I wanted to be with. Ever since meeting you, you're the only one I've wanted."

"I didn't know."

"Clearly." He rolled his eyes. "I'm fixing that now, though."

Grayson scooped her up into his arms, and she squealed. He carried her to his bed and set her down gently and then pulled the tie holding her dress together. It fell open, exposing her lacy black bra and matching panties.

"The first time I saw you like this, I knew it would never be enough." Grayson picked up her left hand and kissed her ring finger. "And now I get you forever," he said as he looked into her eyes.

Reid used her free hand to undo his belt and then the button on his slacks. She looked up at Grayson as she slipped her fingers into the waistband of his boxers, pulling them down until they pooled at his feet.

Her hand slipped under his shirt, her nails trailing along. She felt him shiver under her touch, exciting her. Reid started on the buttons of his shirt, wanting him undressed. He moved her hands aside and worked the small disks through the holes. When he got to the last one, he slipped it over his shoulders and let it fall to the floor.

The mood shifted as Grayson stepped closer to Reid and cupped her face in his hands, searching her eyes. He leaned down and softly kissed the corners of her lips before pressing his lightly against hers. His tongue searched for an entrance as their kiss deepened into something passionate yet gentle. Reid let out a small moan that caused Grayson to pull away slightly so he could look at her incredulously, asking with his eyes alone if she wanted more.

"You are the most beautiful woman I have ever seen." Grayson whispered the words as his lips ghosted across her skin. Goose bumps rose, and she shivered. He smiled in response and began to leave open-mouthed kisses on her body until he was back to her lips. His hands were all over her, caressing every inch of her body. Reid let out a moan, and her head fell back as he cupped her breasts and played with her taut nipples. She shuddered when his grin turned wicked. He was toying with her. She wasn't sure how she felt about that. They'd waited so long for this moment. She was eager for him. But also, she wanted to savor every bit of the torture.

Grayson lifted her effortlessly and carried her to the center of his bed, placing her on the soft comforter. He kissed his way down her stomach until he'd reached the edge of her panties. He looked up at Reid and waited for her permission; she nodded.

He slid the lacy fabric down her legs and tossed it aside. He began to explore every inch of her body with his mouth, tongue, and hands, showing her just how much he loved and adored every part of her being.

Grayson settled between Reid's legs and took a deep inhale of her scent before burying himself in her. She moaned loudly and gripped a handful of his hair as he expertly worked his tongue over her nub.

"Grayson." She arched her back and gripped his shoulder to bring him closer to where she needed him to be. He complied and slid himself into her silken depths, slowly pushing until he filled her completely. His eyes rolled as he inhaled deeply.

"Fuck, Sully," he muttered.

"God, yes," Reid replied as she moaned and dug her nails into his backside, pushing him impossibly deeper. His hips rocked into her, thrusting with urgency to satisfy her. She brought her knees up, giving him a different angle. He hissed at the sensation and thrust harder.

"I'm close," she said breathlessly. He reached between them, pressing into her nub. Her moans became louder, her movements frantic. She muttered words of encouragement and adoration.

"Please, please," she begged him, wishing him to push her over the edge. He kissed her deeply to swallow her cries while pulsing inside her.

They lay there, spent and blissed, their naked bodies intertwined, until Grayson rolled off Reid and inhaled deeply. "Sully."

Her answer was inaudible.

"Yeah, same. We need to do that again."

"'K."

"Except we have dinner reservations with our family."

Reid sat up in surprise. "What?" She looked at a naked Grayson, with his arm over his eyes, breathing heavily.

"Yeah, it's part of the whole engagement surprise."

"Now you tell me." Before she could get out of bed, he wrapped his arm around her waist, pulling her to him.

Grayson chuckled. "Give us a minute. I want to hold you."

She wanted him to hold her as well. Lying back, she nestled into the crook of his neck and slung her leg over his, grazing his slacked penis. The simple touch caused him to flinch.

"Uh-oh."

"What's 'uh-oh'?"

"Seems like I'm about ready for a repeat and longer performance."

"I guess we'll have to wait until we get back." To remind him of what he'd started, she took him in her hand and stroked him. "We can do a little of this when we get back, but just remember, I'm not the one who forgot about the reservation when you started taking my clothes off."

Grayson groaned into the pillow. "Promise?"

"Promise."

They cleaned up, re-dressed, and made it outside to where a limo idled. "That's our ride," Grayson said. "I'm surprised he stayed."

"Grayson!"

He ran his hand through his hair and greeted the driver. "Thanks for waiting."

"No problem."

Grayson followed Reid into the back seat. He reached for a waiting bottle of champagne, popped the cork, and poured each of them a flute. "To us," he said as he tapped his glass to hers. "I love you, Sully."

"I love you, Grayson."

The entire time she drank, he never took his eyes off her. When she pulled the flute away, he leaned down and kissed her. "I'm so damn happy."

"Me too."

She held out her hand, admiring her ring. "It's beautiful, Grayson."

"Does it look familiar?"

Reid's brows furrowed as she pulled her hand closer, inspecting her ring. "Uh, I'm not sure. But I think . . . Is it?"

Grayson nodded. "Reid, I asked your father for your hand in marriage before I even went to look for a ring. I thought we'd look together—at least that's what Pearce says people do now. However, when I was with your dad, he handed me your mom's ring. As soon as I opened the box, I knew that was the ring for you."

Reid cupped his cheek and pulled him toward her. "I love it so much. You have no idea." When she pulled back, she felt wetness on her cheeks.

"Don't cry," he said as he wiped her tears away.

"These are happy tears."

"Yeah? That's good, then."

They pulled in front of the Italian bistro where Grayson and Reid had danced on their first date. He guided her inside and toward the back where their table was, along with the small gathering he had arranged with their friends and family.

Reid went right to her father and hugged him. "Thank you, Dad."

"Anything for you," he said as he held her tightly. When they parted, she showed him the ring and then hugged him again when he teared up.

After she and Grayson had greeted everyone, they sat down to a nice dinner, followed by dessert and dancing. And when they got home, exhausted, Reid made good on her promise. As did Grayson.

Eighteen

Nadia

Halloween was Rafe's thing. He'd loved dressing up with the girls, taking them trick-or-treating, and being the neighborly face everyone on their block loved seeing. It never failed: he would end up with more than his own kids as they walked the sidewalks of their neighborhood, and he never cared. Nadia used to go with him and the girls when Lynnea was still in a stroller, but once she was determined to walk, climb stairs too high for her little legs, and carry her own heavy bag of candy, Nadia stayed home and handed out candy to the kids who came to their door.

Once the first of October was upon them, Rafe would decorate the house, adding orange and purple lights to the eaves and around the columns and spindles on their wide farmer's porch, and he'd always put up fake cobwebs, even though Nadia hated them. Without fail, insects thought they had a new home, and by November 1, she was ready to use a blowtorch to get the webs down. Rafe would spend hours, if not days, making fake corpses who would sit in the two rocking chairs on their porch. The year he added the spooky-sounding doormat almost did her in.

Rafe's favorite holiday, aside from Christmas, was a week away, and Nadia hadn't bought the girls costumes. She hadn't even bought candy to hand out. Nor had she put up a single decoration. As she looked around her at her neighbors' houses, she realized how much she missed the decorations.

The girls piled into the car. Once everyone was buckled in, Nadia drove them to the strip mall where the Halloween pop-up store was. This was part of the therapy Nadia had been going to once a week. Her therapist wanted her to start living the life she and the girls were accustomed to. Something more than being at school.

Inside the store, Nadia pushed a cart and told the girls they needed to hold on to the side. In her head, she begged them not to let go. She feared one of them would run off and she wouldn't be able to find them, which would trigger a panic attack. When she sat in therapy, she tried to convince herself her fear was irrational and that living in fear wasn't the way to live. It was easy to say those things aloud, but to actually shut your mind off to the notion was near impossible.

It took almost two hours, but the girls finally picked costumes. They tried to convince their mom to dress up, but she wasn't going out with them. Kiran would take the girls trick-or-treating, and he would dress up with them, just as Rafe had. This was Kiran's idea, and Nadia couldn't be more grateful for him.

On the way home, the girls persuaded their mom that they definitely needed chicken nuggies to finish out their day. She compromised and went to the drive-through and told them they had to wait until they got home to eat. She didn't want to find nuggets in the back seat or have the greasy odor stay in her car.

When they turned onto their street, Nadia slowed and took in the decorations, mindful of the people outside. Their neighborhood really went all out for the holidays, which drew hundreds to their area from October through December.

"Mommy, look!"

Nadia saw and stopped her car in the middle of the road. "What the . . . ," she said. Her neighbors were outside her home, putting up decorations. The front door was open, and people carried boxes out, while Kiran stood on the porch pointing in every direction. Nadia pulled into the driveway, and before she could shut her car off, the girls had unbuckled and were out of their seats.

Gemma and Lynnea ran right to Kiran. He crouched down and scooped them into his arms. Nadia's heart skipped a beat. Rafe had done this countless times with them. She got out of her car and walked toward him.

"What's going on?" she asked despite the obvious.

Kiran held the girls on his hips. "We're decorating for Christmas?"

"Wise guy," Nadia mumbled. "Did you break in?"

Kiran laughed and set the girls down. "I called Hazel."

"You called Hazel?"

He nodded. "I noticed the lack of decorations and figured I needed to do something about it."

Ever since the first day of school, Kiran had come over at least once a week, mostly on Saturdays, to help out around the house and in the yard. Two weeks ago, she'd invited him to stay for dinner. That was a big step for her to take. It would be the first time they'd had dinner with him without Rafe, and she was afraid she'd send the wrong message to the girls. And even herself. Last weekend, he'd stayed for dinner again, then stayed to share a glass of wine with Nadia. It was the first time she'd felt like life could be okay, eventually.

"Once I started pulling out boxes, they came over to help."

Nadia looked around at the twenty or so people in her yard. They waved and smiled at the faces of people she usually talked to often but hadn't spoken to in months.

"Thank you," she said as she placed her hand over her heart. Tears welled in the back of her eyes. She fought them off, telling herself she could cry later, in the shower, where no one would have to see her, and no one could hear her.

"There isn't anything I wouldn't do to help you and the girls, Nadia. I think you know this by now." Kiran reached out and gave her hand a squeeze.

Nadia nodded and offered him the most genuine smile she could. She told the girls to take their costumes into the house. Kiran asked her what they were going to be. Nadia grimaced and held up the bag in her hand.

"I'm sorry to say, but you're going as a hot dog."

"What kind of dog?" Kiran leaned forward and cupped his hand around his ear. "I don't think I heard you."

"Hot dog," Nadia said again. "Not H-A-W-T either. H-O-T, as in the type you eat. Like a Fenway Frank. Only you're not wearing a Red Sox uniform."

Kiran stared at her blankly.

"The girls are going as ketchup and mustard, if that makes the situation any better."

"It absolutely does not." He turned and looked at the house. "Wow, they actually hate me."

Nadia let out a laugh. It was a sound she hadn't heard in a while, and it caught her off guard. She covered her mouth and met Kiran's gaze. He smiled, grinning ear to ear.

"That was nice to hear."

"It feels strange."

"I imagine." Kiran looked behind him and then back to Nadia. "This is okay, right?"

She nodded. "The girls needed this, and I think deep down, I did as well. This was Rafe's holiday, and I know I should be the one to take the girls out—"

"Stop," he said as he held his hand up. "I've got this. I'm looking forward to spending some quality time with Ketchup and Mustard."

"I'm looking forward to seeing the three of you together."

"Ha. I bet you are." He shook his head. "A hot dog, really?"

Nadia shrugged. "There are worse things."

"Name one."

"The ass end of a donkey."

"Touché."

He reached out and touched her hand before heading back to the decorations. She stood there, with his hot dog costume still in her hand, and contemplated what to do next.

Laughing would be a good start.

She hadn't had a full-belly, side-aching laugh in a long time. It wasn't like she could buy one or make one magically appear out of thin air, but she'd try, even if it only helped her feel some semblance of normality again.

Nadia went into her house and headed straight to the kitchen. She happened to have a couple of rolls of already made sugar cookie dough waiting in her refrigerator. Without taking the girls from their duties as top decorators, she turned on the oven and sliced the dough per the faint cut lines and set the circles on her baking tray. She couldn't do much, but what she could do was bake or offer her neighbors treats.

While the first two dozen baked, Nadia gathered as many cups as possible from her party supply shelf in her pantry and put them on a tray, along with a pitcher of lemonade and liters of soda. For some reason people used soda as a crutch and had brought her copious amounts, along with food, after Rafe died. She hadn't had a use for it until now.

Carrying the tray outside, she had to maneuver around people—no, friends—when she got to the porch. "Drinks!" she hollered. "Cookies will be out in a second." Nadia turned and caught Gemma staring at her.

"You made cookies?"

Nadia nodded.

Gemma ran to her mother and gripped her in a hug. Nadia squeezed her daughter tightly. They didn't need to speak words. This was enough. When Gemma let go, she gave her mom the brightest smile Nadia had seen in months.

When all was said and done, with all the cookies gone, Kiran, Nadia, and the girls stood outside at dusk. Kiran handed Nadia the battery-operated power box that would turn on their lights. She shook her head.

"You do it."

Kiran appraised her for a moment and then looked away. "Girls?" He cleared his throat. "Are you ready?"

Gemma and Lynnea hollered "Yes!" and threw their arms up in the air. Kiran pressed the button, turning on the lights and the ghoulish animatronics Rafe loved so much. Spooky music played, and some terrifying scarecrow tried to entice children to come see him.

"He had the wickedest sense of humor," Kiran mumbled low enough for only Nadia to hear.

"He really did."

"I miss him so much, Kiran, but this"—she pointed to the house—"you really brought him back in spirit for us. Thank you."

Kiran put his arm around Nadia and kissed her temple. She froze. If he noticed, he didn't say anything or seem to care. "It was my pleasure. I'm not on cleanup duty, though. That's all you."

For the second time that day, she laughed. And she really liked how it sounded.

"Girls, shower time." The girls thanked Kiran for putting up their decorations and then ran into the house. Nadia didn't want Kiran to leave yet and motioned toward the stairs. He followed and sat down next to her. It was unseasonably warm for late October, which was a rarity, but it also meant they'd probably have freezing temps for Halloween.

"These past few weeks—"

Kiran held his hand up. "Are you going to ask me to stop coming around?"

Nadia shook her head. "No, I was going to thank you. You've really helped me come out of this funk. I miss him, Kiran. I don't know if I'll ever stop, but with you around, the girls are laughing, and they smile. I smile. You're good for us."

"There really isn't anywhere I'd rather be. I look forward to Saturdays."

She smiled again. "You like doing chores."

"I like spending time with you. If it means I get to do chores, then yes."

"Would you like to have dinner with us on Sundays as well?"

"I'd like that very much, Nadia."

Nadia had no idea what to do next. She wanted him to know she liked having him around, more than she probably should. She slid a little closer to him, until their bodies touched, and she didn't dare look at him out of fear he might see something in her that she wasn't ready to admit.

When she heard Gemma call her name, she turned toward the house. "I should go. Unless you'd like to wait for a glass of wine or something."

"Or something," he said. "I'll be waiting, Nadia."

Nineteen

Grayson

Grayson trailed his fingers down Reid's left arm until he reached her left hand. He lifted it up and admired the ring he had placed on her third finger almost two months ago. Sunlight shone through the partially opened blinds in Reid's room. Her ring sparkled and created a kaleidoscope of lights on her wall. Every time he caught her admiring the ring, he felt proud.

Everything felt right between them. And he was grateful for this second chance at life. It allowed him to do the one thing he had put off forever ago—fall in love—and he was so in love with Reid. He regretted not telling her years ago.

She smiled but kept her eyes closed. Grayson kissed her ring, and then her. "Merry Christmas." Technically, they had one more day, but this would be the only time they were alone. They'd travel to his parents' house tonight, open presents in the morning, and then head to Luther's. It was important to them that they spend as much time as possible with their families. Next year they'd flip-flop and spend Christmas Eve and morning with Luther, and then head to his folks' place. After everything that had happened with Grayson, he and Reid planned to live in the moment. They'd take nothing for granted, and that included the holidays, visiting their parents regularly, and spending time with each other.

"The weatherman said it might snow," he said, groaning.

Reid's eyes opened. Her brown orbs gleamed with excitement. "Seriously?"

He gave a one-shoulder shrug. "It won't stay, fortunately." This was the drawback of living in a cold climate but not one cold enough to snow during the winter like the states north of them. In years past, they'd spent some long weekends skiing in New England, where they were guaranteed to find fresh powder almost daily. If it wasn't natural, the resorts made it. Now the thought of going felt like a chore.

"Since when do you not like the snow?"

Grayson thought about her question for a moment and shrugged again. "I don't know. This sense of dread filled me when I said it might snow. Before . . ." He paused and thought about the heart beating in his chest, wondering if it had something to do with his current dislike for the white stuff. "I guess I don't like it anymore."

Reid sat up on her elbow to look at him. "What else is different?"

"Not my love for you, if that's what you're wondering." He kissed the tip of her nose.

"Good to know," she said as she dangled her ring finger at him.

"I don't know. I think most things are subtle, but some definitely catch me off guard. The other day, at the grocery store, I walked down the aisle and absentmindedly put a can of sauerkraut in the cart. I hate sauerkraut, or I did."

"That's strange. Maybe you should bring it up with your therapist at your next appointment. Make a list as they happen so you don't forget."

"Yeah," he said as he pulled her to him. "We should go to Vermont next month and go skiing. Do you think Pearce would want to come with us?"

"But you just said—"

"You still love it, and I'll relearn to love it," he told her.

Reid kissed Grayson. "Are you only inviting Pearce because he has a car?"

Reid blushed and Grayson kissed her.

"Yeah, that's why I'd invite him too," he said, laughing. "I'll ask. Do you want to make a reservation? Even if he doesn't go, we can borrow my mom's car or rent one for the weekend."

"I'll book something."

Their relationship was easy. Almost too easy at times. They'd fallen into a quick routine, one Grayson didn't even question. After they'd been engaged for a week, Reid had asked him to move in. He accepted and was able to sublet his apartment until his lease expired. The only real issue they had was the size of the apartments. Neither place was overly big, and both were far too small for two people. He'd donated or put into storage the majority of his things, and Reid had boxed up seasonal clothing—items she wouldn't need until spring or summer. They were determined to make the living arrangement work until after the wedding, and then they'd look for a house.

The "making it work" part lasted all of a month before they put their names on the list for a two-bedroom apartment with more space in the same complex. Neither of them wanted to leave the building where they lived. It was close to the train station and easily walkable to downtown, where they could do some shopping. Having full access to a gym was a bonus, as was the washer and dryer. The internet was free, and the complex had controlled access, something that was hard to come by with other buildings.

After the first of the year, they would meet with a wedding planner. Luther had told Reid to plan her dream wedding and to not worry about the cost. When she jokingly said they would elope, Luther was hurt. Grayson promised his future father-in-law they would in fact have a wedding in DC or the surrounding area, and Luther would walk his daughter down the aisle.

Reid wanted a springtime wedding, someplace where the cherry blossoms would naturally cover the aisle. Neither of them had any friends with children, so having a flower girl or even a ring bearer would be out of the question, and neither of them wanted to wait years to get married. A year from next March or April, they'd become husband

and wife. They'd yet to settle on a date but knew it would be after the holidays.

"Merry Christmas," she said in shock. "I can't believe I didn't say it back."

Grayson couldn't help but roll his eyes. Reid insisted on returning sentiments each time he said one to her. It was one of the many things he loved about her. He moved on top of her and settled between her legs, keeping most of his weight on his elbows.

"This is the best Christmas of my life," he told her as he pressed his lips to hers.

"We haven't even had it yet. What if you hate my gifts?"

"You're the best gift of my life," he told her and then paused. "Minus my heart, but because of it I can love you freely and without reservation." Grayson pressed his lips to hers again and then deepened the kiss.

Reid's fingers trailed up and down Grayson's back. His muscles flexed underneath her touch. They settled on the waistband of his boxers. She played with the elastic before pushing her hands beneath the fabric and digging her fingers into his flesh to bring him closer to her. Their tongues danced together wildly, exploring each other's mouths with a fiery, intense passion that grew exponentially every day. Grayson's hand slipped under the hem of the shirt she wore to bed. It was his but looked far better on Reid. He traced circles on her stomach before moving upward to cup her breast.

Reid moaned into his mouth, arching her back as she pressed herself into his hand. Grayson broke the kiss for a moment to admire her flushed face before leaning down to kiss along the curve of her neck. He nipped at her skin gently, making her gasp in pleasure.

He sat back on his knees and pulled her upright with him. In one quick motion he had her night shirt off, and he pushed his boxers off before hovering over her again. Her hand caressed his cheek and then her fingers curved around his jaw, trailing the length until she came to his lips, tracing them.

They never stopped looking into each other's eyes.

"I can't wait to be your wife," she said to him.

Grayson pressed his forehead against hers for a moment, savoring the closeness before kissing her fiercely again. His hand slipped between them, finding the wetness between her legs. This had been the easy part of their relationship. They had a connection, one he'd denied for far too long. Once he let his guard down and opened himself up to loving her, all bets were off. He couldn't get enough of her. He didn't want to. Day and night, his desire for her was like something he'd never experienced before.

He captured her lips again. Reid whimpered softly as he rubbed circles around her clit. Each moan or quiver brought him gratification. Grayson wanted to make her happy, to please her, and he'd do anything he had to in order to make her smile.

When he slipped inside her, he paused and gave himself a moment. Each time for him was like the first time all over again. His heart pounded heavily in his chest, a sure sign it still worked, and as he began to slowly move within her, the moment confounded him. Here he was, making love to the woman he loved more than life itself, on Christmas Eve morning, while she wore nothing but the ring he'd given her as a promise leading up to their future. As far as he was concerned, he was the luckiest man in the world because Reid loved him beyond reason.

Sated and spent, they spent the rest of the morning in bed, dozing in and out of consciousness, making love, and planning for the future. Grayson wanted to look at homes, especially in up-and-coming neighborhoods, or find a condo near a park. A neighborhood to raise their family, but still be close to the things they liked to do. Before he'd asked her to marry him, they'd talked about children. He had always brushed the idea aside because of his health issues. Reid wanted kids, and a dog. She didn't care about the white picket fence, but she definitely wanted a sexy mom car. Grayson would give her everything. He'd give her the moon if he could.

They finally got out of bed, showered, packed for the two days they'd be away, and almost forgot the gifts they'd purchased for their parents. By the time they left their apartment, they looked like two people leaving for a three-month European vacation and were very thankful their building had an elevator.

When they got outside, they were surprised to find Luther coming up the pathway.

"Your dad is here," Grayson said so only Reid could hear him. She looked up, and Luther beamed.

"Hey," she said when he came closer. "Merry Christmas. What's going on? Everything okay?"

"No complaints," he said as he wished them Merry Christmas in return. "I thought I'd give you kids a ride to the Haneys'."

"Thanks," Grayson said. "We appreciate you."

"My pleasure. Besides, I'm heading over there anyway." Luther took the bags from Reid and turned toward the street where his truck was double parked. People honked, among other things, but no one really cared. It wasn't like the truck was going to stay there for long.

"Why are you heading toward Sydney's?" Reid asked. Grayson set the other bags in the back of the truck and opened the door for Reid, holding her hand as she climbed in.

"Well," Luther said when he got behind the steering wheel, "Sydney invited me to spend the night. At first, I told her no because I thought it would be awkward, but she persuaded me and said after everything we've been through as a family this year, she didn't want to see me left alone when they had the extra room. I still balked, but then she said things would be different when you two have children and neither one of us wants to miss out on important moments. So, I gave in."

"Thank you," Reid said as she kissed him on his cheek. Luther smiled but quickly turned so Reid couldn't gush more. She then looked at Grayson. "Your mom is amazing."

"I know. She raised me." He winked and thought about kissing her, but with her dad right there, he kept his lips to himself. And then he began to wonder about the sleeping situation. Even though he and Reid lived together, that didn't mean all the parents were on board with them sleeping in the same room. He glanced at Luther, who kept his eyes focused on the road. Reid eyed Grayson suspiciously, and he shook his head. With her dad sitting next to them, he couldn't exactly tell her he wanted to have sex with her in his childhood bedroom. Grayson would brood about it later. No point in thinking the worst until they got to his mom's house. The rest of the drive, he held on tightly to Reid's hand, almost as if he wouldn't be able to touch her again until they returned to their apartment. If that was the case, they were definitely sneaking out later.

TWENTY

NADIA

When it was time to decorate for Christmas, Kiran had recruited the neighbors to help. He had even offered to help them decorate if need be. This time, Nadia was prepared and turned it into an event of sorts. In exchange for their help, Nadia served lunch, as well as hot cocoa, some alcoholic drinks, and snacks. She played holiday music, started a fire in the fireplace (even though she wasn't used to doing so), and put on a Santa hat, despite lacking any spirit.

Every day she woke up, she tried. She tried to live the way she and Rafe had or the way she thought he would want her to. Mostly because of the girls. She greeted them with a soft smile and tried to act as if everything had been the same. She showered them with love, even though she felt wholly unloved herself, despite the fact she knew the girls loved her. While a child's love was unconditional—it was dependent and naive and came with a feeling of wanting protection from the world—the love from a partner was different. It was all consuming, it was breathtaking, it was butterflies in the middle of the night and morning and a rush of excitement when you received a simple text message or an "I love you." That was how she'd felt with Rafe, and now . . . well, now she felt like she had nothing. The holidays only exacerbated those feelings.

Holiday cards arrived at the house, addressed to her only. The first time one arrived, she'd cried for hours. Rafe had been erased from everyone's mind. Gone and forgotten. She yearned to see his name next to hers, just one more time. And when that card arrived, from someone who hadn't heard of Rafe's passing, she'd spent the day crying. Nadia couldn't win.

Nadia had zero desire to celebrate the holidays, and if it wasn't for Hazel and Kiran, she probably would've forgotten to shop. Her standby excuse was "I'll do it tomorrow." Halloween had been simple. Seeing the girls dress up with Kiran was fun and entertaining. But now, the pain from losing Rafe felt like a ton of bricks on her chest, and she couldn't seem to move them. No matter what she did.

Hazel refused to let Nadia dwell or sit in a puddle of sorrow. She insisted they shop on the weekends, employing her younger sister to watch the girls. She'd drive Nadia to the mall, make lists of things the girls had mentioned when she picked them up after school, and force Nadia to be present. "It's for the girls, not you," Hazel told her repeatedly.

At times, Nadia wanted to disown her friend, yet she was the one who picked up her phone whenever Nadia called and was always the first one to come over when things teetered on the edge of unbearable.

And then there was Kiran. He was there; even on the days when she didn't want company, he was there, making his presence known. Kiran seemed to have a sixth sense, knowing when Nadia needed a break. He took the girls shopping so they could buy their mom presents, made sure the house had been winterized, swapped Nadia's summer tires for snow tires, and came over to shovel the pathway when it snowed. He did everything Rafe would've done, and he did it without complaint or a phone call asking for help. When Saturday and Sunday rolled around, he was there, having dinner, just as he had in the previous months. Kiran wasn't going anywhere.

The one aspect of life Nadia had trouble with was her in-laws. Otto was fabulous, coming around on the weekends to see if Kiran needed help. Cleo, on the other hand, was absent. She had every excuse in the book to avoid coming to the house. Nadia understood, to an extent; the house was Rafe. He'd left his mark everywhere, but the children missed their grandmother, and even though they went to their grandparents' place, Nadia felt slighted by Cleo.

Nadia looked out the kitchen window, pausing while washing a pot left over from homemade mac 'n' cheese. A cardinal sat on the tree, staring at her. At least that's what it seemed like. If she tilted her head, the cardinal did as well. She'd heard (and seen on the numerous sympathy cards) about cardinals being messengers from passed-on loved ones. Prior to losing Rafe, she never would've bought into anything of the sort, but lately, she'd even contemplated visiting a medium. She'd watched enough shows and had seen the reaction of people who'd heard from someone they missed, and she desperately missed Rafe. With those thoughts, fear set in. What if he didn't come through to her; then what would she do?

Hazel told her to stay far away from mediums, for the time being. Nadia needed to heal, to start her life anew, and to move on from Rafe. Those words stung Nadia deeply. At the end of October, she'd sort of thought she could begin to move on, but then Thanksgiving happened, and her brand-new dining room table Rafe had insisted on buying sat empty. Nadia and the girls had taken the train to see her parents in Maryland. Her depression returned with a crushing force.

She couldn't imagine loving anyone other than Rafe for the rest of her life. Deep down, she wasn't angry at Hazel for being honest, but at the situation. Healing would take time, according to the therapist. As would moving on. There wasn't a set timeline of when a spouse had to accomplish anything, other than living. That's what was important. Rafe would want Nadia to live, just as they had been.

She went back to washing the pot and tried to ignore the bird. When she looked up again, he was closer to the window. The branch he was perched on wasn't strong enough to hold a bird, or so she thought. Nadia dried her hands, picked up her phone, researched what cardinals liked to eat, and then ordered everything—including the window bird feeder that would safely bring birds into her home. If the cardinal was Rafe, in some roundabout way, then she'd do whatever she could to take care of him.

When she looked out the window again, the bird was gone. Her heart missed a beat, and a wave of sadness washed over her. She'd bring this up at her next appointment; she'd ask her therapist if she was delusional or if messages from the beyond really did exist. She needed to believe they did. Tomorrow, she'd set up the bird feeder and hope for the best.

The girls came downstairs, dressed and ready to go to their grandparents' house. Their normal Christmas Day visit had changed when Nadia had told Cleo and Otto they were heading to her parents' house. She needed to surround herself with love and affection. She wanted to curl up next to her sister in the bed they'd shared, when they'd talked about boys, life, and heartache, like they used to when they were in high school and home from college. Reuben would be there, eager to spend time with his nieces.

Gemma twirled when she came into the kitchen. Both girls wore matching green velvet dresses that complemented their hair color: Gemma with her auburn hair like Nadia's, and Lynnea's blonde locks, reminiscent of Rafe's.

"Wow," Nadia said as she placed her hand over her heart. "How did I get so lucky with you two?"

Gemma curtsied. Lynnea, on the other hand, tapped her cheek and gazed evilly at the ceiling. "I know about how babies are made."

Oh, God.

"No, you don't, Lynnea. Stop saying that," Gemma said with so much mom sass that Nadia cringed. Gemma had had to grow up a lot in the past handful of months. Something Nadia had never wanted for her daughter. Either of them. They needed to stay babies for as long as possible, and never leave her.

"Yes, I do!"

"Girls, please." Nadia had no intention of asking her daughter *how* she knew where babies came from, until later.

"There's a mommy and a daddy, and they—"

"Lynnea, stop," Nadia demanded. "This isn't something you talk about except with me, got it?" The last thing she needed was for Lynnea to say something to Astrid today. Freya would lose her ever-loving mind. As it was, Freya was none too happy to have to celebrate Christmas early on account of Nadia wanting to be elsewhere. Nadia couldn't win and suspected this would be the last Christmas she spent with her in-laws. Next year, they could take the girls for one day. Cleo and Freya were doing a damn good job of making her feel unwelcome.

Those feelings weren't an exaggeration. When they arrived at the Karlssons' house, the environment was anything but welcoming. Freya barely said hello. Lars couldn't get the day off from work, even though it was Saturday. Leif couldn't put his phone down to talk to anyone, not that Nadia could blame him. Being the only young man in the family had to be boring for him.

When it came time for presents, everyone gathered in the living room while Otto handed gifts out. Freya chose to have Astrid and Leif wait until the actual holiday, since they'd be at the Karlssons' place again. Nadia understood. She gave her niece and nephew their gifts and anxiously waited for them to open them.

"They're going to wait," Freya said.

"I'd really like them to open them now," Nadia responded. "Especially Leif." She'd given him one of Rafe's ties and tie clips, knowing how important it had been to Rafe that young men dress up for occasions. It had taken a lot for Nadia to go through some of Rafe's things and find the right one for Leif.

"He'll wait."

"Astrid—" Nadia stopped talking and nodded. There was no use in arguing. Besides, the kids didn't look eager to open anything anyway.

Nadia was handed a small box. She waited until the girls opened their presents, smiling along with them each time they held up their new toy or item of clothing. When the girls finished, Freya and Cleo left the room, saying they needed to get dinner ready. Nadia sat there, with the small box in her lap and a forced smile on her lips.

"I'm sorry," Otto said. "Rafe's death has been hard on her, and seeing you and the girls—"

"I get it." She didn't. Her children were Cleo's grandchildren. Her son's children. Cleo should've showered them with love and affection, the way only a grandma could. But no, she was cold and mean.

"Mommy." Gemma caught Nadia's attention. She strained a weak smile.

"Yeah, baby."

"I don't feel good. Can we go home?" Nadia wanted to hug and kiss her daughter for being sick. It was the excuse she needed to get the hell out of there.

"Yeah, we can."

"Nadia—" Otto started to say but stopped when she shook her head. Getting out of there had to happen before she broke down. Otto stood, gathered the girls' presents, and carried them out to the car. Nadia said nothing to her mother- and sister-in-law and could barely hug Otto. The first holiday after losing your spouse wasn't supposed to be shitty.

As soon as they pulled away, she looked at Gemma in the rearview and saw her crying. "What's wrong, Gemma?"

Gemma wiped angrily at her tears. "I'm mad at Grandma and Grandpa."

Me too.

"How come?" Nadia asked. "They bought you some really nice clothes."

"It's not that. It's the way Grandma treats you. She's mean."

"It's okay, Gemma."

"No, it's not! You lost Daddy and need her to love you the same way, and she's mean. You didn't even open your present from her."

Nope, because I don't want to know what's in there.

"She didn't buy you much things," Lynnea said. At the stoplight, Nadia turned and saw tears in Lynnea's eyes.

"My loves." Nadia could barely hold back her sob.

"Last year Grandma gave you a million presents."

She didn't, but that's a nice thought.

"It's not about how many presents you get, Gemma. It's the thought that counts."

"Well, her thoughts are mean," Gemma said as she looked out her window.

When they arrived home, Nadia unloaded the car, emptied the boxes, and threw the wrapping paper away. She made multiple trips up and down the stairs when she could've easily asked the girls to come get their stuff. She kept her emotions in check until she went into her bedroom. A waft of Rafe's cologne washed over her. She swore he was in their bedroom, hugging her. Did he know how his mother had acted?

No, he didn't.

"Rafe." She said his name softly. "I need you."

Thirty minutes later, Kiran knocked on the front door. He stood there with a pile of presents in his arms. Nadia let him in.

"What are you doing here?"

"Otto called," he told her. "Said things didn't go very well over there this afternoon."

"That's the understatement of the century." Nadia followed Kiran into the living room. He set the pile of presents under the tree and organized them.

"I know you're leaving for your parents' soon, so you and the girls can open them when you get back or before. Doesn't matter." She didn't miss the "you and the girls" part but intended to ignore it.

"Are you hungry?"

He nodded. "I ordered a delivery," he told her as he looked at his phone. "It should be here shortly."

"For us?"

"Yeah."

"Kiran—"

"I know what you're going to say," he said, shrugging. "This is where I want to be."

She nodded and told him she was going to set the table. He followed her into the kitchen and helped until the doorbell rang. As soon as they had a mini holiday feast set up on the table, Nadia called the girls down. They loved Kiran, and he had gone out of his way to make sure the past three months had been bearable.

"Mommy, did you see the presents under the tree?" Lynnea asked as she crawled into her seat.

"Yep, Kiran brought them over."

"Can we open them after dinner?" Lynnea asked.

"How about we open them after we eat dessert?" Kiran suggested. "Maybe we can get your mom to make us some hot cocoa."

Lynnea agreed enthusiastically, while Gemma sat there, reserved. Nadia noted the way Gemma stared at Kiran. Did she see what Nadia did? Could Gemma sense that Kiran meant more to them than just being Rafe's best friend?

After dinner and dessert, Kiran took the girls into the living room, while she made hot cocoa from scratch. While she waited for the milk to reach the right temperature, she peered out the window at the leafless branches on the tree. She was startled when the cardinal landed on the branch nearest to her.

"Are you my sign?" she asked the bird quietly. "Did my husband send you?" Realistically she didn't expect an answer. That didn't stop her from hoping for one. She stood there until the bird flew away, which he did right when the milk reached the perfect temperature.

Nadia carried a tray with four mugs of cocoa and a plate of cookies into the living room. The girls sat on the floor, with Gemma leaning in the chair Nadia normally sat in. She sat and ran her hand down her daughter's hair.

"Are you feeling okay?" she asked her.

Gemma nodded. "I wasn't sick when we left Grandpa's," she told her mother. "I fibbed."

Nadia's heart swelled. "You didn't have to do that for me."

"Yes, I did." Gemma crawled into Nadia's lap and snuggled into her embrace.

"I love you, my sweet girl."

"I love you, Mommy."

Over the next hour or so, they opened presents from Kiran and drank hot chocolate, and then Kiran told them he'd see them in the morning to take them to the airport for the quick flight to Maryland. Nadia walked him to the door and thanked him for the presents, and to her shock, he leaned in and kissed her cheek softly.

"Merry Christmas, Nadia." Kiran was out of the house and down the steps before she could respond.

Once the house was quiet, she sat by the tree with its twinkling lights and soft music playing in the background. The present from her in-laws sat on the table next to her. Part of her didn't want to open it because the hurt would be too much. Gemma had been right about the gifts, and it was pretty shitty that a child recognized how poorly Cleo had treated Nadia.

She picked up the box and shook it. Something moved around. Knowing better than to open it, she did. Inside the box was a scarf, hat, and mittens. The kind you would buy for the Yankee swap in your office. Nadia stared at the contents and then looked at the wrapping again. The tag read: NADIA. Cleo couldn't even write FROM: MOM & DAD or CLEO & OTTO on it.

Nadia set it aside, turned everything off, and climbed the stairs. She woke the girls up and told them to crawl into her bed. She needed them with her.

Twenty-One

Nadia

The holidays were anything but special. Nadia had struggled emotionally, as had the girls. Gone was the magic Rafe had brought to the morning. They missed him more than they thought they would. The magnitude of her situation weighed heavily on her.

When Nadia had stared at her bank statement and saw the number in her savings account dip lower, she worried. Christmas wasn't easy on one income, and she didn't think it would be fair to Gemma and Lynnea if she had to scale things back. At least not their first one without their father. She was grateful that someone, she assumed the city or the hospital, had covered all Rafe's medical expenses and she didn't have to contend with those bills. There were others, though. The mortgage, which they'd both contributed to. Health insurance, previously obtained through Rafe's employer, was now Nadia's responsibility. What she had through the school district didn't have their old low fees and deductible plan. Still, she was grateful to have coverage.

As she looked at the numbers, she figured since she had the summers off, she'd get a waitressing job downtown. When tourist season was in full swing, the bars and restaurants were so busy that locals rarely went to any of them. She could easily supplement her income. None of that would work, though. Anything she made would go to a babysitter, leaving her back where she was.

Her luck changed when her brother called one rainy afternoon in late February.

"I got a job offer in Boston," he told her.

"That's fantastic." Over Christmas, he'd mentioned switching jobs but hadn't said where. Having him so close would be a relief and a gift. Living away from her family, especially during such a tumultuous time, had been hard. Her mother had stayed with her for some time, and her dad had made numerous trips up north to help around the house and maintain the yard until Kiran took over. Having her brother close would mean she'd have someone, other than Hazel and Kiran, to depend on. And the girls loved their uncle. He'd be able to help out with them whenever she needed.

"I'm going to need a place to stay," he said.

"I can definitely help you look."

Reuben cleared his throat. "What about if I live with you and the girls?" he suggested. "We can convert a space in the basement into a room. There's already a bathroom down there. Dad can help me extend it into a shower. This will give you a man in the house, not that you need a man living there. But also, I'll pay rent. I'd rather live with you and the girls than in some apartment where I'm lonely, and I expect to spend most of my free time at your place anyway. You'd be saving me gas money."

It took Nadia all of three seconds to agree. Now, when she looked at her bank account, there'd be a bit of a cushion, thanks to her brother.

Currently, Warren, Reuben, and Kiran were hard at work in the basement, and her mom fluttered around in the kitchen, making copious amounts of food to freeze later. Lorraine had been concerned Nadia wasn't eating well enough when she saw her at Christmas. She'd commented on how much weight she'd lost, which Nadia had explained away by the pain she felt from losing her husband. She vowed to get better. If not for herself, for her girls. They needed their mother to be strong and healthy.

It was something the therapist had said. Nadia needed to find a way to move on, to start living her life again. For the most part, life had moved on. Nadia and the girls got up every morning, dressed, and went about their day. In her mind, she could almost pretend Rafe was temporarily gone—on a business trip, out with Kiran, or visiting his parents. That was until Kiran came over. When he was there, they smiled and laughed. He brought that out in them, and she truly appreciated having him around. It was when she put her head on her pillow at night and stared at the space Rafe should've been in that her heart broke all over again.

Nadia stared out the window. After Rafe's death, they'd kept the blinds closed. One of her New Year's resolutions was to keep them open to welcome light and nature back into their home, even when it was gray and rainy outside. She wanted to watch the seasons change, see their daffodils and tulips bloom, and witness the transformation from winter dullness to vibrant spring.

The guys came upstairs for lunch. Nadia smiled when she saw Kiran. It was as if the response was automatic. After everyone made chitchat and ate, Nadia started cleaning up.

"I saw that," Lorraine said as she carried plates to the sink.

"Saw what?"

"The way you looked at Kiran."

"What are you talking about?"

Lorraine stood next to Nadia. She shut the water off, forcing her daughter to look at her. "Gemma says Kiran is here a lot."

Nadia sighed. "He comes over on Saturday, does the outside chores, and makes sure everything still functions properly. In exchange, I feed him."

"And on Sunday?"

Nadia stared out the window. "He's Rafe's best friend, Mom. Nothing more." Except when her therapist had brought up moving on, Nadia had refused to even entertain the idea. The notion seemed so far out in left field for her. Until she closed her eyes at night and saw Kiran there.

"It's okay if he's more, Nadia. You're young and you have young children. No one expects you not to move on or remarry. Rafe would want that."

"Would he?" she asked, looking at her mom. "Would he want his best friend marrying his wife?"

"I think he would. If I know anything about my son-in-law, it's this—he would want you to move on with someone he trusted—and he trusted Kiran. He's been a part of your life since the day you met Rafe. He's known the girls their entire lives, and he's never done anything to cause you to mistrust him. Give yourself a chance to be happy again, Nadia."

On the morning of the one-year anniversary, Nadia, the girls, and their extended family woke to a cloudy day, with the sun doing its best to brighten everyone's moods. No one seemed talkative as they sat around the dining room table, sipping their coffee and eating their breakfast. An occasional noise came from Warren, Reuben, or Adam as they rustled their section of the newspaper. Warren was old fashioned. He wanted his news in print and not on his phone.

One by one, they showered and dressed. Nadia went last yet needed the most time. Lately, she'd been strong; she hadn't cried in months. But when she woke this morning, the enormity of the day weighed heavily upon her. Everything about the year before was fresh in her mind, from the way they woke up that morning, to what she and the girls wore, to the last time she saw Rafe alive.

Today, Nadia would come face to face with her mother-in-law again, a woman she hadn't seen in four months. They hadn't even spoken. Otto was around a lot, though, especially when Warren wasn't in town. She suspected her father kept in touch with her father-in-law, or was he now her former one? Nadia had no idea what the rules were there. But Cleo had kept her distance. Nadia had a hard time explaining Cleo's actions. It was one thing to push Nadia away, but not the girls. They needed their grandmother, that connection to the father they'd lost. Cleo had her reasonings, and as much as she didn't want to, Nadia respected them. Just not the way she treated Gemma and Lynnea. At the end of the day, they were still Rafe's children. His blood flowed through them.

When they opened the front door, Kiran was poised to knock. Something he'd stopped doing unless Nadia's parents were in town. "Hey," he said to the family while staring at Nadia. He held his arm for her to take. "I'd like to escort you to the ceremony."

"Thank you."

Kiran walked her to the SUV her father had rented. It was a sleek, black, oversize monster with tinted windows to give her and the girls privacy. For the most part, the local media left her alone. But with the anniversary of the Commonwealth Cup, now known as the Rafe Karlsson Memorial Cup, the media had begun asking Nadia for interviews. She declined each one, having nothing to say. Kiran opened the back door for her and helped the girls in, then shut it behind Gemma. For a brief moment, he conversed with Warren, and then he got in to drive.

Last year, when Nadia had dropped Rafe off for the race, maybe two or three police cars were there. This morning, she lost count after ten. When Kiran held her hand as she exited the back seat, she saw the police were needed for crowd control.

"Why do they need to be here?" The question was rhetorical.

"People like to pay their respects," Kiran said. "The race has tripled in size. The money earned will go to a new playground."

"That'll be nice for the area."

Kiran agreed. "They're going to name it after Rafe."

"Of course they are."

How were they supposed to move on? While she appreciated the sentiment, it was too soon. As it was, Nadia avoided Harvard Square because of the reminders. Now she'd never be able to come to town to shop or enjoy any of the cafés.

Tia, a representative from the race committee, greeted Nadia. She'd spoken to Tia a few times about their opening ceremony. It wasn't something Nadia wanted to do, but she also didn't want Rafe's name all over television and in the news along with mentions of how his family didn't show up.

"Good morning," Tia said. She and Nadia shook hands, and then Tia introduced herself to the rest of the family. She showed Nadia where she wanted her to sit, which was front and center, with cameras pointing at her.

Before her was a photo of Rafe. The sight of him, smiling and happy, caused her breath to hitch. There wasn't a word for how she felt when it came to missing him. Gemma and Lynnea sat next to her, with her parents next to the girls. Two seats remained at the end for Otto and Cleo, although she had no idea if they'd show up. She hoped so.

Reuben, Sienna, Adam, and their boys sat behind Nadia. As did Kiran, who planned to honor Rafe the only way he knew how, by running. Nadia hoped Kiran realized he honored Rafe every day when he showed for his family.

Minutes before the ceremony started, she felt a hand on her shoulder. She looked to find Otto there. She stood and hugged him, and then she saw Cleo. Nadia hated that she hesitated for even the slightest moment. She held her arms out and hugged her mother-in-law, and then smiled as the girls leaped to their feet to greet their grandmother. Nadia's heart soared when her parents moved down two seats and allowed Cleo and Otto to sit next to the girls. If it took this somber moment for them to come together as a family, so be it.

After speeches from the director of the race and the mayor, Nadia went onto the makeshift stage to accept the key to the city on behalf of Rafe. What the hell was she supposed to do with it? She then declared the road race open. It was like an instant flood of people took to the street to watch their friends and family run, while the racers boarded busses to take them to the starting line.

Kiran helped her off the stage. "Meet me at the finish line?"

"Are you going to run in a suit?" she asked him, eyeing his clothes.

He laughed. "No, I have a bag in the SUV. I'm going to change."

She nodded. They were close. Nadia was certain Kiran wanted to be more than a friend, or someone she depended on, but she was nowhere near ready for anything, with anyone. She knew Kiran wasn't dating anyone, despite women trying to get his attention. He went to work daily, texted her in the morning and afternoon, called after dinner, and spent sunup to sundown at her house on the weekends. He was there for them, and she appreciated him more than ever.

"We'll be there," she said as she reached out and touched his arm. "Rafe intended to win last year, so . . ." Nadia shuddered. "Make him proud."

"I'll see you at the finish line," he told her. "I'll be the first one crossing."

Nadia had no doubt.

Twenty-Two

Grayson

Grayson sat in a blue plush chair. It was old, with remarkably great cushioning. Yet it was an odd choice for a therapist's office, although he enjoyed running his fingers along the fabric, feeling the texture change from smooth to rough. He'd done it so many times that it was now an absentminded habit of his, each time he sat there. Grayson had read over and over again that people should seek therapy after undergoing an emergency heart transplant. Even though Grayson was at his one-year mark, he'd kept up with seeing Dr. Littleton because doing so gave him someone to talk to who wasn't related to him. Dr. Littleton listened, offered advice, and didn't judge him when he said he felt overwhelmed with emotion sometimes. Grayson was crazy in love with Reid and often felt as if he wasn't expressing himself properly.

"This is a big week for you," Dr. Littleton said from the other blue plush chair. Grayson likened it to a throne, fit for royalty, and Grayson was the minion or peasant begging the almighty for guidance and reassurance.

"Do I celebrate?"

"You could, or you could go on like it's no big deal."

Grayson shook his head and looked down at his fingers, moving in a pattern-like formation. He tried to stop them, but they continued to swirl and swirl, back and forth.

"What's wrong, Grayson?"

"Nothing," he said as an automatic response.

"I've known you for a year," Dr. Littleton said. "I wouldn't be very good at my job if I didn't notice something bothering you."

Grayson sighed, but no relief came. He shook his head, bit his lower lip, and rocked a bit in the chair. "My heart." He put his fist over his heart and held it there. "It hurts."

"Did you tell your cardiologist?" Littleton flipped through his notes. "I'm sorry, I can't recall his name. Did you tell him at your appointment?"

"Yes. He ran some tests, did the proper imaging, and there's nothing. It's healthy. I'm healthy. No fear of rejection. But I'm sad and I can't explain it, and it's not all of a sudden. The feeling has been there, and I thought it was because the heart needed to get used to me, Reid—you know, my life. The feeling lingers. Sometimes it's strong and I want to cry for no reason, and other times, it's this dull sensation."

"How long have you experienced this?"

"The dullness?" Grayson shrugged. "For a bit, I think. I feel like I only really knew it was there after I woke up crying the other day."

"From a dream?"

He nodded. "I don't even know what it was about, but there were other people there, but they were fuzzy, and then I woke up with tears streaming down my face, soaking my pillow." He was thankful Reid had gotten up early and gone to the gym; he was afraid of what she might have thought or done had she seen this early-morning meltdown.

"Have you felt this any other time?"

"I think so. I have severe moments of sadness. They're random. It's like I have a plan but can't bring myself to do anything. I'm lucky Reid was content to chill for the day, but it was unlike me. I like to be active, be outside, exploring nature. Not sitting in our apartment, cooped up with the blinds closed."

Dr. Littleton wrote on his yellow notepad. Without looking up, he asked, "How is Reid? How are things with her romantically? Physically?"

Grayson blushed. While he loved talking about Reid, talking about their sex life was a bit awkward for him. He wanted to respect her privacy, which Dr. Littleton understood. But Grayson grasped that the questions weren't invasive, only meant for healing and processing the ordeal he'd been through.

"Reid's amazing," he said. "We met with the wedding planner and tasted some cakes the other day. I never knew I was a 'white cake with raspberry filling' type of guy, but I am. We talked about the whole 'cake smashing in the face' thing, and I told her I thought it's a bit disrespectful and I didn't want to do it."

"Why's that?"

"Because she will have spent so much time perfecting her look for the day; I don't want to ruin it because someone along the way thought smearing cake on your bride's face would be a funny tradition. It's rude."

"How did she feel?"

"Grateful. She thanked me, which she didn't need to do, but I get it." Grayson ran his hand down the front of his pants. "I love her, with this heart, my other heart." He shrugged. "But sometimes I look at her and . . ."

"And?"

"I don't know," he said. "There isn't a doubt in my mind she's the one for me. But when my heart aches, it makes me question whether I should even be here right now. Someone died so I could live, and what if I'm not living up to their potential? What if they were this amazing person who walked grandmas across the street, who donated time at the soup kitchen or the clothing drive. What if my heart is telling me I'm failing at being the person it was intended for?"

Dr. Littleton stood and went to his desk. He typed on the computer, strummed his fingers on his desk, and then nodded.

"This is going to sound off, but listen to what I have to say," he told Grayson. "There is zero scientific proof that organs can change your personality, memories, or how you feel. However, it seems to me that your very healthy heart is experiencing some emotions you're unfamiliar with, right?"

Grayson nodded.

"When you're with Reid, what do you feel?"

"Elation, happiness, gratitude, satisfaction," he told the doctor. "Love, desire, like I want to be with her all the time. Everything I denied myself in the beginning, it's still there and stronger. But sometimes, when the ache is strong, I question what's missing, because I feel like something is definitely missing from my life right now."

Dr. Littleton came back to his chair. "I think what you're experiencing is referred to as cellular memory. Many doctors disagree this even exists, as research is limited."

"What is it?"

"Cellular memory allows your body to remember how to fight diseases. In terms of an organ, in this case, your heart, it had to remember how to function in a new cavity. The transplant team made sure you had a normal heart rhythm and blood flow. However, some scientists have taken cellular memory to also mean that donors' memories, feelings, likes, and dislikes are stored in those cells and then remembered by the recipient."

"In my terms, please?"

Dr. Littleton laughed. "In a nutshell, you could be experiencing memories from the donor."

Grayson let the statement germinate. He didn't think it was possible, but then again, he wasn't a doctor, and what Dr. Littleton had said sort of made sense. If that was the case, would someone who drank beer and received a new liver suddenly stop? Could his heart hold memories and feelings of its life before the transplant?

Nah, Grayson wasn't buying it. What Dr. Littleton said didn't make sense. There was no way an organ could remember emotions. Something else had to be going on.

That night, when he and Reid crawled into bed, they lay on their sides, looking at each other, with only the moon beaming its bright stream of light through their window.

"Are you okay?" Reid asked. She ran her hand through his hair. He kissed her palm and then held her hand against his heart. It thumped wildly, passionately for her.

"Ever since the summer, there are times when I'm incredibly sad sometimes," he started. "I've woken up from dreams I don't remember, crying. And my heart." He covered her hand with his. "It aches sometimes."

"Have you talked to your doctor?"

He nodded and then spoke his reply. "I've passed every test," he said. "Every image shows a reactive, healthy heart."

"Are you having second thoughts about us?" she asked, with a hint of sadness in her voice. Grayson leaned forward and pressed his lips to hers.

"Not even remotely."

"Okay. Then what is it?"

He moved closer to her, closing the gap between them. He needed to feel her presence, to be in her space and share in the natural calmness she carried with her.

"I don't know," he told her. "I saw Dr. Littleton today. He suggested that maybe the heart is remembering the donor, and that's what I'm feeling."

"That's not a thing," she told him. "Your mom asked one of the cardiologists if that could happen after your transplant because she feared this exact thing. He said it wasn't possible."

"It's not scientifically proven, just a theory. Others who have received organ donations have indicated a change in their behavior or what they ate."

"Your behavior did change," she pointed out.

"If you're referring to how I feel about you, no, it didn't. I've always felt this way but didn't want to burden you with my issues. Once I knew I had a new heart and the old junky one was out of my life, I did what I wanted to do a long time ago. Telling you how I feel or felt was literally the most exhilarating and scariest time of my life. I was so afraid things were irrevocably broken between us because of how I acted."

"They should've been," she told him. "But I've been in love with you for as long as I can recall. I think the only way I could ever be out of your life is if I were to move away and not tell you where I went."

"I'd definitely file a missing persons report." He smiled, thankful for the moon's brightness coming through their window.

"This feeling you have, what can we do about it?"

"I don't know. I'm not sure there's anything we can do."

"You could reach out to UNOS, find out if the donor's family is receptive to communication or even a meeting. They're the only ones who will know. Maybe this is part of the healing process. What about finding a support group? Someone might have experienced a similar situation and can guide you."

"Thank you," he said as he kissed her. "I don't know how I got so lucky to have you in my life, Reid. But I am truly the luckiest man on the planet."

"And the cheesiest." She giggled when he tickled her side. She moved in closer and snuggled against him, placing her hand on his heart. "Whatever it is, as long as you're healthy, we'll figure it out."

◆ ◆ ◆

The next morning, they sat down to drink their coffee and watch some television before they ventured out for the day. Grayson flipped mindlessly through the channels until he saw the words "organ donations." A multiple-episode documentary was on. He immediately hit record and started watching with rapt attention.

When Sydney called and asked Reid if she wanted to go shopping, Grayson told her to go and have fun. The documentary had captured his attention. He sat there for hours, listening to others tell their stories about their transplants, trying to absorb what he could. Only one recipient talked about experiencing unexplained emotions. Grayson rewound the segment and watched it repeatedly, writing down his own series of questions. The more he listened, the more he thought what he was experiencing was the same. Cellular memory was definitely a thing, and he had it. However, he had no idea what to do about it. He could make a request through UNOS to meet the family, but that could take up to a year, and that was only if the family was receptive.

Grayson couldn't wait a year to hear no. His heart wouldn't be able to take the rejection. Nor could he live any longer with the ache in his chest.

He needed answers now.

When he finished watching, he had a desire to know more. He grabbed his laptop and began reading everything he could on transplant patients, life after a transplant, and where he could find support groups. Either in person or virtual. It didn't matter.

Information was scarce. He only found a couple of blogs that touched on the matter, but one he read was rather intriguing. The recipient had asked to meet the donor's family. They declined. He'd become so obsessed with finding answers for why his heart felt the way it did that he scoured local obituaries during the time he was in the hospital. In the end, he came up short. He never uncovered the issue and still struggled to this day with unexplained emotions.

A year had passed since Grayson's heart transplant. Per his therapist's warnings, he'd avoided seeking out the things he'd missed during his time in a coma. Dr. Littleton had explained that, because of how the mind absorbs and processes information, it was normal for people to miss a day or two of the news but hear something in passing. But missing weeks or even months and then trying to catch up could cause more issues for the patient. Grayson had heeded the advice, except when it came to the college basketball championship. He had to know who'd made it to the Final Four and won the title. Thankfully, he was a fan of neither team.

Grayson typed keywords into the search bar of the internet browser. His pinky hovered over the enter key. He could look, or he could move his finger up two rows and delete everything.

He pressed enter and then spent the next five or six hours looking at everything he could from the days he was in the coma and in the intensive care unit to the days after his discharge. The only time he left his computer was to take his meds and eat, both after hearing reminders that sounded from his phone. Grayson dove into the news, enthralled by how much had happened in the time he was asleep.

It wasn't even a refreshing nap.

The wave of emotions that came over him left him feeling down. He was shocked by what he'd missed, saddened by what he read. It shouldn't have taken him a year to read the news, but he understood why his therapist had cautioned against doing it.

Grayson closed his laptop when Reid came home. He told her how he'd spent his day. "I think I need to take a walk," he told her after they ate dinner. "I need some fresh air."

"Do you want me to come with you?"

He thought for a minute and then nodded. Being in her presence calmed him. Kept him grounded. Grayson waited while she changed into her sneakers, and then they made their way outside.

"Let's walk to the Mall," he told her. "I want to see where we're getting married next year."

Reid beamed. They held hands and traversed their neighborhood until they'd reached the National Mall. The cherry blossoms were in full bloom. The pink canopy of flowers created a beautiful aesthetic. It was easy to see why Reid wanted to be married there.

Grayson did as well.

She didn't know this, but he had a countdown on his phone to the day she'd become his wife. Asking her to marry him was the best decision of his life, except for when he'd kissed her for the second, third, fourth, and how many other times.

"This is perfect and what I want for our day," Reid said when they arrived at the Mall. "Look at the ground. The natural beauty of the way the blossoms fall. I can see myself walking down the aisle here." She beamed up at him, her smile brighter than the North Star.

"It'll happen," he told her as he kissed her. "Let me take your picture."

Reid took a few steps away from him and posed. Every few seconds, she'd change the way she stood, tilt her head, or position her feet. He snapped photos in rapid fire, taking as many as he could, knowing he'd keep every single one because he'd love them all.

When she came forward, he showed her the pictures. Reid frowned at most of them, but he thought they were beautiful.

"I'll delete those later," she told him.

"No, I want them."

She rolled her eyes. "Let's take a selfie."

They turned, and Grayson put his arm over her shoulder. She tucked herself into his side, resting her hand over his heart. He extended his arm, raising it high enough to capture not only them but also the scenery behind them. Through the camera, he saw her look at him. He turned and kissed her, praying like hell his thumb snapped the picture.

Twenty-Three

Grayson

The next week, Grayson sat in the same plush blue chair and recounted the same feelings he'd had the week prior. If anything, the ache in his chest had increased, to the point where he'd cried every day. He couldn't pinpoint the cause, even though he'd tried. Grayson had started a journal after his last appointment, detailing everything, including the new foods he liked. Things he hadn't eaten before, like Italian dishes. He'd never liked ricotta, but his mouth watered when he saw commercials for lasagna, and he had ordered ricotta pancakes with brown butter maple syrup and blueberry compote the other day at breakfast. Prior to surgery, he'd loathed fruit on his food, especially when it was warm. Grayson was not a fan of pie, unless it was a pie made of pudding with a graham cracker crust; then all bets were off.

"Did you talk to your doctor about cellular memory?" Dr. Littleton asked.

"I mentioned it, but he says it's near impossible."

Dr. Littleton nodded. "Impossible to prove, but not improbable to feel. I think one thing to remember is if the science isn't there to support and prove, it's hard to compute. Science needs proof—cold, hard facts—and in a situation like this, it's almost impossible to achieve. We can't ask an organ, and if we ask the patient, the answer would be skewed. Some will be like you and say they've experienced something, while others will say they haven't experienced anything. That brings us back to 'something,' which could easily mean one thing to you and be somewhat different to another."

"This is complicated," Grayson said. "And hard for me to describe." He placed his fist over his heart and shook his head. "This is different, and while I know the heart—my heart—isn't the one I was born with, it feels like mine, and yet I'm reminded almost daily now that it's not." Grayson sighed. "I feel like my heart is broken, and I can't figure out why."

"How's Reid? Did you talk to her about this?"

Grayson nodded. "I did. She's so supportive and understanding. I don't deserve her."

"She feels otherwise," Dr. Littleton said. "We've spoken at length about her role in your life, your rehab, and your relationship. I know you've both done the work to communicate how each of you are feeling. I'm not surprised she's supportive, but you definitely deserve her, Grayson."

He shrugged. "The other day while flipping through the channels, I came across this documentary on transplants. I spent hours watching it and wasted an entire day scouring the web for other stories. And then I searched the news for the time from when I was in the coma."

"Oh?"

Grayson shrugged again. "I know you advised against it, but missing those weeks . . . I thought maybe something would spur a recollection, and my heart would start singing or some shit. I don't know."

"Did you learn anything?"

"The news itself is depressing."

"Sports is more your thing, right?"

Grayson nodded. "I spent a lot of time scrolling through ESPN as a mind cleanser."

"Did you find anything interesting?"

Another shrug. "Not really. I don't know. Nothing held my interest."

"Not UConn winning the college basketball championship?"

Grayson rolled his eyes. "Not a fan," he said with a sigh. "Someday, my Zags will be there." When the Gonzaga Bulldogs had made their first run in the tournament, back in 1999, Grayson became a die-hard fan. He appreciated their tenacity and determination and loved that they were a small school making it big.

For a moment, Grayson's mood improved, and then flashes of what he'd found came back to him. "For the few happy moments, there's been so much death," he said to Dr. Littleton. "And then I remember someone lost their loved one so I could live . . ." He trailed off and looked out the window. "I'm grappling with this knowledge now more than ever."

"What you went through is an experience like no other."

"Except to the family who lost someone," he said. "What's their experience like?"

"It's hard to say. Everyone copes differently. Have you thought about reaching out to UNOS?"

Grayson nodded. "I have, but at the same time, I don't know how I'd feel if they're not interested in hearing from me. The paperwork I have says I can write the family of my donor a letter, and while I think that's nice, what if they don't read it, and then my questions go unanswered?"

"Which are?" Littleton asked.

"What type of person was my donor? What did they like? Is my new love of Italian food something they enjoyed, or did my palate change from surgery?" Grayson shrugged.

"They may or may not have the answers, unless you try."

Grayson nodded. His life had this odd imbalance. If he leaned too far to the left, he'd fall. Same with the right. The problem was, neither side had the answers he sought to understand his feelings.

On his way home from his appointment, he stopped at the bookstore and bought another journal. His current one only had a few pages left, which he figured he would fill tonight before he went to bed.

Reid had started journaling as well. Documenting what was important to them—how they felt, their goals, achievements, and failures—gave them an effective outlet. At times, Grayson had struggled with bouts of depression, often brought on by his daily intake of meds, knowing that if he missed a day, he'd be one day closer to death. His own mortality weighed heavily on his mind. It was scary and at times even crippling.

Before he left the section, he chose another journal for Reid and then wandered over to the self-help section, not knowing what it was he looked for, but he hoped someone had written a book about their journey from transplant recipient to living with someone else's heart. No one had. At least not a book for sale in the store.

It had started to rain while he was in the bookstore. He opted to take the subway home instead of walking. If he walked in the rain, his mom and Reid would kill him for being irresponsible. Saving them from jail time was definitely a bonus.

Halfway home, his earbuds died, and he could hear the conversation taking place in front of him. Two young women sat there, with their heads bent together, talking about how they'd looked up one of their dates online to see what they could find out. Grayson thought the idea was brilliant, and if he had a sister, he'd tell her to do the same thing. Everything was online these days.

A thought occurred, and despite the voice in his mind telling him this was a bad idea, Grayson proceeded anyway. He took his phone from his pocket, opened a web browser, and typed: *people who died on or around April 9th in the United States.*

Casting such a wide net was a crapshoot, especially since he only knew one thing for sure—his donor had come from the US. The other he guessed based on when he'd had his surgery.

The main hit was notable deaths worldwide, and it listed over ten a day. He'd have to figure out a way to narrow his search. There was no way to obtain this information from UNOS unless the donor's family gave him permission. He'd have to do it the old-fashioned way, with the help of the internet and obituaries.

All he wanted to know was what his donor was like, and then maybe he could figure out what was going on in his chest.

Grayson opened another browser and typed in the URL for the local newspaper. He clicked on the obituaries, waited, and then stared at the search bar. He had to know the name of the person he sought. He couldn't put in a date range or a specific date.

Grayson closed the app with a bit more aggression in his finger than needed. He clutched his phone and leaned his head against the window of the train. There had to be a way to find out who had passed locally without having to wait for UNOS.

When his stop was announced, he was so deep in thought that he almost missed it and barely escaped through the closing doors. He rode the escalator up, and when he got outside, he saw a line of taxicabs parked out front of the station, and he made the choice to take one home. Getting home was more important now. Grayson needed to be in front of his computer, with a wider screen, so he could search more effectively.

At the front desk of the apartment building, the receptionist handed Grayson three boxes and a stack of bridal magazines. The sight of them made him smile. Now that they had their location, other things would start to fall into place. They still had time to figure out their guest list, what they were going to feed everyone, and, more importantly, what colors they were going to wear. Grayson thought a traditional black tux would be ideal, but some magazine had told him that black and outdoor spring weddings weren't always the posh thing to do. Reid thought a suit in linen would be good. Truth was, he'd wear whatever Reid told him to, as long as the scar on his chest was covered. It wasn't as gnarly as it was when he'd had surgery, but he still saw it as a bright-red line, even though it had faded.

Somehow, he managed to unlock their door without dropping any of the boxes or the numerous magazines that undoubtedly showed the same dress in each one. They had so many of these catalogs, all with dog-eared pages. Reid had asked him not to look, and he hadn't. He'd never disrespect her by peeking.

After making something to eat, he sat down with his laptop, a pen, and a pad of paper. He stared at the screen for a moment and then typed *Who passed away in Washington, DC*, along with the date range he'd come up with.

A few names came up. He copied the first one into the obituary section of the local newspaper and read, then read the next, and then the next. Each time, Grayson found something to eliminate the deceased—age or disease, or a wording such as "overdose."

He searched a few more newspapers but hit roadblocks each time. Mostly because searching for someone who might have donated vital organs was hard, and he honestly wasn't sure he knew what he was looking for.

And each time he did a search, he grew more and more depressed. On the verge of giving up, he scrolled through a newspaper from beyond DC, and a familiar name caught his attention: Warren and Lorraine Bolton. Grayson clicked and read the first line, about how they had lost their son-in-law, Rafe Karlsson, in a Boston accident.

He'd known the Boltons all through high school but had lost touch after graduation. Grayson had spent many days and some nights, although no one knew about those, at their house, just on the outskirts of the city. He hadn't thought about them in years.

Grayson continued until he saw which daughter had lost her husband.

He swallowed hard when his eyes landed on her name.

Nadia.

The girl he had dated in high school, until they went their separate ways when they'd left for college, essentially losing touch. Nadia had gone to Boston College, far away from her parents and siblings, needing to spread her wings. Grayson had chosen American. It was close to his mom, and while he wasn't a mama's boy, he didn't want to be too far from her. Before they left for school, they'd agreed it would be best to be single so they could enjoy college without worrying what the other thought.

Nadia and Grayson had dated for two years, and while the initial heartbreak hurt, they both had moved on. They kept in touch for the first semester, and then communication gradually decreased. Grayson had never been upset about losing Nadia. They were going in two different directions, and it was easier than having a long-distance relationship.

Grayson continued reading the article. Rafe and Nadia had two daughters, Gemma (eight) and Lynnea (six). Each time Grayson read, he felt more and more sorry for his onetime girlfriend, and he felt a pang of hurt and anger that he hadn't known. He had never checked with his mom to see if she still spoke to the Boltons. They didn't live far from each other. Surely, his mother must've heard from the neighborhood.

He picked up his phone and pressed the contact image for his mom. On the second ring she picked up. "Hi," she said happily.

"Hey. Um, you remember the Boltons, right?"

"Yes, of course. Why do you ask?"

"Do they still live in the area?"

Sydney was silent for a moment. "No, I think they moved farther out about five years ago. If I remember correctly, Warren retired, and I think they either sold the home or their daughter lives in it with her family."

"Nadia?" He had no idea why he said her name. The article he'd read said she lived in Boston.

"No, the other one. Sierra?"

"Sienna."

"Yes, Sienna. She has two boys. I see them from time to time. Why are you asking about the Boltons?"

Grayson enlarged the photo of Nadia and her family and studied it. She looked happy. *They* looked happy. Their older daughter looked like Nadia, while the youngest looked like Rafe.

"Grayson?"

"Uh, what?"

"Why are you asking? Did something happen?"

"Curious," Grayson told his mom.

"Okay. How are you?"

"I'm good. Can I call you back?"

"Okay. Is everything good?" There was worry in her voice, and Grayson chided himself for being preoccupied. He should've texted her instead of calling.

"Yes, I'm good. I promise."

"Okay, call me later."

He hung up and opened another browser. This time he searched for Rafe Karlsson's obituary. As he hit enter, he had no idea what he was looking for. He guessed he was curious because he knew someone who had been affected by the tragedy, which was a first for him. He often counted himself lucky, since he'd never lost a classmate or a friend to death.

Grayson skimmed, soon learning that Rafe had died after saving the life of another runner during the annual Commonwealth Cup. Rafe was madly in love with Nadia. A doting father to Gemma and Lynnea. The only son of Otto and Cleo Karlsson. Loving brother to Freya and uncle to Leif and Astrid. He left behind his best friend and college roommate, Kiran Dunlap.

And then at the end, the sentence that rocked Grayson was there in black and white: *Rafe Karlsson gave the gift of life.*

Grayson sat back and focused on those words. He wasn't a betting man, but if he were, he'd bet his salary that Rafe's organs had been donated.

In another window, Grayson looked up the Commonwealth Cup, which was now known as the Rafe Karlsson Memorial Cup. He read extensively and took notes on what he could. There was Nadia, receiving the key to the city. He recognized her now. She wore a dark wool coat, with a black hat. Her daughters wore something similar. Nadia held the hands of her girls. The cameras followed their every move.

He lost track of how long he sat there, looking up random things, learning increasingly more about the accident, Nadia's family, her, her husband, and anything else he could sink his teeth into. What he found interesting was the lack of interviews with her. In all the searches, he could only find one, and it was recent.

The Nadia he remembered was outgoing, vivacious, and loved having the camera on her. Captain of the cheer squad and valedictorian, she thrived in the spotlight. Grayson surmised life had probably changed when she had children, or her light had dimmed after she lost her husband.

The constant ache he'd felt in his heart changed. It wasn't dull. It now throbbed, and no amount of rubbing the spot made it lessen. Tears threatened as he looked at the faces of Gemma and Lynnea, which seemed silly. Why would he cry for two girls he'd never met before? His mind told him it was from knowing Nadia, for feeling sorry for her. They'd once had a connection, and it was logical for him to experience some sort of sting after learning of her loss.

Grayson hadn't seen Nadia since the summer they'd graduated from high school, when he helped her pack her car. He had mad organizational skills, and she'd begged him to help her. She carried her things to him, while he put them in her car. Warren, her father, wanted to make sure Nadia could see out of her rearview mirror when she drove. Grayson made that happen for her.

Now, instead of pushing her out of his mind, he typed her name into a search engine and watched as her name, along with her husband's, came up. For a fee, he could pay a company to give him her phone number, address, and email. That seemed excessive and invasive.

Yet he did it for no other reason than he had to know. While his mind told him not to do it, his heart pushed him forward. He typed in his information, along with his credit card number, and he fully expected the bank to call him right away with some fraud charge; then he clicked submit.

The screen changed, and her address, along with a picture of her house, showed on his screen. The house was everything Nadia had ever talked about wanting. The craftsman-style home had a wide porch with a white rocking chair. The stairs had potted flowers, blooming and overflowing. She had a home, a family, and had lost her husband.

He told himself that despite her loss, she was doing well.

Or was she?

Twenty-Four

Grayson

"I need your help," Grayson said to Pearce when he arrived at the basketball court. They'd started playing again, one on one, as soon as the doctor had given Grayson the okay. To this day, he hadn't gone back to the game he loved, afraid someone would bump him in the chest and mess up his heart. Pearce, he trusted. The others, not so much.

Pearce dribbled the ball between his legs and made some move that made Grayson roll his eyes. "Things good with Reid?"

"Never better." Grayson finished tying his shoes and then held his hands out, asking for the ball. Pearce passed it, and then they walked toward the hoop. Grayson took his turn dribbling. "She's definitely not the problem."

"Problem? What problem?"

Grayson shot. Pearce rebounded and kicked the ball back to Grayson. He took another five shots and then stopped. "Lately, I've felt this ache in my chest. I've been to the doc. He says I'm fine. Therapist thinks it might be cellular memory."

"Cell phone what?"

Grayson rolled his eyes again. "Cellular memory. It's where the donated organ remembers its former host."

Pearce stared.

And stared.

"Are you saying your heart remembers its former life?"

Grayson shrugged. "I don't know. It's hard to know because there isn't any scientific fact to back up organs retaining memories. But think about it. If you were to get a brain transplant, you wouldn't be you, but the person whose brain you'd gotten."

"Which is one of the reasons people can't get a brain transplant," Pearce said. "Aside from the whole nervous system needing to be reconnected."

"Right, but think about it." Grayson placed a closed fist over his heart. "This heart belonged to someone. It loved someone. It brought joy and sorrow; it felt and ached for people, hobbies, and who knows what else. How do I know I'm doing it justice by existing?"

"That's deep," Pearce said. "I don't think you need to do a deep dive into what this heart did before it became yours. Whoever it belonged to, they're gone. They've left this realm and left you the gift of life."

Gift of life. He'd seen those words in Rafe Karlsson's obituary.

Grayson nodded. "What if what I'm feeling is loss? What if this ache is the heart longing for the people it left behind?" He shot the ball and missed, and neither of them moved to chase it down.

Pearce studied Grayson, and then slowly shook his head. "Do you love Reid?"

"More than anything."

"Where do you feel that love?" Pearce asked.

Grayson appraised his friend and placed his hand over his heart. "Here. Without a doubt. But that doesn't mean I don't feel for someone else."

"But who?"

He shook his head and walked over to where the ball sat motionless on the court. He dribbled, shot, and retrieved his own rebound. "That's just it, I don't know. I can write to my donor's family through UNOS, but they don't have to choose to meet me, which leaves me right where I am now. Or I can follow a hunch."

"Hunches are never good," Pearce said. Grayson passed him the ball. He shot and made it. "They can get you into trouble."

"If I ignore my hunch, then what?"

Pearce shot again and then sighed. "What's the hunch?"

Grayson passed the ball back to his friend. "I think my heart came from a man in Boston who died saving someone from getting hit by a car."

Pearce froze midshot. The ball faltered and never made it to the basket. Normally, Grayson would razz his friend, but not today. The ball bounced away from them. "Say what? How?"

"When my therapist told me about cellular memory, I started looking things up online—"

"What kind of things?" Pearce interrupted.

"Deaths," Grayson said. "I started thinking about the people who died close to the day of my surgery. I looked up obituaries in the area, mostly because I didn't know how far a heart could travel for a transplant. The people who died, though, had cancer, overdosed, or didn't seem like a viable candidate for donation. Then I searched farther out and came across an article about Warren and Lorraine Bolton. They lost their son-in-law in that accident I mentioned. I wouldn't have gone any further except I know the Boltons."

"How?"

"I dated their daughter Nadia in high school, up until we left for college."

Any color Pearce had in his cheeks left with Grayson's statement. "That's a stretch, Grayson."

He shook his head. "I read his obituary. He was an organ donor. None of the others I'd read up until then said anything of the sort."

"Not everyone will make their decision public."

"That's what I thought, but then I searched different keywords and found numerous obituaries from years past and even weeks ago, all using the same line: 'gift of life.' It's everywhere," he told his friend.

"UNOS, commercials, everywhere I turn, I see or hear it. You've even said it today."

This time it was Pearce who went and retrieved the basketball. He didn't dribble it or try to shoot. He carried it under his arm and walked toward Grayson.

"Did you tell any of this to Reid?"

Grayson shook his head slowly. "I will, but not yet."

"What are you waiting for?"

"I want to know if I'm right."

"About what, exactly?"

"About my heart. If I'm right, then when I see Nadia, my ache should go away."

"Did you ask UNOS?"

Grayson shook his head. "It'll take too long. She could say no."

"So, what are you going to do?"

"Go see her."

Pearce shook his head. "Your hunch is stupid."

"Is it, though?" Grayson asked. "What if my heart misses her?"

"Then what? Do you leave Reid for what's her name?"

"Nadia."

"My question was rhetorical, Grayson."

"I'm in love with Reid. That won't change."

"You don't know that. Especially if you have history with this woman." Pearce threw his hands up in the air. "I swear, you're like one of those second-chance romance movies my mom is always watching, where a long-lost love returns home and magically falls in love with their first love because the person they have waiting for them back home is some 'put work first' type and doesn't care about the holidays."

"Take a breath," Grayson tried to joke.

"Face reality," Pearce fired back. "You're playing with fire. Someone is going to get hurt. No, strike that. Multiple people are going to get hurt."

"What if I need this to heal?"

"What if it damages you more?"

Grayson shook his head. He walked toward the bleachers and sat down. Pearce followed. "Look," Pearce said. "I get that you're confused, that you played a game of basketball and then woke up with a new heart. I can't even imagine what your body and mind went through, and continues to go through, but this isn't the way to do things. There's too much at risk. Your friend lost her husband. You can't just show up on her doorstep and expect her to be okay with this. Besides, do you even know where she lives?"

"In Boston. I paid a fee and got their, I mean her, address."

"Jesus, Grayson."

"I know," he said. "I'm in deep, though, and if I don't find out, I'll sit here and wonder, and I'm scared I'll ruin everything with Reid."

"She has a right to know what's going on. Hiding this from her isn't healthy for your relationship."

"Reid knows how I feel. She encouraged me to reach out through UNOS. But I don't want to wait," he said. "I don't want the rejection letter to come in, saying they don't want to meet me."

"So you what, just show up and say, 'Hey, long time no see, but I believe I have your dead husband's heart in my chest; wanna feel?'"

Grayson gave Pearce a sideways glance.

"Well?"

Grayson sighed. "I thought I'd go there and just see if there's a connection."

"There will be, because you dated."

He shook his head. "We haven't spoken since we said goodbye. I wasn't sad when she left. We just had fun in high school. That's it. I never loved her. Not like I love Reid." Grayson pushed loose gravel around with his foot. "I know this sounds ridiculous."

"Understatement," Pearce muttered.

"But if I don't go and this ache doesn't go away, I'll always wonder."

"And if you do go and the ache goes away?"

Grayson shrugged. "I don't know."

"I think you're making a huge mistake."

"I know," he said. "Will you go with me?"

Pearce choked. "To babysit?"

Grayson eyed him and shook his head. "No, for support."

It took him a moment, but Pearce finally nodded.

TWENTY-FIVE

NADIA

As much as Nadia didn't want to admit it, she and the girls had found a routine that worked for them. What she didn't like to admit was that her now nine-year-old was taking on more of a role in the house than Nadia wanted her to have. Now that a year had passed, she worked hard to make the upcoming months better. Nadia got up with her alarm at 5:00 a.m., turned on the TV in her room, and started the yoga program she'd found online. According to the schedule she'd made for herself, she'd do yoga for fifteen minutes, meditate for ten, and then hop into the shower. The goal was to be downstairs by six to make lunches and then get the girls up and ready.

Their nighttime routine had also changed. After showering, the girls picked out two outfits for the next morning, which gave them an option in case they changed their minds in the morning. Doing so created less hassle and gave Lynnea more freedom. She still came downstairs every now and again in an old Halloween costume or one of those princess dresses she had. On those days, Nadia smiled, kissed her daughter, and went about her morning. The fight wasn't worth it, and if dressing as a princess made Lynnea happy, then so be it. Gemma was just like Nadia and rarely changed her mind, which was a relief.

Nadia had long given up on making breakfast and had resorted to cereal. When she'd made that change, she'd cried for days and felt like a failure of a mother. Life had been easier with Rafe. Besides the obvious fact of having her husband, he'd made every day a breeze. His calm and collective approach to the day balanced Nadia's frantic hair-pulling anxiety, which was self-induced. She overthought everything and hated to be late, which often translated into feeling like she was always running behind. The girls never seemed to be on her kind of schedule, but they were slowly getting there. The three of them were working together to find a happy medium to get them through the absence of Rafe.

Springtime in Boston had always been Nadia's favorite time of the year, apart from Christmas, which had always seemed too magical until Rafe's passing. She hadn't done any of their normal outings, from taking the girls to see *The Nutcracker* to ice-skating at Frog Pond. When the email arrived to reserve her seats for the Holiday Pops, she deleted it without even opening it.

Now that spring was in full bloom, she'd taken the girls to the New England Aquarium to see the African penguins, the California sea lions, and the giant Pacific octopus, which happened to be Lynnea's favorite. Gemma's go-to animal was the southern rockhopper penguin. She liked them because of the way the feathers on their heads stood up and the yellow streaks made them look like rock stars.

Rafe had preferred the Atlantic harbor seals because they could visit them whenever they were downtown and do so without having to go inside the aquarium. They were now Nadia's favorite as well.

Nadia stood in the front yard, with the lawn mower in front of her. She eyed it warily and contemplated going inside to get Reuben. He lived in her basement, but his job kept him busy. She appreciated having him in the house at night, but other than that and paying rent, he wasn't able to help out. Then there was Kiran. Nadia could call him, but she needed to figure things out on her own.

Now she regretted wanting to be independent. Nadia needed to be skillful, but she didn't want to be. In her mind, she replayed the visions she had of Rafe, and the many times they'd done yard work together. Her in the flower beds, weeding and planting, while he mowed, edged, and raked. They were an efficient team on Saturday mornings.

As vivid as her memory of her husband was, she hadn't a clue about how to start the lawn mower. She pulled her phone out and, while tempted to call her dad or Kiran, she opened an app and looked up the make and model of her mower and asked the search engine for videos. After a tutorial, things seemed simple enough.

The front door opened, and the girls stepped out onto the porch. Gemma held two glasses of lemonade in her hand. She set one on the railing and then sat in the white rocking chair. Lynnea copied her sister while holding her own glass of lemonade.

"What are you girls doing?"

"We brought you a drink," Gemma said as she motioned toward the glass.

"I appreciate you both," she told her daughters.

"Do you want us to weed like you used to do with Daddy?" Gemma asked, while Lynnea sighed heavily. Weeding was the last thing Lynnea would want to do. Nadia knew this. Planting was her specialty. Lynnea loved putting the perennial seeds or bulbs in the ground, then watering and watching them grow. Or helping Nadia pick out the annual flowers and moving them from the garden tray into the hole she'd dug.

Nadia nodded. It wasn't that she needed the help, but she wanted the girls to feel like they were contributing. "Stay there," she said as she left the front yard and walked to the garden shed in the back. She rummaged through her tools, soon returning with a bucket filled with shovels, trowels, and a rake. Along with the gloves she'd bought the girls last year.

She set the bucket on the step, and Gemma came forward, bringing Nadia's drink with her. Nadia sipped greedily and gave her daughter a soft smile.

"Lynnea, when we're done here, we'll go to the store and buy the flowers. Okay?"

Lynnea beamed and nodded. "Can I dig the holes?"

"Of course. We can get done a lot faster if you help Gemma."

"With what?"

"When she pulls a weed, if you could stick it in the bucket—that way, when she's done weeding and I'm done mowing, we can head to the store."

"Okay, Mommy." Lynnea came down the steps and picked up her pair of blue gardening gloves. They matched Rafe's, while Gemma's and Nadia's were pink.

The three of them set out to make their front yard look the way it had last spring. After rewatching the tutorial on how to start the mower, she managed to get it going on the second pull. The girls cheered, making Nadia feel like she'd finally succeeded at something good in the past year. She supposed surviving was an achievement unto itself.

As she mowed the yard, she took notice of the other things that needed to be done. The white picket fence needed a new paint job, and there was a loose brick in their walkway. One of the clapboards had warped on the house and would need to be replaced. And the house needed to be painted. The fence and walkway she could manage. The rest, she'd have to hire someone for, and that would cost money. Money she didn't have.

Nadia finished the front yard and made the girls move to the back while she mowed there. The section of yard Rafe had removed at first thaw last year for a swing set had finally filled in with grass. The girls had never asked about the swing set, which sat in boxes under the awning of their garden shed. Nadia could sell it, or maybe Kiran could bring some coworkers over to put it together for the girls.

She'd ask her dad about the swing set: whether they should put it up or sell it. In hindsight, she wondered how much Gemma would use it and how long Lynnea would be interested in it. It seemed like a massive undertaking for one or two years of entertainment.

Nadia watched the girls. Gemma used the foam kneepad to kneel on as she thrust her trowel under the weeds. Lynnea lay on the grass, staring up at the sky. Nadia followed her gaze. Clouds moved above them, creating shadows and optical illusions. If she lost focus, it started to look like the sky was shifting overhead.

Instead of restarting the mower, she went over to Gemma, tapped her on the shoulder, and motioned her to follow. Nadia lay next to Lynnea, while Gemma lay on her other side. They held hands.

"Do you think Daddy can see us?" Gemma asked.

"He can," Lynnea said. "He's always watching. Right, Mommy?"

She believed he was. "He is."

They stayed there, staring at the clouds, pointing out what they thought the shapes looked like, and laughing. It was the laughter that warmed Nadia's heart, that told her they were going to be okay. They'd never get back to the time when Rafe was in their lives, but they'd find a medium—happy or otherwise—that would help them move on.

They lost track of time, until Lynnea's tummy rumbled. They laughed and finally got up. Gemma pointed out the impressions their bodies had made in the ground.

"You can't mow us!" She placed her hands on her cheeks and dropped her mouth open, making an O.

"Let's go get some lunch," Nadia said. "I think nuggies are in order."

The girls jumped up and down, cheering.

They ran inside, bumping into Reuben.

"Hey, where's the fire?" he asked as he caught Lynnea in his arms.

"We're going to get nuggies!" she said in jubilation.

"Do you want to come with us?" Nadia asked.

"Nah, you ladies go. I'm going to finish the backyard." He set Lynnea down, hugged Gemma, and then went to his sister. "I told you I'd mow."

"I know, but it's something I needed to do today."

Reuben nodded as if he understood. "Make a honey-do list," he told her. "We'll tackle projects together. First thing: clean the refrigerator."

Nadia's eyes went wide. "What? Why?" She sidestepped and went to the refrigerator, tugging on the door. When it opened, she gasped. "Lynnea," she muttered under her breath.

"That's my guess, but I didn't want to accuse either of them or ask them."

"I'll clean it when I get back," she told Reuben. "I promised them nuggets; besides, they didn't mean it. They were trying to be helpful and brought me lemonade, Reuben. You should've seen them, coming out onto the porch like they were the parents and I was the teenager doing Saturday chores. I can't be mad at them."

"Nope, but we can teach them some responsibility."

Laughter erupted from her. Being the only boy in the family, Reuben had gotten away with everything. One "Mom" from him, and Sienna and Nadia were in trouble, even when they hadn't done anything to warrant it. She patted her brother on his shoulder. "You're hilarious. Leave the mess—we'll clean it when we get back."

She found the girls waiting for her on the front porch. After getting them situated in the car, they drove to the nearest McDonald's. As much as she hated going in, she parked, and they made their way inside. After they ordered, Gemma led them to a booth.

"I miss the playground," Gemma said with a sigh.

Nadia didn't. It was a mecca of germs, filth, and who knew what. Parents had rejoiced when the establishment changed its branding, remodeled, and removed the PlayPlace.

After lunch, they went to the gardening store, and the girls picked out a wide color array of annuals. Nadia gravitated toward purples, while Lynnea opted for yellows, and Gemma went with blues. Nadia didn't care if there was any cohesiveness to her flower beds this season, because knowing the girls had done all the work would make them the most beautiful ever.

"Can we buy a birdbath?" Gemma asked as they walked around the store.

"Birds don't take baths, you silly goose," Lynnea said, laughing.

"Uh-huh, don't they, Mommy?"

"They do." Nadia directed their cart toward the section with birdbaths. They came in all shapes, sizes, and materials. Some were ornate. Some had houses attached to them. Others were a basic oval tub with a pedestal base made of plastic.

"Which color do you like?" Nadia asked the girls. Giving them each a choice was never the best option. They would undoubtedly pick two different colors.

"I like the white one," Lynnea said.

"Me too," Gemma added, shocking Nadia. She stared at them. "White will look good with all the flowers we bought."

Who was Nadia to argue with that logic? She set the top of the birdbath under the cart and then placed the pedestal in the front, where she had her purse. Both girls held on to the cart while Nadia navigated to the next aisle over to get more birdseed. Ever since she'd put in the feeder last year, she'd grown fond of having birds around.

At the checkout, they saw two metal crates stacked on top of each other, each holding a cat. Nadia groaned as soon as the girls saw the friendly felines.

"Can we get a cat?" Gemma asked, already crouched low with her fingers pushing through the slats to pet the animal.

"Not right now." She hadn't said no because that often led to a tantrum, and their day had been going really well. She didn't want to hear how she was mean or how Daddy would've let them get one if he were there. The girls would never know how hurtful their words were sometimes.

Nadia did her best to ignore the girls, who continued to ask and to tell both cats that they were going to love them forever. She smiled at the clerk when she took her receipt and then told the girls to say goodbye.

They moped on the way to the car, and then chattered about how they couldn't wait to get a cat. Or cats, being as each girl wanted her own. All Nadia could think about was the money a pet would cost them, and how a cat would chase her birds away. The latter couldn't happen. She looked forward to seeing the cardinal every other morning, if not every morning. That cardinal was why she'd agreed to buy a birdbath. She would do whatever she could to keep the bird coming back to her home. Nadia needed to believe the cardinal was a gift from Rafe.

A sign that everything was going to be okay.

Twenty-Six

Grayson

Grayson hated lying to Reid. He told himself it was for the best and a onetime thing. She'd easily bought the excuse he'd come up with, of him and Pearce taking a guys' weekend away. It wasn't the first time they'd done something like that, but it was the first since his surgery and since Grayson had started dating Reid. Still, she was very supportive and all but pushed him out the door. She had made her own plans with Melanie. They planned to shop for a wedding dress. Definitely something Grayson couldn't be a part of.

He and Pearce flew to Boston. Grayson had made the arrangements for them to fly right away. He didn't want to wait to prove his theory correct. The sooner he could figure out what was causing the ache in his chest, the sooner he could put it to rest and tell his doctor that cellular memory was indeed the diagnosis.

After they'd landed and checked into their hotel, they took the Red Line subway to Harvard Square. From there, they walked to where the accident had been. The area was marked with ribbons and a cross.

He looked around. The area was busy with cars and pedestrians, most of whom he assumed were college kids from Harvard heading toward the square. They walked back toward the center of town, where the words Finish line were still visible on the road from the most recent race. People went in and out of restaurants and cafés. Music blared from portable speakers and through open car windows.

When the light turned red, Grayson stepped into the road and looked toward the memorial. Nadia easily could've stood where Grayson stood now and watched everything unfold. Had she witnessed her husband dying? God, he hoped not.

Pearce leaned against one of the brick buildings. Across the street, a man danced and tried to entice women walking down the street to dance with him. Grayson approached with a smile on his face.

"What's so funny?"

Grayson nodded toward the man. "He wants to dance with somebody."

Automatically, Pearce responded with "He wants to feel the heat with somebody."

It was as if the man could hear them. The song changed to Whitney Houston, and they continued to laugh. Grayson and Pearce found an open bench and sat down, and Grayson sighed after a bit.

"Well?"

He shook his head. "Nothing. I don't know. I guess I thought if I stood in the spot where he died, I'd feel something."

"Like panic or fear?"

"Yeah, maybe." In the research he'd done, he'd learned that people who believed they'd experienced cellular memory noted that they'd started eating foods they'd previously disliked or listened to music they normally wouldn't. One person noted that she began dressing differently and discovered a love for baseball—a sport she'd previously loathed. No one ever wrote about experiencing an indescribable ache. Only their personalities had changed.

Because they were technically on a weekend excursion, they bought tickets for the Boston Duck Tour. They walked to the Prudential Center, which was another location on Grayson's list of places. He knew this was where Rafe had worked, and yet he felt nothing when he looked at the building. He felt zero familiarity, and the ache was still present.

They boarded the most ridiculous-looking bright-blue boat on wheels and chose seats in the middle. Pearce sat next to the open window and offered to switch seats. Grayson told him to stay where he was. It was the least he could do, since his friend had come with him.

Grayson thought Washington, DC, held a lot of history, but the city had nothing compared to Boston. From the Freedom Trail to the burial grounds from the American Revolution to its successful sports teams, Boston didn't lack anything. Many of the side streets were still narrow cobblestone roads, with town houses giving way to very little sidewalk. The view from the Charles, looking back at the city and along the esplanade, was one of the most breathtaking views he had ever seen. Instantly, he regretted not bringing Reid to experience this with him, and the ache he felt increased. He hated lying to her.

They ate dinner at Quincy Market, walked along the harbor (where Pearce threatened to dump his soda into the water, joking that it was tea), went into the train station under the arena that housed the Celtics and Bruins, and then finally made it back to their hotel room, where they crashed hard, both exhausted from a day of being tourists.

The next afternoon, Grayson drove their rental car to the address he'd paid for online. The entire drive over, he told himself the address was a fake, that he'd been scammed, and deservingly so. He pulled up in front of the home, with its white picket fence, large porch with two white rockers, and a sign that said **Welcome**.

"Am I making a mistake?"

"Yes," Pearce said. "However, if it gets you over this feeling, then it needs to be done."

Grayson stared ahead. Nadia lived in a cute neighborhood. The kind where people sat outside, talked to their neighbors, and probably closed off the street for summertime block parties.

Pearce got out of the car first, and he waited for Grayson on the sidewalk. He took a deep breath and got out. They went through the gate and up the stairs, and he knocked on the door. Part of him prayed she wasn't home, while the other half wanted to see her and find out if she was the reason for the feelings he had.

The door swung open, and Grayson's heart lurched in his chest. He was face to face with Reuben, Nadia's brother.

They said each other's names at the same time, and then Reuben gave Grayson a man hug. "What are you doing here?" Reuben asked enthusiastically.

"I heard about Nadia's husband and was in town. I thought I'd stop by. This is where she lives, right?"

"Yeah, yeah. Come on in. Wow, what's it been? Fourteen, fifteen years?"

"Something like that." Grayson stepped into the house. Warmth and love washed over him as he took in his surroundings. Pictures hung on the walls of Nadia, her husband, and their children. His heart beat a bit faster. He chalked that up to nerves.

Grayson introduced Pearce, and they followed Reuben into the other room. Grayson sat on the couch, absorbing everything around him.

"Wow, Nadia's going to be so surprised to see you. I remember when she left for college and told Sienna and me you guys broke up. We were devastated. We had so much fun hanging out with the two of you. It's a shame." Reuben shook his head.

"Do you live here?" Grayson asked.

"Yeah, I moved in at the beginning of the year to help her out. It's been tough, especially with the girls."

"Two of them, right?"

Reuben nodded. "Gemma and Lynnea, or as I like to think of them, Sienna and Nadia reincarnated."

Grayson grimaced at his usage of "reincarnated" but had a feeling he understood the euphemism. Sienna was a wild one back in high school, and Nadia was always the one with her nose stuck in a book.

They made idle chitchat, catching up on years' worth of life. When Grayson heard three car doors slam shut, he stiffened. Instant regret, fear, and moroseness washed over him. His emotions were all over the place, ping-ponging back and forth. He was about to leave when he heard the newcomers moving around in the house.

"Lynnea is the youngest and a hurricane," Reuben warned. "Gemma is Nadia personified. Quiet, shy, and probably won't say two words to you. Lynnea will want to know everything from who your parents are to what your blood type is."

Grayson hoped Reuben was joking.

He could smell her flowery perfume before she came into the room.

"Sorry, I didn't mean to interrupt."

Their eye contact was brief. Grayson stood as she turned to leave the room. He smiled, hoping she remembered who he was.

"Grayson?"

His smile brightened. "Hey, Nadia. It's been a long time. I'm sorry about your husband," he said. "I should've called sooner."

She came forward and hugged him. He felt nothing. "Thank you. What are you doing here?"

Grayson told her the same story he'd told Reuben, which wasn't a total lie. He and Pearce were visiting Boston.

Before he could sit down, the girls came into the room. He didn't need her to introduce them; he already knew by the way his heart reacted to them being this close to him. The ache had been replaced with longing and pain.

He fought back a wave of tears that threatened to spill if he couldn't keep his emotions in check. His throat closed off his airways, causing him to gasp, which he covered with a cough.

They were the reason for the ache in his chest, the reason he hadn't felt whole in over a year. Those girls were a part of him. They had a hold on him that could never be severed. No matter what.

"These are my girls," Nadia said. "Gemma and Lynnea. This is Grayson. Mommy's friend from high school."

Grayson crouched to their eye level and held out his hand, shaking theirs. "It's truly a pleasure to meet you," he told them.

Twenty-Seven

Grayson

As much as Grayson wanted to leave, he couldn't. Nadia had invited him and Pearce to stay for dinner and sent Reuben out to get all the fixings for a night of grilling. Pearce had done Grayson dirty and volunteered to go with Reuben, leaving him alone with Nadia and the girls. It wasn't Nadia who bothered him; it was Gemma and Lynnea. They were the reason he'd felt empty, and now that he was in their presence, the ache had subsided.

They carried glasses of lemonade onto the back deck and sat at the table. Nadia put the umbrella up and relaxed, while Grayson watched the girls play in the yard.

"So, what have you been up to?" Nadia asked.

Grayson took a sip and then played with the glass a bit while he formulated an answer. "I graduated from American with a degree in graphic design. I wanted to be an architect but couldn't hack the math, which is stupid, since computers do it all for you these days. Anyway, not much math in graphic design, so I went that route and graduated. For the past few years, I've been at the Wold Collective, where I design ridiculously high-end, overpriced boardroom tables."

"Like the tables with the different color inlays?"

Grayson nodded. "Different shine, inlay, wood. You name it, I design it."

"That's incredibly—"

"Boring? Mundane?"

"Safe," she said. "I work in a middle school with hellions. Granted, not all of them are bad, but a handful of them give me a run for my money."

"Did you get your degree in history?"

She smiled and nodded. "I did. I intended to go back to Arlington, but then I met Rafe and things changed."

"I'm sorry" was all Grayson could say.

Nadia forced a smile. "I'm just happy I still have them." She motioned toward the girls. "I can't imagine losing the three of them. I guess if I had, I probably wouldn't be here talking to you right now."

He wanted to tell her not to talk like that, but he had no right. She was entitled to feel the way she had and continue to do so, without reservation.

"Tell me about him," he prompted. "Since he's the reason you never came back."

Nadia laughed. "I came home," she told him. "I just didn't drive down your street or anything." She looked down at her lap. "No offense, but it was love at first sight when I saw him."

"None taken. We did the right thing by breaking up before college. Neither of us were mature enough to handle a long-distance relationship."

Her mouth dropped open. "Hey!"

Grayson held his hands up. "I only speak the truth."

Nadia laughed. "You're right, but still. Anyway, he was amazing, kind, and thoughtful. The type of guy who holds the door and pulls your chair out. He was the kind of man where people say he died too young because when it came to Rafe, that's true. He worked hard, but he never brought work home. Once he came through the door, the only people who existed for him were his family. Work could wait until the morning, was what he always said. The weekends were ours. We'd sleep in, snuggle with the girls, and then make breakfast as a family. Our lives revolved around us. I know, without a doubt, he loved me. And he worshipped those girls." Nadia pointed toward the yard. "It wasn't just us who lost him that day—everyone who knew him lost a son, brother, uncle, friend, coworker, neighbor. When it snowed, he'd shovel the roofs of our older neighbors' homes, so they wouldn't get conned out of their money, and he'd mow their lawns when they went on vacation. Weeks before he died, he was going to run an after-school program for boys who don't have a dad at home, teaching them manners, how to tie a tie, and how to shake hands. That sort of thing. Rafe was this all-around great man who didn't deserve this."

Grayson's chest tightened. If Rafe hadn't died, someone else would have. It was just divine decree that he happened to get Rafe's heart. At least that's what he told himself while he sat there with Nadia, pretending. He was certain he had his answer. His new heart missed the two girls it loved dearly. Even as he sat there and watched them play, he longed to be near them, to be in the yard, basking in their presence. Grayson's mind told his heart, *This is it—a onetime visit.* But even his mind knew otherwise.

"Aside from making ridiculously high-end overpriced boardroom tables, what else do you do?"

Nothing compared to your husband. Grayson had never felt like less of a man until now. If Rafe didn't deserve to die, then Grayson didn't deserve his heart.

"Honestly, my life is pretty mundane," he told her. "I'm engaged. She's not the mundane part, though." Grayson pulled his cell phone out and brought up a picture of Reid.

"She's beautiful. What's her name?"

"Reid. We're getting married next spring at the National Mall."

"Under the cherry blossoms?"

He nodded.

"That'll be so beautiful. You're very lucky."

Laughing, he pocketed his phone. "You have no idea. I almost blew it with her. Somewhere in my life, I decided being her friend was easier than admitting my feelings for her. I'm glad I woke up before it was too late." His statement held an unbelievable amount of truth despite missing one key component. Grayson thought about asking Nadia outright if Rafe's organs had been donated, but he already knew. There was no way two little girls could make him feel like everything was right in the world when he knew nothing about them.

Grayson was thankful when Reuben and Pearce returned. While they manned the grill and Nadia made side dishes, Grayson went down the steps and into the backyard with the girls, who were having a tea party.

"Hi," he said as he sat down, feeling instantly at ease.

"Hi," Gemma said quietly, while Lynnea said nothing.

"What are you doing?"

"Tea party with our dollies."

He picked one up, held it, and put it back down after it winked at him. Dolls were freaky, always watching.

"Do you know our daddy?" Gemma asked.

I feel him. "No, unfortunately I never had the opportunity to meet him. I'm sorry he's not here."

"The person killed him with their car," Lynnea said quietly. Grayson didn't know how to respond.

"Lynnea, don't say that. Mommy will get mad, and she will cry."

Lynnea's expression turned sad. Grayson tugged on the ends of her hair. "Hey, don't be sad."

"I'm mad," she said as she crossed her arms over her chest. "At her!" She glared at her sister.

"She's trying to protect your mom," Grayson pointed out. "You don't want her to be sad, right?"

"She laughed today," Gemma said. "At whatever you said to her up there."

"Oh yeah?"

"'Cause you funny," Lynnea told him.

How could children go from talking about their father being killed, to laughing? Lynnea was right. There wasn't any way to sugarcoat it. Their words went right to his heart, which began thumping wildly, thumping in his ears. He placed his hand over it to quell the noise. Looking at the girls, he waited for them to make eye contact, to ask him why his heartbeat was so loud. They never did. Couldn't they hear it?

Will they want to hear it?

He could do that for them. The pamphlet was at home, describing the heartbeat teddy bears that stored twenty to thirty seconds' worth of sound. They were meant to help families of those who had lost loved ones and had made the ultimate sacrifice by donating their organs.

Gemma set a cup and saucer down in front of Grayson. "Do you like cream in your tea?"

"I—I don't know," he said. "I've never had tea or been to a tea party."

Lynnea stood, ran to a box, and then returned with a hat and feather boa, which she draped dramatically around his shoulders. The hat didn't fit, so she set it on top of his hair.

"You have a big head," she said as she giggled. "Big brains." She shook her head while laughing until she rolled over.

"My dad calls her a hurricane," Gemma told him while she continued to prepare their imaginary tea. "I'll put cream in your tea. That's how my grandma likes it."

"Grandma Lorraine?"

Gemma looked at him sharply. "How do you know her name?"

"Like your mom said, we went to high school together. I know your grandparents and your aunt Sienna as well."

"Do you know my cousins?"

Grayson shook his head slightly. "No, I don't think so. What are their names?"

In a shocking move, Lynnea sat on his lap. He acted as coolly as possible. "Lincoln and Jaxon. They live in Arlington."

"So does my mom," Grayson told Gemma. "Maybe when you come visit your grandparents next time, we'll go to the zoo. We can visit the elephants."

"I like the pandas," Gemma said.

"They're funny," Lynnea told him. "We watch them on the video when it snows. He's always rolling in the snow. He's going to be a snowman."

Grayson couldn't agree more and didn't want to tell them the pandas were no longer at the zoo.

Gemma held up her teacup and stared at him, as if she expected him to do the same. He reached for Lynnea's and handed it to her before picking his up. They clanked their plastic cups together and then sipped. Grayson was out of his element, but he figured he'd watched enough television during his recovery that he could easily play along.

He hissed and fanned his mouth. "Oh, that's hot, but delicious. You must tell me the flavor so I can make it at home."

Gemma and Lynnea roared with laughter. "Our daddy used to do the same thing," Gemma said. "You acted just like him."

"Did I now?"

Tears welled in the back of his eyes. He pinched the outside of his leg to ward them off. He refused to cry in front of them, Nadia, or anyone for that matter.

"Do you have kids?" Lynnea asked.

"Not yet," he told her. "Someday, I hope."

"Do you have a wife?" Gemma asked.

"Almost. We are getting married next year. Do you want to see a picture of her?"

The girls nodded, and he fished his phone out of his pocket and brought his photos up.

"She's pretty," Gemma said.

While Lynnea pointed out the obvious: "She has Mommy's hair."

"What's her name?" Gemma asked.

"Reid."

"That's a nice name," Gemma said.

Nadia called for them. She stood on the deck and waited. Grayson helped the girls clean up and didn't bother to remove his feathered boa. He thought if he did, he might insult Lynnea. Inside, they washed up, and Grayson helped the girls set the table outside. It was a nice night, and as the sun set, strings of white lights came to life overhead.

Grayson wanted this. He wanted the suburban lifestyle. The house with the picket fence, inviting backyard, and friendly neighbors: everything Reid had talked about before she'd given him the chance he begged for. Where they lived now, they said hi to the people they ran into, but they had no idea who they were or what kind of lives they lived. He hadn't cared until now. Learning about Rafe and the man he was made Grayson want to be a better person.

When he sat down, he chose to sit between the girls. He felt at home there, nestled in their warmth and embrace. He didn't care that they picked food off his plate. He accepted the hot dog Lynnea didn't want when she pretended it was an airplane headed toward his mouth. When Pearce brought up his boa, instead of being embarrassed, he asked his friend if he was jealous that he didn't have one. Gemma fixed that for him. After a quick run to her bedroom, she draped a purple one around his shoulders and placed a very elegant tiara on top of his head.

Grayson's eyebrow popped as he waited for Pearce to say something. He didn't. He bowed his head and continued eating.

It had taken less than an hour, and the girls had Grayson wrapped around their fingers. They owned his heart. The ache was gone, filled now with the love and laughter of two little girls who had lost their father way too soon.

He didn't want to leave.

TWENTY-EIGHT

REID

For the past six years, Reid had watched *Say Yes to the Dress*, critiquing every dress, admiring brides on their big day, and wishing her mom were going to be there on her big day. Most little girls grew up playing bride, either with the ever-popular sheer curtains hanging in their living room windows or the handy pillowcase standby.

Reid had done neither.

Being raised by a single father, she'd spent most of her time outside, digging in the dirt, making mountains in their backyard for her Tonka trucks to climb over, or watching whatever sporting event was on television. It wasn't until she'd started going to sleepovers that things changed for her. She learned how to be more girly, as her father called the changes in her. Reid absorbed everything she could from her friends' mothers. How to do her hair and makeup, how to take care of her body, and how to cook. She loved bringing home recipes to try for her dad. It wasn't until she was a teen, when she'd started to dream about her wedding, that she'd learned from her dad that he'd kept her mother's wedding dress.

Now, as she perused the racks, having gone from store to store and feeling no connection to any of the beautifully made gowns, Reid knew which dress would be perfect. "We should go get some lunch," she said to Melanie, whom she'd invited to spend the weekend with her, since Grayson was gone with Pearce.

"You haven't tried on a single dress, Reid. I know you have time, but still. Don't you want to get a feel for the style?"

Reid shook her head. "I already know which type I want to wear."

Melanie threw her hands up in dramatic fashion. "Now you tell me." She made her way over to the section Reid stood in front of. "Which one?"

"None of these?"

"What store, then?"

Reid bit her lower lip and shook her head again. Melanie's eyes went wide. Reid wasn't even going to try to guess what her friend was thinking.

"Reid Sullivan, if you tell me you're going to get married in a burlap sack, I will strangle you."

Reid stifled a laugh. "Heck no. It is vintage, though. Lacy. And in my dad's closet."

Melanie's eyes widened again, and then her head started moving up and down. "Yes! Why didn't we think of this from the beginning?"

"I don't know, but it feels right, ya know? Like, I keep looking at these dresses, and while they are lovely, they're not me. My mom's dress . . ." Reid paused and looked at her ring. "It just makes perfect sense. She'd be with me in every sense of the word."

Melanie stepped forward and placed her hands on Reid's shoulders. "This is perfect. I think Grayson should wear navy. What do you think?"

It took Reid all of two seconds to agree. "He'll love it."

"Perfect. Now lunch. Let's go."

Thankfully, they were in Georgetown, where retail and food therapy were on top of their game for DC. They found a modern yet swanky restaurant that didn't require a reservation. They snagged an outside seat, under a wide umbrella. It was funny: even though it was May and the days were gorgeous, the propane heaters still lingered in the corners. Mostly for the evenings and nighttime crowds, where the chill in the air could ruin a good meal.

They ordered a bottle of white wine, grateful for the convenience of living in the city, where mass transportation was available. While they waited for their meal, they sipped on wine and snacked on bruschetta.

"I made a list of things you need to do and when," Melanie told Reid. "I've shared it with you."

Reid picked up her phone, opened the list, and read. "Thank you," she said. "It feels good knowing most of the important stuff is taken care of. Hiring the wedding planner was literally the best and easiest decision."

"Aside from saying yes to Grayson," Melanie pointed out.

"That was a no-brainer."

"How's the guest list coming?"

"I think we're up to one hundred. We still have time before we do our save-the-date magnets."

"When is your engagement photo session again?"

"In June. We finally decided on the Smithsonian Gardens."

Melanie nodded in agreement. "I swear, this has to be one of the best places to get married. Are you sure Grayson doesn't have a brother?"

Reid giggled. "Just Pearce."

Melanie's nose crinkled at the sound of his name. "He rubs me the wrong way."

"Why? He's a good guy. You guys always get along when you're together."

"Too well, sometimes. I don't know. He gives off brother vibes."

"And that's a bad thing?" Reid asked.

Melanie gave a half shrug and sipped her wine. "Do we get to pick our entrance music?" she asked.

"Yes. Grayson and I are going for a very laid-back vibe, with elegance, though. I want this wedding to be elegant and beautiful."

"Part of me is jealous. I mean, I've known from the beginning he was the one for you. And despite my many—and I do mean many—times of wanting to bash him in the head, I'm happy to be part of your special day. The other part of me is like, no way in hell would I get married. Live together, have babies and whatever, but the marriage thing . . ." Melanie shuddered.

Reid reached for Melanie's hand and squeezed. "I think because of how your parents are, it's turned you off from marriage."

Melanie's parents had been married for ages, yet they fought constantly, slept in different bedrooms, and traveled without one another. She'd spent many nights crying on Reid's shoulder about her parents and didn't understand why they wouldn't get a divorce. All their children were grown and living away from home, so using them as an excuse was no longer valid.

"They're not the picture of what a marriage should be like, but still." Melanie paused to take a bite of their appetizer. "Marriage is a contract with unwritten rules where you read between the lines. Like, you're supposed to know what the other person wants and needs without them communicating. It doesn't sound appealing."

Reid promised herself she'd never look at marriage the way Melanie did. "Communication is key. Grayson and I have worked on this part of our relationship a lot. We've had to."

"The transplant changed him."

"For the better."

Melanie picked up her glass and held it out for Reid to clink. "Sad to say, but true."

After lunch, they scurried to their spa appointment. They opted for a couples massage, mostly so they could talk, while they both realized drinking a bottle of wine at lunch was probably not the smartest thing they could've done. They were sleepy and fighting to keep their eyes open, yet they still had a nail appointment to get to.

"Honeymoon?" Melanie mumbled groggily.

"Somewhere warm," Reid replied with the same vigor. "Grayson's picking. He's taking the job very, very seriously." She yawned.

"Do you approve his time off?"

Reid tried to laugh, but her masseuse hit a knot in her lower back that made her wince and her toes curl, and not in the good way she preferred. "Oh God," she moaned as hands kneaded and pressed into sensitive skin. "That's going to leave a bruise."

"Sorry," the masseuse said.

Melanie lifted her head and looked over her shoulder at her gal. "Don't let her scare you. I don't care about bruises."

"Sadist," Reid mumbled. "The last thing I need is to explain a bruise to Grayson. He'll worry something is wrong."

"I hadn't thought about that. I guess anything out of the ordinary is a red flag for him?"

Reid nodded as best she could. "He worries, and I'm okay with it. I'd rather let him question everything than ignore things. He's very aware since the surgery."

"Like I've said, you're lucky."

"I know," she said quietly as she closed her eyes and gave in to the massage.

◆ ◆ ◆

The next day, when Grayson was due home in the early evening, Reid and Melanie took a rideshare out to Luther's house to ask about Reid wearing her mother's wedding dress. She expected him to say yes, but she also anticipated some hesitation and tears. Her father had never remarried and rarely dated, even though Reid had encouraged him to get back out there. She adored her father, in all his gruffness, and wanted to see him happy. At one time in her life, she'd tried to set him up with different teachers she'd had, purposely getting into trouble so he'd have to come in and talk to whichever teacher she'd felt would make a great partner for her dad. Her efforts failed. Every single time.

When the girls arrived at Reid's childhood home, her father's truck was parked in the driveway, and any hope she'd had that they might catch him off guard were dashed when they found him weeding the flower beds. They had been her mother's pride and joy. She was always planting, growing, and pruning her prized rosebushes, the flower bed full of pink peonies, and the hedgerow of dahlias, which needed peat moss to help keep the soil well drained. As Reid got out of the car, she saw the pinks, purples, and white of the dahlias and made a note to change the flowers she'd chosen for the wedding. She would honor her mother in every possible way.

"Hey, girls," Luther said as he stood. He took off his work gloves, wiped his hands on his pants, and gave them each a hug. He'd always treated Melanie like a daughter and had opened his home to her many times when her parents were at each other's throats. "To what do I owe the pleasure?"

"Wedding talk, Pops," Melanie said, to which Luther groaned comically.

"Come on in, then. I put a pot of chili on the stove this morning. It's probably about done."

They followed Luther into the home, which indeed smelled like cayenne and chili peppers. His chili was famous and often requested at family gatherings. Reid thought it was because relatives wanted to make her dad feel included but had found out a few years ago it was because he had a secret ingredient. One he refused to divulge.

"Dad, this bouquet is beautiful." Reid spun the vase and marveled at the blue dahlias and cream-colored roses. "Where did you get it?"

"Uh, the front yard," he said sheepishly. "I didn't do anything special. Just snipped, added water, and stuck them in there."

"Pops, it's gorgeous. Don't let the bridal magazines catch on that a big ole softy like yourself is actually a floral designer."

Melanie and Reid giggled as Luther cringed.

He ladled out three bowlfuls of chili and set them on the table before going back for shredded cheese and sour cream. When the girls were younger, Luther used to grate the cheese himself until already-chopped everything began to appear in stores. Now, cooking was easy. Precut everything from onions to carrots, celery, and ginger had been a game changer for most families. They sat down, fixed their bowls the way they preferred, and dug in.

"So good, Pops," Melanie said. "I need the recipe."

Luther only shook his head. Reid figured he'd need to give it up eventually. Until then, she and Mel would have to be patient.

"What's the wedding talk we need to have?" Luther asked in between bites. Reid looked at her dad and saw him scrunch his nose. She couldn't tell if there was something wrong with his lunch, which she doubted, or if he thought there was something wrong with her wedding plans.

"We went dress shopping today," Reid told him. Luther's spoon paused midair before he set it down.

"What store? I'll write you a check before you leave."

"No store. At least not yet," she told him as she placed her hand on top of his. "The thing is, every dress I look at, I don't like. Not even enough to try on."

"I saw on *Extra* that women are getting married in pantsuits these days," he told her. Melanie choked on her chili and began coughing.

"Sorry," she wheezed out. "You caught me off guard, Pops."

"Daddy, I'd like to get married in Mom's dress."

The words soaked in, and Luther's eyes went from quizzical to happy as a smile spread across his face. "Are you sure?"

Tears clouded Reid's vision. "Yes, I am. When I think about wearing her dress, it brings me such joy. It's what I want."

Luther nodded, wiped his mouth on his napkin, and pushed his chair back. He left the dining room and returned minutes later with a large white box. He presented it to Reid. The clear plastic cover gave her a glimpse of her mother's dress. It would need to be cleaned, possibly hemmed, but it was in mint condition. It was the one thing Luther had never let Reid play with when she was younger.

"It's perfect."

Melanie came over to look at the dress. "You're going to be stunning in this dress, Reid. This is the right dress for you."

As Reid stared into the box, she imagined herself walking down the cherry blossom–covered aisle, carrying a bouquet of dahlias and roses from her mother's garden. She looked at her dad. "I have one more favor to ask."

"Anything," he said, visibly holding back his emotions.

"My bouquet," she started. "I know I already ordered it from the florist, but I'd like the flowers to come from Mom's garden. Her dahlias are always so pretty, and I'd like them in my bouquet. The roses, the florist can get from wherever, but I want a majority of my flowers to come from the garden."

"Honey, I think that's a great idea, but it's going to depend on a number of things," he told her. "We would need an early spring in order for them to be ready by your wedding date."

Reid's excitement plunged. By this time next year, she and Grayson would be married. So much of their ceremony depended on spring.

"I hadn't thought of that."

"Pops, what if you propagate and start them in the bedroom—turn it into a makeshift greenhouse or something?" Melanie asked with a shrug.

"That's a possibility. I'll ask one of the gals at work and see if they've done something like that before."

"Would one of these ladies be a date to the wedding?" Reid waggled her eyebrows at her dad, who turned a deep crimson.

"Eat your lunch, Reid." Luther picked up his spoon and shoveled a heap of chili into his mouth, avoiding all eye contact with the girls as they oohed him. Reid intended to send her father an invitation to the wedding, even though he was paying for everything, and would make sure it included a plus-one. All she wanted was for her father to be happy.

Twenty-Nine

Grayson

As soon as the **Remove seat belt** light came on, Grayson was out of his seat and heading toward the bathroom.

He closed the door, slid the lock into place, and then broke down. The tears he'd been holding ever since he'd met Gemma and Lynnea came rushing forward tenfold. He could no longer stop them and was thankful for the roar of the airplane's engines for drowning out his gut-wrenching sobs.

From the moment he'd laid eyes on the girls, he knew they were the reason for the constant ache in his chest. Rafe loved those girls beyond measure, and that love had stayed with his heart, and now Grayson was suffering because of it.

He glanced at himself in the cloudy mirror. Tears streamed down his cheeks. Some created a trail over his jaw and trickled down his neck, while some went straight to his shirt, wetting the fabric.

Grayson felt foolish and heartbroken. Two emotions he had trouble dealing with when mixed together. He shouldn't feel this way about two tiny humans he didn't know, or barely knew, for that matter. Yet when he sat there, enjoying his tea, he felt like he'd known them their entire lives. He loved them. Long before he'd even known they existed. That was the only way he could explain how he felt. They were a part of him, and he had to find a way to stay in their lives.

A knock sounded.

"One minute," he said as he cleared his throat. Grayson stared at himself, hoping every answer he sought would magically appear in the mirror. Nothing was there. Except for a man with red-rimmed eyes, a running nose, and flushed cheeks. There would be no hiding this from Pearce, who'd undoubtedly have questions or give him some type of look that would border on disgust.

Pearce had gone with him for moral support. Had done everything Grayson asked of him, but it was clear he didn't approve. No one could understand how Grayson felt. Waking up every day, knowing something was wrong but not being able to pinpoint what that something was until now. Now he knew, but knowing didn't make things better for him. Not with the distance between him and the girls. And while Pearce had cautioned Grayson about seeing his ex, Nadia wasn't who Grayson wanted in his life; it was Gemma and Lynnea. Their presence made him feel whole. Complete. They were the ache he felt.

Grayson apologized when he came out of the bathroom. He made his way back to the row he shared with Pearce, thankful it was just the two of them and not the dreaded middle seat situation. He sat down and kept his eyes trained on the flight attendants as they served drinks.

"You okay?" Pearce asked.

Grayson nodded and bit his lips to keep his emotions in check.

"Do you want to talk about it?"

He shook his head. After dinner the night before, they'd gone back to the hotel and hadn't discussed their visit with Nadia, Reuben, and the girls. Doing so was the last thing Grayson wanted. He'd told Pearce he was tired and crawled into bed. Instead of sleeping, he'd stared at the ceiling, recounting the encounter. He'd hated leaving but knew they'd already overstayed their intrusion.

Grayson was thankful they were on an airplane and not driving. Their voices would have to be elevated to have a full conversation, and anything he had to say, he wouldn't want others to hear. He didn't care what people said; it was a natural reaction to eavesdropping. Not a day went by when he didn't listen to what others talked about. He knew more about the people on his daily trains and in his office than he cared to.

The flight from Boston to DC was quick. They'd spent more time waiting in the airport for their flight than actually flying. Once the plane landed, they were off and through the terminal as if their asses were on fire. Grayson wanted to get home to Reid. He needed to see her, hold her, and confess. Lying to her and withholding his true intentions of taking the guys' weekend weighed heavily on his conscience. He'd made a promise to himself when he pursued her to always be honest. It was the easiest thing he could do with her.

Grayson and Pearce took the subway together until they needed to switch lines. Pearce hugged his friend, patted him on the back, and told him to call if he needed anything. He wouldn't call. Pearce might be his best friend, but Grayson sensed he couldn't grasp the magnitude of how Grayson felt. He didn't blame him at all, especially when he couldn't fully understand things himself.

When he arrived at the apartment complex, he opted for the stairs. He took each flight slowly, delaying the inevitable. Reid would be ecstatic to see him, but she'd notice right away that something wasn't right. She'd instantly think he was sick, or something had happened to his heart. She'd be right, but for the wrong reasons. As Grayson approached their door, he knew he'd tell her everything.

Before he slipped his key into the lock, he paused and listened. Soft music played from their apartment, and he imagined her dancing, and likely pouring them a glass of wine. Reid would've made or at least ordered them dinner, having it there by the time Grayson told her he'd be home. If this were a normal homecoming, they'd share a meal, and then he'd take her into the shower with him, unwilling to spend any more time alone. He'd make love to her there, using his height as an advantage when it came to shower sex. After the shower, he'd take her to bed, where they'd be a little freer with their lovemaking.

But this wasn't a normal homecoming.

Tonight, they'd sit at the table, their wine going untouched, their food turning cold while he spilled his guts about his trip, who Nadia was, and how happy he'd been when he saw the girls for the first time and how heartbroken he'd been when he left them. Grayson had to find a way to express to Reid how none of this had anything to do with her and how it had everything to do with the heart he'd been given.

A heart he hadn't asked for.

Before he turned his key, he closed his eyes and pictured Reid, loving and patient with him. In his mind, he saw her cry. Could feel her sadness, and he hated himself for what he was about to do.

He opened the door slowly. Reid was in the hallway and turned, her smile starting off slowly but spreading wide as they made eye contact, and then it dropped. She rushed to him, placing her hands on his cheeks and peering into his eyes.

"Grayson, what is it?"

He shook his head slightly and pulled her into a hug. As much as he tried to fight back the tears, he couldn't.

"You're scaring me," she mumbled into his shirt. "Are you hurt? Do you need a doctor?"

"No," he told her. A doctor couldn't fix what was going on. Without turning, he reached back and shut their door, then took her hand and led her to the couch. He sat heavily, with a sigh, which released none of the tension he felt.

Grayson cleared his throat and held on tightly to her hand. "I need you to listen to what I'm about to tell you. I need to get this all out, and then I can answer all your questions and talk about everything. The first thing I want to say, though, is that I love you and can't wait to be your husband."

Reid smiled, but it didn't reach her eyes. He couldn't imagine what was going through her mind right now.

"Do you remember the day you went shopping with my mom?"

Reid nodded.

Grayson recounted his actions from looking online at obituaries, to expanding his search, to when he'd come across the article about Nadia's husband—who she was to him, and how he'd gone and seen her.

Reid pulled her hand away from his.

"You went and saw her?"

He nodded as tears welled.

"Did you . . ." Reid swallowed hard. "Ch-cheat on me?" She could barely get the question out without losing her voice.

His eyes went wide and his body rigid. "What? God no, Reid." Grayson moved closer and reached for her. "I am so in love with you. You're my whole world and the reason I am here today. If it wasn't for you . . ." He trailed off. He often thought about that day. He didn't remember everything from it, but Reid had told him the story and how she'd planned to start dating because she needed to move on from the limbo she'd been in where Grayson was concerned.

"Nadia's an ex, nothing more. When we went off to college, that was it. I never pined over her or tried to win her back. I've only ever loved one woman in my life, aside from my mom, and that's you, Reid."

She looked at him and said nothing.

"I went there. I stood where Rafe died, hoping to experience or feel something that would ease the feeling in my chest. When I saw her, my heart didn't soar like it does when I see you. It was like seeing an old friend who, if I hadn't seen her, I wouldn't have missed, if that makes sense."

"A little," she said.

Grayson inhaled. "When I saw her daughters . . . *his* daughters, everything shifted. I wanted to cry, to weep, as if I'd experienced the most profound loss of my life. This"—Grayson put his fist over his heart—"space is yours and theirs. I can't explain it, other than what Dr. Littleton said about cellular memory. My heart—*his* heart—misses those little girls."

"You don't even know if you have this man's heart, Grayson." Reid got up from the couch and went into the kitchen. Grayson gave her a minute and then followed. He stood, leaning against the wall.

"I wish I could let you feel what I feel. I wish there was a way for you to know how seeing and loving you every day makes me feel, but also being with them took away the ache."

Reid stood at the stove, stirring the sauce in the pan. "So, you're what, going to play dad to them, and I'm going to do what? Share you with your ex? Like, I'll get you two weeks out of the month?"

He wiped at his fallen tears. "No, Reid. Nothing like that, but I need to know them. To be in their life somehow. For the first time in a year, I felt complete."

Her head snapped up, and she froze. Before she'd even turned and looked at him, he knew she was crying. "I'm supposed to be enough, Grayson," she said, pointing at her chest. "We are supposed to be enough for each other." Her hand motioned between them.

"You are."

"But I'm not." Her lower lip quivered. "They make you feel complete. Two strangers."

"It's not the same," he told her. "I can't explain it, but that feeling like something is wrong wasn't there when I was with them." Grayson moved closer. "I sat with them, listened to them tell me about their dad, how he died and how they felt. We had a tea party. They embraced me. Made me matter in their world."

"I'm sure they were being polite," Reid said.

He shook his head. "This was different."

"You want it to be different so you'll have an answer. You need it to be different so you can justify what you're telling me." Reid pushed past Grayson, heading into the other room.

"Reid."

She spun around. "Why did you withhold the reason for your trip?"

Grayson hadn't expected her to ask, although he should've. He ran his hand through his hair, tugging at the ends. "Because I wanted to make sure my hunch was right."

"And you couldn't share that with me?"

"I thought you'd talk me out of it."

"Does your ex know why you randomly showed up at her house?"

He shook his head slowly.

"Right, so you lied to the both of us. That's lovely, Grayson." Reid moved farther away from him. "You know what, you're right. I would've talked you out of it, because what you did is wrong. You don't lie to the people you love, and you certainly don't show up at someone's house under the guise of being in town and wanting to pay your respects. I don't know what's worse, lying to me or lying to a grieving wife and two little girls."

"I know and I'm sorry, Reid. I truly am. The last thing I want to ever do is hurt you. Or Nadia and the girls. It's just . . ." Grayson trailed off.

"It's just what, Grayson?"

He didn't know how to answer her.

"Do you plan to see her again?"

"It's not Nadia who I want to see," he told her. "It's the girls. My heart, this heart." Again, he placed his hand over his chest. "It belongs to you. To the girls, Gemma and Lynnea. Not Nadia."

She stood there, looking at the ground with her arms crossed over her chest. Grayson took timid steps toward her, afraid she'd bolt out of the room, out the front door, and out of his life. He regretted not telling her.

"That's the crux of the matter, isn't it, Grayson? That's not your heart." Reid choked on her words as tears fell down her cheeks. "The one you had before, the one you swore loved me, but you were too in your head to make a commitment. The one you lied to me about . . . that one." She pointed to his chest and shook her head. "This one doesn't love me. So, here we are again. Right back to the beginning, just another excuse."

"That's not true, Reid. You have my heart. All of it. But those girls have a piece as well. Maybe the feelings will go away or change, but right now I feel heartbroken because I'm not with them."

"That's great, Grayson."

"My feelings are about them, Reid. Not you. I'm solid there. I'm in love with you and I have been for as long as I can remember."

"You don't lie to the people you love, Grayson." She stepped away from him. "I need some space." With that, she picked up her purse and walked out the front door.

Thirty

Reid

It had been two weeks since Grayson had gone to Boston and come back with a somewhat life-altering confession. After she'd walked out, she'd gone to the park and sat at the playground, where she watched families play. Some children were there with both parents, some with a mom or dad or someone who could've been a babysitter. What Reid did was imagine the mom who was there, pushing her young son on the swing and then taking him down the slide, as Nadia. Reid would refer to Grayson's ex by her name because she was more than his ex, and she suspected they'd know each other before too long. If Reid and Grayson were going to stay together, and if he insisted on being in the girls' lives, he'd have to come clean to Nadia.

The young woman with the baby kept Reid's attention. She watched how she doted on the boy, showering him with hugs and kisses, and not making a big deal when he fell. He didn't cry but showed her his hand, which she kissed, apparently making it all better.

Reid barely remembered her mom, and of what she did remember, she wasn't sure if they were her real memories or stories she'd heard over the years. Countless times, her grandmother or one of her aunts would start a story with "When your mom . . ." or "Your mom used to . . . ," and those stories had somehow turned into moments Reid remembered as happening. The mind is funny that way, creating falsehood and blurring the lines between what's real and what's not.

Sort of like how Grayson felt with his heart. There was very little scientific proof to back up his claim, or others' assertion that cellular memory existed. Reid had done her own research after Grayson told her about Boston. She searched every keyword she could think of, read every article, and scoured the bookstores for reading material on the subject. Very few existed, which scared her in ways she hadn't imagined. Her mind told her Grayson was imagining things or making up answers for whatever validation he sought. It also made her think that he could become a test subject, for that matter, and she didn't like that. What he felt was personal to him and his experience, and she wasn't sure it needed to be shared. At least not with the outside world.

While she sat there, her phone rang, pulling her from her musings as she watched a stranger interacting with a child. Grayson's photo filled her screen. Her finger rested on the silence button as she contemplated whether she wanted to talk to him or not. If she sent him to voicemail, he'd continue to call or text. She answered.

"Are you okay?" he asked her.

She thought for a moment at the open-ended question. Physically, she was fine. She wasn't hurt or in any danger that she knew of. Emotionally, she was a wreck and confused, and she didn't know how to process everything Grayson had told her. Reid wanted to support him, but she thought he'd gone too far.

"I'm okay, Grayson."

"Where are you? Can I come to you?"

She said yes before she could stop the word from coming out. Every fiber of her being wanted to be with him, near him, even though her heart and mind conflicted with one another.

"I'm at the park. Where the playground is."

"I'll be there in a minute."

He hung up. It would take him ten to get there. She called Melanie. When she answered, she told her everything as fast as she could. All

Reid wanted was a little bit of advice on how to handle the situation or move forward.

"Wait, did he hook up with her?"

"No," Reid told her. She believed Grayson when he'd said he hadn't cheated, and she had no reason to say otherwise. Even before they were dating, he'd rarely dated other women, and the few times when he had gone out, he'd end up crashing at her place or calling her when he'd arrived home far too early for a date to be over.

A cheater he wasn't.

What he'd done was so out of character for him that there was no way she wouldn't forgive him, but it wouldn't be easy.

"What do I do?" she asked Melanie.

"Shit if I know," she told her. "I mean, my first inclination is to kick his ass out, but what if this is real, Reid? Like, what if what he's feeling is a legit thing?"

"That's what I'm worried about. What if he wants to be with them? He has a history with her, and now there are these two girls who lost their dad, who apparently have a hold on Grayson. Where does that leave me?"

"I don't know, sweetie. But you definitely have to talk to him. Let him know you're scared. Maybe you should go with him to one of his therapy appointments. A third-party professional will be able to give you more advice than little ole me. I'm the 'dump first and ask questions later' type, which is why I'm the old maid of honor at your wedding."

Reid smiled at what Melanie said. "He's coming this way," she told her friend. "He called, and I told him where I was. As much as I want to stay mad at him, I can't. But I'm scared."

"Grayson loves you, Reid. I highly doubt he'd do anything to jeopardize your relationship. And if he does, he'll be looking for that new heart at the bottom of the Potomac. Believe me, this would be a surgery he'd feel because I wouldn't put him under."

"Brutal."

"Look, you know how I feel. You waited for this dude. If he messes up, he deserves whatever comes his way. I'll remind you of what you told me: communication is key."

"It is, and he lied."

"So, get him on the lying part and help him figure out the rest. Just tell him, no more secrets."

"He's here—I'll call you back."

Grayson approached the bench where she sat. Instead of sitting down, he cupped her cheek and pressed his lips to hers. The kiss was tender but spoke volumes. "I love you," he said as he sat down next to her. She never took her eyes off him.

"Of all the places, why here?"

Reid shrugged and found herself moving closer to him when he placed his arm behind her. "I don't know. I was in the park, heard laughter, and came over. I've been people-watching."

"Anything interesting?"

"Not really. I guess I thought if I watched the other parents with their kids, I'd be able to understand what you've told me."

"And do you?"

She looked into his eyes and shook her head. "No, and I'm sorry for that. I think your situation is unique. You were given this gift of life, and with that came a lot of changes. Not only physically but personally as well. I can't help but wonder—if you knew you were getting a new heart and had gone through the required therapy beforehand, would this still be a thing?"

"I don't see how it wouldn't be," he told her. "I've come to terms with my own mortality. At first, yeah, I was angry, scared, and felt unworthy. But this feeling, it didn't start right away. Or maybe it did, and I chalked it up to those jabs of pain the doc said I'd get. The best I can liken it to is being homesick or going on a long vacation and being eager to get home. Those little girls are home, in the sense it's what my heart needs to heal. It's a testament to the type of man and father he was, who I want to be. For all I know, they need it too. I looked up those heart bears or whatever they're called. I could do that for them eventually. Give them back a piece of their father."

"You make it sound like you intend to be a part of their lives, Grayson."

"I do," he told her. "And I'm hoping you'll be with me."

She shook her head and looked off into the distance.

"Reid, will you talk to me, please?"

Her head turned instantly, and her eyes glared. "Like you talked to me about all of this before you acted? Before you stopped to consider how I'd feel?"

"I—this isn't about you, it's about—"

"It's about us, Grayson," she said, pointing between them. "We are supposed to be doing all of this together, remember? Because before it was you and it was me, and then you promised me things, and now you're . . ." She trailed off and wiped angrily at her wet cheeks.

"I'm what?"

Reid couldn't look at him. Not now. "You're pushing me away. Giving me these excuses, and I fear they're not going to stop, that you'll come up with something else in a few months, and we'll be right back to where we are now—me not trusting you fully—and I hate that feeling, Grayson." She looked at him and pointed. "You've put these thoughts into my head, when I thought everything was good, that we were solid, and now I feel like I'm on the outside, crumbling because you have these other feelings. Feelings I'm afraid you're going to act on, and then what?"

"Sully, I love you. More than I even know how to describe," he told her. "These feelings I have, they're in addition to what I feel for you. I want you to share in this journey with me, to be there and learn as I go. This isn't something I want to exclude you from. But if I don't try to figure them out, I'm going to be sad. This thing keeping me alive yearns for those little girls, Reid. I don't know how to shut that off."

They sat there for a long time, saying nothing. Each wiping away at their own fallen tears. A ball rolled toward them, and Reid watched it while Grayson bent and picked it up. He handed it back to the little boy who'd come running after it, and he received a toothy thank-you. Grayson was kind, always had been. Part of this made sense, but she couldn't wrap her mind around it. Not without thinking she would lose in the end.

She finally broke the silence between them. "I need time."

"Away from me?" he said, his voice cracking.

Taking time away from him would be the smart thing. Reid shook her head. "No, not from you, but from whatever happened in Boston. I can't jump in with both feet, not yet, at least, and maybe never. I need you to respect my stance on this."

Grayson nodded.

Reid fiddled with the ring on her finger and contemplated whether it should come off or not. How would she get over this obstacle? She wasn't sure she could, and she definitely wasn't sure she could share Grayson with the children of his donor.

She had a lot of soul-searching to do, but so did Grayson.

Over the last fourteen days, coming to the park every day had become a habit. Now that the days were longer, she came after work and watched people interact with their children. She was sure they thought she was some type of stalker and not some woman who enjoyed the chaotic atmosphere. This was something she had to do alone. It gave her a reprieve from Grayson and the situation they were in.

She recalled the conversation about Boston, what Melanie had said, and Grayson. Reid had shut the door on bringing it up until she was ready. Every day and night, she worked scenarios through her mind, switching positions with Grayson, with her being the one with the new heart and experiencing these feelings. Each time, she came back to the same conclusion: she'd want the same thing as him.

Then why was it so hard to accept?

Reid knew why.

Because she was afraid.

Afraid of losing Grayson.

Herself.

What they had become.

What if his heart rejected her?

The thought crippled her. Worse now than before. She was scared she wouldn't fit in his life anymore, that there would be no space for her.

Was her fear irrational?

No. There wasn't anything stopping him from pushing her away again.

But would he?

No. Grayson loved her.

When dark clouds rolled overhead, everyone scrambled. Reid walked briskly to the apartment she shared with Grayson, knowing he'd be home. She'd barely made it up the stairs to the entrance of the complex before the sky opened, thunder cracked, and sheets of rain fell as if someone stood above her dumping water from a bucket.

Inside their apartment, Grayson stood at their sliding glass door, looking out, wearing nothing but her favorite pair of gray sweatpants. They had a view. It wasn't anything spectacular, but it was theirs, and they enjoyed it.

Reid set her bag down and slipped out of her shoes, padding over to him. She slipped her arms around his waist and pressed open-mouthed kisses to his back. Grayson shivered.

"I'm very happy you're not soaking wet," he said as he brought her hand to his lips. After he kissed it, he turned and pulled her into his arms. The scar down the center of his chest rested at eye level. The only time she purposely touched it was during their lovemaking; otherwise she steered clear because his nerve endings were tender and her touch caused an unwelcome sensation to spread.

"I made it inside in the nick of time, which is good because I don't have my umbrella, and I'd be sad if I ruined my shoes."

Grayson bent and kissed her. She opened to him and put her arms around his neck, holding him to her. She'd never tire of kissing him, or being with him, and hated that they had this dark cloud looming over them. Regardless, she couldn't help how she felt.

"How was the park?"

"Enlightening," she told him as she stepped back and looked at him. She shook her head and sighed. "You and gray sweatpants should be illegal. I guess it's a good thing you're inside and not out walking among the masses."

Grayson winked and adjusted himself, which she rolled her eyes at. Reid went and sat on the couch, patting the cushion next to her. He sat and pulled her legs over his.

"What's on your mind?"

"How'd you know something was on my mind?"

"I know you, Reid," he said as he pushed hair behind her ear. "I can almost see the wheels turning in your head. What's up? You can say whatever it is you need to say. I can take it."

She opened her mouth to speak, but he held his hand up. She cocked her eyebrow at him.

"I can take anything you have to say, unless you're telling me it's over—then I refuse to listen."

Reid batted his hand away. "It's not over, but I do have something to say," she told him. "I know it's been two weeks since I told you I needed some space away from the situation. Every day I've thought about us, the past year, the past month. How you've expressed your feelings on the matter, how I have. I can never tell you I know what you're going through or how you feel, because I don't."

"Knock on wood." Grayson leaned over as far as he could and rapped his knuckles on the side table.

"Right, but that doesn't mean I don't feel, or I'm not affected by all of this. It took me two weeks to figure out what it is I'm feeling. Needless to say, I'm ashamed and have honestly never felt this way before."

Reid adjusted herself so she could see Grayson better. "My hesitation in accepting that you want a relationship with the girls is fear. Fear you'll want to be with them and not me. That you'll push me away or keep things from me if I don't learn to love this side of you. Fear I won't fit in your life anymore," she said with a shuddering breath.

"You fit right here." He took her hand and placed it over his heart. "This beats for you," he told her. "And those girls, but not in a way you think. This thing keeping me alive beats for them because it's tied to their father. But you own it. They're not taking me away from you. As for Nadia, I'm not interested in her. Not even remotely. I can't imagine the pain I'd be in if I left you. I'm not sure the ticker would survive. You're the only one I think about being with, day and night. I love you, Reid. I plan to be your husband in less than a year. We're going to have babies and grow old together."

"I hate to break it to you, but I'm going to be twenty-nine forever."

Grayson laughed and kissed her. "I love you."

"I love you," she replied.

"Are we good?"

Without hesitation, she nodded. "We are, but I reserve the right to question everything."

"I wouldn't have it any other way."

After dinner, they lay on the couch together, with Grayson's long form positioned behind Reid. Some reality show was on, but she was focused on his fingers circling lazily on her hip, and slowly making their way under the waistband of her shorts. She yawned and snuggled closer to him, loving the way his body kept her warm.

"Do you want to go to bed?" His lips were near her ear when he asked.

"I do, but I'm not tired."

"Me neither." He rose and held his hand out for her, only to have his phone ring.

Reid saw Nadia's name before Grayson could pick his phone up. Not that he'd hide anything from her. He sat down on the couch.

"Don't lose any of those not-tired thoughts," he told Reid and then put his arm around her, pulling her into his side.

"Hello?"

"Hi, Grayson." Lynnea's voice fluttered through the receiver.

"Hey, what's up?"

"Nuffin'," she said. "When do you come here?"

"I don't know. Why?"

"Can you take me to the father-daughter dance?"

Reid's heart sank. The romantic in her wanted him to go, while the logical part wanted Nadia to control what her daughter was up to.

"Where's your uncle Reuben, isn't he taking you?"

"Yes, but he's taking Gemma, and I will go wif you."

Reid saw Grayson's Adam's apple bob as he swallowed. He struggled to hold back emotions that didn't belong to him. It wasn't his heart making him feel this way; it was the donor's. Reid could see this.

"Where's your mom? Does she know you're calling me?"

"No," Lynnea said quietly. "I pressed your name."

"It's okay to call me, Lynnea. But you have to ask your mom first."

"Oh. Can you take me to school tomorrow?"

"I don't live there, sweetie. Remember, I live near your grandparents."

"Wif Weid?"

Reid covered her mouth when she heard Lynnea say her name.

"Yep, with Reid." Grayson reached for her hand. "Where's your mom?"

"Outside."

"Okay, let me talk to her."

The phone jostled and then went silent. "She hung up," Grayson said as he stared at the black screen. "Nadia mentioned she was a little troublemaker."

"Is Reuben not nice?"

Grayson shrugged. "He's fine. Young. Filling the parental role right now. He moved from Arlington to Boston to help Nadia. He's not the problem—Gemma is. The girls are very opposite and butt heads."

He stood and took Reid with him. "Where are we going?"

"Uh, to bed, because neither of us are tired." Grayson winked.

"Oh."

Instead of allowing her to walk, he picked her up. "When I tell you that you're the most important person in my life, I mean it. Am I upset by the call? Yes," he said as he carried her to the room. "Do I want to love on you right now? Also yes."

They fell onto the bed together. Reid scooted onto her side. "You're going to go there, aren't you?"

Grayson said nothing.

She ran her fingers through his hair. "I need you to do something."

"Anything."

"I want you to tell Nadia, and tell her the truth, Grayson. Either call her before you go or tell her when you're there. In private. Tell her what you think and how you came to this conclusion and what her girls already mean to you. As much as I love you, you're being incredibly selfish. They're grieving. Nadia lost her husband, and those little girls lost their father. I know you feel a connection, and Lynnea does as well. However, what if you just happened upon them at a time when they were susceptible, and looking for someone to cling to?"

Reid sat up and added, "Have you thought about what happens if you don't have Rafe's heart?"

To her surprise, Grayson nodded. "I think about it daily, but then I think about those girls and . . . it's so hard to explain, Reid. Do you know how you felt when I had the heart attack, and you didn't know whether I was going to make it?"

She nodded.

"Take that feeling and magnify it. Before I met them, I dreamed of faceless beings and woke up crying, and I couldn't explain it. I knew something was wrong, but I didn't know what until I saw them. And then I realized there wasn't anything wrong, just missing this piece to make me whole."

"But not complete?"

Grayson ran his fingers down the side of her face. "You make me complete, Sully."

"I hate knowing there are secrets out there. She needs to know that you believe you have her husband's heart. Not telling her is deceiving her. It's deceiving the girls, and it's honestly setting them up for more heartbreak."

"I can give you every excuse possible, like it's too soon or it might be too much for Nadia to bear. Honestly, I think you're expecting me to say those things."

Reid nodded.

Grayson sighed. "I don't know if I'm ready to say those words to her, but I will."

"When?"

"After the dance," he said. "I don't want to ruin the night for them."

Reid lay back down next to him.

"What if she tells me I can't see the girls?" he asked quietly.

She turned and faced him, seeing the pain in his eyes. "Then you listen to what she tells you, and you respect her decision."

"That would break my heart," he told Reid.

"And you could break theirs."

THIRTY-ONE

NADIA

When Nadia came in from watering the front lawn, she caught Lynnea on her phone. The girl's eyes went wide with horror as she dropped the phone and ran for her room. Nadia picked it up, saw Grayson's name on the screen, and froze. She glanced toward the upstairs and, in a panic, ended the call.

Maybe he didn't answer. Either way, her youngest was going to pay for sneaking her phone. Not only that, but for calling Grayson.

After his surprise visit, which had really caught her off guard and elated her at the same time, the girls confided to her that they really liked Grayson and said he reminded them of their father. Nadia cried for days at the revelation. While she'd been excited to see him after all these years, she never wanted the girls to replace their father. Just as she had no intention of ever bringing someone home or remarrying. But having Grayson there, even for a day, had brought so much joy to Gemma and Lynnea. When he left, he promised to come back very soon and made sure Nadia had his number programmed in her phone. He told the girls they could call him whenever their mom would allow. It seemed Lynnea had taken that invitation to heart and forgot she needed permission.

Nadia climbed the stairs and knocked on Lynnea's door. She heard rustling, but no answer. "Lynnea, may I come in?"

"Lynnea doesn't live here," a mousy little voice said.

"Oh no, she doesn't? She didn't say goodbye. I'm going to miss her so much. Do you know where she went?"

"No." This time the voice had changed to a deeper squeak.

"Oh well, now I'm sad. If you see Lynnea, can you tell her that her mommy loves her so very much?"

There was some movement in the room. The knob twisted, the door swung open, and Lynnea launched herself into her mother's arms. "Oh, you're here," Nadia said as she hugged her. "I thought I'd lost you forever."

"I was just foolin', Mommy."

"That makes me so happy." She carried Lynnea into her room, shut the door, and sat them both down on her bed. Nadia held her youngest on her lap and stroked her hair. "Now, do you want to tell me why you called Grayson without asking me?"

Lynnea shook her head and then buried her face into her mother's shoulder. Nadia continued to hold her, missing the moments when she was smaller and she could carry her everywhere. She'd give anything to go back in time, to experience some of her favorite memories. To see her husband again. To feel his arms around her.

Nadia still hadn't cleaned out his side of the closet or emptied his dresser. She didn't know when she'd be ready to remove him completely from her life. When Kiran had come over, pretending to be in the area but really to check on her, she'd asked him if he wanted anything of Rafe's. He'd declined but asked for the right to change his mind later, and she'd agreed. It all made sense to her. Each morning, she woke up and stared at the empty side of the bed, praying it was all a dream. She knew it wasn't, but she had hope.

"Did Grayson answer when you called?"

She nodded, and Nadia's anxiety skyrocketed. She'd hung up on him and would have to apologize not only for that, but also for whatever Lynnea had said to him.

"What did you and Grayson talk about?" Nadia tried a different tactic.

"The dance."

Her heart hit the floor with a thud. Last year, she'd ignored the father-daughter dance. The event had happened so close to Rafe's passing that there was no way she could've had the energy to get Gemma ready or even suggest she attend. Her grandfather easily would've taken her, or any of her uncles, but Nadia hadn't been in any frame of mind to get the ball rolling. So, Gemma had missed it, which had added more heartache and devastation to an already brokenhearted girl.

"At your school?"

Lynnea nodded. She was old enough to go this year, but Nadia hadn't given it much thought. Reuben had said he would take Gemma, and that was that. She'd never stopped to think that Lynnea would want to go. She supposed that, had Rafe been there, he would've taken both girls. She'd assumed Reuben would do the same.

"I'm sure Uncle Reuben is taking you. We just haven't talked about it."

"I don't want to go wif him and Gemma."

But you would've gone with your dad and Gemma.

What was the difference?

"Do you want to go with Uncle Lars? I can call him. Or Kiran?"

Lynnea shook her head.

"What about Grandpa Otto?"

Another shake.

She could ask her father, but she didn't necessarily want him traveling that far for a two-hour dance. "Honey, is this why you called Grayson?"

Lynnea snuggled impossibly deeper into Nadia's shoulder, almost as if she was embarrassed. Nadia nudged her and worked to pry Lynnea's viselike hands off her neck. "I want to see your pretty face," she told her daughter, who reluctantly let go. "Ah, there's my beautiful girl. Did you call Grayson because of the dance?"

Lynnea nodded.

"I see. You know he lives by where I grew up, by Grandma and Grandpa. He's not in Boston."

"I know," she said as she fiddled with the blankets on her bed.

"He can't just stop his life and come here, Lynnea. Besides, he . . ." She trailed off. The last thing he'd said when he left was to call him with whatever the girls needed. Not her, which she'd found odd. It was like he'd singled out the girls for a reason. It could be that he thought they needed their own person for moral support or something. She'd seen how they'd bonded during the tea party, and the girls were incredibly upset when he'd left that night.

"Why do you like Grayson?"

Lynnea shrugged. "He's warm like Daddy, and they smell the same."

Nadia hadn't even noticed if they wore the same cologne, which she found odd, because the cologne Rafe had worn—he'd worn it because she'd bought it for him—was her favorite scent. She'd recognize it anywhere, and yet she couldn't recall smelling it on Grayson.

"I get that you like Grayson. I like him too—"

"Is he going to be my new daddy?"

Nadia gasped. "Wh-what? No. Why would you say that?"

Lynnea shrugged and once again burrowed into her mother. "He's just like Daddy," she mumbled. Lynnea's tears wet Nadia's shirt, and she held her daughter tighter. She was having a hard time grasping the notion that the girls thought Grayson was like Rafe. They were nothing alike. Not in looks, mannerisms, or even attitudes. When she'd dated Grayson, he was noncommittal, aloof, and very much "go with the flow," unless it didn't suit him. This was what had made it so easy to break things off with him when she'd left for college. She'd been right to do so because that was where she'd met Rafe, who was the opposite of Grayson. Rafe was daring and adventurous, and when he put his mind to something, he worked at it until he'd achieved his goals. Not once had she missed Grayson, and even now, if she didn't see or hear from him again, it wouldn't be the end of the world. But something told her that he wasn't going to let that happen, and neither were her children.

"Sweetie." Nadia rubbed Lynnea's back. "No one can ever replace your daddy." As she said the words, it hit her. Lynnea would have very few memories of Rafe—and that gutted Nadia. She inhaled deeply and vowed to *always* talk about Rafe, even if she ever dated or remarried. Rafe would always be at the forefront. It was the least she could do as his wife and the mother of his children.

Lynnea lifted her head. She had her thumb in her mouth. A habit she'd picked back up after Rafe died but seemed to have stopped on her own. As much as Nadia wanted to tug on her hand, she didn't. She hated seeing it, but it brought Lynnea comfort, and that was important. "Eber?"

"Ever," Nadia said as she tapped the tip of Lynnea's nose with her index finger. "Your daddy is irreplaceable. He will always live on in your heart."

"I miss him."

"I know you do, sweetie. I miss him more than words can even describe."

They sat there hugging until Gemma came upstairs. She was covered in dirt, head to toe, after spending some time in the flower beds. Ever since she'd taken charge of the weeding, it had become her thing. Nadia appreciated the help and loved that they all had a thing to do together.

"Looks like you need a shower," Nadia said to Gemma.

She nodded. "Look, I have dirt under my nails, and I wore gloves. I just don't get it." She threw her hands up in the air in exasperation.

Nadia laughed and reached her hand out to her, pulling her into her side. "I love you girls so much." She held them as long as she could, thankful that neither of them squirmed. Somehow, they knew when she needed their love and affection. Their lives easily could've gone south, down a hole of depression, but somehow the three of them were pulling through.

"Come on," Nadia said as she stood. "Gemma, you go hop in the shower while your sister and I go make dinner."

"Uncle Reuben and Kiran are making it."

"Kiran's here?"

Gemma nodded. "Yep, he brought beer and steaks," she said, shrugging. "We can't have his beer, though, so he brought us our own beer."

"I want beer!" Lynnea shouted, while Nadia cringed. There wasn't a doubt in her mind, or Rafe's, for that matter, that Lynnea would end up being their wild child, the one to keep them up all night when she went on her first date or lied about going to a sleepover when she was really going to a party. Nadia knew all the tricks, thanks to Sienna, and she hadn't forgotten a single one of them. The bonus when Nadia and Rafe had bought their house was that all the bedrooms were on the second floor, and while the girls had emergency fire ladders, she hoped they wouldn't use them to sneak out. Because sneaking out was exactly what Nadia had done. Maybe it was a rite of passage.

With Gemma in the shower, Nadia and Lynnea headed down to the kitchen and out to the back deck, where Reuben sat at the table and Kiran grilled. He looked over his shoulder at her and smiled before she could even say hello. Reuben smirked, let out a quick chuckle, picked up his bottle, and took a sip.

"This is a surprise," Nadia said.

"I was in the neighborhood," Kiran told her.

"With dinner?"

Kiran smiled sheepishly and shrugged.

Did Reuben's smirk mean something?

Nah, there's no way. Kiran was Rafe's best friend.

But what if?

Nadia shook her head and rejoiced as her phone rang. She pulled it from her back pocket and then showed the screen to Lynnea, whose eyes widened. "Hi, Grayson."

"Everything okay?"

"Yes, I'm sorry Lynnea pranked you."

"She and Gemma can call whenever they want—you know that."

Nadia did but didn't understand why. How had he bonded so quickly with her children? "I know. She still should've asked for permission."

"It's fine. I just want to make sure everything's okay."

"Yep, we're good. You?"

"Things are good," he told her. "Listen, if it's okay with you, I'm going to come up next weekend. I'll take Lynnea to the father-daughter dance, and I'd like to get a head start on the swing set."

"Grayson, you don't have to."

"I know," he told her. "I want to."

"Reuben can do it," she told him. Or Kiran.

"Anyone can do it, Nadia. Lynnea asked me."

She couldn't fight with that logic, and if it made Lynnea happy, so be it. Grayson said he'd text her with his travel details later, and she was to let him know what color dress Lynnea would wear so he could order a matching corsage.

When she hung up, she looked at her daughter. "Grayson is going to take you to the dance." Lynnea jumped up and down. "However . . ." Nadia's voice had a stricter tone to it. "If you are not on your best behavior, I'll hide his number in my phone, and you won't get to talk to him again."

"Okay, I'll be good."

"Thank you."

Lynnea ran off to tell Gemma about Grayson coming back to visit. Nadia sighed and sat down at the table, between her brother and Kiran, who continued to man the grill.

"Who's Grayson?" Kiran asked. At first, his question caught Nadia off guard, but then she remembered he hadn't been around a couple of weeks back, when Grayson had first come over.

"He's an ex from high school," she said. "He'd heard about Rafe and was in town, so he stopped by."

Kiran looked from Nadia to Reuben. "An ex, huh?"

"Yeah. The girls took a liking to him."

"Is that what we call it?" Reuben asked. "He was like a candle, and they were the moths. It was weird."

"What does that mean?" Kiran asked.

Reuben shrugged.

"He reminds the girls of Rafe," Nadia said. "Which makes zero sense because they look nothing alike."

"Zero similarities, and yet they acted like they've known him their entire lives," Reuben added.

"Huh" was all Kiran could say, and he went back to grilling.

As the girls set the table, Nadia made a salad to go with the chips Kiran had brought for dinner. They sat down, made idle chitchat, and laughed together. The days were getting better for Nadia, but the nights were still hard. She hated going to bed alone, and she truly loathed being in her bedroom. She needed to make a change in there, but each time she thought about it, she wanted to break down and cry. The bedroom had been their sanctuary, a place for them to be with each other without interruption. In there, they could be Nadia and Rafe, two people madly in love with each other from the day they'd met. Their love hadn't died when he'd died, and at times, she wished it had. Loving Rafe had been the easiest and hardest thing she'd ever done.

After dinner and after the girls had gone to bed, Nadia sat outside and stared at the darkened sky. Very few stars shone; thanks to being in the city, stargazing wasn't really a thing. They would need to drive out to the Cape or head inland, away from the bright lights.

The sliding glass door opened, and the chair next to her scraped against the decking. "It's a nice night," Kiran said as he sat next to her.

"It is."

They sat in silence for a long while until she said, "Do you think he's up there, watching us?"

"Yes, but I hope not," he told her.

"You hope not? Why?" She looked over at him and found him staring at her.

Kiran reached for her hand. "Because if he was, then he'd see me holding his wife's hand, and he'd hear me tell his wife that I think she's the most beautiful woman I've ever seen, and when she's ready, I'd really like to take her out for dinner."

Her quick intake of breath couldn't be missed. "Kiran."

"I know, Nadia," he said. "People think it's wrong, the best friend and the widow, but I don't care. Around November, I started having these feelings. I thought they'd stop, but they haven't. I suppose if you tell me you're not interested or we never have a chance, then I'll have to figure something out. I'm willing to wait, Nadia. Until you're ready. That's if you're interested in me."

Nadia absorbed his words. His kindness. She smiled. "I'm interested."

THIRTY-TWO

GRAYSON

Ever since he'd had his heart transplant and returned to work, all Grayson had to do was tell his boss he was stressed and needed a week or so off, and he'd get the time off, no questions asked. It was a ploy, one Reid hated but also encouraged because she knew what would happen if Grayson became too run-down. He really had to coast through life, stress-free. Flying to Boston to spend time with Gemma and Lynnea, under the guise of being there for them, was about as stress-free as he could get. They were like natural endorphins for him.

Grayson booked a hotel as close to Nadia's place as possible. Ideally, staying downtown would've been fun for him, but he wasn't there to be a tourist. He was there to do something Rafe would've done himself, and that was take his daughter to the annual father-daughter dance. The idea of getting dressed up, slipping a corsage on Lynnea's tiny wrist, and setting her feet on his while he twirled them around the room filled him with such pride that he had a perpetual knot in his throat. To make things even better, Reid had been very accepting of him going, but he had an ultimatum from her—tell Nadia the truth, or she would. His gut told him that if Reid was the one to spill the secret, things would be over for him. He couldn't do anything to jeopardize the trust he had with either woman. He also didn't want to hurt the girls.

He showered, then dressed in a black suit with matching blue tie to coordinate with Lynnea's dress. With one last look in the mirror, he picked up the corsage and headed out to his rental. He would drive Reuben and Gemma as well, and the plan was for the men to take their dates out to dinner. The girls had chosen their favorite fast-food place, because apparently no one could go to the dance without a tummy full of nuggies.

Grayson pulled up to the curb, shut his car off, and got out. He took the stairs two at a time and could hear giggling on the other side of the door before he even knocked. His knuckles rapped twice against the wood, and the door opened.

He smiled at Nadia.

"Hello, Mrs. Karlsson. I'm Grayson Caballero. I'm here to escort Miss Lynnea Karlsson to the dance this evening."

Nadia beamed, and more giggles erupted from behind the door. "I do believe she's expecting you. Won't you come in."

None of this was rehearsed, which pleased Grayson. He was happy Nadia was playing along. He stepped in, held the corsage box in front of him, and waited for Nadia to close the door. Lynnea stepped out from behind her mother in a navy blue dress, with sparkles and layers of tulle. Thanks to Reid, he knew what it was. Her blonde hair had been curled and pinned to the top of her head, with ringlets framing her face. From the pictures he'd seen of Rafe, Lynnea was his twin.

"Lynnea, you look beautiful," he told her as he dropped down to one knee and opened the box, which contained two white roses wrapped in navy ribbon. "This is for you," he said as he slipped it onto her wrist. "Reid picked it out for you."

"She did?" Lynnea looked at her flowers and then held her arm up for her mom to inspect. "Look, Mommy. Weid did this."

"They're so pretty. Just like you."

"Reuben got one for Gemma, right?" Grayson asked as he stood. Nadia nodded. He stepped forward and gave her a one-armed hug. "It's good to see you."

"You too. Thank you for doing this."

"You don't have to thank me," he told her. "I want to do this." He left out the part where he *needed* to do this to make his heart feel whole.

Reuben came up from the basement and greeted Grayson. He was dressed in a gray suit with a gray tie. Grayson was about to ask where Gemma was when she started down the stairs dressed in a pale-pink dress with her auburn hair loosely braided. She looked identical to Nadia, and for a moment all Grayson could do was stare and remember the girl he'd dated in high school.

"Hi, Grayson," Gemma said, pulling him from his thoughts.

"Hi, Gemma. You look very pretty tonight."

"Grayson called me 'beautiful,'" Lynnea said as she stuck her tongue out at her sister. Nadia's eyes widened.

She grabbed Lynnea's shoulder and turned her toward her. "Stop that, or you're not going," she told her. "You promised to be good, and this isn't how a young lady is supposed to act. Apologize to your sister."

"Sorry, Gemma."

Nadia shook her head. "Sorry about that," she said to Grayson and Reuben. "She's . . ." Nadia inhaled. "As Rafe would say, 'possessed by a demon.'"

"I am," Lynnea said, nodding enthusiastically at Grayson.

"It's because she watches stupid movies," Gemma said as she rolled her eyes.

"Okay, well, how about we keep the demons locked up for the night so we can enjoy ourselves," Reuben said. He picked up the box on the side table, opened it, and took the corsage out. Gemma held her arm out as if she'd done this a million times. Grayson noted that next year, he'd make sure the corsages matched. He saw Nadia turn Lynnea away before she could say something about how hers had two flowers and Gemma's only had one. Parenting was hard, and he didn't envy Nadia one bit for having to do it alone. For his part, he'd try to ease the burden as much as he could or was allowed.

Grayson insisted that Nadia take pictures of them, as well as of her and the girls. She refused at first, saying she wasn't dressed for photos, but Grayson and Reuben wouldn't take no for an answer.

"I think you should print one or two of these," Reuben told his sister. "Frame them and give one to Mom and Dad. They'd like it."

Nadia looked at her phone. "I think I'll print one now and take it over to Rafe's niche. I'd like him to have it, to show him we're doing okay."

Reuben kissed his sister on the cheek and told the girls to give their mom a hug, and then he and Grayson ushered the girls outside to the car, grabbing their booster seats from the porch.

After Grayson had put Lynnea's booster seat in, he held his hand out for her to grip while she got into the back seat. He helped her fix her dress before she sat down and then reached over to make sure she was buckled in before he shut her door. Reuben did the same for Gemma.

Grayson drove them to McDonald's. Not ideal for him, but he wanted to make sure the girls had the night they wanted. He ordered a salad. It wasn't as tasty as it would've been from a different place, but he smiled, laughed, and ate every bite. Thankful no one questioned his odd order. All Reuben said was "I'm not a fan of this stuff either."

Once the girls' tummies were full of nuggets, the four of them headed to the gym at the elementary school. It had been set up like prom, complete with balloon arches, streamers, and a DJ in the corner. A photographer was taking photos with a custom backdrop. Grayson and Lynnea posed for their photo, and then, at his suggestion, the girls took one with Reuben and then by themselves. If anything, Nadia could use the picture for their holiday card or something. Or he could take it and mess around with it, adding Rafe to the background. Digital arts were his specialty, but he wasn't sure how Nadia would feel about it.

Lynnea and Grayson hit the dance floor. He twirled her around once, causing a fit of giggles, and then she spun around and around as fast as she could, to show him how the tulle of her dress fluffed out when she went in circles. She stopped and almost toppled over from being dizzy. Grayson caught her and told her to put her feet on his. He held her hands and waited, feeling very little pressure. She was light as a feather and wouldn't hurt him. With her settled, he began swaying to the music.

When the song changed, she stepped off and started busting a move on the dance floor. Grayson tried to keep up with his own moves—anything to keep her smiling.

"This is so fun," she yelled over the music. "Can you come next time?" she asked him minutes into the dance.

"Of course."

After a couple of times around the room, Grayson danced with Gemma. She copied her sister and put her feet on his, and he moved them around the dance floor. As the night wore on, Lynnea became tired. For their last dance, Grayson picked her up and held her while they danced. All night long, his heart beat in double time. This was where he was meant to be.

"Thank you," she said groggily.

"You're welcome, Lynnea."

On the way home, they stopped for ice cream; even though Lynnea was barely awake, she was adamant that she could eat an ice cream cone. By the time he'd pulled up to the curb, Lynnea had fallen asleep. Nadia greeted them at the door and led the way to her bedroom.

He laid Lynnea down and kissed her forehead. "Thank you for an amazing night," he said to her before leaving the room. Grayson waited for Nadia at the bottom of the stairs. When she came down, her eyes were watery.

"Thank you for doing this."

"It was my pleasure," he told her. "I had the best time." He kissed her on the cheek, said goodbye to Reuben and Gemma, and headed to his car. He made it as far as the corner before he began crying. The night had been emotional for the girls, and for him, but they didn't know that. All they knew was that their mommy had an old friend who was willing to do stuff with them. How would they feel once they found out the friend had their father's heart beating in his chest?

Would they still accept him?

Would Nadia forgive him for the deceit?

Grayson didn't want to find out. Reid's ultimatum would have to wait. He'd tell Nadia soon. He just needed more time.

The next morning, Grayson was there bright and early. He didn't bother to go to the front door, in case they were sleeping. Out back, he began opening the boxes and reading the instructions on how to put the swing set together. Reuben came out of the house, in sweats and no shirt, hair standing on end.

"You're early, man."

"Yeah, I couldn't sleep."

"Give me a minute or sixty," Reuben said, laughing.

"Take your time."

Nadia or Reuben had already removed the grass where the swing set would go. Once it was built, they'd haul in some straw and sawdust to pad the ground in case the girls fell. And Grayson expected Lynnea to fall a lot. He had yet to see it, but according to Nadia, she was a daredevil, and he pictured her doing some crazy shit off this swing set.

By the time Reuben came back, Grayson had everything laid out. He'd be able to build this in one day and mentally questioned why Reuben was there if he wasn't actually helping with the girls. This should've gone up last year for them, to give them something to do.

Another hour later, Rafe's best friend, Kiran, came over to help or take over for Reuben. Grayson wasn't exactly sure. Not that he cared. He was on a mission to build the girls their play set. Tomorrow, once the cement footings had set for twenty-four hours, they'd be able to swing, slide, climb, and play princesses if that was what they wanted to do.

At lunch, they took a break. Nadia had made sandwiches for everyone. As soon as Grayson sat down, Lynnea crawled into his lap and rested against his chest. He didn't mind, but he did wonder if she somehow knew the heart of the man she loved unconditionally still beat for her.

"Nadia says you guys dated in high school," Kiran said to Grayson.

"Yeah, for about two years?" Grayson looked at Nadia for confirmation.

"No lingering feelings, huh?" Kiran looked at Nadia, who shook her head.

Grayson chuckled. "Nah, there aren't any residual feelings there."

"Grayson's getting married next spring," Nadia said.

"To Weid," Lynnea popped her head up to say. No one had the heart to try and correct Lynnea on the pronunciation of Reid's name. "She's very pretty."

Grayson smiled at Lynnea. "She is, isn't she?"

Lynnea nodded. "Mommy said so too."

Grayson glanced at Nadia, who blushed. "Should we call her?"

Lynnea sat up and nodded quickly. Grayson got his phone out and pressed Reid's contact image and waited for her face to appear on the screen. As soon as she did, his heart raced, and his smile went from ear to ear. He was ridiculously in love with her.

"Hi," he said, almost breathlessly. "Someone wanted to call you." Grayson angled the phone slightly to show Lynnea. She leaned into Grayson and waved.

"Hi, Weid."

"Hi, Lynnea. Did you have the best time last night?"

She nodded. "I twirled a lot."

"Your dress was so pretty. Grayson sent me a photo."

He whispered in Lynnea's ear about her flowers. Lynnea popped up. "Fank you for the flowers."

"You're welcome. I'm glad you liked them."

"So pretty. Like you."

Reid blushed, which Grayson loved. He turned the phone back onto himself. "We just wanted to say hi."

"Hi," she said. "How's the play set coming?"

"Good. I have some help, so it'll be done today. The girls should be able to play on it tomorrow."

"Well, make sure you test it out beforehand."

"I will. I'll call you later tonight. I love you."

"Love you too. Tell everyone I said hi." Reid blew him a kiss. He wanted to be in two places at once but couldn't figure out how unless he brought Reid with him. He was just thankful she'd believed him when he'd told her there wasn't anything going on between him and Nadia. It wasn't her he needed to see. It was the girls. They were the only reason he was there, putting himself through all this.

After he hung up, he watched Kiran and Nadia, with their heads bent together. Kiran was definitely interested in Nadia, and she seemed receptive to the attention he gave her. Grief was a funny emotion. If Grayson went by what Reuben had told him, he'd suspect Nadia wouldn't date until the girls were out of the house. By the looks of things across the table, those two had something going on, and if it wasn't happening now, it was going to happen soon.

Grayson and Kiran tightened the last screw just as the sun went down. Instead of staying for dinner, he told the girls he'd see them tomorrow morning, bright and early. Kiran had asked Grayson if he could help fix some things around the house, mainly cosmetic stuff that Rafe had intended to fix last year. Without hesitation, Grayson agreed. He'd taken off a full week of work to spend with the girls, and he'd do anything Nadia needed him to do. He'd be that person for her until she found someone else, and even if she didn't, Grayson would be the person the girls could count on.

When he climbed into bed, he called Reid. Her face lit up his screen, making him miss her more than anything. "I love you," he said as soon as she said hi.

"I love you too. Are you okay?"

He nodded and wiped at an errant tear. “Lynnea has been very clingy these past couple of days. I don’t mind because her presence makes me feel good.”

“And Gemma?”

“She had a friend over earlier, so she was busy. She also keeps her feelings bottled up. Gemma’s a lot like Nadia that way.”

“Did you tell Nadia yet?”

Grayson paused and cleared his throat. “Not yet. I will.”

“They need to know.”

He closed his eyes. “I know. Can we not talk about that, though? I miss you, Reid. Can you come up here?”

“I’m not sure.”

“Because you don’t want to or because of time off?”

“Both,” she said. “This is still very weird to me, Grayson. I’m trying. I truly am.”

“I know, and I love you for that. I just want you here, next to me. You’d like Nadia.”

“I might have to fight her,” she said, laughing.

Grayson shook his head. “I’m pretty sure she’s interested in Rafe’s best friend.”

Reid’s mouth dropped open. “What?”

“Yeah. I’m not sure, though. Just an observation.”

“How does . . .” She didn’t finish her question.

“Thankfully my heart isn’t tied to her. Just the girls. It’s just them.”

“Odd, don’t you think?”

“I don’t know. The girls are physically part of Rafe. It makes sense, when you think of it that way. I told you, when I saw Nadia, I didn’t feel anything, but those girls. Game changer.”

Grayson hated it when the conversation stilled. He trailed his finger down his screen, pretending it was her face. “Please think about coming.”

“I will. Are you taking your meds?”

He nodded. “Haven’t missed a day.”

"Good. Get some sleep, Grayson. I love you."

"Love you," he said as they hung up.

Grayson scrolled through the photos on his phone, stopping on one of him and the girls. He stared at it, allowing his tears to fall.

They were the only people who mattered in all this.

Grayson would tell Nadia everything. He prayed she'd understand and see what really mattered—the girls—because there wasn't any doubt in Grayson's mind that Rafe's daughters had bonded with him.

And if Nadia told Grayson he could no longer see the girls . . . well, he couldn't think about that now.

THIRTY-THREE

REID

As soon as she hung up with Grayson, she looked at flights and cringed at what one would cost tomorrow. Still, she put her credit card information in and processed the charge, and then got out of bed to pack. She could take a couple of sick days and not have to worry about anything. Besides, she wanted to be with Grayson, and she sensed that he needed her there. He was nervous about telling Nadia the real reason he'd reached out, and Reid wanted to be there to support him. Maybe to even prove Grayson was a stand-up guy, although Nadia should already know that. Reid just wanted to be with him.

She got very little sleep and was at the airport by three in the morning to catch her five o'clock flight to Boston. If she'd planned everything perfectly, she'd be at Grayson's hotel by the time he woke up, surprising him. Of course, for everything to happen as she'd planned, her flight and rideshare would need to be on time. One could hope.

As soon as her flight touched down, she got off the plane as fast as the people in front of her would allow and rushed through Logan, following the signs to the rideshare lot. She dodged people, bumped shoulders, and apologized profusely for being rude. When she finally made it outside, she saw a line of cars waiting for passengers. She got in, gave the address, and then watched the clock like a hawk. Grayson would call her when he woke up, and she wanted to be anywhere but in the back seat of the car.

Reid ran from the car, through the lobby, and into the elevator. She got to his floor and speed-walked until she came to his room number. With her hand poised to knock, the door opened, and Grayson stood there, in shock. Slowly, his face morphed. He didn't ask any questions as he reached for her and brought her into his room.

Grayson spun her around, cupped her face, and pressed his lips to hers. She dropped her bag and pushed her hands under his shirt. He tugged her sweatshirt and shirt over her head and unclasped her bra, freeing her breasts. He pressed his warm hands against her lower back and lifted her off the floor. She hooked her legs around his waist and pulled them even closer together. Grayson cupped her ass in his hands and squeezed. She moaned against his lips.

"I'm so happy you're here," he said in between kisses as he set her down on the bed.

"Me too."

He ran his hands over her smooth body and then sat back on his knees, pulled his shirt over his head, pushed his shorts down his legs, and tugged her favorite yoga pants down her legs, then took off her shoes and tossed everything onto the floor. Reid laughed at his urgency but welcomed it too. He hovered over her, looking into her eyes.

"Best surprise ever," he told her.

"The best." She smiled.

Grayson pressed his lips to hers and then to her neck, stopping to suck on the skin of her neck. She shivered at the sensation. He continued his way down, between her breasts, and then circled each of her nipples with his tongue.

Reid groaned and arched her back, pressing her breasts against his mouth. Grayson took one breast into his mouth, and then the other. He sucked on her nipples until she begged for more, and then he kissed his way back up to her lips. He looked into her eyes and smiled.

"So beautiful," he whispered as he kissed a line down to her belly button. Reid moaned out loud, shifting once again. She tangled her fingers in his dark, soft hair.

He positioned himself at the entrance to her body with one hand while he used the other to hold himself steady against her as he slowly pushed inside her. Grayson swore as he moved his hips, creating a steady rhythm for them, drawing out a slight moan from her as she arched into his movements.

Grayson smirked, which only turned her on more.

"You're so full of yourself," she managed to say in between thrusts.

"No, honey. You're full of me."

She intended to roll her eyes, but instead they fluttered, which resulted in a chuckle from the man doing things to her body that only he could do. He could make her feel like the most beautiful woman in the world when he looked at her, but also make her feel like a vixen when they were together like this. He knew how to make her body do things she'd only read about in books.

They peaked, and as they came down from their euphoric high, sunlight blasted through their window. Reid looked toward the beam of light and gasped. "The curtains were open this entire time!" She scrambled to pull the comforter over her body.

Grayson looked over his shoulder and chuckled. "Oops."

She slapped his chest. "Oops?"

He shrugged and pulled her to his body. "I'm sure no one saw anything, and if they did, they're definitely jealous."

"Of you or me?" Her eyebrow raised.

"Definitely me." Grayson kissed her and seemed ready for another round until his phone rang. He groaned and covered her body with his while he searched the floor for his phone.

"Who is it?"

"Kiran," he told her as he silenced the call. He moved back to his side and tucked her in next to him.

"That's the best friend, right?"

"Yeah, nice guy. I like him. I'm helping him do some stuff around the house—fixing some loose boards, cleaning out the gutters, and doing basic maintenance. Things her brother should've done but hasn't. Which I honestly don't get."

"Maybe he's not handy."

"Maybe, but figure it out." Grayson shrugged. "I can't wait for you to see the neighborhood they live in. It's cute and something I'd like us to work toward."

"You want to move out of the city?"

He nodded. "Eventually. We want to start a family, and while I enjoy what we have, I think kids need a place to play. Yes, there are parks, but yards are nice to have as well."

Reid ran her fingers through his hair. "We should get going."

Grayson groaned again. "Honestly, I'd rather be a tourist today."

"Tomorrow," she said as she kissed him.

"Tomorrow it is, then."

They dressed, grabbed breakfast, and then headed to Nadia's with a dozen doughnuts. Reid was nervous to meet the girls. Grayson was all about the kids and had stressed how important they were to him, which also posed a problem because he still hadn't told Nadia why he was truly there.

Grayson parked along a curb but didn't turn the car off.

"Are we here?"

"No, their house is up the street," he told Reid. "I've been thinking about what you've said and how I need to tell Nadia. I agree with you: she needs to know, but I'm not sure if I can do it alone."

Reid reached for his hand. "You're not alone, Grayson. I'm here, and we can do it together. But it has to be done. No more secrets; no more hiding. Remember what you said to me last year, how you felt like you have a second chance?"

Grayson nodded.

"Don't be upset with what I'm about to say, but you're only taking the 'second chance' part to heart when it conveniences you. That's the same thing the old Grayson did. That guy, he used to hide his feelings and push me away under the guise that he was protecting me. And then you had this miraculous gift given to you, and you wanted to make a change. This part needs to change, Grayson. If you tell me how much those girls mean to you, then be the type of man their father was. Be someone who's open and honest with the people he loves, and accept that they can handle the truth."

Grayson gripped the steering wheel and looked forward.

"Can I ask you something?"

He nodded.

"Besides fearing she'll tell you to take a hike, what are you afraid of?"

Grayson turned and stared at Reid for a long moment. His mouth opened and closed. He went to speak, but his voice cracked. Another minute passed, but it felt like an eternity while Reid waited.

"Rejection," he finally said. "I remember when we first met, I thought you were out of my league." He laughed. "Strike that: you are out of my league. But you liked me, and yet, I was a ticking time bomb. You know there was never the right moment to tell you about my heart. It's not something you bring up when you first meet someone or after you've fallen madly in love with them. I couldn't ever tell you, so I hid it. It was easier that way.

"Now, here I am, hiding it again, because I'm afraid they're going to reject me or find me unworthy of their love or not want mine in return."

Reid brushed her fingers through Grayson's hair. "Want to know something?"

"What's that?"

"They love you without knowing how you came to be in their lives, and something tells me they're going to love you after you tell them. The bond you share will only strengthen."

"You think so?"

"Grayson, deep down, you're a good man. You just take the wrong path to get to the right road."

Grayson sighed. "In hindsight, I wish I'd done things differently. I didn't expect—"

"For this to be what you thought it was?"

He nodded. "Yep. I thought I'd come here and feel nothing. Sometimes, I wish that were the case. Now, I'm attached. I've known them for weeks, and it feels like I've known them their entire lives."

"It'll be hard all around. The best we can do is be honest and go from there."

"Yeah," he said with another sigh. He pulled back onto the street and drove around the corner, then parked in front of a house. Reid stared out the window, noticing not the home but the two girls who lit up as soon as the car parked. They raced down the stairs and ran to the fence.

"Gemma's a bit shy."

"Not Lynnea, though," Reid said.

Grayson nodded. "Don't be jealous of her," he joked. "She really likes me."

Reid laughed. "I'll try to rein it in."

They got out of the car, with Grayson carrying the box of doughnuts. He reached for Reid's hand when he met her on the sidewalk and guided her over to the girls.

"Weid!" Lynnea screamed her name and jumped up and down. She fumbled with the latch on the gate and finally got it open but didn't pass the threshold until Grayson was there. She launched herself at Reid.

Grayson's mouth dropped open, and Reid smirked.

"Hi, Lynnea," Reid said as she gave her a hug. "It's nice to meet you in person."

"Me too. Come on." Lynnea grabbed her hand and started to tug, but Reid told her to wait up a bit.

"Hi, Gemma, it's nice to meet you as well." Reid held out her hand.

Gemma stared at it for a moment and then looked at Grayson. She beckoned him forward and cupped her hand over his ear, and then he nodded. Gemma smiled and then wrapped her arms around Reid's waist, catching her off guard.

Reid hugged her back.

"Grayson talks about you a lot," she told her.

"He talks about you girls as well."

"Oh no," Lynnea moaned.

Everyone laughed.

They took the girls inside, where Grayson made introductions to Nadia and Kiran. No one else offered any hugs, which Reid was okay with. Hugging kids was one thing. Adults were a whole other thing. They joined everyone at the dining room table for breakfast, and as soon as Grayson sat down next to her, she leaned into him.

"You have a type."

"A what?"

Reid motioned toward Nadia, who was busy putting plates in front of the girls. "We have the same color hair."

Grayson looked from Reid to Nadia, and then at Gemma. "I have nothing to say for myself," he told her, laughing.

"Were all the girls you dated in college red haired?"

He shook his head. "Nope. You and Nadia are the only ones."

"Ah, I see. Start with red, end with red."

"Is there anything better?"

Reid smiled and said, "Nope. We're literally the best."

"Reid." Nadia said her name to get her attention. "Grayson says you work together?"

"We do. I work in Human Resources."

"We fear our HR department at work," Kiran said. "Anytime we get an email from them, I think we lose a year off our lives."

"Oh no, it shouldn't be like that," Reid said. "Where we work, we try to make HR approachable and part of the team. Everyone but our director is an employee advocate. We each have teams. Our director speaks for the company; we speak for the employees."

"I'm surprised you're not unionized," Kiran said to Grayson.

"The setup at Wold is different," Reid said as she looked at Grayson. "The owners really value their employees and make sure we receive an annual cost of living increase and bonuses, and we always give out merit awards for productivity, closing sales, things like that."

"I'll be honest, I'd never heard of someone designing tables until Grayson told me what he does," Nadia said. "Now I look at this table differently."

"Same," Kiran said. "I went into a board meeting the other day and looked at the inlay." He shook his head. "Grayson's ruined me." He laughed.

"What can I say?" Grayson held his hands up. "Anytime you want to come tour the facility, let us know. Everything happens on-site. Nothing is outsourced. From start to finish, the product is made at Wold."

"Maybe we can take a visit this summer," Kiran said to Nadia.

Reid didn't miss the exchange between them and agreed with Grayson that Kiran definitely had a crush on Nadia. She tried to put herself in Nadia's shoes, having two young kids and losing her husband. Would she move on after a year? It was hard to say. The heart made people feel things differently. The situation Grayson was in was the perfect example. He'd loved two strangers from the moment he'd met them and couldn't imagine his life without them. Maybe that was the same for Nadia, with Kiran being Rafe's best friend. They'd known each other for years, and falling in love could've been a natural progression. And then Reid imagined herself with Pearce and quickly changed her mind. He was nice and she liked him, but she knew far too much about him and his ways to think he'd ever be a good fit for her. But then, if you lost someone you loved, grief could really change you.

When Kiran and Grayson declared it was time to work, Nadia asked if Reid wanted to go to the mall. Before she could answer, Lynnea stated yes: Reid absolutely wanted to go to the mall with them. If Reid thought things would be awkward, she was mistaken. Within minutes of being with the Karlssons, she could easily see why Grayson was so smitten with the girls. They were nice and kind and treated Reid like she was part of the family.

Throughout the day, Lynnea never left Reid's side, and Gemma asked for her opinion on clothes or jewelry she liked.

"Grayson speaks very highly of you," Nadia said when they stopped for a caffeine pick-me-up. They took their coffee and the girls to the indoor play place and sat down. "I'll be honest, when he first showed up, I thought he was there in an attempt to rekindle things. You read about long-lost love and all that, and I came home one day and there he was. But as soon as I asked about his life, he showed me pictures of you. When he says your name, there are stars in his eyes, and you can tell how much he loves you."

"I've loved him for a long time," Reid said. "We've only been together for a year."

"When you know, you know, right?"

Reid looked down at her ring and nodded. "He couldn't commit . . ." She trailed off, wishing she could take the words back and fearing the conversation was headed toward a path it shouldn't.

"Because of his heart?"

Reid looked at Nadia, who kept her eyes focused on the girls.

"He got sick a couple of times in high school, and I remember his mom really freaking out. I saw the pills in the bathroom, and she used to harp on him about germs, taking the meds, and being careful. Grayson would never come out and say something was wrong, but I saw the names of the meds and figured it out."

"Nadia—"

"My girls love him," she continued. "Lynnea, she's struggled a lot since Rafe died. My dad and Reuben have been there a lot for the girls, but it's not the same. Then Grayson shows up a couple of weeks ago, and my angry little girl who lost her father has light in her eyes again. I try to warn her, to tell her he's got his own life, but she tells me he reminds her of Rafe. Gemma says the same thing. And then I see it:

the way Lynnea sits with Grayson, always pressing herself up against his chest, and I wonder."

Reid was at a loss. She had no idea what to say or if she should say something at all. Was it her place?

No, it wasn't.

"I think you should talk to Grayson."

"I'm afraid," Nadia told her. "I'm scared to know if what I think is true."

Reid reached for her hand and gave it a squeeze. "Let's go back to the house."

Nadia nodded and told the girls it was time to go home. The drive back should've been silent, but Lynnea and Gemma sang along to the radio, with Reid and Nadia following them. As she turned toward the back and sang with the girls, Reid surmised that if someone had told her yesterday that this was where she'd be, she would've laughed. She didn't want this—not for Grayson, for herself, or for this family—but there they were, weaving lives together in the most chaotic and yet beautiful way possible.

When they got home, they found the men hammering away on the porch. Nadia paused, looked at Grayson and Kiran, and asked them to meet her in the dining room. Grayson eyed Reid, who nodded, hoping that was enough to tell him Nadia had her own suspicions.

The three of them went into the dining room, while Nadia got the girls situated with a movie in the catchall room. She returned with a folder, set it down on the table, and then took a seat.

"On April eighth, my husband set out to run a ten-mile road race from Heartbreak Hill to Harvard Square. Something he'd done for years. Last year, he was determined to win. It would take him fifty minutes from start to finish. Blocks away from the finish, a car somehow made it through the crowd after losing its brakes. There was a runner who wore those big over-the-ear headphones and didn't hear the honking. Rafe pushed her out of the way, but he was unable to get himself to safety.

"When I was waiting for him at the finish line, I heard the screaming and the horn honking but didn't think anything of it until I saw the ambulance blocking everyone's view. I knew my husband was there. I could see his location. So, I went there, but I couldn't find him. One spectator said the man in the ambulance wasn't going to make it. I watched on my phone as my husband's blue dot moved farther and farther away from me. Deep down, I knew the spectator was talking about Rafe, but I didn't want to believe it.

"One of the police officers drove me to the hospital, where reality set in. Unfortunately, Rafe was brain dead and put on life support until they could notify next of kin. My Rafe, my strong, healthy husband, was gone. He died a hero. In more ways than one. I made the decision to donate his organs." Nadia opened the folder. She kept her eyes on the paper.

"I asked that the people who received Rafe's organs were people who had something to live for, someone who took care of themselves, and weren't someone taking an organ from someone who truly needed it. I wanted whoever it was to receive this gift from my husband to be someone who could thrive." Nadia picked up a piece of paper and cleared her throat. "On April ninth, my husband's organs, some tissues, and blood stem cells were harvested. On or around April ninth, my husband's heart was transplanted into a viable male." Nadia read the rest of the donations Rafe had made. When she finished, she set the paper down.

Reid reached for Grayson's hand. He squeezed it.

"In the early hours of April tenth, I had a heart transplant," Grayson said quietly. "A month prior, I'd collapsed after a basketball game." He looked at Reid. "We were leaving the gym, and she'd given me some news I didn't care for. She saved my life by being there. I was in bad shape. My heart had quit. Time had essentially run out."

Grayson looked at Nadia. "A year later, I started feeling this ache. It's a feeling I can't describe. I tell my cardiologist, we run all these tests, do the scans, and everything comes back clean. I tell my therapist, who tells me I might be experiencing cellular memory. Of course, very few people believe in this. Reid and I discussed it, and she encouraged me to reach out to UNOS. But before I can do that, I come across this documentary on transplants and things people have experienced. It got me thinking, and I started doing a deep dive. I'm reading obituaries from people in my area, and nothing seems to be fitting. I expanded my search, and that's when I saw an article about your parents losing their son-in-law."

He adjusted in his seat and cleared his throat.

"The timeline fit. I began to wonder, ya know, all while praying the ache would stop because I feared something was wrong with me. That's when I asked my friend Pearce to come to Boston with me, because I had this ridiculous hunch, and waiting for UNOS, not knowing if the family of my donor would even want to meet me, could take a year. I thought if I saw you, I'd get my answer. I did."

Nadia met his gaze.

"The ache stayed until I heard the girls. The relief was instant, and then I saw them, and everything changed. The ache turned into something I can only describe as pure happiness. Elation. Love. And then sadness. It hurt me to sit there and talk to you while the girls were in the yard. That's why I had to go sit with them. I needed to be in their space, to feel their presence. They calmed me," he told her. "They made me feel complete in a way I can't explain."

Grayson put his fist over his heart as tears streamed from his eyes. "I am deeply and truly sorry I wasn't honest about why I came here the first time. I wasn't sure how to say 'Hey, I think I have your dead husband's heart' without making things sound outlandish."

"Do you still believe you have Rafe's heart?" Nadia asked.

Grayson nodded.

"After you left, the girls told me you reminded them of their father. I didn't see it, as you're nothing alike. And then the other night, when Lynnea called you, she said something that made me wonder but still didn't make sense. She said you smelled like Rafe—and you don't. I would know because I smell his cologne every day. I see her with you, clinging to you like you're a life source for her. It doesn't matter how you're sitting: when she sits with you, her ear is pressed to your chest. It's like she knows, and logically that doesn't make any sense."

"What if you don't have his heart?" Kiran asked.

"There's always that possibility," Reid said. "But that doesn't explain why Grayson has bonded with the girls so quickly. For me, when I found out about Nadia being his ex, I thought for sure I'd be the one losing Grayson, but he doesn't feel anything for her, other than friendship. If he did, I wouldn't be here right now."

Kiran looked at Grayson and then Nadia. He shook his head, making Reid wonder what was going through his mind. A door opened, and the four adults sat up straighter. The patter of feet came down the hall and into the dining room.

It was as if she knew.

Lynnea went to Grayson and crawled onto his lap. She held his head between her tiny hands. "Why are you sad?"

"I'm not," he told her.

She wiped his tears and then rested her head against his chest. The contented sigh she let out was enough for everyone to believe what Lynnea already knew.

Rafe's heart had found its way back to them.

Epilogue

"Your mother would be beside herself," Luther said to his daughter as he stood next to her. Reid's decision to wear her mother's wedding dress was the right one, even though she'd had to battle through alterations. The fabric had aged, but overall it was in good condition. She kept it mostly the same, except for the neckline. While her mother had preferred a higher neck, Reid went with a swoop neck and had the removed fabric turned into her garter and used in her bouquet.

The bouquet was courtesy of her father. He had taken Melanie's advice and created an indoor greenhouse, growing the flowers Reid wanted on her wedding day. The bridal party carried flowers Reid's mom had planted many years prior. The pink, white, and orange arrangement of peonies, dahlias, and roses couldn't have turned out prettier.

In the past year, so much had changed between her and Grayson. When their lives could've turned everything upside down, they hadn't. Reid chalked that up to communication. So many things could've gone wrong, such as Nadia thinking Grayson was lying about having Rafe's heart. That day had been an emotional one, but therapeutic. They cried a lot, laughed a little, and vowed to be a family. It didn't matter if anyone on the outside understood why former exes became incredibly close; it was what it was. Everyone was happy.

When all was said and done, Grayson sent his letter to UNOS, and Nadia reached out. It wasn't that they needed confirmation, because they already knew what Grayson had suspected. It was because they eventually wanted to be able to tell the girls and didn't want anyone saying otherwise.

Nadia approached in her pink off-the-shoulder gown. She gripped Nadia's hand, smiled, and then kissed Luther on his cheek. He'd become an honorary Pop Pop to two very rambunctious, fun-loving girls who doted on him. For his part, he'd opened his home and heart to Nadia and the girls and happily spent the holidays at the Boltons' place in Arlington. It was the biggest celebration any of them had been to. The same went for Sydney and Gilbert. She reveled in her new title as Pippy, while Gilbert happily wore a T-shirt that read My granddaughters call me Poppy. With four sets of grandparents, the girls were loved unconditionally.

Over the past year, Nadia and Reid had grown close, almost like sisters. Nadia had confided that she loved Kiran but she wasn't sure if she could love him the way she'd loved Rafe, and at one point she'd encouraged him to move on. He refused. Their relationship hit a new level after Kiran ran in and won the Rafe Karlsson Memorial Cup, to honor Rafe. This year, he'd been assigned Rafe's number, which Nadia took as a sign, and she finally let the last wall she'd put up crumble to the ground. Kiran spent the night, for the first time, that night. In the new bed and newly painted bedroom at Nadia's. She called Reid the next morning and told her all about it. Being like sisters and all.

"He's one lucky guy," Nadia said about Grayson before heading down the aisle. Reid watched Kiran Dunlap never take his eyes off Nadia. He was a patient man, waiting for the woman he was madly in love with to love him back.

Melanie walked next. She kissed Luther and then Reid, telling her she loved her. When she got to the end of the aisle, she stood there, waiting for her best friend to finally walk down the aisle to wed the man she loved.

Gemma was next to walk. She gave Reid a kiss on her cheek, hugged her Pop Pop, who promised to dance with her later at the reception, and then rushed toward the front of the altar, despite everyone telling her to slow down. Gemma hated the attention and had told Reid a time or two that she wasn't sure she wanted to be in the wedding. No one was pressuring her to do so. She'd decided this morning she would.

From behind the false wall, Reid could see Grayson. This was important because she wanted to see his reaction to the girls walking down the aisle. After Reid had met and fallen in love with them, asking Nadia, Gemma, and Lynnea to be in the wedding was a no-brainer. Reid and Grayson wanted them there on their special day, and in their lives.

Lynnea stepped forward. Reid crouched to hug the young child. "You are so pretty."

"So are you," Reid said as she touched the replica of her dress. "Do you remember what to do?"

Lynnea nodded. Reid kissed her, and Lynnea made her way to the aisle. Everyone oohed when she started dropping more cherry blossoms onto the ground. When she got to the end of the aisle, instead of standing next to her mom and sister, she stood with Grayson, tucking herself around his leg. Their bond was unbreakable.

The music shifted, and Luther reached for his daughter. "I'm only loaning you to him," he told her. "You're still my baby girl."

"Always, Daddy."

After the reception, Grayson, Reid, and Nadia took the girls to a private room. On the table sat two boxes, wrapped with a giant red bow.

"Why do we get presents?" Gemma asked.

"It's a party," Grayson told her. "Everyone gets something." He wasn't wrong. All the guests would go home with some sort of gift or party favor representing the bride and groom.

The girls approached the table, each taking the box with her name on it. Gemma opened hers slowly, while Hurricane Lynnea tore into her package.

"A bear!" Lynnea said happily.

"Press his hand," Nadia told her.

Grayson sat on the ground next to them. He helped Gemma take hers out of the box and showed her where to press.

"It's not doing anything."

"Oh," Grayson said as if he'd forgotten to tell them. "Put your ear to his chest."

Lynnea did, but Gemma eyed him warily and shook her head. "I know what this is."

"Yeah?" Grayson asked.

She nodded. "Maybe I don't want this."

"It's okay if you don't," he told her. "You can keep it in the box. Save it for later."

"Why does my bear have a heartbeat?" Lynnea asked.

"It's Daddy's," Gemma said as she fought back tears. "You can listen to his heart whenever you want now."

"Oh." Lynnea pressed the button again and put her ear on the bear. She smiled from ear to ear.

"Why are you giving these to us?"

Grayson's eyes watered. Reid came over and put her hand on his shoulder, while Nadia went to her oldest.

"Sweetie," Nadia said smoothly. She reached for Lynnea and held her as well. "Do you remember walking down the hall with your daddy, and all those people were there?"

Gemma nodded.

"When your daddy died, he was so strong and healthy, he had a chance to help others, even though he was no longer going to be with us. He gave others the gift of life. He lives on in others out there."

Gemma looked at the bear, then her mother, and finally at Grayson. With her eyes full of tears, she asked, "Do you have my daddy's heart?"

Grayson nodded as he wept.

"Why did you give us the bears, then?"

"What do you mean?" Grayson asked.

Gemma shrugged. “I guess what I’m asking is, Why do we need a bear when we have the real thing right there?” She pointed at Grayson’s chest.

“No thanks.” She put the bear back in the box, much to everyone’s surprise, and then crawled into Grayson’s lap. Lynnea did the same, although Reid was sure Lynnea had no idea why. “This is much better.”

Reid agreed. Hearing the real thing was much, much better.

Acknowledgments

This book all started with a what-if . . . What if a heart transplant patient had feelings that didn't belong to them? Then the research began!

Thank you to my amazing team at Montlake. Being in this family is such a blessing. To Lauren, having you in my corner has been life changing. Lindsey, remember when we met for breakfast in Texas and I told you my idea . . . thank you for making this one shine!

Yvette, every word, every story—you've touched them all. I wouldn't do this without you. And yes, I know, this is the same as last time, but seriously, nothing has changed. You're my bestie, and I love you dearly.

Thank you to Erik, Madison, and Kassidy for always being patient and understanding.

Thank you, Michelle D. Our daily and nightly sprints have been a game changer. I appreciate you and your wisdom, guidance, and friendship.

And finally, thank you to my readers. Some of you have been with me for the past ten-plus years, and some are new. I appreciate each and every one of you and thank you for taking a chance on me with each page you turn.

About the Author

In 2012, Heidi McLaughlin turned her passion for reading into a full-fledged literary career. She is now the *New York Times*, *Wall Street Journal*, and *USA Today* bestselling author of the Beaumont Series, the Boys of Summer, and the Archer Brothers. McLaughlin has written more than twenty novels, including her acclaimed first novel, *Forever My Girl*, which was adapted into a film starring Alex Roe and Jessica Rothe that opened in theaters in 2018.

Visit the author at www.heidimclaughlin.com, and keep up with new releases by signing up for her newsletter at https://landing.mailerlite.com/webforms/landing/x4t5g9.

You can also follow Heidi on Facebook (AuthorHeidiMcLaughlin), X (heidijovt), Instagram (heidimclaughlinauthor), YouTube (HeidiMcLaughlin), and TikTok (heidimclaughlinauthor).

teacher who befriends her, Chehade immerses readers in a culture blown apart by sudden conflict, minutely recreating the surreal stretches of foreboding, violence and tedium that a city-turned-war-zone inflicts on its residents. How she turns words into Sensurround, allowing the rest of us to feel the bewildered horror and rare joys of these two people as if we shared skin and nervous systems with them, can only be called a tour de force of observation and empathy. What Chehade conveys about the pain of not belonging—whether as sensitive misfit or refugee—eliminates the barriers of time and nationality, directly connecting 1975 with today's widespread religious/political turmoil and masses of displaced persons for readers who are likely never to wonder again what the plight of immigrants could possibly have to do with them."

—Carolyn Jack, author of *The Changing of Keys*

"'The war engulfs and dwarfs everything,' writes Thérèse Chehade in *We Walked On*, her novel of two families disrupted by the Lebanese Civil War. In the same novel we read, 'War cannot break the dance of life.' These are the antipodal themes that *We Walked On* dramatizes so vividly. Essentially a war story, *We Walked On* forsakes sensational war story tropes in behalf of something more subtle: the quality of life ceaselessly moving forward even as bombs fall and bullets fly. Elsewhere in Chehade's novel we read, 'War was many things: animal terror, loss of control, and obsessive attention to daily details.' *We Walked On* illustrates, with singular authenticity, how the first two are made endurable by the third."

—Peter Selgin, author of *Duplicity* and *The Inventors*

"With an exceptional pen, Thérèse Soukar Chehade draws a tranquil, richly layered world that is destroyed by war. Chehade's heart-rending, beautiful prose propels the reader through the spectrum of emotion with unforgettable power. A poignant, beautifully written tale of tragedy, loss, and hope."

—Morgan Howell, author of *The Moon Won't Talk*

We Walked On

Thérèse Soukar Chehade

Regal House Publishing

Published by
Regal House Publishing, LLC
Raleigh, NC 27605

ISBN -13 (paperback): 9781646035205
ISBN -13 (epub): 9781646035212
Library of Congress Control Number: 2023949031

Cover images and design by © C. B. Royal

A slightly different version of the prologue to Part I (pages 2-5) appeared in *Big Big Wednesday*, Issue 5, 2017 under the title "Red Pistachios."

Regal House Publishing, LLC
https://regalhousepublishing.com

Printed in the United States of America

For Nadia

And for all children of war

I am going to die.

You will not die.

The bombs are close. How they wail before they explode! I hear the crying of the wounded. Next time, it will be us.

Come away with me.

I have covered my ears. I have squeezed my eyes shut and made myself small. Should I kneel? Should I pray?

You must do everything in your power to survive.

What will happen if we get hit?

It will be quick, and we will not feel anything. But we won't get hit.

How can you be so sure? Do you have powers of divination?

I refuse to give in to the war. When it storms in with its fury and its violence, I look away. As long as I can do that, I can cope.

Refuse, refuse. You think you can outwit the war? The bombs will find us. We will be blown to pieces. Our bones will be trampled to dust, and no one will hear our screams.

Stop with these thoughts.

How can I stop? War is everywhere. (*A pause.*) I feel sick.

Be brave. Form a barrier with your mind.

The bombs are too loud. They have taken over everything. (*A pause.*) Do you think they will stop if it rains?

Yes, I'm sure of it.

That's a foolish idea.

Then what do you want me to say?

I want you to tell me the truth and stop treating me like a child.

I want you to admit that the world is burning. War has become our rain and our sun and our moon.

I will not do as you say. Instead, I will gather what is at hand. Memories, inventions, anything I find I will give you and you will live on them. You can dodge this, but you must apply yourself. When the world grows dark around you, you must look away.

I am not myself. See how I'm changing? The war went into me.

Look at me.

My hands won't stop shaking. Give me back my hands. I want my hands back.

Take mine.

I can't tear myself away. Will you pull me?

It's the season of green plums. You love green plums with salt.

We're not even in a proper shelter. Why don't we have a shelter?

We're fine here, away from the windows.

What time is it?

It must be morning.

Oh, I don't care. I will either die now or spend my life in hiding.

She weeps.

Tell me what else you see.

You'll be rude and tell me to shut up.

I won't. I promise. What do you see?

The sun on the slopes.

Yes.

Your father buying you raw pistachios from the peddler across the street. You thought it meant you were his favorite.

The skin stained my fingers red. It was so soft. A tiny pressure from my fingernail, and it split open.

> Remember that Easter dress, with the white ruffles and tiny beads? How you hated it?

What did you say? I can't hear you.

> *Louder:* The hot salty world. Sea urchins and grilled fish, the sea in your throat. Do you remember the grapevine in your grandmother's garden? You always left for the city before the grapes ripened. You picked them when they were still sour and ate them with salt. Remember stopping by the side of the road after the beach for ice cream? Apricot and lemon and pistachio and walnut and sugar-apple…

I remember my grandmother weaving yarn on her fingers. She's winding it into a ball. Now she's gone. Now I see a watermelon we left in the fountain to cool. The water came straight from the mountain streams and poured into the pipes of the old house and the fountain in the garden. It was so cold it split the watermelon in two. What else do you see?

> A toad sits on a rock. I think it's sleeping. A frog lies still on a stone wall shaded by fern. Farther out, water cascades from a hole in the rocks into a stone basin. The water is recycled by a large black contraption in the middle of the basin. I am mildly curious about the inner workings of the contraption, but I am more interested in the toad and the frog and why they haven't moved.

The sunlight streaming through the grapevine dapples the tablecloth. In a shady spot, there's a coffee stain and crumbs and an ashtray full of cigarette butts. The cat sleeps on the ledge next to the geraniums. A sentimental French song plays on the radio. The church bell rings.

> A leaf heaves itself off a tree and spins. One branch points to something in the distance. Another branch from the same tree shoots straight from the trunk, then climbs over a rock and finds soil to enter.

Nothing happens in your story. And why did you bring up that ugly Easter dress? We posed for pictures on the balcony after the Sunday Mass. I am smiling, but secretly I hate the dress. Those moments are gone forever. They were false. I can't say, *Oh, the good old times, how we were happy!* I can't say, *What I wouldn't do to have these moments back!*

> Of course they were real. They live in you still.

No. The war has erased everything. I am ashamed of my smell. I don't want to be mangled parts and blood on the wall. I don't want to be a nameless casualty in tomorrow's newspaper. I have got to commit myself to memory. See, right here? A freckle next to my belly button, another on my left palm right below the thumb. The second one might be a mole because it's raised and darker than the first, but both have been with me since the beginning. I have a decayed tooth that I haven't seen to, and split ends and flat feet and a bit of roundness in the stomach.

> I want to give you the future so you can put yourself in it. But I only manage these wisps from the past and threads no thicker than the imprint of a fingernail on red pistachio skin. I am tired and I have my limitations. Take what I give you and survive by it.

I remember holding my father's hand in the markets of Beirut. It didn't matter how small we were, roaming around and complaining about everything. We looked up, drew the sky close, and sailed. Our own magic carpet… My poor father. Now I'm remembering things I don't want to remember. Where have you gone? Hush. We are done for.

The explosions grow more furious. The shells pound in quick succession, shattering the breaking dawn. Then the bombs move on to another sector of the city.

In the eerie calm, the twisted shadows of the dead wring their hands. They never got to say goodbye, and now the world awakens without them. They see their faintly recognizable selves, the breath they left behind, their cells afloat, their dust in the golden light, and people passing through them, and they are not being touched, and they are not touching.

"I will die soon," she sobs.

In the distance, the bombs continue their assault.

A Few Weeks Before

1975

1

Hisham

It was the end of February, and the unusually warm temperature had packed the schoolyard trees with leaves. The flower beds were bursting with color, and the jacaranda trees planted in front of the dormitory that housed the nuns and boarders provided shade to a cluster of girls sitting on benches beneath their sweeping branches. To the east, two tall pines on either side of the secretarial and bookkeeping school, commonly called Technique, shielded more students, as did the covered hallway that ran opposite. With the sheltered spots taken, the rest of the girls spread out on the steps leading to the parking lot, preferring the open sky to the demeaning prospect of mingling with the middle grades in the covered court.

Hisham, the Arabic teacher at Sacré-Coeur and Monsieur Bassil to his students, stood at the window of his ninth-grade classroom and observed the scene below. A nun emerged from the Technique and walked toward the dorm in a swirl of black fabric. Two teachers were talking under the basketball hoop, just a few steps away from a game of dodgeball that was winding down without a clear winner. The clock struck the half hour, and as if on cue, the afternoon buses entered the large gate and rounded the flower beds, coming to a hissing halt under the window.

Two hours until dismissal. The heat made him restless, eager to get on with the rest of the day. He wished he could hold class outside and recite poetry that wasn't in the curriculum. But the thought of Mother Superior's disapproving face dissuaded him. When their paths crossed, she would nod absently in his direction, her eyes looking past him as though he were made of air.

He debated whether to scrap his lesson and lecture. Why not simply tell his students what to think? They would love nothing better. The discussions he insisted on having caused everyone great anguish—him for their silence, for which he faulted his own teaching, and them for knowing they had disappointed him. It was easier to lecture while they took down every one of his words, their lips pursed in concentration as their pens flew across the pages.

His gaze retraced the path, resting again on the dodgeball game. The two girls facing off were his students. He liked them both—Rita, his smartest, and Amal, who had transferred from a neighboring public school and was still without friends four months later.

Rita swaggered back and forth with the ball in her palm, taking her time to strike. What was she up to? He usually avoided taking sides. But the way Amal stood, with her legs bent as if crouching in the fields, tipped the scales in her favor. He saw himself, an unwashed village boy covered with cuts and mosquito welts, clinging to his mother while she foraged for wild greens. Roaming the hills, playing pranks on the priest and staying out until dark, taking the time when he got home to brush off the dust from his clothes and leave his shoes at the door before entering the small house. These were futile precautions—they were rugged children, he and his brother, Fuad, with dirty fingernails and leaves caught in their hair and clothes. The outdoors trailed them, holding fast even as they bathed in the tin tub in the courtyard, the loquat tree dropping its leaves in their bathwater and the birds making a racket in the branches. The outside world was an extension of home. Hisham thought nothing of the two worlds intertwining until one day he felt a resentment welling up within him for the intrusions on what had turned overnight into a consuming passion, books filling his fantasies, keeping him hooked for pages.

His first book fell in his lap. He'd gone with his mother to the neighboring town. They'd spent the morning searching the novelty shops for fabric and thread, and by noon his patience had worn thin. He saw his chance between stores, let go of his mother's hand, and ran—smack into a display of used books. He lay sprawled on his back, squinting against the sun, covered with books. He grabbed each book and examined it closely. One cover caught his attention. It had the black silhouette of a man's profile. Over the next few weeks, he would read the complete Sherlock Holmes series in Arabic. He fed on mysteries for a while, and then on Ibn al-Muqaffa's *Kalila wa Dimna*, the fables unspoiled by his teachers' dull explanations. He discovered Tah Hussein and Najib Mahfouz, the satire of Al-Jahiz, the irrepressible poetry of Abu Nuwas. His body, once restless, could now sit still for hours in the shade of a tree with a book pressed to his knees. It was his mind that soared and tumbled, all grace and muscle. Yet the land was always there, other people's land he was expected to farm now that he was of age, stealing him away from his newfound love, siphoning his soul. He felt unable to breathe, threatened with extinction. At eighteen he fled to the city to join his brother. He left knowing that one day he would have to return, because in a country as small as Lebanon, there's no breaking free.

He stepped away from the window, leaving the two girls to their mysterious games, and erased the board. Ever since he accidentally parked in her spot, the chemistry teacher had been leaving him her leftovers. But most teachers at this school didn't clean up after themselves. He didn't mind it last year, when his afternoon class followed that of the French teacher, Monsieur Gidéon; and Hisham, who had attended the village public school and later the public university, would study the excerpts on the board to improve his French.

He reached for his textbook and looked for the poem he had assigned for today's lesson. He would have no trouble finding a volunteer to read it out loud. It was later when they would clam up, while he stood in front of the class with his arms folded across his chest, waiting for a finger to rise and break the silence.

He skimmed through the poem. The narrator reflected on

his companion's melancholy. Was it the evening twilight that made her sad? He urged her to find beauty in the fading day before it was too late, while the young Salma remained immersed in her sorrow.

He listed two questions on the board: What literary devices does the poet use to describe the natural world? Does the narrator correctly interpret Salma's state of mind?

The second question brought to his mind the image of his wife sitting reclined against the pillows the night before and lambasting the speaker.

"Postulations of an idle man," Gisele had said, her chin jutting out at him. "Salma is probably exhausted. Too much work and no help, yet there he is, going on about the sun and the moon."

He knew she was angry. He had spent the afternoon writing his article for *The Station*, a small journal that paid him with free copies, and had forgotten to clean the kitchen. When Gisele came home, she took one look at the mess, then slammed doors, stripped bed sheets, and took the curtains down in the room where he was working. To distract her, he asked for help he did not need with his lesson. She had dropped out of the university in her second year, unable to decide between accounting and philosophy, while he finished his degree in Arabic literature, and the difference between them bothered her.

She criticized the speaker of the poem, who embodied Hisham's most grievous flaws: his bookishness and impracticality, his endless wallowing in abstract thought while clutter piled up in the rooms.

He apologized and cleaned the kitchen and was forgiven. But his wife's words had unsettled him. He lay awake, thinking about the quiet Salma. The morning found him wondering how he might shed light on her silence for his students.

His finger scrolled down the page. He once considered Salma to be little more than a vehicle for the poet's ideas. Now she demanded explanation.

One must always see others as they really are, he thought

in a sudden fit of passion. Especially the quiet ones, whom we distort with our projections.

We are impenetrable to each other.

Rubbish! His wife's voice snapped inside his head.

He slammed the chalk down on the tray. Leave it to Gisele to muddle up his thinking right before a class because of a dirty kitchen!

There is a different reading, he shot back. There is such a thing as the politics of optimism. The poem, published after World War I, was the exiled poet's attempt to console his compatriots during the Great Famine, which drove many of them to seek new lives abroad.

He was annoyed with himself. A few words from Gisele, and a familiar poem broke apart. He was so easily influenced by others. He was like a screen with the air running through it. But he always listened to his wife, who was infinitely sensible, while he drowned in the tangles of daily existence.

They had met at university, two transplants, he from a small village in the north and she from a town in the Chouf region. He was shy with women. But she had a way of tilting her head and fixing her gaze on him that put him at ease. They saw each other daily after class for coffee and a walk on the corniche. He enrolled in one of her accounting classes and failed it. Gisele said he was hopeless, but her eyes shone with love, and her smile silenced the voice in his head that whispered it was only a matter of time before she saw through him and was disappointed.

A few weeks after their wedding, Gisele circled an ad and handed him the newspaper. "Make an appointment," she said, reminding him of his derisory income from writing and the odd jobs that he occasionally secured at the university, thanks to a good track record and a few kind professors. He followed through, secretly hoping he had botched the interview. Mother Superior had seemed bored and vaguely annoyed by his answers. To his surprise, he was hired.

The mystery was eventually solved. Gisele's cousin was dating the physical education teacher, who happened to be Mother Superior's niece. Strings had been pulled. Hisham owed his employment to wasta, the cronyism he so despised.

If Gisele had only used her connections to get them a phone line! Four years since they applied, and still no response. He would gladly have traded his principles for a phone.

They had a big fight.

"What did you expect? Who would have hired you?" she said. He didn't know how to answer. He had no experience or interest in anything besides writing book reviews, and that produced so little money and so much satisfaction, he wasn't sure he could call it work.

But he was a good teacher. These are fine questions, he thought, looking at the board.

In a few minutes, the bell would ring, and his students would flock in with their flushed faces and sweaty bodies. He opened more windows. Even after four years of teaching, his stomach still knotted up before a lesson. These girls, who had been taught to obey him because he held the power of the report card and had their parents' unwavering support, could still make him nervous.

He reached for his sandwich and made notes about the day's lesson. On the blackboard he wrote Al-Wasf—description—in big letters, then sat at his desk and waited for them to start filing in. Only when they had taken their seats would he stand, their cue to rise. This was the one indulgence he allowed himself, this small, stupid vanity, to see a class rise before him. They would face each other, and with a long look at their young faces, he would gauge how far he would take them, and wonder if today they would follow.

Rita

I clutched the ball. Across the yellow chalk line Amal watched me, hopping on her toes like a boxer. I dropped my arms and paced, cradling the ball in my palm, a swagger in my stride saying I could drop the ball and walk away, or just as easily turn around and deliver the knockout blow. I was that good.

I got into shooting position, narrowed my eyes at Amal, then pretended to change my mind and resumed my pacing, and I did this a few more times until she stopped bouncing and fixed me with a puzzled look. I felt sorry for her. She was new and gullible, and none of her teammates seemed willing to intervene and order me to stop stalling or surrender. But winning was winning, and our abilities at the sport being equal, she at throwing the ball and I at dodging it, my only option was to bluff my way to victory and bring an end to the stalemate.

When she started pacing, heel to toe, head bowed, I saw my chance. I got back into position and hurled the ball straight at her legs, a perfect shot that would have sealed my victory. But at the last minute she pivoted, and with bated breath we watched the ball whizz past her, then fly over the gate and disappear into the bushes.

Maybe I had lost my aim. Maybe she had been on to me all along and countered with her own bluff. Before I understood what was happening, the whistle sounded, and the game was over.

Somewhere in the Stone Age, a cruel soul must have decided that ten minutes of downtime before the bell were needed to tighten the reins lest we got any ideas after we'd been let loose to play in the sun. Every day, at 12:35 p.m. on the dot, the whistle went off and we threw balls, badminton rackets, and Hula-Hoops back in the bin and played nicely in small groups.

Since lunch and recess lasted a mere forty-five minutes, we rarely managed to finish the games we started.

Our protests did not sway the thieving teachers on watch. I stood looking down into the crowd of girls, hoping to find my friend Seta to vent to her. She lived across the road and was my best friend, though if she had read my thoughts, she would have gently downgraded our friendship to best of friends. I loved her, but she was fickle—one day we were inseparable, and the next I was barely there. She didn't mean to hurt me. It's just that we weren't equally important to each other.

When I didn't find her, I stalked off toward the garden. Even though it lay in full view, we called it the secret garden because it was off-limits, separated from the corridor by a black fence the nuns kept locked. I knelt and pressed my face against the pickets. Climbing the fence was child's play, but nothing about the garden enticed insubordination. It was modest and jumbled, with spiky foliage in shady spots, dwarf palm trees in random places, and clumps of lopsided flowers along the lawn. Yet it seemed like a place where my resentment might find release, and I gazed at it with deep longing.

I would have happily stayed with my back to the world, but my legs became numb after a while, so I stood up to shake them and get the blood flowing. Turning my gaze back to the schoolyard, I saw Dina holding court on the parking lot stairs with a flock of admirers. I knew what had them smitten: the soft clusters of brown hair falling around her face, and the great legs she kept naked under the shortest uniform a girl at Sacré-Coeur had ever gotten away with.

Dina was one of a handful of rich Muslim girls at Sacré Coeur. She arrived in the middle of March with a horde of relatives, and we gawked, speechless. She was beautiful. The older females in the group wore headscarves, but not Dina. She walked in her miniskirt and high-heeled boots, beaming at the air around her. Even though it was late in the year to register, Mother Superior took them on a grand tour, swayed by obvious signs of their wealth.

What were Muslim students doing at a Catholic school? "Why not?" my sister said. "I should introduce you to some of my friends, broaden your horizons." Rasha was in her first year of university and thought she knew everything. But I wasn't being narrow-minded. If it were up to me, I'd be in a secular school. No Mass, no catechism. My Muslim peers were exempted from both. Perhaps that's why they had joined, to seek in the halls of Sacré-Coeur the freedom of the unaffiliated.

I made my way back to the schoolyard, where Seta was playing hopscotch. I sat down on the ground, tucked my knees to my chest, and watched her hop on one foot across the chalk-drawn boxes, avoiding the lines as she kicked the stone to the top of the grid and back. She completed several courses successfully, and just as I was getting tired of watching her, she put down the foot she had until now kept raised in the air, looked at me, and began frantically pointing to her pockets. I had no idea what she was trying to tell me, and to my puzzled expression she gave a sigh, put her hand to her heart, and began reciting *Antigone* in French. I finally got it.

Even though there'd never been an official statement to that effect, we had always believed that we were not allowed to speak Arabic during recess. We refused to comply—only the wealthy and aspiring spoke French in everyday life, and we were middle class and ordinary. No one had ever been caught, as far as we knew, so we continued to break the unspoken rule. Yet it persisted, lurking in the shadows of our thoughts, occasionally rearing its head. We heard stories about spies patrolling the schoolyard, taking down names and slipping the dreaded "signal," rumored to be a small wooden red block, into the pockets of unsuspecting offenders. Because the punishment was unclear, gory images of rat-infested dungeons and starvation circulated, temporarily bringing us back in line.

"It's all a big sham!" I yelled with a conviction that I didn't fully feel. But the sun was hot, and I was in no mood to obey a phantom order no one had bothered explaining.

While Seta resumed her hopping, my mind wandered to

Arabic class and Monsieur Bassil, who looked like Franco Gasparri, the Italian actor in the photo novellas my sister and I consumed by the dozens. He was tall and dark, with skin the color of caramel when the sun touched it. Classical Arabic was hard, but Monsieur Bassil explained the difficult words. When we clammed up, he seemed discouraged. He said our ignorance pained him, but he forgave us because we were the victims of post-colonial self-loathing. One day we would be proud of our mother tongue. In the meantime, he must double his efforts and give us extra homework, which, no matter how he put it, seemed an unfair fate to inflict on the children of past oppression.

I noticed Amal standing alone near the steps on the opposite side of the court. I was still feeling bad about the dodgeball game, so I waved at her when she looked my way. She ran up to me and sank to the ground, then started talking while I only half-listened. She had short blond hair and a pretty face full of freckles, and she smelled like unwashed armpits and the mint lozenges she sucked all day. When she invited me to lunch, I happily accepted. She lived across the street from the school and had lunch at home every day. As her guest, I'd receive three thirty-minute passes to leave the school grounds. It was not to be missed!

The bell rang. We filed back into class, took our seats, and turned to the assigned poem in our textbooks. Monsieur Bassil picked Amal to read. Her voice was raspy and melodious, and she sounded exactly the way I imagined the narrator, old and gentle and a bit of a nag.

We had ten minutes to answer the questions on the board. The first question was easy. The poem was rich with symbolism. The sun frowned and the scared clouds scudded to the sea. At the end of the ten minutes, I raised my hand and said that the narrator sounded old. Monsieur Bassil wanted me to elaborate. You would mention the beautiful weather, and Monsieur Bassil would still ask you to say more.

"He sounds kind and caring, like a father or an uncle," I began.

"I think he's old. He doesn't let her speak," Amal tossed out.

"It's true," I said. "Salma never says a word. How does he know what she's thinking?"

Monsieur Bassil kinked his right eyebrow, a sign of interest. The narrator saw beauty in the evening, he explained. For Salma, the dying day represented old age and decay.

"You're right. We don't know what Salma is thinking," he added. "Is she sad? We only have the speaker's word. Do you trust him?"

Opinions were divided, but mostly we had no idea. Encouraged by Monsieur Bassil's example, we were not afraid to say we didn't know.

"Hope is a cheap way out. What if Salma had a good reason to be sad?" I asked. I went on. "In *Les Fleurs du mal* the young lover does not look away from the carcass on the side of the road. Baudelaire does not spare us the ugliness of decay."

Baba said we were an emotional people and could learn from the West how to look squarely at the truth without flinching or making up pretty words to smooth the edges. Baba was born in Palestine of Lebanese parents, who had moved there when the Levant was a collection of Ottoman-controlled provinces. The French and the British drew new borders and divided up the region in 1920, after the collapse of the Ottoman Empire. We got the French, Palestine the English. We were a mixed breed, part Lebanese, and part a tangle of foreign influences. Baba's parts were different, and this made him an enigma. He wasn't afraid to speak his mind. Did the English bring out his forwardness? Perhaps that was a purely Baba thing, and the English had nothing to do with it.

"Escape, Mademoiselle Sfeir, or survival?" There was a brief pause before Monsieur Bassil continued. "In Baudelaire's poem, the carcass is a blooming flower. What do you make of his exquisite language? Does it mask the terrible truth? Yes, his young lover doesn't look away from the rotting corpse. But Baudelaire's art gave him immortality. So, tell me, Rita: how is his lover bolder than our narrator?"

I slumped in my seat. He usually liked to end discussions with a rhetorical question, and I didn't rack my brain for an answer.

Our next assignment was to write a descriptive poem. We grumbled. But it was free verse, and at least we weren't diagramming sentences. Pens tapped the desks and eyes darted around looking for inspiration. I let out a series of yawns.

Monsieur Bassil collected our work. I blushed when I handed him mine: *The sky is blue / Rejoice, my heart, while it lasts.* We cleared our desks and made our way to the library. I checked out a few Agatha Christies, then found a quiet corner and pulled out my sister's copy of *Madame Bovary.* When the bell rang, it was as if only seconds had elapsed. Yet poor Monsieur Bovary had already fallen for Emma, and the first Madame Bovary had conveniently died and left him with a comfortable inheritance to sweeten his prospects.

Escape, Mademoiselle Sfeir, or survival? Why did Monsieur Bassil have to ask me that? On the way home, the question rattled on in my brain. I was no closer to an answer when I got off the bus or walked into the apartment to find my little brother, Tony, playing with my records, and yanked them from his hands and made him cry. I scribbled the question in my journal. I had a few riddles in a corner of my brain, and I added Monsieur Bassil's question to the lot. Years from now, the answer could appear like a match struck in the dark.

Hisham

He sat at his desk, planning the next day's lessons. Escape or survival? How did one answer that? He hoped Rita could tell him. Her good, brilliant mind. A trenchant quality to the mind of a fourteen-year-old, even if muddled with stereotypes about East and West. Poetry started before your Baudelaire, my dear girl. One day he might explain the influence of Baudelaire and Eliot on the moderns, and of Abu Nuwas and al Ma'arri on everyone.

Oh, Rita! Who doesn't need a little sweetener to the days? One can't look at God's face and live. Haven't you read your Bible?

What would he teach them tomorrow? Shall he say that the old man in the poem was brave to find beauty in the dying light? At thirty he felt like an old soul, gravitating to tales of old men at the tail end of their existence. He was not a gloomy person. But he liked sunsets and sunrises, all the in-between spaces, the pauses where one took stock. Drove his wife crazy. She found him passive, dormant, a pupa forever in the making. She didn't call him that to his face, but the thought was clear in the way she rolled her eyes and sighed. She was wrong. His mind was always working. His skill set was not what she had hoped for in a husband, and his salary was a pittance. But he could make beauty out of the sordid world.

Escape was a form of survival. What's wrong with that, Rita?

Rita

It was the time after dinner, with the clean dishes stacked in the cupboards and the glass panes beaded with steam; the time to savor zhourat tea and sesame cookies, the scent of lemon used to brighten stained fingernails, and light gossip at the kitchen table.

I filled a bowl with pumpkin seeds and washed Baba's ashtray in the sink while Mama and Rasha whispered at the table. From the way they leaned toward each other, their heads almost touching, it was clear that tonight's gossip was of the highest secrecy. I washed Baba's ashtray under a thin jet long enough to catch snippets of an affair between a married neighbor and a worker in the ground-floor carpentry shop. I continued to listen until the jingle signaling the start of the wrestling match came from the family room. As I was drying the ashtray with a cloth, Rasha said, "You know it's all an act, don't you?" I shrugged. She was missing the point; the game was merely an excuse to spend time with Baba. "Then it's all harmless fun," I said before exiting the kitchen.

In the family room Baba was lying on the sofa, propped up by pillows. I placed the ashtray and pumpkin seeds on a small table at his side and sat on the sheepskin rug with my back to the wall. The Russian twins made their entrance with a flourish of red capes, snarling at the booing audience. Thunderous applause greeted the Lebanese brothers as they stepped on stage in black tights and gym suits, waving at the adoring crowd. They were not twins, but except for a slight difference in height, it was difficult to distinguish them from each other. I named them One and Two in ascending order. The Russians I just called *this Russian* and *the other one.*

As soon as the referee sounded the whistle, One climbed

the ropes, sprang off, and dove down on the Russian, who lay sprawled out on the floor beneath him, getting punched in the face. The referee issued a warning.

"No, you idiot!" my father yelled.

"Do you think they paid him off, Baba?"

I was secretly rooting for the referee. But I was willing to give Baba a pass because he had competed in amateur boxing in Palestine, and I still didn't know the rules despite his best efforts to teach them to me. In an old photograph that seemed to have been taken from a hilltop, the two boxers in the ring looked as small as thumbprints. I recognized Baba's sloping shoulders and balding head. I had his muscular limbs and a way of moving that was both lumbering and smooth.

My grandfather had been a cook at a seaside café in Beirut. After tasting his Siyyadiyeh, a wealthy Palestinian businessman offered him a job at his restaurant in Nazareth. My grandfather was a newlywed. It was a good offer. The young couple packed their bags.

They had two sons in the years that followed. My grandmother crossed the border twice to give birth on Lebanese soil. But between the joys of reunion and her condition, she forgot to register the newborns. During the war of 1948, the family escaped Nazareth on foot and settled on the outskirts of Beirut. There were no birth records, nothing to prove the boys were Lebanese. My father, the youngest, was seventeen. The move left him with a permanent Palestinian accent and a sense that wrongs committed by the powerful were seldom righted.

Refugee passes and aid from relief agencies were offered, but my grandfather declined. His sons had the right to citizenship. Work permits were not available to the refugees. The policy was intended to discourage settlement; everyone assumed it was only a matter of time before the refugees returned home. According to Baba, there was a secret motive: most Palestinians were Sunni Muslims, and to naturalize them would have tipped the voting balance. For once, Christians and Shiites stood united.

The Palestinians never left. The poorest among them are still in the camps. The middle classes have either left to work in friendlier countries or integrated by marrying locals or making fortunes that overcame prejudice. Over time, bereavement turned to anger, and from the Nakba grew an armed resistance that waged attacks on Israel from the south. Many Muslims supported their struggle. Most Christians wanted them out.

My grandfather's persistence paid off and identity cards were issued. My father worked at a construction plant during the day and attended university classes at night. He got a job and married my mother. Of Nazareth, I knew little. It was hilly. My father loved it. Every now and then a question rose to my lips, but I would put it off, then forget to ask.

The second round started with Two pinned down to the mat. He wriggled free, and after a few backflips, it was the Russian's turn to pound the floor with his fist while Two's foot pressed into his neck. Mama came over and sat next to Baba, who turned and stroked her cheek while the Russian leaned into a back bend and released himself.

In one of his rare expansive moods, Baba told us how the two of them met. He had gone to his ancestral town in search of a bride. He did not want a headstrong Beiruti girl and sought a nice bride from the mountains. This was his first visit to Tarawa. He went directly to the home of a well-connected relative. The town's waterfalls and red tile roofs enchanted him. But he was a city man through and through and made his wishes known to the matchmaker: only someone willing to move to the capital would do.

They made the round of prospective brides, but no one caught his eye. He was ready to give up when he spotted my mother promenading with friends in the town square. She wore a flouncy summer dress. The relative made the introductions. My father was lovestruck. My mother had big, sad eyes and a gap-toothed smile. Why was that gap so appealing? He loved the beauty mark on her lower lip, a purple bud that set her apart. He expected a blooming future.

In a photograph taken during their engagement, she's wearing a flowing dress with a wide black belt. With her shades and darkly painted lips, her white clip-on earrings and short wavy hair, she looks fashionable and a little aloof, unlike the mother I know. My father is in his late twenties, his hair already receding. He's grinning, youthful and handsome in his summer suit, with his arm held out, his hand resting on the tree behind them, the gesture possibly an invitation for my mother to lean back into that offered arm.

Baba told us girls we should be modest and selfless like our mother. Saintly, they said about my mother, a fate she could not escape even if she tried. But she believed the world held unspeakable dangers, and even though I was already too much like her, I aspired instead to my father's equanimity, his belief that the dice would always fall in the best possible arrangement, and the world, while not benign, had a way of sliding back into place even after great hardship.

One pirouetted across the rink, slipping through the Russian's fingers, who made as if to catch him but caught only air, much to the joy of the cheering and clapping crowd. In his black tights and gym suit he danced like an elf, so light on his feet and so enchanting, that the wrestling was forgotten in the general revelry, until a gong rang, signaling the restart of the match.

Baba stroked Mama's hand. They didn't look anything like the glamorous young couple in the photo. He'd gained weight over the years, and she had a thing for shapeless housedresses that could withstand the rigors of housekeeping. But she was leaning into his hand, and the smiles on their faces were pure sweetness.

To my delight, the match went into overtime.

Hisham

His old Opel was heating up. He turned off the engine and rested his hands on the wheel. It was useless. In the rearview mirror the highway was streaming with cars as far as the eye could see, and up ahead the tunnel's entrance was clogged with more cars. He dreaded being trapped inside the tunnel in a riot of blaring horns, the motorists making a racket for the thrill of hearing it echo against the walls, in the way the Lebanese have of escaping unpleasantness with boisterous noise.

A swarm of seagulls swooped down from the sky to his right, feasting on the bounty littering the beach. The setting sun cast ribbons of light across the water. The sea was constantly moving, making you doubt your own steady feet. He thought of summer, with its thick haze on the horizon and riot of colors, everything sky and water, the brilliant light wavering in the heat. He'd always resisted the national urge to flee to the mountains during the hottest months, just to be in that light and feel the blue wrap around him.

He started the engine, joining the chorus of blaring horns, then turned on the radio and flipped through the stations. The news was reporting on the riots in Saïda. Private capital had taken over the fishing industry, and the fishermen were in an uproar. The army had intervened to put an end to the protests, resulting in clashes that had already claimed many lives. The country was divided, with both sides enraged at each other: one at the army for shooting at the protesters, the other at the protesters and the Palestinians who had sided with them.

Hisham sympathized with the protesters, but the violence made him nervous. His brother, Fuad, believed in radical change and the cleansing power of riots. Hisham's government of choice was a benign authoritarian regime, a strong institution that would satisfy people's dual need to be led and live freely. And the only way to get there was to move slowly and cautiously, like a mouse gnawing at a wall.

But this crop of politicians should be drowned at sea.

The traffic started moving, and he was soon out of the tunnel and speeding ahead, the wind whipping through the window. He passed the harbor and drove through the city, steering with one hand while going the wrong way down narrow streets, blowing the horn to warn oncoming traffic. A few minutes later he was parked in front of the clothing store in the Hamra district where Gisele worked as a salesclerk.

He found her arranging sunglasses on a metal rack, while a few feet away a man and a woman were urgently whispering to each other next to a heap of clothes on the counter. The woman held up an angry face toward her older companion, who leaned toward her, twirling an impressive mustache, perhaps intended to distract from his baldness.

Gisele looked up as he strode toward the waiting area, smiled at him, then frowned furtively at the squabbling pair. He smiled back and sat down on the round sofa to wait. Aside from the couple and a man and his teenage daughter browsing in the junior section, the store was empty. There were flowers on the tables and tall plants with big glossy leaves in bronze and earthen pots. A crouching female statue in a marble fountain poured water from a jug hoisted on her shoulder.

He suddenly remembered Gisele's birthday and got up to browse the racks. A silver chain-link belt caught his eye. He picked it up but dropped it quickly when he saw the price, and made his way back to the sofa, looking around sheepishly to see if anyone had noticed. The woman with the mustachioed companion had put on a purple summer dress and was admiring herself in the mirror while Gisele squatted behind her and took up the hem. When she finished, she cut the thread with her teeth and stood up. The woman cocked her head, unable to decide. Tired of waiting, Hisham caught Gisele's eye and pointed to the street as he headed for the door.

In the doorway he hesitated, then released the doorknob and stepped into the roaring street. Lately he'd been planting himself in the middle of bustling streets, standing still while the crowd surged past him, as if remaining motionless would save him from the sweeping tide. He looked at the mountains and sky, so close he could draw them to him. His small country, the size of a thumbprint on a map, a thin coastline surrounded by mountains. Crammed together, leaderless, the Lebanese made a mess of things, always complaining about their government while eulogizing their country's landscapes and their seafaring forefathers.

The people were as varied as the landscape. Palestinians and Lebanese fleeing Israeli bombs in the South poured into the capital, and rural migrants came knocking on doors looking for jobs scarce in their mountains, while a sizable Armenian population clustered in the inner souks and on the city's outskirts. There were at least eighteen religious sects spread across the country, all clamoring for a say. New political parties sprang up like mushrooms, and not one day went by without demonstrations or shootings.

Beirut exhausted him. Images of an idealized past roused up longing for his village where he had lived in blissful ignorance. Except for his father and brother who fought about politics, he knew nothing about the conflicts lying the length of a mountain away.

When Beirut stifled him, he reminded himself that he had wanted this. At eighteen he had fled his mountain with a few liras in his pocket to join his brother, and ran into the arms of the city, eager to see his life finally begin.

He scanned the sidewalk cafés in vain for a free table, then turned and examined the display windows. Swiss watches, cassette players, and cotton bedsheets flicked through his mind as possible gifts for Gisele. Peddlers of novelty items accosted him from the sidewalk.

He bought two jellabs from a juice vendor and was munching on pine nuts when Gisele appeared. She was beautiful in her turquoise skirt and white sleeveless blouse, her dark hair swept up in a ponytail. A church bell rang. As if on cue, the call to prayer wafted from a nearby mosque. He got down on one knee and bowed, joking that the heavens had conspired to break out in song upon her arrival. Laughing, she pulled him to his feet. They walked toward the sea, arms entwined, as she told him about her colleague, Siham, and her affair with their boss.

On the way, he bought roasted peanuts in paper cones, and they strolled along the corniche, stopping to lean over the guardrail and look at the sea, their lips salty from the peanuts and the mist of the waves. He put his arm around her shoulders, and she leaned into him. A fisherman stood on a flat rock jutting out into the water, his line cast into the frothing waves. In a few weeks the beaches would be swarming with people. Sailboats and motorboats with skiers would crisscross the water, and the Pigeons' Rock would lure the daredevils and suicidal to leap from the top.

He turned and faced the street. Families with children clutching cotton candy strolled by in the pink light, young people made eyes at one another, and ka'ak bread vendors wove through on their bicycles, beeping their bells in warning. Cheap gold jewelry flashed from a stand. He plotted a devious plan in his mind: inexpensive jewelry packaged in an elegant case procured from his cousin who worked at a pricey jewelry store. He'd be caught in an instant! Better to take her to dinner at El-Ajami and to see Shushu's new play.

"I can't wait for summer," she said. He heard her yearning for the beach cabin she wanted to rent at a private resort that would cost him a bundle he didn't have. Old resentments rose in him. All her money went to clothes, while to him fell the burden of their living expenses. The raise he got after the last teacher strike had barely made a dent.

He pulled away and headed to the stands for sandwiches and drinks. When he returned, she resumed her talk about money—

the extra they would have if she was promoted, her plans for spending it, the Italian living room set she had her eye on, the parties. He took a long swallow from his drink and looked away. He didn't want to see her like this, so covetous it embarrassed him. His attention drifted. He pretended to be shocked when she told him about her boss's wife's surprise visit and Siham's face reddening violently. As long as he nodded and chimed in at the right moment, she didn't notice that he was half-listening.

They got in the car and drove to the market. Funneled by the crowd, they wove through narrow alleys lined with stalls sheltered from the sun by shredded awnings and small shops whose doors were clogged by piles of plastic shoes. The walls were hung with cheap merchandise—nylon garments, long-handled brooms, loofahs, carpet beaters. Fishmongers with tall wicker baskets hoisted on their shoulders bartered heatedly with shopkeepers. Souk led to bustling souk—jewelry, fabrics, flowers, spices, produce. She bought coffee and perfume, Armenian sausages and cheese, putting up a strong bargain, her mountain accent sneaking back into her speech and confounding the merchants. He told her about his students who had delighted him by speaking intelligently and without coaxing and the hour that flew by. It was her turn to listen distractedly.

The sky had darkened by the time they arrived at the small chapel. She tied a headscarf around her neck and walked inside while he followed, fumbling with the grocery bags. Aside from the small ceiling lamp, the only source of light was a bank of flickering candles close to a wall covered in paintings of the Virgin Mary in various incarnations.

He found a pew in the back, then slid in next to a man with prayer beads in his hands. A pleasant drowsiness overtook him. He must have dozed off. When he opened his eyes, Gisele was kneeling on the footrest next to him, deep in prayer. He had confessed his atheism a few months into their relationship and waited for the verdict. She shrugged and never brought up the subject again. He breathed a sigh of relief, but later wondered whether her silence was a sign of acceptance or an unspoken rebuke.

The prayer ended. Crossing herself, she stood up and headed for the door, and he staggered to his feet and followed her to the street.

They walked in silence. A few persistent peddlers yelled out their pitches, their day-old produce already too old to sell. In the dusky light of the lampposts, people hurried by, seeking entertainment in the restless city. Hisham felt a surge of tenderness for Beirut. How much longer before it collapsed in exhaustion? But a city had reserves of energy not available to a mere mortal like him, who was looking forward to the book he'd left on the nightstand and hoping that his wife would find something to watch on television and let him be.

2

Rita

At the beginning of March, our grade was invited to a three-day retreat at the nuns' summer convent. Brochures promoting the event's goal of "cementing Christian values" were sent home. The older girls cautioned that it was a ploy to extract our darkest secrets. But a good time could still be had: the trick was to pretend to bare our souls while saying nothing at all and show piety we didn't feel while still having a good time. When I found out that Seta was going, I was in.

There were enough girls in the school parking lot to fill a bus when I arrived early Friday morning. Seta was busy with her friends, so I approached a group of girls who debated the potential of seeing the sisters without their habits until the signal for us to board the bus sounded. As I passed Seta in the aisle, I touched her shoulder, and she smiled at me and said a few words before turning back to the girl next to her.

It was a short drive to the small village, known for its springs and wild meadows. After climbing a small hill, we stopped in front of a gate that revealed a large stone building. A cobbled path wound down a large grassy field all the way to the monastery, and following it, we passed a side courtyard enclosed by arched walls offering a view of the sea in the distance. Further to the left, a garden planted on a terrace teemed with tall plants and fruit trees and sunflowers on the verge of blooming in the early heat. The monastery was covered with purple bougainvillea that cascaded profusely as if sprung directly from the stone. At the front entrance a young nun escorted us to a long hallway on the second floor with beds lined up against the walls. She gave a few instructions, then left after announcing that there were snacks in the kitchen.

There were at least thirty beds, each with a small brown crucifix hung on the wall over it. With its white walls and gleaming terrazzo tiles, the long, narrow room had the feel of a hospital ward. We fought for prime spots near the windows. The beds near Seta were quickly taken before I could claim my own, and I found myself settling in next to Nicole, a classmate whose joy at seeing me made up for my disappointment.

The morning passed slowly, with visits to the chapel and the library, and free time to roam the grounds. After lunch we received our assignments—mine was to set the table before meals and sweep the floor after—then were escorted to the garden, where we were put to work weeding and hoeing. Thanks to the hot weather, the plants were very near to yielding their crop. The day concluded with a short Mass and another meal.

The next morning we were woken early by the bell and led to the lawn. We gathered sleepily in a circle to the news that Monsieur Sami, our shy and pimply math teacher, would be leading the meetings. He was new to our school and had been bullied into giving up his weekend. We'd been awful to him since the beginning, passing secret notes in class and bursting out in laughter behind his back. Seeing him now, visibly terrified, made us crueler still. We tittered to hear him stutter. We yawned in plain sight and refused to answer his questions.

I kept an eye on Seta. A few weeks earlier, she had confessed her crush on Monsieur Sami. I was shocked by her poor taste—was it the lost puppy look? But she seemed so serious, and I was so grateful to be included in her confidence, that I said nothing. Watching her now, with her closed and furious expression, her white-knuckled hands pulling at the grass, I feared her next move.

It was worse than I could have imagined. She jumped to her feet and strode to the middle of the circle. With her eyes fixed on our shocked teacher, she said, "Je t'aime!" and then screamed it again and again. She roared and stomped her foot, her face turning a violent crimson, and her declarations of love startled the silence. We watched, stunned, our eyes pendulating between them. Monsieur Sami's pimples had swollen alarmingly with the blood that flooded his face. I found it difficult to look at him, and even more difficult to watch my friend. I wanted desperately to pull her aside and knock some sense into her, but I watched helplessly without daring to move. She finally burst into tears and ran across the yard to the lawn's edge, where she hunched into herself sobbing.

Monsieur Sami cast his eyes desperately around the circle as if pleading for instructions. We looked away. At last, he heaved himself up, and with his head sunk between his shoulders, staggered out toward Seta. He took a few steps, stopped, and then started again. He did this a few more times, stopping and resuming his walk until he reached her. He must have been practicing his speech during all that stalling, because as soon as he stepped in front of her, he began to speak. Even from a distance, we could tell she had stopped crying and, with her face raised up to him, was listening.

When Sister Marie-Anne appeared in the doorway we turned sheepishly toward her, terrified for Seta but hopeful that she would put an end to this incident before it ruined our stay. She scanned our faces, then followed our gazes across the lawn, where Seta was sitting under a tree, and Monsieur Sami stood with his back turned to her, gazing at the sea.

Sister Marie-Anne cut across the lawn, and my heart dropped. But nothing happened. After a short conversation with Monsieur Sami, the sister pulled Seta to her feet and led her across the cobbled path, and the two of them walked arm in arm, while the sister waved her hands as if showing her the sights.

We understood that the incident was closed. Despite our relief, the anticlimax was a letdown. We swooned and yelled *je t'aime* in jest at each other until a sister reprimanded us.

The retreat went on as planned. We met in small groups. The school priest attended the afternoon sessions. Our revelations were hardly scandalous. A girl confessed to a breach in her faith, carefully, to test the waters, and instantly Father Simon's rosacea flared up and the sisters' eyebrows shot up in alarm, prompting the girl to quickly change course and pledge unwavering faith. Seta sat apart from the group, drawing sketches in her pad. The rest of us winked and smiled at each other. Eventually we stopped noticing her presence.

After lunch we gathered in the common room. The hours rolled. We had enough free time to enjoy ourselves. I spent the afternoon reading and taking long strolls in the garden. My attempts to talk to Seta led nowhere. She kept to herself, and although she did not rebuke me when I sidled near, her closed expression kept me at bay.

On the last day of the retreat, Seta discovered me with my hands clasped to my heart, crying out Monsieur Sami's name to a group of giggling girls. I apologized. I stood before her with my arms dangling and my words brief but true, but she swiveled on her heel and walked away, and it was like a door shut in my face.

The thing was, even as I laughed with the others, I understood Seta. I knew how powerful emotions could cloud your good judgment. The previous summer I had vowed to enter the convent on my eighteenth birthday. Intense stirrings would suddenly overtake me, and I would drop everything and kneel before the many icons in our apartment. Which saint I chose hardly mattered. I prayed to Jesus at the last supper; to Saint Therese, "the Little Flower"; to Saint Maroun kneeling at the mountaintop and pointing a foreboding finger at the sky; and to an exalted Saint Rita, my patron saint, marked for sainthood by a thorn that shot out from the crown of Jesus and lodged in her head.

I prayed and prayed, until one day I suddenly stopped. The optician who leased the space on the ground floor of our apartment building had hired a new apprentice, a handsome Alain Delon look-alike who banished God from my thoughts. Alain Delon came out to the courtyard between customers to watch me play tennis against the wall. My solo game improved. The ball slammed into the wall as I flew across the court. At night, I kissed his imaginary lips on the back of my hand. Then school started. The shop was always closed by the time I got home, and after a few weeks of pining I moved on.

As a result, I did not take Seta's feelings for Monsieur Sami seriously. I believed they would pass, the way mine had come and gone without leaving a trace.

The retreat came to an end. On the bus taking us home, Seta walked straight to the back seat without giving me a glance. I turned and gazed at her, sitting alone with her forehead tipped to the window. My heart was heavy with regret. I had ruined a friendship, and I couldn't figure out why.

At school she continued to ignore me. The following Thursday, a well-known politician, shot during the Saïda protests, died from his injuries. Announcement of our early release sent us into a frenzy of speculations. We knew the politician's name. We had heard it on television and in our parents' conversations. That was all we knew. Why the early release we were not sure, but we were not complaining.

We waited for the buses, jittery with excitement and trepidation. Seta stood apart from the others, clutching her books to her chest. I saw parts of her face, her chin, the thick tangle of curls across her cheeks. When my bus arrived, I sat in the first row to avoid running into her. She walked by without looking at me. I opened my copy of *Le Grand Meaulnes* and resumed where I'd left off that morning. François Seurel was walking through the woods, hoping to find the enchanted castle that his friend, Meaulnes, had discovered on a stormy night. Meaulnes had tried to retrace his steps, obsessively drawing one map after another, to no avail. François continued on his way, hoping to complete his mission, even if it meant losing his dear friend.

I'd read the novel before, and I knew the outcome of François's walk: a clearing, then a meadow, and the house of the school guard at the end of it.

"I found nothing," François said.

Poor François, sickly and introspective. Watching from the sidelines as his friend vaulted into his life.

When the bus stopped, I let Seta off first and watched her go inside her building, wondering whether she would ever forgive me. Because if she didn't, I'd have to learn not to care.

I entered our apartment and ran to Mama to tell her the bad news. She was mopping the living room floor and paused while I spoke, and when I was done, she picked up the bucket and walked to the bathroom without saying anything. I followed her as she emptied and filled the bucket, washing and wringing the mop until the water ran clear, her eyes narrowed and shrouded with dark fear, and I realized that this welcome break from school might not be such a wonderful thing after all. She'd been praying more lately, an aura of fear around her that sparked my own scary thoughts. I rattled off my questions. Will a state of emergency be declared? Will the army step in and the schools close, and will we stay in Tarawa at my grandmother's house to wait out the events? But my questions remained unanswered, and her fear lingered in the silence after she left the room and was now mine to bear.

I went to the bedroom and raided Rasha's closet. I slid into the mustard-yellow corduroy pants and ruffle-sleeved blouse she'd bought on a recent shopping trip with Baba, where we'd come home with bags full of spring and summer clothing. I struck several poses in front of the mirror before diving back into the closet, where I found a box of Swiss chocolate under a mound of shirts and helped myself. I looked around some more, finding pictures and ticket stubs but nothing I could use to blackmail her with. I had happy memories of my mother forcing my sister to bring me along on all her outings in the hope that my youth would keep her virtuous. Fortunately, my presence made no difference, and my early education in the world of older teens took place in Beirut's coffee shops and dark movie theaters, where I watched my sister and her friends flirt with idle young men and exchange furtive kisses, silly smiles, and innuendoes.

She walked in when I was removing the top and flew in a rage. "How many times have I told you?" she screamed before grabbing my shoulders and shaking me. I tried to get free, but she shoved me down, and I found myself pinned to the floor, squeezed in a tight grip between her knees, as she spat her fury at my face, called me thief and liar, and added, pointing to her top in a heap on the bed and the chocolate wrappers all over the floor, that she had been vandalized. I tried wiggling out from her grip, but she was immovable. We went on like this until our mother came to remind us that our father might walk in at any moment. Rasha reluctantly let go of my arms, locked her closet, and left the room with one last furious look.

I lay in bed after she left, leafing through a photo novella. But Franco Gasparri couldn't take my mind off the ache in my arms where her knees had dug. I dropped the novella and stared at the ceiling. We were sisters, full of fierce love and sudden waves of anger. I knew that I had done something wrong, and that in the morning I would forget about our fight as if it had never happened. But I was sorry to let it go, this anger that made me feel alive. I had lain weak and half-repentant and humiliated in Rasha's grip. But strength was something that grew like a house, stone by stone. One day I would be fearless, and with this thought I dropped off to sleep.

Hisham

The wounded of Saïda succumbed to their injuries. On Thursday, the deaths of a deputy and an army lieutenant sent the country into bedlam. The deputy was Muslim, the lieutenant Christian, a combustible juxtaposition. Protests broke out and were followed by bursts of gunfire. Burned tires blackened the air with thick palls of smoke and soot.

By Monday the country was getting back on track. When Hisham woke up, Gisele was already gone. She'd mentioned an early errand in town, but he couldn't remember where it was. He'd been distracted recently, obsessively following the news in order to predict the future and detect signs that this, too, would be buried, swept away by a national temperament that loved pleasure as much as it did squabbles and religion.

He crossed into the kitchen, lit a fire under the kettle, and waited for the coffee to boil before he poured himself his first cup of the day. Gisele had set a bowl of olives on the table alongside a plate of bread and cheese in order to entice him to eat breakfast. He sat beside the window, ate a few olives to make her happy, and stared out at the shoeshine boy who had set up shop under the barbershop's awning and was soliciting business from passersby.

His mind traveled back to his boyhood, and he remembered picking olives with Fuad in late autumn and bringing them to the press. In the winter they worked at the village store after school. In the spring they tilled and planted the ground, and in the summer they harvested the tobacco. He despised every second of it. The hard times left their imprint on the brothers. Fuad fumed about the government's indifference to the poor. He knew the shoeshine boy's name and brought him a gift every time he came to visit—fruit, coins, and once a ticket to see a Bruce Lee movie. And Hisham? He believed that only a thin thread separated him from ruin. When a beggar approached him, he threw a few piasters in the extended palm and fled like the devil.

A clamor drew his attention back to the street. A brawl had erupted over a parking space, and two men were lunging at each other, screaming and shouting insults, while peacekeepers held them back in the honking traffic. Suddenly a car drove onto the sidewalk, scattering the terrified pedestrians, and came to a halt with grinding brakes. A man in military fatigues emerged, pulled out a gun, and fired into the air. People screamed and ran for cover. Hisham drew back from the window. Another round of gunfire was followed by whistle blows. Then the guns went quiet, and someone shrilled out orders. Somewhere, a voice: "I intervened when help was late arriving."

Hisham peered from behind a corner of the curtain. The crowd was trickling back. A police officer was directing the traffic. On the sidewalk, a militant leaned against the hood of his car, smoking. He threw the butt to the ground, climbed back into his car, and sped off in front of a crowd of frightened bystanders.

Hisham arrived at school a few minutes before the bell rang. In the hallway Sister Marie-Anne stopped him. "Your grades, Monsieur Bassil. By noon tomorrow." He'd have to correct forty tests by day's end. The morning dragged on. He sent three eighth graders to the office for speaking out of turn. The ninth graders were at recess when he sat at his desk with a stack of unmarked tests. He crossed out entire paragraphs and deducted points for mistakes he might have overlooked on a better day.

He shifted his attention to the reading assignment, a play excerpt. In the opening scene, a government official was negotiating a hit with an assassin. When he discovered his target's identity, the hit man refused to carry out the job. He would not assassinate a political dissident or a defender of the poor.

Hisham drew three columns on the board, labeling the first

Hero, the third Villain, and leaving the middle one blank. It was one way of introducing the lesson. They might not be able to get to the columns today. He'd first have to shake up a few entrenched beliefs and introduce the notion that the moral needle oscillated, that clarity required a bit of sorcery.

He riffled through his notes. Most of his students would pick the villain's column. A few would listen before taking sides. Then there were the ones like him, with their burrowing instincts and seducible, vagabond minds, who would frustrate everyone with their fickleness by insisting on seeing multiple sides to everything.

They trooped in, red-faced and sweaty, and he began the lesson. They scanned the text in search of answers. The minutes passed, and when he thought he could no longer bear the silence, he walked to the window and stood with his back to them, resisting the impulse to have them grab pen and paper and take dictation. But when he turned around, a few hands were raised, and off they went. He congratulated himself on giving them meaty topics, even though the scope of their thinking often left him disappointed. He had to remind himself that they were young, but they were his prize students. With them he trespassed into critical reasoning beyond their years, while with his younger students he stuck to the textbooks, with their nationalistic poems and moral tales, their nostalgic pictures of peasants in traditional sharwals and tasseled fez hats playing the flute in the shade of trees.

The official elicited no sympathy, but then the government never did. The hit man didn't fare much better. They wouldn't exempt a killer, even a golden-tongued populist with unlikely ideals.

"He's a hero. By turning down a powerful man he's risking his life," someone offered.

They broke ranks. He assured them it was all right to change their minds, even when they couldn't explain why. They issued their verdicts. The middle column began to fill.

The bell rang. It had been a good discussion. He beamed at them as they walked out, his beautiful, smart pupils.

After school he drove to Fuad's office. As a rule, the two brothers avoided politics, but one of them always slipped. Hisham would get an earful, and he would scramble to keep up with his well-informed brother. But you wouldn't know there was trouble by looking at the people around him, driving with their roofs down, eager for summer. It wasn't until he'd parked the car that he noticed he'd been gripping the wheel.

Karam Agricultural Company, a major grain and poultry supplier, occupied the third floor of a downtown office building. A well-lit corridor lined with glass partitions led to Fuad's office. The work area behind the partitions was buzzing with activity. Fuad's office was at the far end of the corridor. Hisham put his ear to the wooden door, listening for any signs of Walid, Fuad's meddling colleague and the reason he didn't visit more often, then twisted the doorknob and walked in.

A single light bulb hung from the ceiling. In one corner of the room, a floor fan recycled the stale air. Fuad and Walid sat at their desks, punching numbers into electric calculators and making entries into ledgers. Stripped down to their undershirts, they looked startlingly similar, with their paunches and receding hairlines, and their chest hair curling up from the necklines.

Walid was the first to raise his head. Leaping to his feet, he hugged Hisham, uttering a string of greetings before stepping out to buy coffee from the janitor, who had a thriving side business in the lobby selling coffee, cigarettes, and candy.

Fuad motioned that he'd be a few minutes longer. Hisham sat in a chair and watched as his brother lined up his pencils in a neat row on the desk. When they were children, homework was nightly announced at the kitchen table with a session of pencil sharpening. Hisham had been perplexed, but asking Fuad for an explanation would have been an intrusion, and in their tiny house the two brothers guarded their privacy with the zeal of monks. He could only speculate on his brother's motivations.

Perhaps it was Fuad's way of clearing his mind. Maybe he collected sharpened pencils to ensure a steady supply in case he was interrupted. There was something excessive about all that preparation. It revealed a fear of setbacks and the belief that they could be avoided with careful planning. When homework was finished, the same pencils were lined up and sharpened again, a parenthesis closing.

Hisham watched his brother with a mix of affection and impatience. Was this the same man who wanted to save the world? This slow, deliberate nitpicker, with his pencils neatly pointing to the wall?

The door swung open. Walid had returned and was handing out the coffee, the dreaded question on his lips. "Anything on the way?" he said, and both Fuad and Hisham knew what he meant. The local custom was to pry the secrets out with circumlocutions.

"No, no children yet," Hisham said weakly. He and Gisele had been married four years, and everyone seemed to be counting.

Not yet. Not ever. In the first months of their marriage, they tiptoed around their hearts' true desire. *In a few years, no hurry,* until... Who said it first? No children, not ever. He adored his niece and nephew but had no desire to have children of his own. Gisele was an only child. She grew up watching her aunt raise six children while her mother lived a relatively leisurely life. Gisele decided that if having fewer children was good, having none was even better. Sometimes Hisham had his doubts. What was wrong with them that they rejected what other people considered to be the best part of life? She seemed to be plagued by the same thoughts. Who knows what the future will bring? We might change our minds in a few years, she said, leaving the door open. But they hadn't yet, and they didn't seem to be any worse for it.

"What are you waiting for?" Walid shifted his gaze to Fuad, pleading with him to talk sense into his younger brother. Laughing, Fuad buttoned his shirt and led Hisham to the door.

They walked toward their favorite pastry shop, with Hisham griping about Walid (Bearish! Meddlesome! Insupportable!), and Fuad laughing and stopping every now and then to catch his breath. He'd gained weight. Were these rings under his eyes? Hisham used to tag along when they were children. Fuad would run out of the house, always angry about something—corruption, the useless Arabs, Palestine and Israel, the high prices and low wages, the fouda, chaos everywhere. Hisham feared for his brother, made fists behind his back, and prayed he would not have to use them. The gods listened and the bullies steered clear, even though Fuad was short and slight, and anyone could have easily taken him down. But his tongue cut like a knife, and no one took him to task. Everyone predicted he would go far, become a lawyer or a journalist. Instead, he became an accountant with an unhappy marriage. But to Hisham, he remained formidable. The mundane circumstances of his life did not alter his essence.

They walked past shops and restaurants with queues of people at the entrance. Fuad bragged about his children—Layla's excellent grades and Karim's mastering of the Moonlight Sonata—and made no mention of Grace. The couple weren't getting along, and they no longer cared who knew it.

The coffee shop was full, and they had to wait for a table. Waiters brushed past with trays, yelling orders. Pastries filled with nuts and clotted cream were displayed in trays behind glass panels. A young waiter escorted them to a table near the window and arranged their chairs away from the sun. They ordered coffee and a pastry and made small talk: how they seemed to have gone straightaway into summer; their mother's garden, which must be in full bloom; and their plans to spend Palm Sunday in the village.

Hisham was happy. It must be this coffee shop, he thought. One felt good here, lulled by music on the radio and the thud of backgammon stones slamming the boards.

What, then, compelled Hisham to break the enchantment?

Was it a desire to confront the inevitable that made him drop his fork and dive straight into the latest riots? He complained about the violence and disruptions, the protesters blocking traffic and causing chaos.

"The powerful call civil protest a mutiny, then go on to rule forever," Fuad said.

Hisham felt hopelessly inadequate, his mind misty and slow, filled with half-formed ideas. Of course, he sympathized with the fishermen of Saïda. One always felt sorry for the poor, until they started smashing windows.

He wanted explanations. Not because he thought Fuad had to account for his thoughts, but because he needed answers to mend the rift in his own soul. Fuad sipped his water and appeared ready to change the subject.

"Why burn tires and blow up shops?" Hisham persisted.

Fuad saw it differently. Not thuggery running riot, but an eruption long in coming, self-affirming anger, the last resort of a desperate people.

"The army shooting into a crowd of peaceful protesters is barbarous," Fuad said.

It always came down to this. Enough blame to go around. When everyone was a sinner, who were the victims? Hisham fell silent. How could he explain? Something terrible was being unleashed. The difference between him and Fuad was vast: free, messy speech for one was anarchy for the other, the beginning of the end.

"Make calm, rational demands," he heard himself say. He didn't believe a word of it. "We are being hurled into war," he continued. Militias of all factions had been training. Once again, the country was on the brink of disaster. One time too many made for bad odds.

Fuad released a sigh. "The army shot at peaceful demonstrators. It was a mistake to deploy the army in Saïda and a mistake to order it to fire at the crowd, and *this*, my dear brother, is what will start the war."

Bring in the army, don't bring in the army. A debate as old as independence. Bring it in and it would break along religious lines and ignite a civil war. Don't bring it in, and the Lebanese would still kill each other.

"It's not clear who shot the first bullet. Things got out of hand. Some of your peaceful demonstrators were well armed."

Fuad gave him a dark look. "I'll tell you what got out of hand: the rich and their government cronies. And how do you think the people are feeling? Up to here. Up to here!" he repeated, bringing his hand to his brow, palm down, like a lid on a boiling pot.

He was angry. I have made him angry, Hisham thought, and he will lose the argument. He remembered the girls at school walking in a single file and standing to attention when he entered the room, and the nuns keeping a close eye on things. His heart filled with fondness. In this atmosphere of calm restraint, he was able to teach his students how to reason and ask questions, so that one day they would realize the senselessness of burning tires and chanting slogans no one would hear. They would become slow to anger and grow up to correct wrongs with the power of cool reason. For his brother, the violence on the street was what you put up with for the greater good, the accidental dead be damned.

A memory came to him. During his student years he used to take part in demonstrations. He told Fuad how one day he found himself held up at the end of the line. By the time the slogans reached him, they had become distorted and stripped of meaning.

"It was like a silly game of Pass the Message," he continued. "Still they carried on, making fists and puffing out their chests like stupid roosters and yelling at the world. It was funny, but I didn't laugh. The whole thing devolved into another scuffle between the Christian and Muslim students. One minute they were chanting together for Palestine and lower tuitions and higher wages and cheaper cinema tickets, and the next they were fighting. I decided never to take part in another demonstration.

I didn't see the use. I was better off attending class. And now, I fear the riots are taking us to a bad place."

Fuad drummed the table with his fingers. He looked bored, but Hisham wasn't done yet. "How will the riots save us?" At the same time, he felt a pang of envy. For there was his brother leaning forward and saying something Hisham didn't completely understand because he was spellbound by Fuad's eyes, which were shining with a blazing conviction Hisham would never know. His brother was free of the doubts that paralyzed Hisham, whose mind was always watching from a distance, judging like a strict, supercilious uncle, repeating, *This will not do, these outbursts. Cooler heads must prevail*, preventing him from feeling anything fully. How safe it was, yet how frustrating, to live with doubt, to always find a counterargument and have a ready excuse for inaction.

"For which good will you fight?" his brother was asking. "What wrong will make you so angry that you will run to the streets without giving a toss whether people are on their best behavior or if you're doing the right thing? Silence will harm you, and silent is how they want you, begging in a corner for the crumbs they throw your way. When we protest, we are fearless. Things get smashed and mistakes are made and the house burns down, but the house is no good so let it burn."

Fuad looked handsome and strong. A chasm separated them. Hisham spoke about teaching the young to think for themselves instead of running wild in the streets, and about using words instead of guns.

Fuad asked Hisham about his classes.

He mumbled something in response. He didn't want to talk about his students, who would not, he realized, grow up to save the world. But Hisham was not interested in revolutions. He wanted to be left in peace to read and write. This was it, his contribution: teaching, doing good. None of it would make any difference. For Fuad, a conscience without a doctrine to back it up was a rudderless ship, a waste of time. Hisham wasn't sure he disagreed.

"You know this might end badly," he said after a pause. "The country hasn't seen eye to eye on anything since we came together to expel the French. That was a long time ago."

"We are more alike than you think, my dear brother. We all need to eat. Speaking of which, I'm still hungry," Fuad quipped, patting his own large stomach while summoning the waiter.

It was too easy to call on our basic humanity, Hisham thought.

And yet, we tried to make a go of it, he thought. Together the Lebanese kicked out the French and created the National Covenant. In exchange for the promise of a country, the Christians let go of their dependence on France and Muslims dropped their dreams of a united Arab nation. To fulfill their pledge to each other would be the most radical of revolutions.

They made their way back. When they entered the building, they saw the janitor weeping in his chair over the death of his brother-in-law in a car accident in Syria. Hisham expressed his condolences and drifted to the entrance, leaving Fuad to comfort the bereaved man.

It was getting dark, and the air was starting to cool. He leaned in the doorway, his gaze drawn to the cinema marquee across the street where two young Egyptian heartthrobs were locked in a tight embrace. Cooking odors issued from fast-food carts, reminding him that he was expected at home. As he turned to leave, he noticed a girl sitting in a chair in a dimly lit corner of the lobby, her back to the door. He hadn't seen her when he walked in, and he wasn't sure if she'd been sitting there the whole time or had just emerged from one of the ground floor apartments. Her chair was angled so that the natural light from the glass fell on her left side. As he edged closer, he made out her shoulder-length hair and the white and blue uniform of a nearby public school. She sat motionless, engrossed in the book on her lap, her ankles crossed under the chair, exposing the threadbare soles of her shoes pockmarked with holes.

(He was about eight. He had been handed a secondhand pair

of leather shoes at the start of summer and instructed to make them last. By winter's end the soles were worn so thin, he might as well have been barefoot. He was always cold, as if the holes left him permanently exposed to the elements. In school he sat by the brazier, warmth slowly spreading through him. He could have stayed there all winter, but the bell would ring, and he'd have to leave and stagger out into the wretched cold.)

He was about to reach her when, sensing his presence, she looked up from the page and met his gaze. She appeared to be about thirteen. Her birdlike face, half in shadow, jutted out sharply toward him.

He smiled and asked what she was reading. She frowned and seemed to think about his question for a few seconds. Then she lowered her head, her hair falling like a curtain over her face. When he didn't move, she slammed the book shut and raised her glaring eyes at him. He was confused—he was usually good with young people—but he pressed on, providing his name and occupation, and was met with the same stony silence in response. Mortified, he muttered an apology, then swiveled around and walked to the bulletin board, pretending to read the notices.

Fuad beckoned him from the elevator to show him a picture of Karim from his most recent recital. When the doors closed, Hisham inquired about the girl. Fuad looked at him with surprise and told him that her name was Jumana and that she was the janitor's daughter. Hisham's cheeks flushed with shame. He had intruded on a girl in mourning. He decided to buy her new shoes and leave them on her father's table with an anonymous note. It was the least he could do.

Hisham wouldn't have minded charity when he was a child. Had anyone offered, he would have tucked the new shoes under his arm and made a run for it. He would have worn the shoes and put the incident behind him. He grabbed all the books he could find and read and clawed his way to a better future.

He praised his nephew's photo and left. The lobby was deserted, and Jumana's chair had vanished. He left the building and walked to his car, his thoughts drifting to the novel he was reviewing for *The Station*. The novel, told in the elegiac voice of a female narrator who had left her native village for the capital, chronicled the stories of her friends who had remained behind to lead lives constrained by narrow conventions. She intrigued him. Unable to break free, chained to her village by tales of injustice, she never revealed her own story. Her voice was muffled, and one had to lean in close to hear it.

He quickly got into his car and drove away. Dusk had given way to night. His thoughts went back to Jumana. She'd probably mistaken him for a sexual deviant. He was furious with himself.

To his left, the sea was dark. He felt a sudden yearning for a hidden beauty lying outside his reach, and a sense of melancholy settled over him. What if his revelation never came?

Rita

We woke up to thunder. Lightning split the blackened sky. The streets were white with hail. In school we were restless. It was all the teachers could do to keep us from jumping out of our seats at every howl from the angry sky.

To our dismay, we were dismissed at the usual time, not a minute earlier. The school bus skidded through the slushy streets, marble-sized hailstones battering the roof.

When we got off, Seta motioned for me to follow her. Beside myself with joy, I trailed her to the puddles thick with hail. The thunder had quieted down, but the sky was gloomy, and the lashing rain blinded my vision. No matter. Fallen from grace, now I rose again. I was with Seta.

She bent forward, scooped up a handful of hail, and worked it into a ball.

"My cousin plays with real snow," she said, her fingers wrapped around the ball.

Her cousin lived in Montreal and sent her pictures of snowbanks high as small hills and smiling snowmen sitting crookedly on their haunches. She tossed the ball into a puddle and walked across the street to her apartment. Pausing at the entrance, she turned to give me a wave.

Flushed with joy, I ran up to my apartment. I peeled off my uniform and wrapped it in a tight bundle, then threw it on the floor and looked for my mother. I found her at the kitchen window, scanning the street for my father's car. Rasha and Baba rode home together after she finished her classes. They weren't expected for another hour, but my mother's eyes were already dark with worry. On the radio the announcer listed car accidents and extensive damage.

"One thing after another," Mama said, making the sign of the cross.

"It's only hail," I answered in a small voice.

She glared at me. "Sugar rationing. Israel. Demonstrations, burnt tires, and the angry mobs. And now this," she said, ticking off disasters on her fingers.

This, I thought, remembering Seta, was a wonderful day. But my mother's fear had leaked into me. In my room I sat on the edge of my bed and thought of Seta, and once again happiness bubbled up inside me. Was this it, then? Forgiveness?

But the next minute I saw my mother's fingers stabbing the air. Mama was right: one thing after another. I paced the length of my room. I imagined the car rolled on its back, Baba and Rasha's lifeless bodies by the side of the road, pummeled by hail. I closed my eyes, but the terrible images kept coming. Mustering all the willpower I possessed, I summoned my father. *There is nothing to fear, my little lamb,* his voice said in my head, and I breathed.

I set off toward my parents' bedroom. My mother was saying the rosary, upright in her favorite chair by the window, her spine a taut line pulling her heavenward.

"They'll be here soon," I said to reassure her.

She waved me off impatiently. I had made her lose her place.

In the kitchen Tony was eating his way through a pile of candy. He looked up at me in alarm when I leaned over him, fingers hovering. I grabbed a chocolate bar. He made as if to cry, then changed his mind, deciding to absorb the loss rather than fight a losing battle.

My good-looking brother: curly hair, long eyelashes. He was only four, but he was heir to the family name and a thorn in my side. My parents loved me. But when Tony was born, my father danced in the corridor, and his screams of joy rang like a betrayal. My mother was now Um Tony, Tony's Mother, as if until then she had been mothering ghosts.

The sound of the key turning in the lock jolted me out of my resentments. I dashed down the hallway, and there they were, Baba and Rasha, looking agitated but unharmed. My mother brewed zhourat tea and worried about the end of the world.

"There is one millennium," she said when she was in her end-of-the-world mood.

"The end of the millennium is in another twenty-five years!" I tossed back.

Rasha complained about her statistics class at dinner, and Baba promised to help. I tensed up. *Kojak* was on and my sister was hijacking our father. I wanted to see Telly Savalas eat his lollipops and catch the bad guys without reading the subtitles in order to improve my English and impress my father.

Kojak was taking a long drag on his cigarillo when my father arrived. I filled him in, then got off the sofa and sat on the sheepskin rug. The day had been a success after all.

I couldn't get to sleep that night. I only wanted to think about Seta, but I couldn't shake the dark thoughts. Every day brought new conflict. Violence had spread to universities and public schools, which were attended by students from all walks of life. Our Muslim classmates continued to show up, but we suspected their days with us were numbered. How could it be otherwise? The country was breaking apart.

But none of these things were happening near me, and if I ignored the news, I could easily pretend that life was still normal.

The next day at school, I reminded Amal about her lunch invitation, and a few days later, I had my passes. I was overjoyed. At my request, we took the long route to her apartment, soaking in the brilliant light and the sweet air of freedom.

Amal and I began to spend a lot of time together. Everything was going well at first. But Amal clung to me, and I felt trapped and smothered by her attention. I also missed Seta. She must have missed me too, because she invited me to her house to look at the new magazines her relatives had sent her. Like many Armenians, she had relatives all over the world. She had visited Paris, Nice, and Brussels, while I had never left the country.

I loved her room, with its white lace curtains on the windows, bright scarves hung from the bunk beds, a Beatles poster on the wall, and family photos from all over the world. Her bed was littered with pencil sketches. Claire, her older sister, had the top bunk. She was the family's brain, and I was a little afraid of her.

We sat on the floor cushions. Seta inserted the cassette, and Aznavour began to croon, lamenting the passage of time and his lost youth. I found a picture of a shirtless Patrick Juvet and asked to have it for my fan journal. The Partridge family smiled at me from the page of another magazine, all toothy grins.

"She's beautiful," I said, pointing to Susan Dey. Seta's eyes flitted to the picture. She seemed distracted. I wanted to tell her that everything was going to be all right, but the words sounded fake, like a line from a fairy tale or an American movie.

Instead, I told her about the American hippies who came to Tarawa every summer. My uncle invited them to the garden, where he slept on a cot under the vine trellis during the summer months. He'd built a full bathroom and brought down a small stove for cooking. I told her about my crush on Bob, who looked like Jesus in *Jesus Christ Superstar*, and how he had told me in broken Arabic that one day I would be beautiful, and I was devastated. What did that make me in the meantime? He only had eyes for Rasha, my pretty sister who had more admirers than she could handle. The two of them struck a deal: she taught him Arabic and in exchange, he gave her guitar lessons. They traded lessons under my father's strict gaze, who knew all too well that this was a ploy to flirt with his daughter.

Seta listened intently, her eyes never leaving my face. I kept talking until her mother called us to the kitchen. Auntie Sylvie handed Seta a bowl of popcorn and inquired about my family. Like many older Armenians, she mixed her gender pronouns and word endings, and I didn't blink when she addressed me as a boy.

We ate the popcorn in Seta's room while Aznavour sang. Seta was silent. I saw her eyes wandering. There was so much she withheld from me. I didn't believe she meant to keep me out. She just didn't see the point in sharing her life.

I'm sorry I made fun of you, I said silently.

"I like Monsieur Bassil," I blurted in the silence.

She sat up, her eyes wide with wonder.

"No, no, not that way," I laughed, when she pressed me for more, nervous about the turn this was taking. I'd be the laughingstock of the ninth grade if word got out that I had a crush on Monsieur Bassil.

"I just think he's a good teacher. Not as good as Monsieur Gidéon," I added quickly. The French teacher was a god.

She reclined. "I don't know. Arabic is so hard," she said.

"I think he's the best Arabic teacher," I insisted. "Arabic is a great language, you know. The language of science and philosophy." It's what Monsieur Bassil had said. It irked me when the girls didn't even try. They would rather die than confuse their French subjunctives.

We eventually got to talking about our favorite TV shows. I knew we were back on track when our conversation would pause for a few moments without either of us rushing to fill the silence.

I left Seta's apartment with Patrick Juvet's picture tucked under my arm. The sky had darkened, and a light rain was falling. When I got home the gossip session was already underway. Lamia, my next-door neighbor, had stopped in on her way back from a party. She looked beautiful in her gold sequined dress and her hair done up. Her parents were from Bethlehem. They were a good deal older than my parents, but the couples were fond of each other because of the connection to Palestine. As a child, I had spent countless hours in their apartment, trying on Lamia's makeup and following Auntie Nur as she hobbled around on crutches, a stroke a few years earlier having left her paralyzed on one side.

I sat next to Lamia and grabbed a cookie. Rasha cleared her throat and drummed the table with her fingertips, something she was dying to tell. Normally I would have been checking on Baba, who was watching TV in the family room, but I stayed put, curious to hear what my sister had to say. But Lamia had news of her own she wanted to share first. Straightening her shoulders, she grinned and came out with it: at long last, and after several tries, she had finally passed her driving test. As of tomorrow, she would be the proud owner of a convertible Mini Cooper. The car was at our disposal. We thanked her effusively. It was no trouble at all, she said. She needed the practice. In fact, we would be doing her a favor.

Fantasies of our outings piled up in my head. The beach, the mountains, the city at night. I felt a rush of affection for Lamia, who now towered in my esteem over everyone except Baba. I gazed at her lovingly.

Then it was Rasha's turn. She told us the following story:

She had been held up on campus and decided to take a shortcut to Baba's office. She was soon lost. She asked for directions and was given conflicting answers. Frantically she pushed on to the next street and the next after that without finding her way.

Finally, she reached a street that had nothing special about it except for the odd feeling it gave her. She hung back for a while, then decided to press forward. Suddenly, the clouds swarmed in, as though someone had flicked a switch.

"It was a warning," she insisted, her eyes darting around the table at our faces.

Men scurried by, giving her sly glances. She noticed the absence of women and quickened her pace. She had the uneasy impression that invisible eyes were observing her.

Laughter sounded from a point above her head. She slowed her pace and looked up. Three women stood on a balcony, chattering loudly. They wore short dresses with plunging necklines. Their long hair cascaded in heavy waves across their shoulders.

Rasha realized that she had ended up in the red-light district. The big signs on the buildings—Laila the Blond, Miriam from Aleppo, and the famous Marica—at last made sense. She looked down at her feet, broke into a run, and didn't stop until she had reached Baba's office.

Rasha stopped and took a sip from her tea, then glanced at Mama and Lamia. Her face was red with excitement.

Mama didn't know what to say. Contradictory thoughts were clearly waging war on her face. Some chastising might be in order. But for what reason, exactly? It was clear that Rasha was shaken by the incident, if a little too excited. My eyes turned to Lamia. I trusted my neighbor to get it right. But Lamia was tight-lipped, waiting politely for Mama to speak first.

I was disappointed with my sister. I didn't recognize the frightened girl who bolted at the sight of a few prostitutes. The sister I knew crossed lines, sneaked into the city at night, was the life of the party. Why the scandalized virtue? Could all her rule-breaking be nothing more than a thin coat that cracked with the first contact with real life? And if that was the case, wasn't it the epitome of unfairness to shower her with all these adventures, while I sat home moping and shackled with the restrictions of youth? A huge longing overtook me. I wanted to wander the streets of my city alone, to be in complete control of my destiny. Should I one day stumble into a brothel, I'd be sure to stay and take a closer look.

But my sister's nervousness had rubbed off on me, and in my mind, my city became a place of hidden dangers.

Mama said, "Don't tell your father."

Drawing a cursory map on a napkin, Lamia showed Rasha a shortcut to Baba's office.

And just like that, she gave me back my beloved city.

Hisham

The sun had just risen when Hisham and Gisele rang the doorbell. Fuad was badgering Layla and Karim to get ready. In return, the siblings argued for the window seats, their just compensation for waking up at dawn. "Not a chance," their father said. They kept at it, but Fuad would not change his mind. Gisele and Grace would never agree to take the middle seat, and he was already in enough trouble for pestering everyone to hurry up so they could leave early for his parents' house and beat the traffic. In retaliation, Layla dressed in mismatched clothes and Karim took a long time in the bathroom. Even the thought of their doting grandparents didn't soften their resentment. From across the room Hisham mouthed the name of their favorite holiday treat, a specialty of their grandmother's, and their faces brightened. From then on they ignored their elders.

Fuad sped down the empty autostrade, stealing glances at his wife and children in the back seat. No one was speaking to him except Hisham. I'm drowning, drowning, drowning, crooned Abdel Hafez over the radio. Grace and Gisele swayed their heads to the music in the back seat, Karim and Layla scowling between them. Hisham reckoned they'd be given the silent treatment until they arrived at the village.

Before long they had left the coast and were winding up between the hills. Hisham rolled down the window and took a deep breath. You could almost pinpoint the exact spot where the sluggish city air gave way to a crisp and lovely breeze, as though a thin curtain separated city from mountain. From this altitude Beirut looked hazy, smudged by the khamsin, the dry windstorm that blew in from the Egyptian desert. It had descended on them the day before, blanketing everything in dust.

Slouched in his seat, Hisham swallowed to clear his ears. On his right the road dropped, a guardrail separating the car from a steep descent covered in thistles and fern. Even where the vegetation was abundant the land looked arid in the heat, with the leaves airbrushed with silvery gray strokes like ash.

"No politics with Father today, all right?" he instructed his brother.

"I will keep the muzzle on," Fuad replied, laughing sharply.

It was all he would get out of his brother, but it might be enough. Chastened by his wife and children, Fuad would tread carefully. Hisham felt sorry for him, but he was too sleepy to start a conversation.

He had been up most of the night working on his review. He'd been at it for weeks, but it wouldn't write itself. He didn't know much about the narrator, and what little she did reveal was only partially acknowledged. What secrets or inhibitions kept her quiet? He was a fine one to talk, he thought. He went to great lengths to please his mother, who had no idea that he was an atheist, or worse, that he and his wife had decided not to have children.

His mother must be at the stove dicing vegetables into a pot. He imagined his father walking in the door with mint from the garden. They fretted about their sons, the firstborn involved in dubious politics, the younger one childless.

The village must be bustling with the Palm Sunday preparations. Jordan almonds, sweet liqueurs, and the jasmine necklaces sold on the side of the road. Ma'amoul dough resting in a cool corner of the kitchen, giving off smells of butter and yeast and rose water. The bulk of the Easter cookies would be baked later in the week, but they would enjoy a small sampling today.

The land, lined with flowering olive and almond trees, flattened as they approached the village. The two-lane road narrowed. Cars honked in warning at the bends, taking turns to pass. A man on a donkey moved to the side to let them through. They stopped to buy jasmine necklaces for the children. Houses appeared, their shutters opened to the breeze, the terraces filled with people eating breakfast. They looked up and waved when Fuad rolled through, beeping the horn in greeting.

Despite its crumbling roads and sprawling summer residences commissioned by absentee immigrants, the village was beautiful. Tall umbrella pines towered over the hills terraced for farming. Low stone walls edged the paved alleyways, which took on a haunting beauty at night in the yellow light of the lampposts. In the daytime, these same alleyways led to the village center, where taxi drivers and ambulant vendors congregated, and housewives gathered at the water fountain after Mass to gossip and wash the lamb tripes for Sunday's lunch.

His parents' house sat between a clutch of old trees and a path that wound down to the neighbor's orchard. Fuad parked by the stairs. They rolled up the windows and exited the car, stretching in the early morning sun. Two flowering apple trees framed the flower beds, the beautiful garden a startling prelude to an ugly house. With its neat rows and climbers and dark soil that had been tilled and thoroughly weeded, the vegetable garden in the back was only slightly less ornate.

They were met with a flurry of greetings and led to the table under the grapevine trellis. Hisham's mother grilled him about the trip, his job, and why he was so skinny. Patting him on the belly, Gisele declared him to her satisfaction. The older woman shrugged dismissively; this boy needed more meat on his bones, and no one was going to tell her otherwise.

The meat pies disappeared. The second kettle of coffee was put to boil on the stove. His mother puttered about between kitchen and terrace, talking nonstop. Poor eyesight and bad knees had slowed her down, but she remained lively, and today, with her entire brood here, she was in her glory.

Hisham had always felt closer to her than to his father, to whom he bore a striking resemblance—both tall and stooped, with the same mop of black and unruly hair. These days the older man sat in an office pushing paperwork; Hisham wasn't quite sure to what end. He had been a customs officer before becoming a land surveyor. Somewhere during these shifts, Hisham lost track. A lifetime of struggles had left its mark on the older man's face, the weathered skin crisscrossed with deep lines.

After breakfast, Hisham's father rolled a cigarette, then sat back in his chair, stretched out his legs, and began telling stories. The children perked up their ears for the village latest. There was always something in it for them—spooky cats and small disasters, and every now and then, tales not meant for children's ears.

When Hisham was growing up, his father reserved his storytelling for company. The rest of the time, when he wasn't fighting with Fuad, he kept silent.

Hisham couldn't understand why they fought. All Fuad did was talk; he pontificated and got hot under the collar, then sat down at the kitchen table and sharpened his pencils. When he disappeared for days, their father assumed he was making trouble. Hisham disagreed; Fuad was probably blowing off steam, telling anybody who would listen how bad the world was.

These days, Fuad still marched in demonstrations and wrote the occasional op-ed for the local paper.

Their father beamed when Fuad laughed at his jokes. Perhaps all he'd ever wanted was for his firstborn to shut up and listen.

Hisham got up and went to the bathroom, pausing on his way to peer into their old bedroom. The wall paint had faded, and the curtains were frayed and yellowed. The same fringed spreads covered the two twin beds. The night table hadn't been dusted in months. He remembered the icy cold of the bedsheets in winter and curling into a ball, blowing warmth on himself. He walked in and opened the wardrobe. Dark spots where the silvering had peeled covered the mirrored door. He found his old slippers in the corner and put them on, leaving his shoes by the door.

On the terrace, the table was cleared. Passersby paused at the gate, exclaiming about the children. The peal of church bells sent his mother into a frenzy. She searched the house frantically for her key and rosary. Tired of waiting, the children left with Grace and Gisele. His father stood in the doorway, rolling his eyes and urging, "Yallah! Yallah! Let's go."

At last she was ready. She took hold of Hisham's arm, and they made their way to the church with their neighbors, greeting one another and exchanging news in low tones as if the church bells had placed them in a trance. The whole thing was to Hisham's liking, the air saturated with the smells of jasmine and wild thyme, the footfalls on the pavement a soft percussive beat keeping time with the bells.

At length the church appeared, a big white building with red-roofed steeples, tall wooden doors, and stairs wrapped around it. The courtyard was full of children running and riding their bicycles. The women tied headscarves around their necks and summoned their children and husbands. Hisham and his mother were the last to arrive, his mother struggling up the steps and then down the aisle to the pew where his father had reserved two spots for them. She knelt on the padded knee board and closed her eyes. When the priest appeared and the whole congregation rose for the start of Mass, Hisham kept his mind distracted until the final benediction returned them to the bright morning and the same fragrant alleys.

At home, the children ran around the terrace while the women cooked, and the men worked in the garden. "Give me the trowel. These are weeds, son. Have I taught you nothing?" The older man was grinning.

The women called them to the table. The clang of utensils was the only noise for a while. Then the music on the radio stopped, and the jingle of a news flash sounded. They fell silent as the newscaster spoke of unrest spilling from the capital to the north of the country. In Tripoli, members of leftist groups clashed with security police.

Hisham looked down at his feet. A great dread overtook him. The day would be spoiled.

"There's a new militia office in Bismat," his father said, naming the men who had enlisted.

Across the table, Fuad stiffened. Hisham's mind raced. He used to be good at deflecting attention from the crisis, and if not, at hiding. He reached over and stroked his mother's cheek.

"Is this makeup I see?" he quipped.

She played along. "Makeup at my age!" She slapped his hand, chuckling. "Listen to this boy!"

"Why don't you join?" their father persisted. "Who else but your fellow Christians will look after you in times of need?"

"The man has lost his mind!" their mother said, poking her husband in the shoulder. "You want your son to join a militia?"

But he ignored her and continued. "You'd carry a gun, wouldn't you, son? Would you point it at the right people?"

"We are on opposite sides when it comes to the right and wrong people, Baba," Fuad said, his face flushed with suppressed rage.

"I knew it. You would take up a gun against your own people," their father exclaimed.

"Yes! Are you happy?" Fuad screamed before storming inside the house.

They fell silent. Fuad couldn't have meant it. Surely the words flew out of his lips in rage, but he was still his brother, nothing but talk and grand ideas, but deep down harmless.

Gisele brought out the Easter cookies, and a new, forced lightness settled down on them. The older man got up and went inside the house, and a few minutes later, father and son came out, speaking calmly.

Later, Hisham joined his father on the divan. The older man's head drooped down onto his chest. "Go lie down, Baba," he said gently.

"Just resting my eyes," his father replied. The next minute he was snoring.

A hand on his arm interrupted his thoughts. It was his mother. If Fuad's words had bothered her, he could not tell. When Hisham was a child, she'd summon him in the evening to admire the stars with her. It usually happened after a fight between his father and Fuad. Hisham would put his head on her lap, and she'd stroke his hair with her hand that smelled of soap and cooking. For many years, a great peace would overtake him at nightfall, as though his mother's invisible hand still caressed him at the exact moment the stars overtook the sky.

He smiled. She had dyed her hair and missed a few spots. His parents were going to spend Easter with them in Beirut. He would ask Gisele to take her to a hairdresser.

"When will you give me a grandson? Gisele isn't getting any younger."

"Don't let her hear you!"

"I was nineteen when I had your brother." She pointed to his father. "He's a stubborn old fool but he means no harm. Sometimes he tries too hard to knock sense into your brother." She added, turning sideways to look at him, "At least I know where I stand with Fuad. But you are so quiet. I never know what you're thinking."

He shrugged. They smiled at each other.

"Is there anything you need, Mama? Anything I can get you?" he asked. He meant to make up for being gone. He expected her usual answers: have children, come and live in the village, go to church. Instead, she asked for her shawl.

After a while Grace and Gisele returned from their walk, the children in tow. His father woke up. Fuad emerged with the car keys.

They got in the car, laden with Easter cookies and leftovers, and drove off as their parents waved from the steps. Before long the village was behind them. The trees on the hills sagged with berries and spring blossoms. The sun was setting over the horizon. By the time they reached the coast it had already disappeared. The sadness that suddenly assailed Hisham was perhaps nothing more than the flicker of a letdown the twilight brought out in him. It had been a long, tiring day. It was most likely that too.

Rita

We awoke on Palm Sunday to the dreaded khamsin. We took the car to church instead of walking in the hot, hazy air. After the service, the priest led us outside for the procession. My mother thrust a decorated candle into my hand. I tossed it onto a bench before hiding behind two women. We made our way to the courtyard, then to the small garden that separated the church from the hospital to which it was annexed. We walked the cobbled path edged with flower beds and tall trees. Black-railed balconies stretched along the hospital's main building. We exited the hospital grounds and spilled out onto the street, squeezing together to let the traffic through.

I liked being carried along by the crowd. Children dressed in pastel colors were perched on their fathers' shoulders, clutching candles festooned with garlands and colored ribbons. The crowd obstructed my view, shielding me from the swirls of dust that were suddenly rising as the wind picked up. I did not have to see the path to know where we were. The trees themselves were known to me, as were the signs and the buildings.

Then something shifted, and the press of people tightened around me. I found myself squashed against the man in front of me, his jacket grazing my cheek. I pushed him away, but the crowd was pressing on me from all sides and marching on. I looked up and saw a wedge of sky, the tree crowns above flapping in the wind. In my growing panic, the world spun, and the signs and buildings blended into each other, now slowly, now more quickly.

I'd always disliked being in a crowd, but I'd never felt so helpless before. Images from the last several weeks flashed before my eyes: burned tires and angry mobs, blown-up shops and buildings, and the desolation of a place emptied out by fear. I looked suspiciously at the faces around me. Were there killers among us? *Don't be ridiculous, my little lamb*, my father said in my head. I took a deep breath. On market days I survived the crowds by keeping up with my mother, the task of synchronizing our steps capturing my attention and distracting me from my growing panic. Now I searched the river of feet on the ground, trying to find a suitable pair to follow.

A pair of white Mary Janes caught my eye. Based on the size, I guessed the owner was close to me in age. I matched my pace with hers, and even when I lost sight of her shoes in the crowd, it was easy to get back into the same coordinated cadence once they reappeared. This exercise distracted me for a while, but just as I was starting to enjoy the morning, my rescuer vanished. In vain I looked for the gleam of white in the marching feet. I searched for her in the faces surrounding me, but I had no idea what she looked like. I tried to get away, but the crowd pushed back harder, dragging me in one direction while I struggled to go the other. I panicked. I could die of suffocation or fear right then, in a church procession.

At last, traffic was rerouted, and people spread out on the street. I took deep breaths until my heartbeat returned to normal. I searched the crowd until I spotted my family. I looked at Rasha, who was wearing her new sunglasses; Tony, who was perched on Baba's shoulders; and Mama, who held her hand up to block the sun. I felt as though I were watching them from a great unbridgeable distance, and I began to cry.

Then the church bells stopped ringing, and we came to a halt. I made my way through the crowd, and when I reached my mother I linked my arm with hers and didn't let go until the procession had made a full circle and we were back inside the church for the benediction.

Later we posed for photos. My mother gave out chocolate eggs and sesame cookies. On the way back we stopped at the butcher's shop for cutlets. I was calmer now, and despite the pesky khamsin that blew dust in our mouths, the morning was beautiful.

Mama's shopping list was getting longer, so Rasha and I decided to go ahead. Curtains of flowers trailed from the balconies. A plane left a white line in the sky. Flowers sprang up on the grassy divider between the two streets leading to our home. We stood at the curb, preparing to cross. The traffic was heavy now, and no one slowed down for us. We saw our chance and ran. Upstairs in our apartment, we plopped on our beds, replete with cookies and flush with effort, and waited for our mother to come so that the festivities could continue.

Hisham

The racket jolted him awake. He crawled under the covers, but whatever Gisele was doing wasn't going away. When he staggered into the kitchen, the countertops were covered with packaged food, and Gisele was scrubbing the empty shelves from the height of a chair. She turned and gave him a look that said it was high time he came and pitched in.

He poured coffee from the kettle and handed her a cup. She declined, asking for a bucket of clean water instead. He returned with the bucket and set it on the counter, and she bent over and washed the sponge.

"Everything must be in perfect condition. Operation Frustrate My Mother-in-Law," she joked. He said she looked nice in her red apron and rubber gloves and ponytail, and she asked him to make himself useful and restock the clean shelves before she disappeared halfway inside a cabinet.

They were expecting his parents for Easter, and his mother was a snoop who rummaged inside their drawers and under the sofa cushions, triumphantly displaying coins and dust bunnies and other signs of sloppy housekeeping. He found the whole thing funny, but Gisele was not amused. He spoke with his mother. She stopped snooping, but Gisele never got over it.

After he was done with the shelves, he tidied up the bedroom closet and the mess on his desk, leaving the review he'd been writing on top of the pile. School was out for two weeks for Easter break, long enough to finish the piece. He hoped his parents would decide to stay at Fuad's to be with their grandchildren. Hisham would help with driving and errands, but he'd still have enough time to squeeze in a few hours of writing each day.

Gisele was silent during lunch, nodding absentmindedly to

his attempts at conversation. Her instructions multiplied—eat over your plate, don't let water drip on the floor when washing your hands. "You are not the one who has been cleaning since daybreak," she snapped when he complained.

When his patience ran out, he went and stood on the balcony to flee her dictatorship, her Royal Highness of the Mop and Castigating Mouth. Propping his elbows on the handrail, he looked down at the street. The cloth trader across the street was hauling his bolts inside the shop. A woman cleared the clothesline in the building opposite.

When Gisele joined him, he was in a better mood.

"It's going to rain," she said.

"Not likely," he answered, pointing to the clouds skimming toward the horizon.

Her hands gave off a pleasant smell of lemon and soap. He turned to her and smiled.

"I'm almost done with the piece," he lied as a way of keeping himself on track. One day the trick would work, and he would live up to his deception.

"Is it about Nizar Qabbani?" she taunted. It was their ongoing joke. She loved the poet, while he pretended to mock her poor taste.

"I'm working on serious literature!" he joked.

"You're a snob," she said. "You don't like him because he writes about women and publishes in women's magazines."

They went to a reading once. The poet read well, revealing music in the vernacular Hisham hadn't grasped on the page. But he loved their banter too much to admit his change of heart.

She took a book from the shelves and read a few verses. He made a funny expression and pretended to cover his ears. She jumped on his back and wrapped her legs around his waist as he careened with her to the bedroom.

During lovemaking, she closed her eyes. Shyness, she explained when he asked early in their marriage. But it's me, your husband who loves you, he said, wounded. Still, she said. She tried atoning, but the damage was done. The feeling that she was withholding herself from him leaked into their lovemaking. A new distance opened between them. He suspected her of lying; her supposed shyness did not fit with the woman he knew, who loved to impress people and put them in thrall to her, and who relished men's attention.

Something must have turned her off once, some neediness in him she could not abide. Bitterness rose in him. He wanted absolute faith in their love. He wanted her to see him fully, with all his faults, and still love him. Otherwise, what was the point?

"Look at me!" he whispered. He felt her stiffen. But she turned and faced him. In her eyes there was love, but also weariness.

He collapsed on top of her. She tapped his arm. He rolled onto his back. She drew close, resting her head on his chest. His fingers roamed the length of her spine, stroking the short hairs at the nape of her neck and squeezing her nipples. She pushed him away, then turned and lay on her side.

Afterward, she changed the bedsheets and showered. The clouds had disappeared. They decided to go for a stroll. She grabbed light jackets from the closet and a bag of mandarin oranges.

The evening wore on. They glimpsed the sunset between buildings. The store windows lit up. A movie they wanted to see was playing at the neighborhood cinema. They bought their tickets and entered the empty theater. The lead actress was wonderful.

Later, Hisham complained about the ending.

"Stop your bellyaching, dear," Gisele said.

On the way home he wanted to talk about the movie, but Gisele was eyeing a pair of shoes in the Bata window.

"They'd be perfect for Layla," she exclaimed. His niece's birthday was coming up. Gisele's, too, he remembered suddenly. He had yet to buy her a present.

A black pair of patent leather shoes roused Jumana's memory in his mind. He remembered the girl's scowl and her battered shoe soles. He had not thought of her since the day in the lobby when he accosted her like a fool. Now her image flashed with an insistence that reignited his shame. He resolved to return later and purchase the black pair. He wouldn't tell Gisele. He couldn't explain his reasons for spending money on a stranger. Charity? Atonement for his intrusiveness? Or something less laudable, a desire to put her in her place and return the humiliation?

They resumed their walk. The dings and clacks of pinball machines blared from the arcade store. Gisele yawned. The world receded. Figures passed them in the darkness. They were alone, entwined in each other. Peas in a pod, he trilled. A pot and its lid. You and I.

He whispered a few verses from Qabbani into her ear. She rested her head on his shoulder, his apology accepted.

Rita

Traffic came to a complete halt on our way to our friends' house in Keserwan. The line of cars stretched without an end in sight. Baba used a handkerchief to wipe his brow and the back of his neck. In the front seat, my mother's chignon was unraveling. The three of us kids sat thigh to thigh in the back, Tony sprawled out in the middle, Rasha obsessively rearranging her face in a small mirror, and me breathing deeply to get rid of my nausea. Even on short trips I got carsick.

"Do you want to go out for a stretch?" my father asked. I had thrown up in his car once and he'd been on the lookout ever since. I shook my head. Normally, I would seize the opportunity to leave the car, but not today. Something bad was going to happen at any moment, and I didn't want to be caught in it when it did.

My father turned on the radio and flipped through the stations until a voice announced widespread protests and road closures. Cars began to climb over the divider and accelerate in the opposite direction. Baba followed their example, and we turned around and headed back home.

"Always something," Rasha grumbled, snapping her mirror shut. All week she'd waited to see Marc, our friends' firstborn. He had a crush on her, and she liked the attention.

I took a deep breath. A lukewarm wind whipped my face. Images of what we were missing flicked through my brain: the mulberry drinks that would have greeted us upon arrival, the big living room with its cream-colored furniture, the Limoges and Lalique ornaments in the glass cabinet, and Boule de Neige, their aloof white cat lounging on her pillow throne at the window. By now the adults would have finished gushing over how tall we had grown since the last visit and would have sent us to the garden. Tony and I would sit with the twins by the cherry tree, staring longingly at the unripe fruit. Or we might be abusing the rickety deck swing, mercilessly pumping our legs to hear it creak. Rasha and Marc would have found a quiet spot and would be deep in conversation. She'd put on airs when he asked her about St. Joseph University, where she was a first-year student and where he'd be studying physics the following year like his father. There would be purple salvias in the flower beds and gardenias in earthen pots. Further down, on the patio, a round table would have been set for lunch. The twins would bring out their remote-control race cars and completely ignore me, while my brother would fare much better by virtue of the stupid pursuits he shared with the rest of his sex. I concluded that I was not missing much after all, and I had the demonstrators to thank for it.

A few minutes after we got home, my neighbor Lena rang the doorbell. I didn't like her. She had made me touch her brother's penis a couple of years earlier, and I had avoided her ever since. But Seta was boycotting me again and I was bored. I told my mother I would be back soon and walked out the door with my corruptor in tow.

Lena made my skin crawl. She had the look of someone who could see through to my dirty secrets. She had pinned me with that look just before handing me over to her brother Joseph, who was standing with his shorts halfway below his hips and a stupid grin on his face.

I wanted her where I could see her, so I let her go first on the stairs. She was dressed in pink shorts and a white top. Her greasy ponytail swung back and forth about her back. Maybe I was walking right into another trap. The thought of Joseph waiting for me with his pants down sent shivers up my spine.

The memory of her guiding my hand and whispering, *Touch*, still disgusted me. I did as I was told. I hated how his penis felt in my hand, warm and damp like a small animal. Afterward, I couldn't sleep for shame. Not only had I touched a boy's privates, I had blindly followed orders. Why did I not stand up for myself? The question haunted me. Nothing in Lena appealed to me. She was a poor student. Her father was a lout, and her mother was the neighborhood gossip. And I, a coward.

But here we were on the rooftop again because I was bored. A part of me hoped that she was plotting something. I'd show her this time. But when I looked around, I saw nothing suspicious.

We sat with our backs to the parapet. I got to my feet and looked down the air shaft. In the darkness, I made out the outlines of the small bathroom windows we rarely opened because of the cockroaches. I imagined the insects scurrying across the walls, then lying in wait, wings rustling, the females heavy with eggs, and pulled away in disgust.

Lena pulled out two cigarettes from her back pocket and lit a match. We smoked in silence.

"I'll probably do Technique next year," she said after a while.

Good, I thought.

I leaned over the parapet and looked down at the autostrade, then across the way at Seta's room. The lace curtains were drawn. I remembered the day I'd helped her pick them out of a catalog she'd gotten from her aunt in France, how we'd passed over the florals and heavy velvet drapes in favor of a fabric that streamed the light. When I mentioned privacy, she said she liked having the light shine into every corner of her room, which surprised me given how secretive she was with me.

We paused to peek inside the room where Lena's brother had flashed himself. The janitor had started building the room as a storage space but abandoned it midway. Twisted metal and buckets of dried lime mortar lay in one corner. We had whitewashed big sections of the wall, then broke off chunks of mortar and drew flowers and sunsets and wonky stars on the unpainted walls.

To the west was the candy factory. Despite the demonstrations, it was open. In the parking lot we saw workers loading empty wooden crates onto a truck. I imagined Nawar women standing over large cauldrons and stirring quietly, their pallets sticky with liquid caramel. Nomadic women, almost never seen with men or children, the Nawar moved in packs, dressed in full skirts and baggy pants, their hands and wrists tattooed with mysterious inscriptions. No one knew where they went after work. They drifted through the streets, melting where the road met the sea behind the factory.

Lena's mother called her from the balcony. Before she left, she gave me another cigarette. I put it in my pocket and went home.

Auntie Hala, our neighbor, was in the family room when I walked in. She had been orphaned in childhood and started working very young, first in Egypt, where she was born, and then in Lebanon, her ancestral land, where she moved following the Nasser takeover. Now she occupied a small apartment on the top floor in the next wing, alone but not lonely, thanks to her doting neighbors. A bespectacled despot who liked to read coffee grounds, she was also very devout, and she and Mama were always hijacking Rasha's and my room for hours for their prayer sessions. In May, Mary's month, we gave up all hope.

I started off toward the back balcony, then changed my mind when I saw the empty coffee cups upturned on their saucers. I was curious to hear what new fortunes the coffee grounds held in store. Auntie Hala picked up Mama's cup and twirled it. My father should expect a promotion. "See that thick line? It's money flowing into his open palms." My grandmother would be cured of her diabetes, and my uncle would find a good woman and settle down.

I was grateful, I was, for this island of sunshine on this gloomy day derailed by trouble. I had been crushed by the weight of failed expectations—not the visit to Keserwan itself, for which I did not truly care, but the abrupt end to a Sunday excursion and the sense that, had we been any closer to the protests, we would have been helplessly trapped in the stifling heat and the angry mob. I wanted to be swayed by Auntie Hala's good omens, but the day's events had darkened my mood.

I went to the balcony after Auntie Hala left. I looked through the cardboard boxes where Mama kept her leftovers, buttons, scraps of fabric, and ruined zippers. I flipped through the pages of *Tabibouka*, a medical journal where I occasionally came across articles about sex. I dug out the long strips of wool my mother used to wrap around our bellies at bedtime when we were little to ward off the air drafts. If we disobeyed and removed our belts, we were plagued by stomachaches the next morning. My mother tended to us without blame, but with the look of someone who knew all too well what happened when you left yourself open to the night winds.

And this was how I spent my afternoon, nosing through my mother's discards, finding much to distract me from the fact that, despite all my claims to the contrary, and the immature twins who would have excluded me from their games, I would have liked to have spent the day in Keserwan.

The weekend that never happened felt like a missed opportunity. The sky was gray and muggy, and the street had emptied. Everyone had gone home. Everyone, it seemed, was waiting for something to happen.

3

Hisham

Sitting at his desk at home, he stared at the open window where no breeze had blown since the start of a heat wave worthy of the heart of summer. The Khamsin left as abruptly as it came, then the temperature dropped before sharply rising again. A spring like no other. For days he had been in a stupor, spread out on the bed, barely moving, the touch of his own skin unbearable.

Even under normal conditions he disliked spring in Beirut, the sudden shift in weather a shock to his system. "Old man," Gisele teased while she went about her day, happy to turn her back on the rainy season.

But this spring, even Gisele wanted to get away. With school out for the Easter break, and Gisele's boss agreeing to a vacation, their minds were made up. His parents' visit had come to an end without a major incident, and he called and offered to drive them back the next morning. He and Gisele planned to stay in the village until mid-week, and even though he hadn't made enough headway with his review to deserve a real vacation, the cooler temperature would fire up his brain, and maybe he could wrap it up quickly and enjoy his stay.

Silly to waste time on unpaid writing, but he liked worrying the same thoughts and shunning reality for the sake of what truth lay at the other end, something pure and bright that flooded his brain with new understanding. The rush, the great relief after a piece of writing was completed! A hand pointed the way, a fear receded. But this was still a long time in coming.

He looked through the manuscript. Ten pages of fragments and false starts it had taken him weeks to write. Lured by the promise of his name in print next to a lineup of better-known reviewers, and hoping for a permanent and paid column, he had been pursuing an article that so far had proven elusive.

The suitcase sat on the dresser, with his half already packed. There was nothing for him to do except write, and then get dinner so that Gisele wouldn't have to cook. He picked up his keys and left the apartment with the manuscript in hand.

At a seaside café, he requested a table on the terrace. The waiter offered to seat him inside, but he declined. He needed the water to think clearly. An umbrella was put up for shade. He ordered coffee. With the building behind him blocking the busy street, and nothing obstructing his view of the sea, he was filled with a sense of freedom.

He uncapped a pen and scoured the skies for inspiration.

Troubled by the narrator's disembodied voice, we see her as a non-character. We know very little about her life… The past has her in its grip, and she disappears in her tales… As she peers through the curtain of time, and the stories pile up, there's a sense that she functions as an archivist, documenting injustices. Perhaps the telling keeps her, if not fully alive, then in suspension.

He wrote a few more paragraphs before checking his watch. He still had enough time to get dinner and run a few errands. He got cheese and sausages, then went to the Bata store to buy the black patent leather pumps in what he hoped was Jumana's size. He hid the box under the spare tire in the trunk, then drove to Gisele's favorite beach resort and bought her a season's membership and arranged the lease for a beach cabin with a private shower for her birthday. She was going to be thrilled.

He sped down the autostrade, music blaring. He was happy to be leaving for the village. He'd have enough time to set his thoughts in order and produce a cohesive work. No need to feel irresponsible for leaving reality behind for a while; soon enough, he'd be returning to the same awful world.

The village was ablaze with greenery. Every day he spent hours walking through fields of poppies and wild daisies. His favorite trail was hedged with laurel and led to a creek where he would wade for a while, then come out and sit on a bench and write. He savored every scent as though he'd been starved for sensations. He brought a book to read under a tree. The constant thrumming and the chirping birds filled him with a wondrous feeling.

The narrator of the novel he was reviewing was stuck in the past. *Her reluctance to disclose her present life keeps her readers at arm's length. One's eyes are drawn to the point of distraction to the blank spaces.*

In truth, he didn't want to write this review, but so much time and effort had already gone into it, and then there was the good company he would be keeping at the time of publication.

He was coming awake here. Home was home, he thought, nothing more or less than he remembered, although he came and went as he wished, like a tourist. Everyone respected his desire for solitude and writing, and Gisele and his mother were getting along royally, and when he returned to the house the meal was cooking on the stove and there were bowls full of green plums and raw almonds, and his father waited for him with the backgammon board laid out on the table for a game before dinner.

The review would get written. He made his way idly home.

Rita

I sat in a corner of the landlord's living room harboring grievances.

Grievance 1: Seta was mad at me again. I could swear a bell in her brain rang every time I uttered Monsieur Sami's name. First day in school after the Easter break, and Amal and I passed the time making fun of our math teacher. I caught sight of Seta too late storming away. Five days later, I was still in Siberia.

Grievance 2: All week I had looked forward to this: my first invitation to the annual party thrown by the landlord's sons, who had a band and looked better than they sounded. But this party was a bust. Only Joseph had invited me to dance, and I'd sooner eat my hand. Lena was giving me the side-eye from across the room because I had turned away rudely when she came over and started chatting as if we were the best of friends. I could go home and watch television. But I decided to stay. Here, at least, I was a part of something Seta had no idea existed.

The furniture had been pushed against the wall to make room for a stage. The music was loud, and it took everything I had not to cover my ears.

We lived in a building where it was easy to stick your nose in your neighbor's business. It was a hollow cube, with an inner courtyard in the center that connected the northern and southern wings. A landing on each floor overlooked the courtyard. For many years, I stood on the landing and watched Rasha climb the stairs to the landlord's apartment to attend a party to which I had not been invited.

While Rasha danced, I ate pretzel sticks and prayed that the evening would end soon but also last forever. Yet I was wearing my new skirt. It was long and flowy with pink flowers and a lace border and was perfect for dancing. Seta had called it "Tzigane" because of the new show with the gypsy characters that was all the rage.

Then came an invitation from a boy. His pimpled face looked beautiful to my thankful eyes. The invitations poured in after that. I'd barely taken a breath before I was dragged back onto the dance floor. I was no longer Rasha's plain younger sister, but someone else, wild and free, with endless possibilities before me.

When the first gunshots rang out, I didn't want to stop dancing. I stood in the middle of the living room, refusing to heed the obvious, until Rasha grabbed my arm and pulled me to the back room where the rest of the guests had gathered. I slid down to the floor, fuming with resentment. Like Cinderella, I'd been pulled from the dazzling night and thrown back into my rags, all because some fool felt the need to shoot something.

Rasha's nails dug into my palm. The shots sounded like they were being fired from inside the building, and I realized that we were in serious trouble. We sat in stunned silence. I heard the bullets ricocheting off the balcony railing right outside the door and the thud of empty shells hitting the courtyard. There could only be one explanation: someone was shooting at us. It made no sense. The room spun around me. Then it came to me that this mad shooter might have already harmed my family and was now after us, and I burst into tears. Rasha gripped my arms and said something I couldn't hear because I was weeping so hard, but the sound of her voice gradually calmed me down. When the gunfire stopped, she went to check with the landlord and returned with the news that the shooter had been detained. He was visiting one of our neighbors and became so irritated by the noise we were making that he fired at us from the landing.

We staggered back to our apartment. Our terrified mother met us at the top of the stairs with incense and holy water, sweeping us inside while our father locked the door behind us. We went to bed immediately, exhausted by the night's events. But it was a while before I could fall asleep. The images of the night tumbled through my head, the dancing and the shooting saturating my dreams, so that I slept in fits and starts and woke up drenched in sweat.

The next morning I staggered out of bed, feeling as though I had not slept at all. During Mass, I felt dizzy to the point of fainting. I did not take communion. Earlier I had refused confession, and I was not allowed to take the body of Christ into my sinful heart. Mama gave me pleading looks. Despite the tenderness she showed me after last night's ordeal, she was firm: I was expected to see the priest after Mass, who would be in his box waiting for stragglers like me. Confession, according to her, would wash me of both my sins and the awful memories.

But I held my ground. Last night a veil was torn, and I glimpsed a wickedness in my soul. I had a dream about the shooter falling from a great height and bursting into flames when he hit the ground, and his screams of agony thrilled me. I dreamed of Seta crying and pleading for my friendship because Monsieur Sami had broken her heart. All that lawlessness breaking into the boundary of our existence, all the burned tires and shootings and angry protests, appeared in my dreams, as though a vital part of me had been tainted and all bets were off.

These were no words for an old priest.

Year One

April 13, 1975 - April 15, 1976

4

Rita

The first round of gunfire rang out while my mother was baking an apricot crumble, Baba was lifting weights in the living room, and Tony was playing with marbles. While Rasha was out with friends, and I danced in the bedroom with the door closed. I stopped dancing. I remembered the shooting at the landlord's party a week earlier, and terror seized me. I told myself not to worry. There could have been a variety of reasons: a wedding, a funeral, a birth—we were a trigger-happy people.

The shots appeared to be coming from the city center. I looked out the window at the distant mountain range and the sunlit trees along the autostrade. The sky stared back at me, imperturbable and blue, as if what was going on in one part of the city was of no consequence here.

As the gunfire got louder, a memory came to me, and an old fear resurfaced. I was seven years old. I'd stayed up late, sneaking into the family room just in time to watch planes streak across the sky and tanks barrel into the desert on TV. Terrified, I hid under a bureau, refusing to come out until my father knelt on the floor beside me and stated that wars took place at the borders, far away from people. "There's nothing to fear, my little lamb," he said. I imagined soldiers advancing and retreating across a chalk line at a place called the border. I took his hand and came out of hiding. A few years later, I learned that I had seen footings of the Six-Day War. Through the years I would see more images of violence: Vietnam, Chile, the war of 1973. I realized that my father had lied to me: war spread like a sickness, destroying everything in its path. But I was grateful. At seven, I had no use for that kind of truth.

The guns ripped through the morning in rapid bursts. I turned up the music and danced, partly to distract myself and partly in defiance. Violence had stopped me from dancing for the second time in a few days, but this time I was determined to keep going. When I turned, there was my father, grinning in the doorway. How long had he been standing there? I gave him a weak smile and turned off the radio.

"Don't stop," he said. But I didn't feel like dancing anymore, and he let me be. After he was gone, I sat down on the sofa. Something big was taking place. These weren't the usual handgun or machine-gun rounds we'd gotten accustomed to in recent months. They came in long, unbroken spurts, as if someone were holding the trigger too tightly. I was back to being a frightened child, crouching in a corner, waiting for a lie to save me.

My mother's figure flashed in the corridor, pulling Tony behind her. I shot to my feet and followed her. The three of us stood in the doorway while Baba sat on the edge of his bed, turning the radio knob in his lap. We didn't move, as if there were treacherous quicksand extending between us and Baba. Perhaps if we stood perfectly still Baba's search would be fruitless, the radio would not broadcast what we feared most, the music would continue playing, and everything would be as before.

But our wish was not granted. The killing of four Christian militants by unknown gunmen sparked a shooting rampage. The Christian forces attacked a bus transporting Palestinians back to a nearby camp, killing most of the passengers. Now the world was on fire.

There was a steady buildup, like the first rumbling of an earthquake gathering force. You could run. Or stay nailed to your spot. Who knew what you were supposed to do?

We moved closer to Baba, who led us to the vestibule, away from the windows and stray bullets. I sank to the floor, pulling Tony to me as he shook in my arms. Mama kept an ear to the door as if in auscultation. Baba paced around, surfing the stations.

Voices drifted outside. When we opened the door, our neighbors were in the corridor with chairs and radios—the Attars; Madame Krikorian with her husband and their twin daughters; the Baloghs from Hungary with their daughter, Anna; and Auntie Hala with her Bible. The Attars looked beseechingly at Baba, while Lamia pressed him for answers he didn't have.

Mama kept bringing up Rasha. Baba said Rasha staying put was the sound thing to do. As if on cue, my sister called to say she was fine and would come home as soon as she could.

But things didn't quiet down. We heard the first bursts of heavy artillery in the distance. We brought two mattresses to the vestibule, and for the next three nights we moved between the vestibule and the landing, jumping at every sound. We clung to the radio. The same sectors in the city kept coming up. If we looked one way we saw clear skies, while on the other side, the city's skyline was black with smoke. But we harbored no illusions. When you live in a small country, you know that sooner or later your turn will come.

I worried about Rasha. Every time Mama let out a low wail, I knew she was thinking about my sister. The telephone lines had stopped working, and we had been without news after that initial call. Her friend was closer to the fighting, a small forest of pines separating her from the last stretch of autostrade before the violence. I searched my brain for words to appease Mama's panic and mine, and when I seemed to have reached the limit of my resourcefulness, my sister appeared, looking weary but unscathed. Mama took her into her arms as I stood back, shyly patting her back. She said they had hidden in the underground shelter where the pitch darkness was nearly as hard to bear as the bombs. Then she gave Tony a big kiss on the cheek, crashed on the mattress, and was lost to the world.

Eventually there was a cease-fire, and on day four, we were back in our beds.

Hisham

The time it took to sit at the table with the tray between them was the time it took the world to explode into madness. A great noise of guns rattled the cups and saucers on the brass tray. Gisele gripped the table's edges, her eyes darting frantically across his face.

They dashed to the entryway. In 1973, it had served as their hiding place when Israeli agents sneaked into the city and killed three PLO leaders, and the Lebanese army pounded the Palestinian camps to prevent retaliation, and the country, split between pro- and anti-Palestinian factions, ripped open.

Their neighborhood lay close enough to the city center to house the whole gamut of religions. As it happened, it was also on the front line.

They knew what to do: move the mattress to the entryway and fill the space with books, writing pads, pencils, candles, flashlights, and Gisele's sewing to keep everything within reach and limit their trips to the bedroom, a land mine with three street-facing windows. There was a gilded mirror on the wall with an umbrella stand in the corner and a chair next to a small round table. From here they had easy access to the kitchen, with its single window overlooking an inner courtyard, and to the bathroom, which had no windows. The layout must have been conceived by a far-sighted builder, who predicted that a country with a propensity for trouble needed rooms nestled inside other rooms, shelters within shelters.

The wait began, in the screeching shells and crashing glass, and the blare of ambulance sirens. The walls reverberated. Sometimes they were able to sleep, but most of the time they lay in the dark with their hands entwined, counting the explosions. They knew what to expect. The terror, if not attenuated, was at least familiar.

On day two, tired of being cooped up, they joined their neighbors on the small landing. But Gisele couldn't stand the crying children. Back in their apartment, she let out little wailing sounds, and he covered her face with kisses. "This will not last long; remember the last time—strife comes, and strife goes. This, too, will be over," he said again and again.

He didn't let her out of his sight. He rushed her when she was in the bathroom, and insisted on preparing dinner while she sat on the mattress, tapping her foot impatiently on the floor, because it was now her turn to worry.

During brief periods of calm, he would remember the hours before the mayhem and try to cling to that happiness: Gisele standing at the sink in a sleeveless orange dress he liked, her hair catching the glint of the midday sun angling from the kitchen window. How she turned her bright gaze toward him after she finished with the dishes, untied the strings of her apron, and hung it from a hook on the wall, then brewed the coffee.

On day four, a cease-fire. Classes would resume on Monday. He had a couple of days to find his way back to the world he knew.

They swept the broken glass and returned the mattress to the bedroom. She slept in his arms. Dawn found him with his eyes wide open, wondering what he would discover when he walked out into the daylight. An hour later he looked out the window and had his answer: rubble, broken glass, a balcony railing dangling over the street. From the gas station he called a glass mender to replace the broken panes in the living room and kitchen.

There was dust everywhere. It took hours to clean the apartment, wash anything that could be stripped, and vacuum every section. On Sunday night, a few hours before he was scheduled to go back to school, the harbor burned. A giant blaze burst from the ground and engulfed the night. He watched the leaping flames from the rooftop, a blanket of black smoke rising like thick vapor to the starry sky. He pictured boxes snapping open and spilling their contents, the ships rocking in the water.

The fire smoldered for days. The harbor was looted while the militants turned a blind eye. The material loss was considerable, but the investigation revealed no foul play, and the case was closed. Something there had been ready to ignite.

School reopened. He was gentle with his students, reading them poems and stories aloud until their eyes closed in contentment, their heads on their desks like children at sleep. All week he read, asking more from them each day until they started to respond, and their chatter once again filled the hallways between classes. During recess, he stood in his usual spot at the window, watching his students slowly come back life. He noticed that a few of the Muslim girls in his classes were gone. Whether this was a sign of things to come, he could not tell. Perhaps the logistics of crossing a city embroiled in repairs kept them away.

There was a lot of cleaning and repairing in the days that followed, and many burials. The Palestinians promised neutrality. But Lebanon was a place of deep entanglements, a small country swinging wildly like a weather vane in the wind.

5

Rita

The battles came and went like the tides. Sometimes the cease-fire was over as quickly as it started. Sometimes there was time to come out of hiding, fix the damage, and breathe. The second round came in May. How did they know when one round ended and another began? It seemed important to know, even as it struck terror in our hearts. We stayed glued to the radio: snipers, random checkpoints to inspect IDs for the wrong religion, people living or dying for an accident of birth. We latched the windows and debated the future.

Rumors spread. The fish we ate was poisoned by the corpses and trash we dumped in the sea. Outside forces fanned the flames of discord. Any time life resumed its normal course, unidentified gunmen blew up something. A "third force" was interfering. There was a "plot" to divide brothers and sisters. Despite the absence of gunfire, markets and schools closed without warning, only to reopen a few hours later.

The schools were now open, now closed. We zipped through lessons to make up for lost time. I did poorly on tests. I didn't care how many tons of wheat China produced. School was a relic from an old life that no longer made sense.

We spent a lot of time on the landing. We learned to locate where the rockets were falling. Seta's building housed the nearest shelter. We hadn't needed to hide there yet, but we kept a suitcase next to the door just in case. We felt safe on the landing, which was surrounded by walls except for a small opening on one side with a railing overlooking the inner courtyard. I looked up nervously at the square of sky above the courtyard. To land near us, a rocket would have to make a high arc over the roof and then curve at a sharp angle, an unlikely trajectory. Still, I pushed my chair back far enough to block out the sky.

It wasn't all bad, since most of the time the fighting was confined to the city center. The school closures were a bonus, and we were no longer required to attend church. I liked spending time with the neighbors on the landing. We had coffee and pastries, swapped books, and played board games. I learned to knit. Anna Balogh gave me tips on my tennis serve and loaned me books and magazines. I read my first book in English. It wasn't very good, but I read it without help from the dictionary or my father.

Other changes were less positive. Baba worried about money. His office was in a war zone. Even during the lulls in the fighting, it was dangerous for him to drive there because he was of the wrong religion. The Christian party ruled our neighborhood. They kept things running and banned any publications that did not follow the party line. We used to be proud of our freedom of expression. Now, getting caught with the wrong newspaper could get you killed. People accepted the ban. It was critical to stand together and fight as one.

Most of our neighbors stayed in their summer homes in the mountains, which had so far remained peaceful, commuting to work when necessary. But Baba hated the long drive to Tarawa. For someone who followed the news as closely as he did, Teta's house was on the moon, too far away for a TV signal and strong radio reception, and the newspapers arrived a day late. When we complained, he offered to take us there, but only if he could leave the next day. Mama refused. This was not the time for us to be apart. So we stayed with the Armenian families and our Hungarian and Palestinian neighbors, immigrants without ancestral homes.

I didn't know what to believe. In my part of the country, Palestinians were the bad guys, sowing division to weaken the government and carry out their armed struggle against Israel from the southern border without restrictions. But I had a father who had fled a stolen country, and he saw things differently.

Auntie Hala became a frequent visitor. She arrived in the evening, hoping to pick Baba's brain and change it. She may have been illiterate, but she kept her ear glued to the radio.

Their talks always took place in the family room, after the initial politeness protocols had been exhausted and Mama had rustled up enough snacks in the dark. She and I listened quietly. Baba and Auntie Hala had very different opinions, and Mama seemed to be on the lookout in case things got heated and she had to step in. But Auntie Hala respected my father too much to cross the line, and there was nothing Baba liked better than a good debate.

Things got a little more intense one evening. The two maintained a civil tone, but they seemed more entrenched than ever in their opposing views. On the news, the Palestinians were either gods or devils, depending on who was speaking, and that scenario was playing itself out in our family room.

Auntie Hala had a tendency to start with something she had heard on the radio about yet another overreach by Palestinian forces. Tonight she brought up the checkpoints they had been setting up in parts of the city, asking for IDs and deciding who could cross and who couldn't.

"The Palestinians: good, bad. They are part of who we are," Baba said, dismissing her outrage. "When you don't give people any rights, you can't expect their loyalty in return."

"We have contributed more to their cause than all the Arabs combined." Flushed with indignation, she reminded him that King Hussein had expelled the guerrillas from Jordan, causing yet another wave of refugees pouring into Lebanon and the PLO moving its headquarters here.

There was no disagreement on Baba's end. Arab leaders, as far as he was concerned, were all talk and no action when it came to the Palestinians.

"They are destroying the South," she added.

"Israel is destroying the South."

"Tell it to the southerners who are dying and losing their livelihoods for someone else's war." I heard a little sneer in her voice, and Baba must have heard it as well, because he looked as if he was about to launch into one of his speeches.

"Your fury would be misdirected, and it's not someone else's war," he said. "Say we put aside our essential oneness and forget that there was once only one borderless Galilee. Then Europe said, 'This is where the line falls,' and broke the land. Say this is ancient history, and what's done is done. Let's ignore for a moment the plight of the Palestinians who live among us. To prosper, we must live peacefully with Israel. But, Sitt Hala, we both know that Israel's idea of peace is the complete annihilation of the Palestinians by any means necessary. Tell me, Sitt Hala: how can there be peace without justice?"

They both made sense to me, and their respective views sat side by side without meeting. I couldn't pick one or blend them together like a handful of different spices you shook in a bag to arrive at a full layer of flavors. I wished the truth shone brightly as the songs said or clanged like a gong someone sounded at the hours of revelation or was massive and weighty so you couldn't miss it. Instead, it skittered out of sight the instant you thought you had a glimpse of it. But in the end, all of these doubts would vanish the moment the bombs started to fall, because if anything was ever loud and massive, it was war.

I was always afraid that the Attars might ring our doorbell in the middle of one of these sessions. Auntie Hala wasn't one to keep her mouth shut. Even if she stayed quiet for my mother's sake, she'd give the Attars long stares that made it clear what she was thinking. But our neighbors had walled themselves off from the world, and the chances of seeing them at our doorstep grew slim. When I rang their doorbell, Lamia opened the small door window without inviting me in. We spoke for a while, but I couldn't concentrate because of all the questions I wanted to ask her but didn't dare. I wanted to tell her how much I missed her, but how could I, with the bars of the window between us? I didn't insist. I could only wait for my friend and hope she would find her way back to me.

6

Hisham

After two months of warfare, their survival hinged on being busy and remaining well stocked. During cease-fires, he stocked up on flashlights, batteries, gallons of drinking water, and canisters of cooking gas. The mattress was back in the corridor. Gisele darned socks, sewed buttons, and fixed zippers. A dress pattern lay on the kitchen table next to her sewing tools. During the lulls, she measured and snipped, her fingers flying. Hisham could have sat there for a long time watching her tilt her head to the side and squint in concentration while the treadle and needle clicked and whirled.

A pile of books lay untouched in the corner. He skimmed the pages without absorbing the words. His typewriter sat on the small console table with a blank page in the carriage. He'd managed only a few notes scribbled quickly by candlelight. They were highlights from newsflashes: the electricity was out. Sixty dead, two hundred, thirty-five. Scuffles broke out in the long lines at gas stations and bakeries. People left the city on foot—Lebanese, Kurds, Palestinians.

He missed the freedom to come and go as he pleased. Every action required careful thought. Hiding made him feel like a cripple. The militants didn't hide. They whipped through the neighborhood in their jeeps, flashing their headlights. Depending on which faction controlled the streets, the militants wore kepis and keffiyehs, or dark hoods and crosses around their neck.

At night he lay awake wondering if there was a grand plan, a chain of command, someone yanking the strings and taking the pulse of the people's terror in all its phases, so that the city lay open, known as a map. Gisele slept next to him, out cold on Valium. Every night she offered him a pill, but he declined. He wanted to stay awake. Thinking, he felt like himself again. He hated the way fear blotted out thought and reduced him to his animal instincts. When he fell asleep, he dreamed about the sniper on his street.

In his dreams, the sniper was godlike, invisible and omnipresent. Hisham saw himself through the scope of the sniper's rifle, a part here and there, sometimes whole, small enough to hold in the palm of a hand, in the eye of a gun. He woke up flushed with cold sweat.

The sniper fired from the rooftop of an apartment building. His job was to keep them in a constant state of terror. Hisham imagined a faceless figure jumping from the rooftops and crawling across the walls while they slept. A hot rage pushed up inside him. He imagined the sniper lying in the street's gutter, riddled with bullets. He saw himself kicking the lifeless body. But he wouldn't look at the sniper's face. He was afraid the image would stay with him forever.

The sniper's first victim was Ibrahim the greengrocer. Ibrahim had raised the metal shutters and swept the debris after the cease-fire announcement. He had crates of chicory, spinach, tomatoes, and green almonds ready to go, as well as an early harvest of loquats and sour green plums. He arranged bouquets of daisy, oleander, and hyacinth in buckets and filled a plastic basin with herbs—mint, parsley, basil, coriander, and purslane.

The rest of the shopkeepers began to arrive. Ibrahim offered them coffee and fruit. Fairuz sang on the radio. The grocers stood under Ibrahim's awning making small talk. After a while, they nodded and walked toward their stores.

Hisham and Gisele cleaned the apartment and ate breakfast on the balcony as the street slowly came to life. Just as they finished, the first explosions were heard in the distance. They quickly cleaned up, then went inside and stood at the window.

The street quickly emptied of pedestrians. Shopkeepers gathered outside to confer. Ibrahim watched them as they locked their doors and lowered their metal shutters. After they were gone, he swept the entire sidewalk. He was returning to his store when the bullet hit him. His knees buckled, and he sagged to the ground.

Gisele and Hisham peered out from a corner of the window. The grocer was on the ground, a hand clamped across his thigh, his blood staining the sidewalk, while the bullets skidded off the pavement. His screams tore their hearts. Gisele covered her ears. Hisham held her to him.

A door slammed. They heard footsteps in the stairwell. When Hisham pushed open the door, he saw people filing down the stairs in the dark. He dashed down the steps after them, slamming the door shut behind him.

They found a safe spot in the lobby to observe the street without being shot. They glanced nervously at each other. They didn't know what to do and they didn't move.

Cries rose from the building across the street. "Over here! Good man!" the voices yelled, and the grocer lifted his torso, pressed down on his elbows, and crawled toward them. He moved slowly, and the bullets snapped around him, and he gathered himself up and crawled on his back, and the trail of blood stretched out ahead of him. A man emerged from the shadows, hoisted the grocer onto his back, and ran with him to a parked car before speeding away. Hisham and his neighbors left the lobby and climbed the stairs to their apartments without looking at each other. Hisham could still hear Ibrahim's pleas, and he doubled over and threw up in the dark stairwell.

People grew even more cautious. After what had happened to Ibrahim, they knew better than to rush outdoors at the first sign of a truce. They crawled out of hiding with each cease-fire announcement, hugging the walls for protection. The sniper would occasionally open fire on the empty street to remind them of his presence. He had not claimed any new victims. Hisham knew it was only a matter of time.

Power kept changing hands. Lately the hooded men had been patrolling the street, keeping vigil behind sandbags. He felt a rush of relief—they were Christian like him—then a stab of guilt. What would a Christian rule mean for his Muslim neighbors? For his brother and his family, who lived on the other side of the city, where the hooded men aimed their cannons?

He knocked on his neighbors' door and asked to use their phone. He already knew the lines were down, but it was merely an excuse to check on the elderly Muslim couple. They invited him in, clearly pleased with the company. There was a bad smell in the apartment. The food rotted quickly because of the power outages. They lived on the fifth floor, and with the elevator out, taking the stairs at their age was a challenge. Short of throwing the trash out the window, there was no easy way to dispose of it. Sitt Farhat apologized for the smell, then hobbled up from her chair and opened a window. With her bad knees and ill-fitting dress she reminded him of his mother, and he felt a surge of relief knowing that his parents were safe in the village. He told them that this would pass quickly and gave examples of similar upheavals that had ended just as quickly as they had begun.

But he was lying. He had insisted to Fuad that the '58 and '73 flare-ups were nothing compared to what lay ahead.

"Cities must burn to the ground before they can rebuild," Fuad had responded. The recklessness had infuriated Hisham.

He left the couple's apartment with the trash and a shopping list, promising to return the next morning with market supplies. But the fighting broke out before he could keep his promise, and once again they holed up and waited out the madness. There was no response the next time he knocked on their door. A neighbor peeked her head out to tell him they'd left with their son a few nights before, and he felt both relieved and saddened by the news.

A cat yowled on the street. A car zoomed by. Over the counter he could see the moonlight slanting from the kitchen window. Gisele sighed in her sleep. He stroked her hair gently. The war had brought them closer together. He would cover her body with his if it came to that, take a bullet in her place without hesitation.

The power returned, flooding the apartment with light and sounds. The refrigerator whirred to life. The wrong hour blinked on the digital clock. He crawled around the apartment, turning off lights and checking for damage. He reset the clock. He had been doing that a lot lately, fast-forwarding time, entire hours lost between power outages.

He went to the bedroom window and gazed out at the full moon, which was as beautiful as it had always been and filled his heart with longing and sorrow. The fires had died out, leaving behind a stench of scorched earth. He saw the new sidewalk planters installed prior to the violence as the municipality's latest effort to beautify the neighborhood. He saw his car parked against the curb, right where he had left it a lifetime ago, with Jumana's shoes in the trunk under bags of summer items, towels, flippers, and goggles he had bought as part of Gisele's surprise gift.

He had meant to deliver the shoes to his brother's office. But things kept coming up to foil his plan. Then the violence erupted. He hadn't told Gisele. He wouldn't know how to explain the impulse that sent him to the Bata store to spend hard-earned money on a gift for a girl he didn't know. Would Gisele believe him if he told her he'd had a premonition of the violence to come and hurried to get this gift before the walls went up? That he had predicted this wretchedness and contrived a shelter for it?

He had asked the universe to allow him this kindness. Now he had no way of getting the shoes to Jumana.

He would think of the shoes at odd moments. There would be a close blast, and he'd panic because he couldn't remember a small detail, the color of the buckle or the height of the heels. The shoes were the only tangible thread connecting him to that girl and to a time before the madness. Without them, she was someone he'd dreamed up. Sometimes he would crawl to the window to watch the tracer fire arc across the night sky. The thought of Jumana in her new shoes made him smile. Be good, do good. As though it was as easy as that.

He was seized by a sudden flare of optimism. He would write. He'd never had a chance to deliver his review. He saw the narrator in a more benevolent light now. Stuck between two worlds, like a deer in the headlights, behind her the sheltering woods, while ahead lay the open road, rife with danger. One might stay a long time like this, in a soft daze, thin threads keeping you holding on, holding in.

He returned to the entrance and lay down next to Gisele. Suddenly, his bout of optimism seemed foolish. Who cared about literature at a time like this? He thought of the hooded men in control of his street. He didn't like them. They walked around swinging their rifles, commanding the street. Yet the sniper became quiet when they seized control. And if closing ranks was what he had to do to survive, he would do just that, even if it felt like selling his soul to the devil.

These were thoughts for the morning. He tried to sleep. But he wanted to roar, stand at the window and howl at the men in hoods and the men in keffiyehs and frighten them into oblivion. His eyelids grew heavy. When sleep came, he slowly released his fists.

Rita

We sat up abruptly in our beds, sleep torn away from our eyes. Everything shook. The sky sparked, and the windows rattled with every explosion. Thick clouds of smoke billowed behind the line of trees. I looked at Rasha. In her I saw how I must have looked, my chest heaving, my face pale as bone.

"Hurry," our mother yelled from the vestibule. We grabbed our slippers and dashed over to her. She was already dressed and stood at the door with a candle. Rasha and I were still in our pajamas. "No time to change," she said, reading our thoughts.

Tonight we would hide in the basement. We were ready. We knew the day would come, the fighting at our doorstep. Weeks ago, we stacked blankets on the porte-manteau shelf and left a suitcase by the door. It took a while to decide what to pack. We made lists. We were ruthless. "We are not going on vacation," my mother said.

My mother's eyes darted around the apartment, looking for anything she could have forgotten. She put out the candle and handed Rasha a flashlight, grabbed the blankets from the portmanteau, and tucked them under her arm. My father lifted Tony to his chest with one hand and the suitcase with the other. After we filed out, Mama locked the door and rapped a knuckle to the frosted glass windows to make sure they were locked.

We poured down the steps. Rasha led the way, shining the flashlight at an angle. Red and orange flashes cut across the square of sky above our building. A shadow appeared on the balcony across the courtyard. It was Lena's mother. They were staying put. "Here or the shelter. Whatever will be, will be," she said, her voice trailing off in the explosions. I was relieved. The last thing I wanted was for Lena and Joseph to remind me of my dark secret on the rooftop just as I was about to die.

We stopped in the lobby. The driveway lay ahead, followed by the sidewalk before the autostrade. I knew this path well. I used to walk it when Seta wasn't speaking to me, pulled by an irresistible desire to see her. I always stopped before reaching her building, not daring to enter. Tonight the path and the empty autostrade ahead were deadly. Yet we had no choice. The shells landed in the next sector, behind the belt of trees. They would get to us soon. It was either now or never.

My mother made the sign of the cross. We hunched our shoulders and surged forward, Rasha first, followed by my father and Tony. My mother and I went last. We ran into a blast of heat and soot, our eyes glued to the ground. We didn't want to see the shells arcing through the sky and their exploding light. We looked down and ran.

I tore away from them. I left them behind and reached Seta's building first. I stood in a corner of the lobby against the wall, and my father didn't see me when he entered and had to call my name.

A door opened onto narrow steps that led down to the shelter. We stopped midway for my mother to catch her breath. I slumped against her, releasing quick puffs of air to still my heart. Below us Rasha made wide impatient arcs with the light, pressing us on. I relieved my mother of her blankets and linked my arms with hers as we descended the stairs.

The shelter was bathed in the dusky light of fuel lamps. At first, everything was a jumble of shapes. We walked slowly, picking our way through the figures on the floor. A few rows down, a small space appeared. We collapsed on our blankets, exhausted.

We sat up a few minutes later to examine our location. When our eyes adjusted to the darkness, we saw women with babies and children sleeping on their stomachs and men pacing the floor with transistor radios pressed to their ears, looking for good reception. We recognized a few familiar faces and exchanged nods in greeting. We were as solemn as churchgoers.

I sat with my back against the wall. On my right, a man kept looking at my chest. I wasn't wearing a bra, and my pajama top was missing a button. I folded my arms across my chest and glared at him until he looked away.

Mama was searching the suitcase for socks for Tony. I clasped my top and reached out with my free hand to help her look. I found the socks and tickled Tony's stomach as I slipped them on his feet. He squealed and wriggled free from my grip, then went and fastened himself to my mother.

Every now and then the men with the radios looked up and recapped the news. The cabinet had declared an emergency meeting. The major routes were impassable. Fighting had spread to most of the city. Bodies were floating in the sea. We listened in silence. When the batteries in one radio ran out, we turned our attention to the next man with a radio.

I recognized the names of familiar neighborhoods. My city was being destroyed—the Rivoli, where we used to watch Egyptian movies; the Automatique, where waiters served chocolate mousse in long fluted glasses; the seaside boardwalk; Le Petit Poucet and the Lafayette stores, where Baba took us shopping. I would never know the real Beirut, the way my parents and Rasha knew it, in its secret alleys and shortcuts and bordellos and nightclubs. I would remember it the way a child remembered things, through the intermediary and interdictions of adults. A feeling of immense loss washed over me.

I rolled onto my side and pulled the blanket over my face. I slept like this at home, in the dark under the covers. I closed my eyes tightly. But a fire blazed behind my eyelids, the floor shook with each explosion, and rage burned in my chest. I hated them, I hated them all.

We were anything but safe here. How could we have thought otherwise? We were like rats in shallow holes. I rolled into a ball and started sobbing. I heard my parents' voices over the bombs, but nothing they said could comfort me. We were the almost-dead. Above us the bombs thundered, sirens screamed, and fires raged. The trees thrashed and dropped their smoldering branches.

A voice inside my brain said, *You will die today*. Another got cross when I fell apart. *Stop*, she snapped when I made a spectacle of myself. *Remember the happy times and breathe into them a second life.*

The memories unrolled in my head:

I stood on the rooftop of our building. The sea stretched behind the staggered buildings. Everything but the blue of sky and water vanished.

I saw Dalia, my friend in the seventh grade. She wore a red bikini. We were at her uncle's chalet at the beach resort with the octagon pool and beaded shower curtain. She danced an African dance she had learned while growing up in Ghana. We grilled fish on a small coal grill, then jumped in the pool. I climbed on her shoulders and she threw me backward in the water. When her uncle was away, we climbed the shoulders of boys. But our play was innocent because it happened in the water, where it was normal to be half-naked, with your thighs clasped around a boy you hardly knew and your crotch gently rubbing the back of his neck and your legs knee-deep in the glory of summer.

The bombs crashed. But I was in that wave of time, and a voice said, *Stay there. Time is running out, so grasp it, grasp it now.*

Then it was quiet. I hid under the covers and waited inside my bubble. I could hear hushed voices and crying babies. I drew myself up to a sitting position and rubbed my eyes.

Men were chatting in a corner. Before joining them, my father pulled out a loaf of bread and divided it between Rasha and me. I tore into the bread, suddenly hungry, and then lay down and waited for sleep. But the air stank of fermented garbage and unwashed bodies, and even though I was exhausted, my eyes remained open. A foul odor rose from somewhere around me, so revolting I couldn't breathe. I sat up and looked around me, trying to figure out where the stench was coming from. A few feet away a man was sleeping on his side, his hands tucked between his legs. His clothes were filthy. Even though there was a mound of trash in the corner and several babies in diapers, I determined he was the vile culprit who had made an already difficult situation intolerable, and I looked at him with hatred and wept.

"Go to sleep," my mother snapped when I complained bitterly. Wounded, I gave her my back and fell asleep.

I woke up later to the noise of shrieking children. It might have been hours or a few minutes, I could not tell. The fighting had stopped. My mother told me to fold my blanket. I obeyed, something normal in the way she gave orders I was eager to return to.

The entrance to the stairwell was crowded. When I saw Seta, I called her name. She raised her head and waved. I hadn't looked for her, and I resolved never to seek her out in the shelter. She wasn't someone to turn to on those days of terror and shrieking despair. Maybe it was pride. Perhaps I didn't trust our friendship to survive this degradation.

We shuffled slowly toward the door. I needed a bed, food, a toilet. "Rita," my father warned. Even Tony was better behaved.

We finally emerged, squinting in the light. The air was sharp with the smell of burned things. Broken branches lay scattered in heaps on the green space between the two autostrades, the light slicing through the shell-struck trees. The earth was gouged, chunks of it gone. Our building was perforated with bullet holes. I had worried about the carpentry shop on the ground floor catching fire, but the metal curtains were down and the shop looked unharmed.

In the lobby the stairs looked huge, the way they appeared at the end of summer, when we returned from our month-long vacation in Tarawa to find the familiar world altered. Our footsteps echoed in the deserted building.

Mama unlocked the door and we walked in, inspecting the damage. Except for the broken windows, everything was exactly as we had left it. "Keep your shoes on," my mother cautioned as she swept glass shards onto the dustpan. My father covered the windows with thick plastic sheets. Tony found a piece of shrapnel wedged in my mother's armchair, the one where she liked to sit at the end of the day to say the rosary. I snatched it from him and held it in the palm of my hand, tracing its cold, ugly edges with my fingertip before tossing it in the garbage. He burst out crying. My mother fished it out and gave it back to him.

"You're a terrible mother," I yelled and stalked off to my bedroom, falling asleep in the same pajamas I had worn to the shelter.

When I woke up, my two favorite magazines were sitting on the night table next to a chocolate bar. When I was little, Baba would always leave little gifts by my bed to cheer me up—Little Lulu comic books, Pez dispensers, jewelry-making beads. He hadn't done that since I turned twelve and told him that I no longer liked Little Lulu.

I ran into my parents' bedroom. Baba sat on the edge of his bed, with an open magazine draped across his knee. He was staring at himself in the mirror and didn't hear me come in.

His office was in a hostile zone, and he had no way of contacting his clients. I overheard him discussing money with my mother. "God will provide," she said, and he brightly agreed. I was surprised to find him so easily comforted. He never prayed. In church, he went through the motions, but I could tell his heart wasn't in it; he was half in, half out. A day after that conversation with my mother, he announced his intention to start looking for work closer to home.

As I watched him stare at himself, intently as if he were staring at a stranger, I wondered if his sudden bout of optimism had been a ruse to protect us from his despair. Timidly, I knocked on the door.

"Yes?" he asked, without taking his eyes off the mirror.

"Thank you for my magazines," I said in a small voice.

"You're welcome, my little lamb," he said, turning to face me.

He gave a weak smile before returning his gaze to the mirror. I'm not sure why, but I thought he was seeing his own ghost, and I wanted to cry.

Hisham

Hisham and Gisele opened the windows and stretched in the flooding light. A truce had prompted hours of house cleaning. The furniture was dusted and the mopped floor gleamed. The dirty laundry waited in a heap in the bathroom for the power to return. They boiled water for their bath. In the tub, she lay loose-limbed, cocooned against his chest. During lovemaking they felt good to each other, like newlyweds in the thrall of early passion.

They left the balcony for last. They paused at the door, cleaning tools in hand. On the floor were bullet shells and glass, broken pots with desiccated plants clinging to clumps of dried earth. Construction noises rose from the street, along with voices crying out instructions and children squealing in the open air.

They took heart and went to work, wiping the rails and sweeping the floor. Suddenly Gisele dropped the broom and collapsed, weeping. He knelt and hugged her. She pointed to the buildings across the street, with their broken balconies and bullet scars. Everything is falling apart, she sobbed. She wanted to know what had happened to the people she used to watch on Sunday afternoons from her chair on the balcony, where she sat snacking on lupini beans and whiling away the time. She gripped the handrail and lowered her head between her arms, her shoulders shaking. What happened to the little girl in the flowery dress who played hopscotch on the sidewalk? And Monsieur Vartan, the photographer? And the bearded Greek writer in his wheelchair? And the old man with the evil eye?

He softly hummed in her ear until she relaxed in his arms. A new resolve gripped him. He would remain strong. The peace would not last, and they would cower in the corners until the next day, when it would all start again. It would take all his willpower, but he would make it, and he would pull her along with him.

She sat on the couch while he finished the cleaning. But her mood had affected him. The rush of life was gone. After breakfast he said, "Why don't you pay the hairdresser a visit and I'll see to the groceries?" Her face lit up. He put his hand on her cheek, and she leaned into it and closed her eyes. "I heard that Ibrahim is back," he lied. She didn't ask how he knew, when he'd been cooped up here with her. She gave him a broad smile, as if the grocer's recovery was a good sign for the country.

After she was gone he cleaned the dishes, took out the trash, and dumped it on the sidewalk next to a two-week-old pile. He passed workers drilling through a smashed section of the pavement. The walls were spray-painted with war slogans and pictures of dead militants. Officers from the Security Forces stood guard behind sandbags once attended by militiamen. Stalls of street food issued familiar smells. A ka'ak seller zipped by on his bicycle; a wooden cart laden with bread hung from the handlebar. The fava beans place had lost its neon sign but not its faithful customers. The roadside stalls were brimming with cocktail juices and coffee, with street food, grilled kafta and falafel balls dropped into cauldrons of boiling oil. Laughter rang out from an open window, people called out to each other—normal life.

He bought a kilo of raw pistachios and conversed with the peddler for the first time in his life. He noticed the man's thick brows and the chipped black fingernails on the hand that weighed the nuts. Hisham memorized every detail so that he could tell him apart from the other peddlers the next time. When he asked for his name and how he had fared during the fighting, the older man mumbled. Hisham began ranting about "these crazy times and the plot to divide brothers," and the poor man grew increasingly uneasy as Hisham's mind raced with ideas to reassure him that he was not connected to the hooded men. But the peddler now appeared terrified, and Hisham quickly paid and left.

Seized by a sudden premonition, he entered a grocery store and dialed his brother's phone number. He said, "I watched rocket launchers on my street fire at the city."

"The bastards," Fuad said. He could have meant anyone: the militias, the government, Israel, the Arabs, the West. Grace and the children would go to the village if things deteriorated. He sounded sure that they would. "Do not talk to me about leaving," he warned.

"Who needs Israel when we keep killing each other?" Hisham said. "Come and stay with us until this is over. Think of your family."

There was a moment of silence.

"My family is not in any danger. No one cares that we are Christians," Fuad said at length.

"That's not true. People are leaving mixed neighborhoods to live with their own kind. This is our life now, whether you like it or not." He thought grimly, *If I take you where my eyes can see you when the bombs rain, if I can gather you and everyone I hold dear in my grasp, we might be able to lie unnoticed until the long, cold night is over.*

A sudden clap of thunder made him jump. Rain in June. The world was going mad.

"Have you ever considered that I belong here?" Fuad asked, raising his voice. "Even my name is a little Muslim, a little Christian. Don't talk to me about leaving. This is a class war disguised as a religious war. It's no coincidence that your leader blames the communists."

"You're making a mistake," Hisham said.

"I'll send you the kids, then," Fuad joked. "You can also have Grace. Don't worry about us," he added after a while. "Grace and the kids will be safe in the village. I must go now. Keep in touch."

Hisham put the receiver down. The rain had stopped: a flash of thunder, a deluge come and gone in the blink of an eye. They were not a country of monsoons, but they were plagued by quick tempers and brothers who made rash and selfish decisions. Fuad could go to the devil.

He bought loquat and green almonds, two of Gisele's favorite fruits. From another store he picked up French pastries and a bottle of wine. He summoned hope to him. They would celebrate tonight: being alive, the sun, and the gardenias blooming in pots all around the neighborhood.

A memory flashed. It was summer and he had gone out for a walk by the river. In the water, a garland of leaves strung together with vine slid past him. When it met with driftwood, it wrapped itself around it and conformed to its shape. Entwined, the two floated together for a while before the garland untangled itself and drifted away, uncoiling, intact.

Something similar had happened to them. Swept by a great force, they had skirted it. And now it had left them, and they had gathered themselves to shake free. How they contorted to adapt and survive! How small their lives had shrunk! Sleeping in the hallway, hugging the walls, glued to the radio. Perhaps they were done with all that. This was likely more optimism than honesty would allow.

But something had sprung up within him, an urge to throw himself feverishly into action. He decided to create a survival plan, something he would put in writing that would include both practical advice and exhortations to persist, which he might share with others—he was a better writer when he thought there was an audience on the other end—and to which he would turn when he lost faith. He wouldn't try to dress up his prose. It would sound like a voice speaking from the edge of a cliff, saying just the words necessary to keep him from falling into despair. He might add more pieces later, or not; he didn't know yet. But it would be a step in the right direction, a model for resistance. He felt a great sense of freedom, and he laughed as he entered the apartment and directly went looking for Gisele and wound his arms tightly around her.

That night, he wrote his guide.

A Guide to Surviving War

By Hisham Bassil

Now that it's here, start by calling it a war. Not the "situation" or "the events." It's a war. A goddamn war.

Keep close to home. You'll soon be able to tell which sectors of the city are under attack, and whether the sporadic blasts you hear are the end of a battle or merely a pause. If you must go out during the lulls, stick to small alleys with shelters along the way. You never know when you might need them. You despise being crammed with all these strangers? Get over it. Your life is worth the inconvenience. And cover your nose. It's a cesspool down there.

Keep your past close to your heart. The memories will remind you that you were once more than a shapeless, trembling mass cowering in a dark shelter. You say the bombs are difficult to ignore? I assure you that it is precisely at this point that you must welcome the interference of your brain.

When the bombs go silent, you might start doubting your memories. What appeared to be seared in your brain in the shelter may turn out to be nothing more than fantasies you made up to quell your heart's sharp longings. So what? You don't think twice about the sea melting into the sky at the horizon. The two are indistinguishable, and so are your musings. All fantasies? This is not the time to be preoccupied with the truth. If your dreams can distract you from danger, they are the most solid and welcome of realities.

But I must warn you about the massacres. I have no solution for those. They are terrible. People who look at a stranger's eyes before slitting his throat—I do not wish to go on. Do not read the newspapers. They describe every gruesome detail. That kind of knowledge is useless to you.

You've probably realized by now that war is a massacre orchestrated by monsters, not an abstraction triggered by unseen forces. I'm not talking about the militants who only carry out orders. I'm referring to the higher-ups. Everything is decided by them. Someone lights the first match and adds fuel to the fire. If you must despise, despise the masters with blood money in their pockets, who praise the heroism of the masses before ordering their slaughter.

Pity your people. You are the trodden of the earth. You flee with nothing but your clothes on your back. You eat food given to you by kind strangers. You stuff your fist in your mouth to swallow your cries, then cry anyway.

The people on the other side are your brothers and sisters, stricken by the same hell, so pity them as well. But when the bombs start falling and death looms, you'll be filled with hatred. That's how it is. War is where everything good goes to die.

Rita

Back in school after a week of fighting, and we had a history test first thing. You'd think Monsieur Labaki would show some mercy. But when we walked in and saw him standing behind his desk clutching a stack of paper to his chest, we knew we were in for an unpleasant morning.

"Textbooks away!" he ordered. We knew the drill like it was only yesterday we were on the school benches. Like we were expected to cram between one bomb and the next till all of it was encrusted deeply in our brains—famous battles, treaties, intrigues. The whole useless litany of a history that kept repeating itself, kept circling back into self-destruction and then rising from its ashes and too stupid to know it was better off staying deep down in the ground.

Monsieur Labaki walked the aisles, keeping us honest. When his back was turned, I poked my desk-mate's leg with my pencil, and she slid her notebook down so I could copy her answers. Politely, I shared mine, but nothing there was worth her trouble.

Monsieur Labaki walked up the next aisle, then wheeled down again, up and down. If we had known about the test, we would have arrived with notes hidden in our brassieres, the seams of our uniforms full of scribbles.

After history came music. Monsieur Haddad introduced the new visiting teacher. She had a lovely face and a big bottom and sang "Embrace Me" in a beautiful soprano. The two teachers made eyes at each other and paid us no attention, and the hour drifted by pleasantly.

It was hot during the morning recess. We squeezed together in the covered schoolyard. I sat on a bench next to a bunch of seventh graders. Seta came by to ask if I wanted to see a movie this weekend. "I don't think so," I said curtly. My tone took both of us by surprise.

I had been in a state since I got up this morning and learned that school was open. Tony spit the news in my ear and ran. I threw a book at him. He sounded so smug and happy with himself for being the bearer of bad news. When I walked into the kitchen, my mother was boiling the coffee kettle. "Too soon," I said and waited for the words to sink in. But she didn't give me any notice.

Too soon, and I meant it. It wasn't going back to school that was the problem, but how to do it with a steady heart. How to shift from the bedlam to these gleaming corridors and the sisters rushing you with their shrill voices—*Vite les filles, pas de retardataires*—without going mad at the incongruity. All morning, I sat in my chair staring at the sky outside the window, expecting the bombing to start any minute. I bit my nails trying to make sense of it. That it was still possible for our music teachers to serenade each other, for the garden gate to have a fresh coat of paint, and for me to worry about a grade on a history test. To answer Seta spitefully because she'd hurt me the other day when I said I thought the prostitute in the book we were reading was right to consider her occupation a calling, and Seta said, "Are you mad?" We were in my room during one of those long afternoons when everything seemed to be on hold, the air thick with anticipation. I said at least she had no illusions about her place in the world. I was in a bad mood, and Seta drew back and changed the subject.

How was it possible for mere words to still have the power to hurt, when only two days ago the city was being pounded and the radio announcer read the names of the dead, the list going on until I covered my mouth and swallowed a scream? I hadn't taken a proper shower in weeks, and it didn't matter how thoroughly you cleaned yourself squatting down and pouring tepid water from a bucket; it was not the same. Everyone was leaving: the optician's apprentice in my building and the Muslim girls at my school, and many more, gone to the four corners of the world.

The bell rang. In French class we filled out pen-pal forms. I chose a German girl who wanted to practice her French. The gym teacher passed around forms for tennis lessons and the swimming program. After lunch, it was Arabic class. Monsieur Bassil said, "Write your thoughts about the war," then went and sat behind his desk.

All day I had waited for this.

The words barreled into each other. Monsieur Bassil stared out the window. He looked scruffy and vacant-eyed. Bewildering, right, Monsieur Bassil? Confusing as summer rain to be back in the swing of things and no one except you asking us how we got on all this time under the bombs.

So, I'm angry, Monsieur Bassil. So angry, my thoughts are a jumble, they bang against each other as though I've suddenly gone mad. I want to reach in and find the thread, unspool it on the page. Then you and I will know the truth. You are lost in your thoughts, gone somewhere no one can reach you. I know I don't have to fancy up my writing for you. Something broken and sweet in the way you look tells me that you will not mind the ranting of a fourteen-year-old girl.

I tell myself beginnings are important, but I don't know, Monsieur Bassil. Maybe they're an illusion. Maybe there isn't one single tip but several, like these formless sea creatures that spread every which way with no beginning or end.

Yet I want to know: Who started this, Monsieur Bassil? Who struck the match? Plenty of people rushing to carry out the orders, but who was it who gave the first order? Wouldn't you like to find the head of the snake, Monsieur Bassil, so you could smash it and be done with evil?

All the dead, dumped on the side of the road. Maybe someone somewhere is shooing away the dogs or throwing a sheet on top of a corpse or digging up a quick grave. I hold on to this image, Monsieur Bassil. Human decency is too scarce to waste when it comes by.

My father says there are war profiteers, arms dealers, businessmen trafficking on the backs of the dead. Makes my gut twist. It's where I feel the obscenity most, Monsieur Bassil. My stomach heaving like it can't keep anything down from that wretched world.

Kissinger is the cause, my mother and her friends say. Wheeling and dealing, changing the map of the region.

It's Syria. It's Israel. They're in desperate need of water and have their eyes on the Litani River.

It's a Muslim conspiracy to drown the Christians at sea.

It's the Palestinians who've dragged us into their war with Israel and won't stay put when we say *enough*. We have paid enough for your war. And it's the Muslim Lebanese who've sided with them because the enemy of your enemy is your friend, and heaven forbid they should see eye to eye with the Christians even once.

My father says it's what the right wants you to believe.

But who's firing at us? I ask him. Tell me whose bombs are crashing on our street and I'll show you our enemy.

He says it's more complicated. Then he drags me into the house of mirrors. My head hurts, Monsieur Bassil, because when I think I found the beginning, it slips away and then it's back to square one.

I want to be like the three wise monkeys.

Some things you can't contain, my father says. Injustice spreads like ink on paper.

This might surprise you, Monsieur Bassil, but I'm also angry at things that have nothing to do with the war. I'm angry at the nuns for going on as though nothing's happened. A history test first thing after all this, Monsieur Bassil? What were they thinking? And the way they badger us about the smallest things. Walk in a straight line, les filles, and being all in a huff if we so much as talk with our neighbor during assembly or wear lipstick or hike up our skirts. Be modest, les filles, as if modesty will open the doors of heaven. Sometimes I want to say, Why don't we all form a line for you and take our oaths of obedience? Will that make you happy? Since you insist on binding us in a garment we didn't choose to wear, we might as well make it official.

I'm angry because I've had to carry so many gallons of

water from the communal tap, I swear my arms grew a few centimeters longer. Angry at having to spend time in the shelter with smelly lecherous men and angry with the blasted snipers running rampant and shooting at innocent passersby. Scum of the earth. And at Sister Marie-Louise who came barreling in, that was a while before the war, and she rapped a girl's knuckles with a ruler and the girl just slumped as if this was nothing and gave the sister the other hand. Underneath her insolent exterior I could feel her hot humiliation, and I cheered for her. I hate bullies, Monsieur Bassil.

And I hate it when best friends are fickle with their affection. Seta still loves me and loves me not.

My head hurts so I think this is enough for now, Monsieur Bassil.

I handed Monsieur Bassil my paper. There was enough time for him to read it. When the bell rang, I jumped up and raced out the door. I was aware of his eyes on me as I passed him, and my cheeks burned as though I had gone and pulled a Seta and declared my love. But all I had done was speak my mind. Perhaps anger tore away the veil same as love, and on the bus home I felt exposed and foolish and thrilled all at once, and then what remained at the end, after my heart had stopped thudding and weariness had settled in, was my panic at the sudden realization that I might never dare to look Monsieur Bassil in the eye again.

The next day he handed me a folded paper. I slipped it in my bag without daring to read it. Not even the smile I glimpsed on his lips before I lowered my eyes could quiet my racing heart.

It took a full day before I worked up the courage to read it. And then I was happy.

25 June 1975

Dear Rita,

Thank you for your heartfelt essay. I agree with your sentiments completely. Know that you express the thoughts and feelings of many in our wretched country.

War is senseless. It confounds our innermost need for rational thought and order. There is absolutely nothing redeeming about it, despite the many justifications we might give ourselves. There is little to understand in that compulsion for annihilation and destruction. Almost anything is better than war.

I agree with you that one is tempted to take sides, for the will to survive is strong. But the religion stated on our ID cards is a mere accident of birth. In taking sides, we are forgetting half of ourselves, Rita. Those people on the other side are also our brothers and sisters. To fuel itself, war exacts of us not only our humanity, but our honesty as well. The head of the snake is us, Rita.

Of course, I write these words in the relative luxury of peace afforded us these days, when pondering about such things is possible. When the hell resumes, as it certainly will, my thoughts will be preoccupied with survival. Such is always the tragedy of war—it stymies our souls, and our capacity for self-deception is endless.

I wish all of us peace in the months ahead. Use your summer wisely, go away if you can, and read, Rita. There is nothing more humane and uplifting than a good book.

Yours in peace,
Monsieur Bassil

7

Hisham

One day, they would look back and see the patterns and decide where they fit in the big story of the war. The peons would fall into their slots, and the march of history would look unstoppable. But for now, they moved with their noses pressed to the rolling minutes. Their resilience was lauded by the world, as if they had any choice. They were recruits in a war they had not chosen. Life went on. But a life stripped down to the basics did not inspire him.

War was always just around the corner. Any minute, things might start again. But the latest cease-fire held long enough for the rich to return from Europe. The beaches and restaurants were packed, and the streets once again teemed with traffic.

Gisele went back to work in the city. Her birthday came and went. Before the outbreak, he had leased a beach cabin at a summer resort. But the place was bombed, and all he had was a key he couldn't use. Still, she threw her arms around him. Her dream was buried beneath a heap of rubble, but she thanked him for the thought.

During lovemaking, she screamed, and he worried that he was hurting her. Her sounds confused him. She said it gave her a good feeling to surrender to the wave of emotions and scream with abandon. Perhaps pain had always existed beneath the surface, and after months of clinging to each other for their lives, she was finally letting him in.

She still tried on new outfits for him. He said she looked beautiful, but he sounded distracted, and she gave him wounded looks.

No matter how hard he tried, he couldn't snap back into

his former life. School was back in session, and the year had been extended until the end of July to make up for lost time. But he was not the same teacher he had once been. He gave his students busy work while he sat at his desk writing. After a brief creative outpouring, his pen ran dry. He continued to write short phrases without verbs to try and come closer to the thing itself in its purest form, without the intervention of action. *Leaf in frenzy behind a spider web. Empty acorn caps. The claw-like tip of a branch.* When he was in a bad way, he brought back the verbs as a call to action, a summons to go on. *Reach out, focus on the positive, sleep, forget.*

Except for his lists and the guide that had come to him in a rush but in the end proved to be useless, words no longer served him. Language, until now his foundation, was failing him. A veil hid a crucial truth, a substance essential to life that eluded him.

His students' papers bored him. Mother Superior forbade any mention of the war. It was best avoided. He didn't argue. He'd never had that kind of courage. He acted covertly, hiding behind his insignificance to do as he liked.

He told the ninth graders to write about the war.

The essays disappointed him. "The Plot," a foreign hand exploiting existing divisions; France, Lebanon's "tender mother," intervening behind the scenes to protect the Christians; and Kissinger was to blame; and partition was the only solution. Rita Sfeir's paper stood out, the words rushing out in a furious torrent. He wrote her a response.

Every night he sat down to plan the following day's lesson, but all he could think of were more worksheets. The curriculum was stale and outdated. The books had to be rewritten.

On the phone, Fuad said that this was a just war.

His earlier pledge to resist was a thing of the past. He awoke every morning with a silent gasp of horror in his throat. When the garbage trucks stopped coming, trash piles were set on fire. He imagined creatures writhing in the flames and crying out in long, throaty screams that hurt his ears. At night he dreamed of raging fires and bombs dangling from the ceiling of a laboratory, ticking under a cold light.

He recalled nearly drowning when he was twelve. He'd swum far enough away from the beach to feel completely alone in the world. He rolled onto his back and closed his eyes. He was startled when a boat rushed by, causing large waves. He drank a large gulp of water and immediately began coughing. The more he coughed, the more water he swallowed, until he choked and went under. He thrashed around, desperately looking for a way out. But everywhere he looked there was water. Finally he saw light above and kicked himself toward it, breaking into air.

His street was rebuilt with amazing speed, but traces of the violence remained. He was stuck between two competing realities. *Must focus on the positive.* That his building escaped almost unscathed was surely a good sign. *Must forget. Do not be afraid.*

Life after the violence seemed to be about erasure as much as rebuilding. The stray dogs vanished and were replaced by cats. Gone, too, were the Muslim girls at his school and the shoeshine boy. He asked Fuad about Jumana's father and learned that the family had fled to Syria. Her shoes remained in the trunk, waiting for her return.

On his shelves were books by Palestinian writers he might have to hide from view.

He didn't trust the calculating part of him that was always watching, coaching him back to health—making love to his wife, Jumana's shoes, his sudden interest in the poor on his street—all part of his survival plan.

An idea occurred to him. Where was the harm? Even though it had been years since they'd spoken. Abbudi. Why not invite him for dinner?

A Muslim friend to heal him like medicine. Another ingredient on the list of his daily upkeep. Abbudi to shatter the walls of their divided city.

He remembered Abbudi's affectionate teasing, and nostalgia rose in him. Why not renew their friendship, which had faded as they grew busy and lost sight of each other?

When he called, Abbudi sounded surprised but happy to hear from him. They set a date for the following Saturday.

Gisele quizzed him. Why had he never mentioned him before? "What will I feed him? I'm exhausted. You know I need time to plan for dinner parties." Hurt by his silence, she became difficult.

"We were friends in school," he explained with a shrug.

She had a way of standing in the doorway with her hands on her hips.

He fired this poisoned arrow at her: "Is it because he's Muslim?"

She shot him an angry look.

"Will you tell your friend how desperately you wanted the Christians to win?"

A mocking smile pulled at the corners of her mouth. She, too, was capable of cruelty. But he had deserved it. He extended his hand as a peace offering, but she left the room, and he didn't have the strength to go after her.

He leaned down on his desk. On the wall, a print he had picked a thousand years ago at an outdoor market: a pair of wings, words tumbling from a cloud, a red inverted heart in the lower corner against a yellow background. The wings white, feathered, angelic. The words black and airy, tumbling toward the heart. The image became his trinity: flight of the imagination, a ready supply of words, and a heart to stay the course.

All futile now. The war had contaminated him. He had hoped for a Christian victory. Gisele had known. She had read his heart like an open book. Struck, she remembered.

Abbudi was his only Muslim friend in a small nation, a tiny dot on the map. How was that possible?

They became friends when Hisham started going to school in the same city as Abbudi in the tenth grade. Small tuition and strong academics persuaded his parents to pay the extra cost.

Hisham and Abbudi hit it off immediately. They loved books and spent hours in coffee shops trading novels and volumes of poetry. Abbudi was well read. He introduced Hisham to Darwish and Kanafani, and to Eliot and the Russians.

Every day Abbudi accompanied Hisham to the station, where Hisham took a shared taxi back to the village. Hisham didn't invite Abbudi over. He was ashamed of his house and narrow-minded parents.

Abbudi's apartment was filled with lovely Persian rugs and trinkets that his mother had bought from the city's well-stocked souks. It smelled of cardamom and rose water. Abbudi's older sister flirted with Hisham, then broke his heart by becoming engaged to a rich shop owner.

If religion entered their thoughts, it didn't linger. They were just two long-limbed boys who loved books and enjoyed each other's company.

Hisham's parents re-enrolled him in the village school for the eleventh grade. Abbudi relocated to the capital that same year to live with his uncle and enroll in a prominent private school. Hisham was sad for a long time. He read and reread Abbudi's favorite authors. The thread eventually broke. But Abbudi had given him a priceless gift: Hisham took charge of his own education and stopped relying on his teachers and his mediocre school. He developed a liking for Western literature, even though his French, which had improved briefly at his new school, relapsed when he returned to the village.

When Hisham moved to Beirut, he called Abbudi. His friend was studying civil engineering at the American University there. They met at a coffee shop downtown. Abbudi wore trendy clothes. Next to him, Hisham felt like a peasant.

They kept in touch through the years. Abbudi frequently traveled to the Gulf and Arabia, where the oil boom drew new workers. They met for drinks. Their encounters were always warm, but it was obvious that Abbudi was now moving in different circles. It was Hisham who always called and initiated their meetings. He didn't mind. He was fine with being left behind. He thought of himself as the guardian of the grail.

The morning of Abbudi's visit, Hisham bought semi-prepared food so that Gisele wouldn't have to do any cooking.

She'd already made it clear that she wouldn't. As a peace gesture, he invited her on a walk. They parked the car on a grassy area next to the water. They held hands, their rift forgotten in the magic they always found at the sea. They saw the city center in the distance across the water. They missed it terribly. Here they felt on the outside, cut off from the flow of life.

They arrived home in time to get ready for Abbudi's visit. An hour later, they heard the first explosions. Hisham grilled the kafta and dressed the salad. He put more beer in the refrigerator and prepared small plates of mezzeh and filled the ice bucket.

The kafta grew cold, and the fighting continued. Abbudi would not be coming tonight.

Hisham and Gisele sat for many moments without speaking. Finally Gisele rose and set the table. They ate quietly while picking at their food, then threw the remainder in the garbage and went to bed.

Rita

In the shelter we tried to follow familiar rules of behavior. As above, below. We kept to our spots. The flashlights went out at midnight. Food was shared. Smoking was restricted to designated areas.

The thing with war—the masks fall. Evil was loosened above, but there was plenty of ordinary people's evil down here.

The Attars had consistently refused to come to the shelter. The stairs were too difficult for a woman on crutches, they claimed. Then they walked in on a day from hell.

We had been there two full days. Our breathing was strained with the stale air we had been taking in and letting out so many times our lungs wanted no more. When I saw them, my heart made a leap in my chest.

I ran over to help. Auntie Nur bore down with her full weight, collapsing in my arms as I lowered her to the ground. I leaned her crutch against the wall, wiped her face with a wet tissue, and covered her with a blanket. Her head fell to one side, and in her frail condition she appeared shattered, her crippled hand lifeless in her lap. I put a pillow between her cheek and shoulder and walked back to my blanket on the floor.

When Lamia finished helping her father, she came and joined me. It was pointless to talk through the explosions. I took her hand in mine and thought of her room, with the cream jars and perfume bottles on the dressing table and the love letters she kept in the drawers. There were sparkly gowns and scarves in the wardrobe, and a blond wig hung from a hook in the wall. I had once danced in that room. While Lamia watched, I threw myself into every movement. Because she defied the rules and did whatever she liked, I didn't feel self-conscious around her. But she grew busy when she started working at the Australian Embassy, and I saw less of her.

I looked at Lamia's strained face and at her father, who was fanning his sleeping wife with a newspaper. All the anti-Palestinian talk had driven them into hiding until this last battle forced them out. I didn't understand why they had cut my family out of their lives, but maybe once you dug a hiding hole, you were afraid to leave it for anyone.

Lamia's hand in mine was my rope out of the shadows. With it, I could daydream of brighter days.

Then the intervals between one bomb and the next widened as the fighting shifted to another part of the city. People stretched, cleared their throats, and brushed the dust off their clothes. "We shouldn't have come," Lamia said. I followed the path of her gaze. People had moved away from us, leaving an empty space between us and the next row of families, who packed together across the gap while we sat as if on an island cut off from the rest of the world. Mama, who was busy with Tony, had missed the change, while Baba and Rasha had gone to be with friends in a different section of the shelter.

I saw the hard stares and sidelong glances. A woman picked up her toddler and spat on the floor. People talked amongst themselves, switching their cold gazes to us, and their words broke around us in terrible shocks.

Yet some of them resisted. They shifted uncomfortably and glanced at the others with eyes that said, *Go easy now. These are the Attars, our neighbors who have been with us forever. There's Palestinians and then there's Palestinians.* Maybe I imagined their discomfort because I was desperate for signs of kindness to stem the tide of hatred. I wanted to call Baba, but I was afraid that his Palestinian accent might make him a target. I placed my arm around Lamia's shoulders, but she slid out of my embrace and went and sat close to her parents.

We returned home in the evening. I visited the Attars many times over the next few days. I sought to seal them off from the hatred with my friendship. They indulged me, took me in with polite smiles, and let me have my fantasy.

Over the next few days the temperature soared, and we went

to the rooftop at dusk looking for relief from the heat. The breeze blew in from the sea and the setting sun left big patches of shade where the children played. We flopped on chairs and hiked up our skirts to feel the full effect of the breeze. The heat had made us irritable, but now we were jovial. We brought radios and listened to music between news reports.

One afternoon, our favorite music program was interrupted by news of an attack on a church. The assailants had defecated on the altar, raped the nuns, and murdered them along with the priest. After the first shock, the women gathered their rosaries and stood to pray, their voices swelling with grief. I stood there in the deepening darkness, terrified of what might happen next. Auntie Hala marched up to the parapet, her eyes gleaming with rage. She yelled angrily, her fists rising to the heavens. There was no doubt who was in her line of fire, and my anguish for my friends overshadowed all other emotions.

I begged my mother to do something. She walked up to Auntie Hala and led her away from the parapet. Her face was twisted in disgust, but she was too polite to openly criticize an old woman. "You are better than this, Sitt Hala," she said flatly. The rest of the women joined in, and Auntie Hala, feeling outnumbered, picked up her rosary again and rejoined the prayer group.

I stared at the Attars' balcony. The door was closed, and the curtains were drawn. My friends had closed in on themselves, and even though I knew they would open the door if I knocked, I recognized the first signs of the heart leaving. I wanted desperately to free myself from all this, the hatred and the violence that was costing me my friendships, but I didn't know how.

A month later the Attars left for Australia. Thanks to her job at the embassy, Lamia was able to obtain immigration visas. Tearfully, I made her promise to write. I waited for several months, but nothing came. The post had stopped working. Maybe she did write. But I wouldn't be surprised if she just turned her back and put us out of her mind.

Hisham

He counted:

Five people hiding in the small bathroom in the Kantaris' ground-floor apartment.

On the other side of the cheap particleboard door, a corridor leading to the living room with its glass façade overlooking the street.

That made two walls.

Above them the entire building.

That made six floors.

Which might be either a good thing or a deadly trap.

He stood between Gisele and the door, a shield. A candle flickered on the sink. They'd brought it with them, Gisele screening the flame with her cupped hand in the dark stairwell. Because the building lacked an underground shelter, ground-level apartments were their best alternative. A wonder Emile Kantari heard them knocking through the blasts.

The Kantaris' five-year-old daughter, Sara, stood in the corner winding the hem of her dress round her fingers. Her parents paid her no attention. Emile Kantari rubbed his pregnant wife's back and kneaded her belly while she sat on the toilet, moaning. Gisele reached into her pocket for a piece of candy and offered it to the child, who chewed on it hungrily with her eyes closed.

The workings of the body are tyranny in war, Gisele said one day while from the window of their car they watched a long line of people leaving on foot. There were pregnant women with children in tow in that file, men and women bent with age. She was always terrified of getting her period in the shelter.

Hisham cracked the door open. The Kantaris had abandoned the safety of their mountain home and stayed in the city in order to deliver their child in one of the top hospitals of the capital. It would be the height of irony if Marie Kantari gave birth on the bathroom floor.

Hisham felt defenseless, his boundaries overrun, one with the convulsing earth. He stuck his face out the door and sucked the air into his lungs, then opened the door and walked along the corridor, stopping just before the entryway, where there was still a wall to his left to protect him.

From there he could see the light of the explosions burst onto the wall adjoining the glass doors. He had eyes only for that light with its terrible beauty and strangely tangled patterns. He peered behind the wall and saw, as the light jumped across the living room, in the seconds before the flash had faded, a clock, a sewing basket on a small table, and a child's school uniform hanging from a hook. Shards of light burst as if with their own radiance, illuminating more objects—a vase, a tray full of cigarette boxes, a stack of books. He observed these disparate objects, trying to piece together a picture of his neighbors' apartment, even as the light shifted and swirled, revealing to him, in the brief span of an explosion, the fleeting everyday pictures of a life. When the images became obscured, he held on to them, and as they piled up and gained solidity, becoming flesh pressing against his retina, substantial enough that he was certain they would not slip away, he returned to the bathroom.

Gisele nudged Emile Kantari toward his daughter and took over fanning Marie Kantari. Hisham felt a deep pang in his chest when he looked at her. She had grown so thin and frail.

"Selfish like your brother," Gisele said when he refused to flee to the village.

"The looters and squatters will move in the moment we turn our backs," he responded. In reality, he was afraid of leaving his brother behind. They hadn't spoken in weeks. Fuad had joined the militia. "All this time, it was more than just talk," Grace said when she broke the news. Hisham imagined, and his stomach heaved. In a way, he had been expecting it.

If he stayed, his brother still had a chance. But leave? It was as if he was throwing his hands up in the air, waiting for Fuad and the city to perish. Beautiful, ugly Beirut. Who would pick up the pieces if everyone decided to cut and run?

"Go. You go," he said.

She refused. "Where you stay, I stay."

And now, eyeing her from the doorway, he thought, *My poor darling. These bombs might be gifts from my brother.*

But they survived. And in the morning, they went home. Broken and distrustful of windows. But they lived. And the following week, Marie Kantari gave birth to a girl.

Gisele spent her time reading old magazines and smoking. Hisham went grocery shopping, stocked up on drinking water, and cleaned the apartment. For a while he cooked. When he stopped, they ate sandwiches. They had crossed the line into a world he did not understand or like but had to endure without protest, because when something broke you did not fault it for its inability to cobble itself back together as fast as you would like it to. You waited until you no longer noticed the cracks, and then you went on living.

Rita

My father was driving home when a bullet passed very near him. It grazed his ear, leaving a pink narrow cut. It was all he talked about for days: the piercing whistle, the flash of pain, the frantic honking as more shots rang out and cars climbed the grassy strip in the middle of the road and zoomed in the opposite direction in a mad dash to get away. He laughed nervously, his eyes darting, haunted by images of the terrifying moments when he jammed the accelerator and the car careened through the weaving traffic, scraping up against the lamppost before he straightened the wheel and escaped. We sat stunned as he spoke amid billows of incense smoke, my mother's exorcisms having doubled in the aftermath of the incident; then we stopped listening, unable to bear the thought that we had come so close to losing him.

Did this brush with death trigger his heart attack a week later? I was on the landing getting a lesson on how to fix a dropped stitch in my knitting when Mama's screams burst into the fading daylight. A deep stupor overtook me. The neighbors were already rushing to help, but I sat paralyzed, with my heart thumping and my mind drained of all thought except the dreadful notion that death, which had attempted to strike my father once before and failed, might have now succeeded. I dropped the scarf I had been knitting on the floor, where it puddled at my feet, and seeing it, awry and raveled, somehow unfroze me. I leaped through the hallway and into our apartment, then straight to my parents' bedroom, where I paused in the doorway, not daring to go in. People had gathered around my father's bed, blocking my view, and although I ached to see him, I also dreaded what I might find. I glimpsed my mother seated on the edge of his bed, and a neighbor standing nearby.

Across the room, Rasha was digging through the wardrobe, tossing clothes in a small suitcase, and from the same wardrobe but on my mother's side of it, a neighbor was doing the same. Someone said to give Baba some air, and people started leaving. Then I saw him.

He lay on the bed, staring at the ceiling in mute astonishment. The sight of his chalk-white face and glassy eyes, and the mound of bedsheets tangled at his feet like wreckage from a battle he had waged alone, devastated me. His right hand rested on his chest, and I kept my eyes fixed on it as it rose and fell with his breathing. With every new intake of breath and exhalation I took heart, as though a thread had unspooled between us, tethering him to me and me to him, and there was my father, helpless, crushed by a stunning blow, but alive.

I brought a chair for the neighbor. I squeezed my mother's cold, limp hand. I held my tearful brother in my arms and stroked his back until he relaxed. I carried him to my room and laid him in my bed when he fell asleep. When I returned, the doctor had already arrived and was examining my father. When he was finished, he asked to speak with us alone, and in a quiet corner of the corridor, he said that my father had suffered a serious heart attack and warned that the next one would be fatal unless he quit smoking. My mother clung to the wall for support. But despite his grim prognosis, the doctor had given her hope, and her voice was firm as she swore that my father would never smoke again.

My father was carried from the building on a stretcher and loaded in an ambulance. Rasha and Mama followed in the family car, while I stayed behind with Tony. When they were gone I went upstairs, climbed into the bed next to my brother, and braced myself for the sleepless night I knew lay ahead.

We went to see him in intensive care, and then in the room where he stayed for a week before they discharged him. When he came home, we helped him up the stairs, which he climbed slowly, pausing frequently to catch his breath. He'd lost weight. It took some getting used to the new, trim Baba, who was a pale shadow of his former self. He quit smoking and followed a strict diet until the color returned to his cheeks. Beirut had remained calm during this period, and we rejoiced in our good fortune, as if the country and my father were healing together.

It wasn't long before he was reaching for his cigarettes again. The doctor had been clear. But there was no convincing Baba. He would rather die young rather than suffer through a lifetime of restrictions. Cheating death had made him reckless. We eventually let him be, but the doctor's warning haunted us, and we lived in fear of the future.

Life went on. July was calm. You wouldn't know it from the military grandstanding. Every day, roofless jeeps with mounted weapons and men standing in the back flying the party flag raced through the streets, young and cocky men with thick beards and gold crosses around their necks. I knew some of them. They stood straight and grave-faced, like soldiers in a good war. I imagined them running across enemy lines, roaring their battle cries. Then I saw them playing with their little sisters and snuggling with their grandmothers, and the memories collided against each other.

In school we were flooded with tests, the nuns keen on sorting out next year's promotions and mindful of the parents who had paid a hefty tuition for life to continue as usual. I read constantly but didn't bother studying and barely passed my exams.

In late July, witnesses reported seeing the Virgin Mary looking down on Beirut and weeping. Auntie Hala came to get us, anticipating another apparition in the coming days and requesting our presence when it did. My mother gathered her rosary and prayer book and led us to the stairs, while Baba rolled his eyes from his chair.

We flocked to the rooftop to keep vigil. We faced east, where Mary was said to have appeared, although in the magnitude of the terrace we were as if atop a mountain, and she would have been hard to miss in the open sky.

Auntie Hala organized a prayer group. I followed along in my mother's prayer book. We chanted, *O Mary, take pity.*

Dusk fell, but still we were without Mary. At night, we descended the stairs back to our apartments, our eyelids heavy with sleep. Our lips continued to murmur prayers that by now we knew by heart, the black starlit sky that was to be Mary's canvas still swirling in our brains. Our dreams were filled with images of Mary, and everything, our skin and the rustling leaves and the cicadas serenading the summer, reverberated with our longing.

The next morning we were on the terrace again, clutching our rosaries and prayer books and beseeching. The weather was mild, even though it was the middle of summer. We took this as a sign that Mary was looking out for us.

Yet day two also proved fruitless. When we lapsed at dusk, exhausted after a long day of prayer, and our lips fell to mumbling, Auntie Hala beat her chest with her fingertips, and her example sparked us with new energy. Then darkness fell and the same scene repeated itself. Exhausted, we sidled back to our apartments. A few hardy ones remained into the late hours of the night. Auntie Hala was the most resilient and she never left her post, her eyes narrowed as she searched for the tiniest spark that would signal the answer to our prayers.

At the end of day three our disappointment was great. Bereft, we had the sense of having missed our chance, of being alone and helpless. We shuffled, muttering our prayers, and even the young children, for whom these gatherings had been great occasions to go at it while the adults paid them no notice, were quiet.

I pulled away from the group, placed my hand on the edge of the wall where the heat of the day had accumulated, and whispered Mary's name. By now I was convinced that I must look for signs not easily recognizable, and I scrutinized the sky for clouds perhaps clustered to form her shape, or flashes of light in places lower than the heavens. It wasn't like Mary to be ostentatious. When I called her name, the breeze picked up, and to me this sounded like the beginning of a response, as though she was picking up her forces, the way heat gathered, building up at midday. Perhaps she was in all things. I peered over the parapet and watched the street. But all I saw were the cars parked against the curb and the dying trees and the haze of pollution on the horizon.

At home I wandered, unable to shake off my disappointment. It gave me solace to think of Mary spilling tears on our behalf. Without that image of her appearing to raise our spirits, we were defenseless.

Yet we recovered. We continued to believe that she dwelled behind the thick clouds and the cresting moon, somewhere in the folds of that sky, standing watch and looking out for us. If she had refused to show up, it was because we were undeserving. But as the days wore on and more of Mary's life story floated in my brain, I began to think that perhaps it had never been her intention to appear. Coming into view would have meant rustling up the past to be once again overwhelmed by sorrow. I envisioned her facing her son's empty tomb, and wondered why in the world she would want to revisit this. Even after he was dead she still worried, imagining the worst, wild beasts tearing him limb from limb, the angry mob coming back for more. Then he appeared, and her first instinct as a mother was to tend to his wounds. But as usual he ignored her, and she did not solicit what he could not give.

Did his rejection tear her heart? I would have gone mad with the pain. Even if we did not impose on the gods a mortal's sensitivity, something of that aloofness must have scorched her once human heart. Why, then, would she have looked back? It was better to stay out of sight, her image conjured up when needed.

I had hoped for Mary, not only to dull the darkness of the last months, but also to ask her to protect my father, who was still smoking despite the doctor's warnings. And when she didn't appear, feeling distraught, I went to my books, dug them out from the shelves and spread them on my bed, and lay down on top. Slowly I slipped a foot, then the other, under a pile, waved my arms and scooped up a bunch and dropped them on my chest, and buried my face in their pages. I breathed and cried and felt defenseless and small, but the world was unresponsive, and in the silence my fears grew and choked me.

Then Rasha came. Clearing a spot beside me, she lay down and took my hand. "There's nothing to fear, my little lamb," she whispered, and the hot tears poured from my eyes.

Hisham

The city, splintered, was rearranging itself and severing bonds. In mixed neighborhoods, one after another, people abandoned houses they had inhabited for life to come up on the other side to be with their own kind.

But Fuad refused to leave his neighborhood, part of a defiant minority unwilling to give up on a dream. When his phone calls went unanswered, Hisham drove to his brother's apartment. Despite the cease-fire, he was nervous. When he reached Fuad's quarter he slowed down. There was a power outage, and he couldn't see clearly, and once or twice he drove over an object on the road. Finally, he pulled over in front of the building and stood on the sidewalk, staring up at the façade, relieved to see the pale light of oil lamps glowing in his brother's living room window.

He was winded after climbing four flights of stairs, and paused to catch his breath at the door before knocking. Fuad's eyes lit up when he saw him. He had lost weight, and he looked thin and gaunt. Hisham hugged him and laughed.

When they were seated in the living room and the air between them was warm, Fuad asked about Gisele and school, and Hisham gave long-winded answers, delaying the moment when a heavy silence would settle between them after the small talk had run its course, and they would have to work up the courage to broach the unsaid.

Fuad looked almost unrecognizable without the weight. But it was him, with the scarred knee, the faint mark of an old vaccine on his upper arm, and the hairy chest sticking out from under the unbuttoned shirt. He appeared distracted, but every now and then something Hisham said elicited a chuckle, and a glimmer of light flashed through Fuad's eyes, and his cheeks reddened as if a warm breeze had blown through him. But the moment passed, and the same absent expression returned, his attention straying. He was too polite to cut the visit short. *Yet he perseveres*, Hisham thought, his throat tightening, *as if my presence is a painful ordeal he must endure.*

Fuad eventually excused himself and went to get two beers from the kitchen. They sat opposite each other, taking long swallows in silence, the flow of talk now interrupted, until Fuad set the conversation back in motion with a question about their mother's refusal to see an eye doctor, and Hisham, who'd never been chatty, felt he could go on for hours, drawing from some formerly undiscovered reserves of light banter, the subject of their mother's stubbornness that seemed to have smothered their father, and from there to stories from childhood about this impassible, silent father, and avoiding, avoiding, the reason he had come in the first place.

Fuad kept getting up to bring more things from the kitchen—peanuts, olives, an empty bowl for the pits—as if he hadn't learned anything from that first interruption about the difficulty of picking up where they had left off, or, on the contrary, as if he was trying to pile up the silences until the visit ended by natural death. Every time Fuad left the room, Hisham looked for evidence that would directly link his brother to the war. Fuad had never mentioned his involvement with any guerillas, and they might have been too quick to accuse him. Hisham found nothing, no weapons or drugs hidden in plain sight, and when he scanned his brother for bloodshot eyes and needle marks for the drugs the fighters were said to use, he came up empty-handed, and Hisham knew that this proved absolutely nothing.

Now it was Fuad who broke the silence. He mentioned his children, who had been spending the summer with their mother at her parents' house in the village, and how difficult it had been for him to visit on a regular basis due to the gas shortage. He went on about the cost of things, the peace talks, and the weather. "You shouldn't have come," he said abruptly. When he noticed Hisham's pained look, he added, "The roads are too dangerous. I'm worried about you."

This last kindness gave Hisham courage.

"What are you doing? You have children!"

Despite his mounting panic, he spoke, gesticulating in persuasion, painting a picture of Layla and Karim fatherless, or, if not, being misled by their father's actions. How could he have done it? Kill. Take another person's life, even if he believed he was on the right side. It was one thing to have a father, a brother who was involved, an activist who held strong opinions and acted on them peacefully, which was something Hisham had always admired about his brother. But to kill for his views? That was crossing the line into something Hisham couldn't accept.

Fuad listened in frigid silence.

At last Hisham stopped and looked expectantly at his brother, examining the inscrutable expression for signs of the impact his words had made.

Fuad leaned forward and said, "I'm going to explain myself one last time. I am fighting for justice, not religion. Compassion without action is useless. Our politicians are corrupt, and our structures oppress the poor. Neither will disappear magically. We must use force to demolish them, and this requires sacrifice. There it is, my thinking. Do you understand now?"

He drained his bottle in one swallow before rising to his feet and retrieving his keys. "Follow me. I'll drive ahead," he said as he dashed out the door. Hisham scurried in tow, slamming the door shut behind him. He stopped at the foot of the stairs, then stumbled ahead when Fuad did not slow down.

They embraced on the street. "Don't stop anywhere. Go straight home. I'll drive until I can go no further."

But you must know that the checkpoints are unmanned, Hisham wanted to say. Isn't that why I found you at home, on your day of rest?

They got into their cars, and Hisham followed through the streets that were starting to come alive as the electricity was restored. Soon they would be clogged with traffic. At least this was the same, on this side as on the other—there's an initial skepticism after the first announcement of a cease-fire, then the streets brim with noise, as if optimism is a difficult habit to break.

When they were as close to the demarcation line as they could get, Fuad swung to the side, wheeled around and drove up to Hisham. "You'll be fine from here on out. But keep going and don't stop." A wave, and he was off.

Hisham sat hunched over the steering wheel for a long time before he reached for the ignition key. He sat with the engine ticking, fighting the urge to go back and beg his brother to come to his senses.

He stepped on the gas and rolled up the window. He had forgotten to give Fuad Jumana's shoes. Now they remained his burden alone, his purpose, a promise he had made to himself. He had to deliver them to a ghost girl he barely remembered: a tumble of hair, tattered shoes, a fierce desire to protect her solitude.

Sometimes he looked for Jumana's features in the faces of girls her age he saw on the street. The chance of finding her in these parts were nonexistent, but he still looked. Maybe he would start looking for his brother in the same sad and hopeless way, snatching from disparate features of strangers he met on the street recollections that would grow less distinct in time. In his imagination Jumana still wore her school uniform and the white shoes with the holes. He tried to see her in a different light, but his brain held fast to that one image, and every time it felt like a new and unnecessary violation. Sometimes weeks went by, and he didn't give her a thought. Then he remembered, and the lapse carried its own sadness. She was slipping away. One day he would forget her. Her ghost was entwined with the ghosts of an entire city crisscrossed with impassable lines, a brother who had wandered beyond reach. Forgetting her was like losing hope. A janitor's daughter. The wall between them is not as thick as that, he who came from poverty. He had reached out and invited damage. He claimed they were alike. She knew better than to play along with his nostalgia. Perhaps harm came from looking back. More likely it came when he forced upon a girl a version of herself she rejected.

One day, back when he and his brother still talked about real things, Fuad said that anger was life affirming. Sometimes violence was the only way for the aggrieved to come out into the light and be seen. Hisham argued passionately against the necessity for violence. Now he remembered Jumana's anger when their eyes locked briefly in the lobby of Fuad's office building. Something there had prevented him from crossing another line. Told him he'd caught a glimpse of something she meant to keep hidden. Yet he stood there. Then, embarrassed, he turned away and pretended to read the bulletin board notices.

When did he lose sight of Fuad's anger?

Black patent leather shoes with gleaming buckles. Through them, he tried to scramble back to what was lost.

8

Rita

The end of July brought grapes and peaches, tomatoes and watermelon, and at long last, the end of school.

In August we headed to Tarawa. Red-roofed houses, staggered on the hills below street level, greeted us when we crossed the town line. A shrine to Mary stood on the side of the road, far enough away from town to earn extra points with God for making the journey. After a bend, a string of coffee shops and grocery stores led to the center. People stopped to stare, curious to see what marks the war had left. I sat upright, gazing ahead with a look I hoped conveyed courage and a burden well shouldered. I had been feeling so small lately, crushed by great forces, and all this attention made me feel important.

My grandmother greeted us at the door with lemonade. Teta was overweight, had diabetes and high cholesterol, and suffered occasional fainting spells that kept her bedridden for days. But she sneaked pastries behind my mother's back and faithfully smoked the three cigarettes prescribed by her doctor to ease her nerves. She had a persistent suitor who called her *mi amor* and sent her love notes. When Rasha and I teased her about him, she laughed and threw in a few spicy details to get a rise out of Mama, her prudish daughter. She was my only living grandparent, the others having died before my birth. I hadn't seen her since Christmas, and it felt great to be swept into her arms and smothered by kisses.

She seated us in the living room, then put Tony on her knee, took my hand in hers, and narrowed her eyes at Baba. "An entire house at your disposal, and you choose to stay in Beirut in the middle of a war," she scolded. Baba cleared his throat and muttered a few words while the rest of us watched silently. I felt sorry for him. But a little chastisement might be just what he needed to get him to listen to reason.

Feeling tired after the long ride, I finished the rest of my lemonade and leaned my head against the gold and plum velvet armchair. A large rug hanging on the wall showed deer grazing by a stream, behind them the dense woods. In the foreground, separated from the herd, a lone deer stared at something beyond the rug. As a child I used to think it was trying to tell me something, and I'd lie down on the floor, swing my feet over the armchair, and stare at it, waiting for a message that never came.

Laughter sounded from the street. I sat up and stretched my neck to look out the window. A group of young girls walked through the square waving bunches of raw chickpeas. My feet tapped against the floor. "Why don't you go see your friend Rima?" suggested my mother. I didn't need to be told twice. I left my empty glass on the table and dashed out the door.

Rima lived a short distance away, in a stone house that lay below street level in a narrow alley lined by houses looking out onto the valley. We had become friends the summer before, when she summoned me from her balcony while I walked down her street, admiring the flowers and the view of the valley I glimpsed between the houses. I answered her call immediately. I had seen her before in the square, where she caught my eye because she was always with a large group of friends and seemed to be the center of their attention. I appeared to be destined to seek the company of girls far more popular than I, and they in turn liked me, or at least felt an urge to take me under their wing. Unlike Seta, though, Rima wasn't fickle. Or maybe I saw too little of her to experience anything but her devoted attention.

Rima's mother, a beautiful woman with the same piercing green eyes as her daughter, opened the door. At the sound of my voice, Rima emerged from the kitchen, her eyes lit with happiness, and led me to the couch, where we sat with our fingers interlaced. I gazed with affection at her face, with its dimpled cheeks and pixie haircut. She was a year older than me and had established her seniority early on in our friendship by teaching me how to smoke. Since then, she'd eased up on the coaching, issuing occasional advice on how to dress or style my hair to attract male attention. I agreed, but by the time we were ready to leave for Beirut, I was usually itching to get out from under her shadow.

Her mother joined us on the couch, and the two of them began grilling me on the "events." I felt uncomfortable with all the attention. I explained that my neighborhood had fared a little better than others in the city, but while the devastation was not as severe as what they might see on television, the war had made daily life difficult, and I described all the ways in which that had happened. My heart sank when I saw their disappointment, and, desperate for their sympathy, I changed course and gave them what they wanted. I spoke of hunkering down with the neighbors while the shells arced in the night sky and the explosions stunned my ears, how I could still hear them when the night fell quiet. This rekindled their interest, and their eyes and ears soaked up everything I gave them, which, while true, felt tinged with self-betrayal. I could see that no matter how hard they tried, the magnitude of the horror eluded them, and my inability to communicate it clearly weighed on me.

When I got back to the house, I headed straight for the garden. My uncle's cot was unmade, and an empty coffee kettle sat on the small stove. I saw no sleeping bags and wondered if his American hippie friends had decided to steer clear this year. I sat on the cot and hugged my knees to my chest. The afternoon sun filtered through the grapevine trellis and fell in small circles of light around the water fountain. Teta's flowers had shot up. There were shoots of parsley and mint in the herb garden, and the row of tomato plants was lined with sticks.

The knot in my stomach dissolved, and at last the tears flowed. Even though my neighborhood had fared better than many, the hiding, as well as the fear and uncertainty about the future and the sadness I felt for all the lives lost, had taken their toll. I cried some more, then headed upstairs for dinner.

The next morning I awoke to the mournful bleating of a lamb. I drew the covers up over my head but couldn't get back to sleep. I finally sat up and looked out the window at the poor creature tied to a rope outside the butcher's shop. How did it know its fate with such wrenching lucidity? What instinct drove it to hurl these pitiful cries into the chilly morning air, having never experienced what was about to happen? I could only hope the melancholy that had settled over me wasn't a sign that something equally bleak was about to happen.

I lingered at the window for a while, and as the sun warmed the square, which became increasingly crowded, a sense of calm washed over me. I was happy to be here.

Mama and Teta were in the living room when I headed downstairs. I rested my head on the chair, drifting in and out of sleep to the sound of their voices. I desperately wanted to sleep again, but the sound of a car door slamming woke me up. Baba came in the next minute, looking pleased with himself as he unloaded bags of walnuts and apples onto the table, then returned to the car for more.

His family owned a large plot of land that had been passed down through generations of farmers. City dwellers like Baba and his family, who had no knowledge of farming, were barred from reaping their share of the harvest because they contributed neither money nor labor, and the only thing binding them to the land was their name and the laws of inheritance. Baba had long been irritated by the oversight. For years he talked about paying visits to his cousins and demanding his fair share. But until today he had never stayed in Tarawa long enough to complete his mission.

He was overjoyed with the gifts he was bringing and agreed to stay in Tarawa when Mama suggested it, perhaps in the hope of getting more crops before his cousins' goodwill ran out. But in the days that followed, we saw no new fruit trophies. Instead, he spent his time sketching Mama and painting a flower field next to a little pond he'd seen on one of his walks. It looked cheerful, with dabs of bright reds and greens against a blue sky. Happy to find him looking so well despite his smoking, we rested easy and enjoyed our time.

Mama and Teta worked in the kitchen for hours while Tony played nearby. Rasha was gone all day with her friends. I slept a lot. In Beirut I had become a poor sleeper, kept awake, if not by the bombs, then by worry. Even as my need for long hours of sleep eventually waned, I spent my days reading or listening to music in the solitude of my room or the garden. Occasionally I hung out with my uncle, who was a projectionist at the local movie theater, and watched him wheel around on his stool, splicing films and threading them onto spools.

A week into our stay, Baba decided to return to Beirut, and no amount of pleading could persuade him otherwise. But he looked healthy and rested, and the news from Beirut remained good, so we watched him leave in his car and hoped for the best.

I was ready for company again, and Rima and I went on daily walks through town, pausing to speak with her many acquaintances to whom she introduced me as her Beiruti friend. This is how I met Fadi. He was tall and slim, with a shock of brown hair that flopped over his face like Davy from the Monkees. I was instantly smitten. He and Rima started talking, and I observed her eyes shining as she laughed at his words. He turned before leaving and invited me to join them on a hike on Saturday, which I accepted, trying not to seem overly joyful.

"You have an admirer," Rima said after he left. I couldn't tell if she was joking. Watching them flirt, I was convinced something was going on between them. Still, I basked in my joy. Rima filled me in. His family owned the hillside villa I'd admired for years. It seemed like an icon of Tarawa, beautiful and remote, standing against the mountain with its arched porticoes and sprawling red roof. His family had fled Beirut, but unlike mine, they had settled in and were not eager to return.

If the conflict continued, Fadi would most likely finish his studies in Paris.

"Hurry up and reel him in. He will not be here for long," she added. Once again, I couldn't tell if she was serious.

Over the next three days, I teetered between feelings of excitement and terror. There was the agonizing question of what to wear. I played scenarios in my head, in which I either clammed up or laughed loudly and humiliated myself. I wondered whether Baba expected to find me home when he arrived on Saturday. I dropped hints to Mama about the outing. When she said nothing, I considered her notified.

I came down to the living room early on Saturday morning, hoping to get ready and leave before Baba arrived. But a stack of newspapers on the coffee table, along with the sound of familiar voices and a waft of cigarette smoke, led me to the kitchen, where I found him at the head of the table, surrounded by Teta and Mama and the breakfast dishes in front of them. Bending over, I kissed him on the cheek and slid in the chair across from him, glancing wearily at the newspaper splayed out before me, its headlines screaming at me—THE SINAI AGREEMENT IS LOOMING. ISRAEL ATTACKS THE SOUTH. LEBANON SUBMITS A COMPLAINT TO THE UNITED NATIONS. THE PALESTINIAN RESISTANCE RETALIATES BY FIRING KATYUSHA ROCKETS AT ISRAEL. Even though there was no mention of Beirut, the war had followed us here. We'd always thought of the South—poor, neglected, and decimated by Israeli violence—as a distant place whose problems did not directly affect us. But what was happening in Beirut was related to the South. I wasn't sure how, but I felt that by looking steadfastly, one could unlock the ties between past and present.

The prime minister had stated unequivocally that there wouldn't be a fourth round. Baba said the calm on the ground seemed to back him up, and this positive update cheered me up a little.

"I hope you'll stay this time. You've looked better," Teta said.

"It's the heat and the long journey. There's nothing a nap can't fix," he replied, tapping his cigarette on the ashtray.

I made a quick assessment. He had bags under his eyes, and he was dressed shabbily, without the care he usually took with his appearance. My heart sank to see him so clearly unwell. At the same time, my eagerness to go hiking with the dashing Fadi pushed out all other thoughts. I asked Mama to pack my snacks and ran upstairs to get dressed, eager to leave before something happened to thwart my plans.

An hour later I was with Fadi, Rima, and two pretty girls my age, twins with easy laughs and cute little noses that turned up at the end. They introduced themselves, but their names went through one ear and out the other as my brain raced with questions about which of the two was Fadi's girlfriend.

We walked in a single file, with Fadi leading the way and the twins bringing up the rear. A steep drop with a series of wide terraces cascaded toward the valley to our right. For a while the only sounds were our footsteps and steady breathing. Then our pace slowed, and the group began to talk and make plans about the upcoming Assumption Feast. I remained silent. But when the twins let out long bellows that echoed across the valley, I joined in and delivered my own sounds to the mountain, with my voice roaring back to me on the swirling wind.

We stopped for a break a couple of hours later and sat on a flat ledge jutting out from the mountain and offering a beautiful view of the gorge. I wedged myself between two rocks and drew my knees to my chest. Fadi took out his harmonica and played a tune. When the twins launched into singing, the one belting out long wistful notes and the other harmonizing, I understood why they had been invited. Feeling better about my romantic prospects, I leaned back and watched the twins, gorgeous with their long dark hair and radiant skin, sing their incantations, which surged with aching purity, vibrating in the open space and inundating us with warmth. I gazed around the valley, admiring the waterfalls, when I remembered one of Baba's drawings and wondered if he had made it from here, and the thought of him laboring down the narrow path with nothing separating him from the deep fall sent new waves of worry through me. But the twins were laughing, and my father was forgotten once more. A shepherd and his goats made their way up the path above us, trailed by a black dog who frisked happily behind them, valiantly patrolling the herd. The twins climbed the path to pet the dog, who nuzzled their necks until his owner whistled. When they returned, chirping happily and calling for food, we produced fruit, nuts, and pastries from our bags, along with a good supply of beer.

For a while we could hear only our chewing and the songs of the birds, and now and then the long and whiny bleating of lambs. When we were ready to talk again, Fadi told us about the monks who lived in the monasteries on the hillsides and the hermits who had fled persecution centuries ago and came to live in the caves cut into the cliffside. One of the twins pointed to a modest dwelling fronted by a cultivated terrace at the bottom of the valley and told of an old hermit reputed to be a holy man who foretold the future. Rima, laughing, said she had tested the rumor by dragging her younger brother there and asking the hermit, who was ill and bedridden, if she would marry the young man in her company. When the hermit said yes in his frail and husky voice, the brother and sister burst out laughing and ran out of the modest house, followed by his caretaker's angry curses. We teased Rima about the dashing couple she and her brother must have made.

Drowsy from the beer and sun, I lay down on my back and closed my eyes, using my bag as a pillow. Fadi accompanied the twins on his harmonica as they sang a beautiful ballad. Then there was silence. I must have nodded off. A light touch on my arm jolted me awake. When I opened my eyes, Fadi's face was leaning over mine. I was only aware of his warm breath on my face and my body rising toward him. With a start, I sat up, my cheeks on fire. He held a lizard in front of my face. "It was climbing your arm," he said.

On the way back, exhausted from our long descent, we fell silent. I thought about his gesture, and the memory of his warm breath on my face still made me giddy. But he was ignoring me, and I gave up on getting him to be interested in me. Time was no longer on my side, and I could feel the minutes ticking away toward the dreaded moment when we would part ways before I could think of something intelligent to say.

The moment came all too quickly. I picked my way sadly through our belongings, which we flung on the ground upon exiting the valley, looking expectantly at Fadi. To my surprise, he grabbed my hand before saying goodbye and gave me a spot to meet him if I made it to the Assumption Feast. Rima's snarky "He's not in your league" warning before we parted couldn't dampen my joy.

The festival was scheduled to take place on Friday. I decided to avoid Rima and spent the next few days frantically planning my outfit and wondering if Baba would decide to join us. In previous years he would take the day off and drive up in time for the festivities. I missed Baba, but his presence would derail my plans, and as I prayed for his absence, I was overcome with guilt and worry. Then I remembered Fadi, and everything else faded away.

At last the day arrived. Much to my relief, Baba stayed in Beirut. We piled into my uncle's car early and drove up the winding road to the mountain peak. Early fireworks exploded in multicolored blooms across the sky, drawing our excited shrieks. Bonfires lit up the mountain. A band of traveling musicians was getting ready to lead the dancers into the dabke with tablas, flutes, and tambourines.

My uncle had barely parked the car when I bolted out the door and ran to the ski lodge where I was meeting Fadi. He was standing by the long food counter, holding a soda can. When he saw me, he tossed the can in the trash and handed me a walking stick. It looked like we were going on another hike.

The mountain smelled like grilled meat and corn, dust and wild thyme. Girls and boys stole kisses behind trees. The musicians shook their tambourines by the clearing. We clasped hands and moved back and forth like a human wave, advancing and retreating until the line seemed to encircle the mountain. A man broke away from the line and danced alone. He tapped his foot on the ground and puffed out his chest before leaping off the ground, a handkerchief twirling in his outstretched palm.

We skipped through the briars. "You're strong," Fadi said. He took my hand on the rocky passages, and even though I didn't need it, I accepted his help. We finally made it to the top. Smoke rose from the fires below. Fadi took me in his arms and gave me my first kiss. I breathed him in. He smelled like hope. Something special was happening to me; I had entered the charmed circle of adulthood. And if, as he kissed me, my parents' lifetime of warnings about the weakness of the flesh echoed in my head, I was also acutely aware of the deprivations of the previous months, and I clung to him with all the willful fury of my body, which was demanding its due before it was too late.

He dropped me off at the ski lodge after our walk. The next day I floated in a state of happy stupor, reliving his kisses over and over. Two days passed with no sign of him. I avoided Rima and went for solitary walks in the hopes of running into him. Finally, my efforts were rewarded. I discovered him playing pool at the coffee shop on the outskirts of town. When he looked up and saw me in the doorway, a flicker of surprise crossed his eyes, but he turned away as if I weren't there. I returned home, confused and despondent, and went straight upstairs, where I burst into tears.

The next morning, I went to see Rima, who took one look at me and drew me into her arms, where I sobbed bitterly. "Poor darling," she said as she patted my head. "He does it all the time. I should have protected you." Her words triggered a new bout of sobbing.

Being brought out of obscurity and then abandoned without

explanation devastated me. I failed to hide it from my mother. She sat on the edge of my bed, muttering words of comfort, her mind full of dreadful scenarios, and when she finally asked the question, I assured her that my virtue was intact, then asked to be alone.

It was the last week of August. Baba, who was tired of making weekly trips to Tarawa and whose health was deteriorating, wanted us to return home. I had a temper tantrum. I desperately wanted to stay in Tarawa. Hope had wormed its way back into my heart against all logic. Every day I stood at the window, waiting for Fadi to come and clear up the misunderstanding. But Mama wasn't having it. We piled into the car one Sunday morning and drove down to Beirut. In the back seat, my heart was breaking.

Hisham

He took a sip of beer and watched the sparrows race between the straw parasols before swooping down to the beach. It was the end of August, and the temperature was soaring. Hisham and Gisele had come to a seaside resort in a coastal city untouched by the fighting. Fifteen kilometers north of Beirut, and it was as though they had landed on a different planet.

From the shallow end of the pool came the excited screams of young children—*look at me, holding my breath underwater, swimming to the edge, touching the bottom*. Teenagers cannonballed from the diving board. He wanted to take a swim in the sea, but Gisele, who was lying on her stomach on the lounge chair next to him with the straps of her bikini top unclasped, had specifically requested his presence so he could rub her back with oil and get her drinks from the bar.

He peeked at the newspaper headlines on the table opposite from him. There was trouble in the Bekaa Valley. Israel and Egypt were on the verge of signing the Sinai Accord. It remained to be seen what impact this would have on the war. Everything, near and far, always affected Lebanon.

He wondered what Fuad had to say about these talks. He would probably criticize the notion of peace when it was carried out on the backs of the downtrodden. On the phone he always sounded as if they were about to face a major reckoning. But the war dragged on, with rival parties winning and losing battles and the number of casualties rising. Hisham wanted specifics, but Fuad wasn't talking. Hisham suspected that his brother knew no more than the rest of them. Grace said he hadn't been home in days. His disappearance meant only one thing: they were getting ready for the fourth round. The happy shrieks of the children receded, and war once again blotted the sun.

Gisele rolled onto her back, fastening her bikini top and slathering suntan lotion on her skin. Since he wasn't permitted to bring up politics, he asked what she wanted to do for lunch and suggested a swim in the sea. She said she wasn't hungry but could use a soda, and that a swim later would be nice, but she wanted to continue tanning for the time being. In the two hours she'd been lying on her stomach, she'd done a number on her back, but he didn't say anything. It was their first trip to the beach in a long time, and she wanted to make the most of it because who knew when they would be able to return? In any event, she wouldn't have listened to him. Things had been a little tense between them. They hadn't made love in weeks. For a while after the battles began, desire flared, then, inexplicably, stopped. Combat fatigue, he said half-jokingly when, once again, he did not respond to her desire. She shot him a wounded look. He loved her with all his heart. But the war had passed into him like poison.

He got her a bottle of soda, and when she was ready, they went for a walk on the beach before diving into the sea. He jumped, truly happy now, abandoning himself to the water. She swam to him, and he reached out and pulled her, wrapping her legs around his waist and dancing with her in the bobbing waves until the noises around them faded. She read his desire in his eyes and her eyes flooded with tenderness. They bounced gently in the waves before untangling, drawing a deep breath, and immersing themselves, leaving the outside world behind.

Gisele slept on the ride home, and the town's lights gleamed behind them in the night. He could see himself living there, with all the beach resorts and coffee shops, and taking leisurely strolls in the old town. But they could never afford the rent. Besides, the rich who had flocked to the area to escape the bombings had created a housing shortage in addition to driving up prices. He thought about the destruction just a few kilometers away. Suffering, according to Fuad, was everywhere and was kept hidden only by willful ignorance. But Hisham was tired. It took too much work to survive each day. Today he had been happy. He could still feel the happiness even as they approached their apartment and the darkness grew deeper in the absence of electricity, and the lingering haze from the bombs hid the stars and moon.

Gisele woke up. "We should do it again," she muttered drowsily.

"Yes, we should," he said. The town would not be spared indefinitely, and we must hurry, he thought, but he didn't say anything.

9

Rita

My uncle's wife took a deep drag on her narghile stem, reached for a cookie from the tin on the coffee table, and said, "France will protect the Christians."

"France is Lebanon's tender mother," Mama concurred, rotating the coals with small tongs.

We are not children. France is not our mother, and she isn't tender, I thought.

Why did I answer the door when she rang the bell? When Rasha and Tony heard her voice, they vanished, and now I was stuck playing hostess. I twirled the tassel on my armchair. The living room set had been reupholstered in a hideous fabric the color of onion skin. My mother was hopeless. She liked only discreet, sober colors. In addition to black and white, her palette included shades of beige and gray, browns and buttercreams.

My uncle's wife left smears of lipstick on the coffee cup and the half-bitten butter cookie. Her lap was full of crumbs.

"Everyone wants a piece of poor little Lebanon." She took another deep draw on the stem, setting the water in the base to churning.

"Poor little Lebanon," my mother echoed, sighing while eyeing the coals in the little tray.

"There will not be a fourth round," my uncle's wife said, imitating the PM's nasal voice.

"Inshallah," my mother guffawed.

My uncle's wife recited names of people who had left for Europe, Brazil, North America. My mother had never met any of them. They belonged to my uncle's wife's considerable circle of acquaintances. It was clear that she did not approve.

"A cot in our own country is better than a castle abroad," my mother concurred.

I leaned forward in my chair and gave her a dark look. I wished she was less agreeable toward a woman who exaggerated her own importance and treated us as her inferiors.

"There is no better climate," Mama added, her eyes flitting to the balcony. Potted plants were lined up against the glass doors and the small adjacent wall. Despite their numbers, they made a weak impression. My mother had a green thumb, but her garden had never completely flourished. Except for a gardenia that flowered every spring, there was something unfulfilled about my mother's garden. She favored plants that had an inconspicuous beauty, small begonias and spindly snake plants, thorny succulents in small painted pots. When the pots started to peel, she repainted them the same color as the railing.

My uncle's wife had the accent of her region. It was assumed that she held the reins in the marriage. When he met her, my uncle shed his Palestinian accent and spoke like a native.

My uncle's wife resumed her nibbling, showering crumbs down onto her lap. "Israel is a necessary evil," she pronounced next. "My enemy's enemy is my friend. The more they tighten the controls on the PLO, the sooner we can be done with them," she said, shaking her head scornfully.

My mother glanced uneasily at the door. Baba was at work, but she was afraid the words might still reach him, stick to the walls, and reverberate their evil. I cracked my knuckles in exasperation. I wanted Mama to speak up. And I wanted Baba here, filling the room with his Palestinian accent. But he was doubling down at work, making up for lost time.

From the street came the rumble of traffic, the trucks sounding out their marine horns in shrieking renditions of the "Für Elise" and "Happy Birthday" tunes. My chest tightened. It was my birthday, and I felt miserable. How could there not be a fourth round? I was trapped in my apartment, my life empty and joyless, without any hopes for the future. Every night I drowned in sleep, and every morning I woke up feeling cheated.

School was starting soon, and with it my freedom ended. I had not gotten over Fadi. I still pined for the happiness that was briefly mine before he dumped me like a pair of old shoes. I hated him. Fadi, with his unlimited prospects and bright future. He was probably in Paris by now, talking with his French classmates about the things French teenagers were interested in, light years away from any war. Or he was still in Tarawa, breaking the hearts of more gullible girls like me.

Next to me a cabinet housed a large, broken radio. On top of it was a doily, a broken clock, a vase with artificial flowers, and a tray full of packs of cigarettes for guests. I called it "the corner of dead things." I reached for the plastic flowers and plucked a rose, bending the petals in my hands and digging the blunted thorns into my skin.

I was turning into my mother. I will wear beige. I will sit with my knees pressed together. I wondered if Fadi had smelled it on me, a kind of mutilation of the spirit, and left.

My mother cleared her throat. She opened a box of candied almonds and offered it to my uncle's wife, who put an almond in her mouth and worked the candy with her tongue, making sucking noises. Mama sighed with irritation. She hated eating noises. She got up quickly to fetch more coal from the kitchen.

My uncle's wife turned to me and listed her children's accomplishments.

Then she asked, "Where are your brother and sister?"

"Sleeping," I lied.

She asked how I did on the state test. I said it was canceled on account of the events.

"Your skirt is a little too short, yes?" she asked, looking at me sidelong, her lipsticked mouth puckered thoughtfully.

"Your skirt is a little too pink, yes?" I wanted to say. But I tucked my hands under my thighs without saying anything.

When Mama returned, my uncle's wife turned her attention back to the narghile. Mama packed fresh tobacco in the bowl, then spread the coal, setting sparks. My uncle's wife was a veteran smoker, so neither of us thought to remind her to wait before taking her first draw. She put the mouthpiece between her lips and inhaled and was instantly seized by a coughing fit. Her face turned red, and her chest heaved. I fetched water from the kitchen and waited while she took sip after sip and returned to normal.

After she was gone Mama called Tony and Rasha to the kitchen. She had baked a birthday cake. She made the same one every year. Today she added frosting and canned pineapple slices.

I blew out the candles. I was fifteen. I felt old beyond my years. At the same time I was still a child, and I had missed my life. The things I knew were of the wrong kind; they might be able to see me through in the long run. But what good were the long views if all I wanted to do was enjoy my youth? I might live a long time. Or I might not make it to my next birthday.

I finished the cake and went to my bedroom. Lying in my bed with the transistor radio on my pillow, I drowned in music. Little by little I escaped.

Hisham

Three weeks later Fuad was still gone. Grace said over the phone that she had recently spoken with him and that he sounded well. But she kept sighing, and the children missed their father. Hisham decided to pay them a visit while the last cease-fire was still holding.

It had been several weeks since his last trip, and he wanted to start with a walk at the seaside. He parked on Bliss Street and made his way to the water. He could see the sea blazing blue as he drew closer, and he ran to the corniche in a burst of joy. Gripping the handrail, he inhaled the sea air, exposing his face to the splash of the waves. The palm trees, the dear cadence of the sea. A ribbon of haze tinged with the light of early dusk capped the horizon. It had been an eternity.

A few men watched the sunset from the rocks below. He could hear bicycle bells, the cries of the peddlers, and children laughing behind him. He stood there for a while longer, and when the sky began to darken, he turned around and headed for his car.

In the fading light a sudden fear gripped him, blotting out every sight and sound. Faces of dead militants peered at him from posters on the walls covered with slogans, striking terror in his heart. A jeep roared past. He gazed ahead. He knew how to do this, freeze his face and still his racing heart. He walked quickly, trying not to draw attention to himself. What a fool he was! After a break in the fighting, he lost his mind and came back to the forbidden city before the next round began.

He got in his car, turned the ignition, and pulled into the streaming traffic. But many streets were blocked by debris, and in his panic he found himself going around in circles. In rage, he struck the steering wheel. After twelve years he still couldn't find his way around Beirut! He found himself at Martyrs' Square, and pulled over to get his bearings. The familiar cacophony of buses pulling in and out and taxi drivers shouting out their routes, and the martyrs' statue at the end of the terminus bolstered him. He got out and walked to his brother's office. Beirut was no longer the city he remembered, but he could still navigate its map in his memory, and recognizable landmarks guided him until he arrived at his destination. He peeked inside, pressing his face to the glass door. The lobby was empty. What did he expect? That he'd find Jumana still reading in her chair, with a book on her knee? He got back in his car and drove to his brother's apartment.

When Grace opened the door and saw him, tears of joy streamed down her cheeks. She took his hand and led him into the living room, where candles flickered on the windowsills and side tables. She lit an oil lamp, crossed her arms, and smiled at him. "Did you have a hard time getting here?" she asked.

"Not at all," he lied. He could sense her loneliness, and his heart wrenched for her.

She lit a cigarette from a pack on the coffee table and ran her fingers through her hair. She looked exhausted, stooped where she used to stand tall. He noticed the old slippers and the frayed sleeves of the housecoat. She had once been fastidious about her appearance, and if not particularly beautiful, she had been striking.

She paced the length of the living room, taking long drags on her cigarette. She had no idea where Fuad was or what he was doing. He sent her money regularly, and he sounded cheerful on the phone, but it was a ghastly cheerfulness she knew was fake. They didn't bring up his activities when they talked. It was their dirty secret that had to be kept hidden beneath layers of silence, or she wouldn't be able to hold herself together for Layla and Karim. There were long stretches when the phone lines were down and she didn't hear from him, and she felt alone and abandoned. She paced and fretted, picking tobacco flecks from her tongue and rambling. She tapped her forehead and apologized for not asking about Gisele. Then she brought up Fuad again. Even before this recent disappearance, he was rarely here. Perhaps it was better that way. The children would have seen it in his face. But maybe she was deceiving herself, and they already knew. Her face softened when she mentioned the children.

As if on cue, they appeared, shrieking with excitement. Layla jumped onto his lap and began listing her accomplishments. "I have a new doll. When I squeeze her tummy, she laughs. I can do a cartwheel. Would you like to see?" She was on her hands before he could respond. Karim sat on the seat across, watching them with a solemn expression. Hisham reached into his pocket and pulled out a gold clip music bookmark, a late birthday gift that put a big smile on the boy's face. Hisham ruffled his nephew's hair before taking a handful of candy from his pocket and giving Layla the lion's share in compensation.

He twisted her onto his back, then stood and flopped onto the couch, pretending to buckle under her weight. "You're hurting my back, girl. What did your grandmother feed you?" She let out a squeal of laughter and tried to escape his grasp. Karim came to her rescue, and the two of them tickled their uncle until he begged for mercy.

Grace laughed. "I'll go make the coffee," she said.

In her absence the children sat down, their faces conspiratorial as they darted glances at the kitchen where their mother had disappeared.

"The village school was awful, Ammo!" they whispered.

"They had no piano. I knew more math than my teacher! The kids were dirty!"

"It could not have been that bad!" he said, pretending to frown. "Of course it was!" he added, tapping his forehead. "I was there, remember?"

Their eyes widened. Did he really attend this terrible school? "Baba too?"

They talked until Grace arrived with the coffee and carried on as the grown-ups sipped. Then Grace said it was time for bed. Their protests went unheard, and they hugged their uncle and mother before sagging their shoulders and dragging their feet to bed.

"His eyes are dead," she said when they were gone. "I can't stand looking at him. I look at his hands and I think, these are the hands of a killer. What should I do?"

She was not asking him about Fuad, who had become a lost cause to her, but about the children and her life and how to manage in the middle of a war.

"Have you thought about going back to the village?" he asked.

"I might do that," she said thoughtfully. "But the school is awful. Still, it's not out of the question." She stubbed out her cigarette in the ashtray and lit another one. Then she glanced at her watch and said, "It's getting late. You really must leave. It's not safe."

"Move in with us," he said. "It isn't much safer, but at least you wouldn't be alone, and Gisele would love to have you."

She shook her head. "I don't want to leave without a plan. But, really, you should get started."

Before he made it to the door, there was a burst of gunfire, followed by the thud of distant artillery. They stared at each other. "Maybe you should stay the night," she said. They returned to the living room, where Layla and Karim were sitting on the sofa counting the explosions. Before long the noise of the bombs grew louder as they started falling close to the apartment. They hid in the stairwell before moving with a few neighbors to the janitor's room on the ground floor. The small room smelled of turpentine and stale trash, and the neighbors quickly headed back to their apartments. Hisham drew the children to him. Where was his goddamn brother? Bombs were raining on his brother's street, on his brother's children, who were shaking and calling his name. He thought of Gisele alone and cursed Fuad under his breath.

The shelling stopped early the next morning and they returned to the apartment. The windows were broken, and there was a big hole in the living room wall through which they could hear their neighbors. He swept the broken glass while the children got ready, and Grace packed a suitcase and stocked up on fruit and bread for the road.

Karim and Layla fell asleep right away in the car. There were no barricades, and he sped through the empty streets. He had to stop twice to pick up debris from the middle of the road. When he approached his neighborhood he veered right, taking a shortcut to his street. He turned off the car, grabbed the suitcase from the back seat, and sprinted upstairs to his apartment. Gisele was asleep in the entryway, curled up on herself. He drew back the blanket and stroked her hair. She opened her eyes and burst into tears as she wrapped her arms around him.

He made coffee and heated milk for the children, while Gisele packed a suitcase. "You're coming," she said as she snapped the buckles shut, holding his gaze. He sighed and shrugged his shoulders. Fuad could go to hell.

Life erupted from all sides the farther north they drove. They stopped for ice cream, even though it was still morning. They were exhausted when they arrived in the village. His parents had been up all night listening to the news. They asked about Fuad, and his mother broke down in tears because no one could tell her where he was.

They fell asleep and woke up in the afternoon and had lunch on the terrace. A taxi driver arrived with a message from Fuad urging them to stay in the village. The fourth round was here.

They'll do exactly that, Hisham thought. Life and beauty will hold them up here. There will be more deaths when they return. But for the time being, life.

But he couldn't stop thinking about Fuad. In his absence the village stifled, life stifled. Life was a lie masking a horrible truth.

He made his way back to Beirut a week later, with Gisele angrily in tow. He returned to the horror, the one thing he still shared with his brother.

Welcome back. Beirut greeted him with her fury.

The air blazed. The sky was covered in smoke and the moon

was nowhere to be found. He thought of clearing the tiny glass fragments protruding from the frames around the plastic sheets covering the empty panes. But the days passed, and he never did.

They hid from the bombs. To stay distracted, they kept their eyes fixed on the shadow of the candlelight convulsing on the wall. When Gisele wasn't looking, he reached for the flame and took his time removing his finger. A blister formed, the skin pink and teary.

Here it came, the whistling and the blast. He saw the blinding light, and the flames shooting, licking the scorched sky. Somewhere there was a tumbling of breaking glass and concrete, twisted metal and mangled buildings and trees toppled to the ground. There were dusty corpses that would grow bruised and swollen. Even to these horrific visions, his eyes refused to close.

Rats scrabbled in the walls. He told Gisele they should have the walls checked, leave poison in the holes. Anywhere a rat came to the light to feed, they should seal it with death.

Here was his pounding heart, his moldy skin, the taste of ash on his tongue. The smell was overwhelming. Here was his shame. He couldn't get rid of it. His perspiration, the stench of his own body in captivity, its animal terror.

A flash of pain in his finger when he popped the blister, clear liquid oozing. He examined his palm in the candlelight, his lifeline long and unbroken. The skin was puckered up and white around the cracked blister, as though it had been in water too long.

He put his hands between his knees and pressed. A rush of relief flooded him. He squeezed his knees once more, again and again until he cried.

And here was his love, his wife, pale in the infernal night. Here was her hand, cold as ice, her trembling fingers, her nails bitten down.

They were alone in the world, the last living creatures. Here was their terrible loneliness. Should death come, would it hurt? Or would they be swaddled by that same white heat, that same piercing light? Would there be silence afterward or a steady sweet purling? Or would that last loud imprint of the world play repeatedly upon their sleep? Should they die this minute, would this awful, broken world remain with them for all of eternity?

And now she squeezed his hand. Here was the burning city. But all he saw was his wife with her lips shaped around his name, calling him back.

One night of horror. Here now, then gone the next day. Today was rainy, tomorrow sunny. They licked their wounds, plugged the hollows, and moved on. Until the next time.

10

Rita

Mama hosted a farewell lunch for Seta and her family two weeks before they left for Canada. On the morning of their visit, Rasha and I were summoned to the kitchen.

"Don't bring up politics," she said, handing us the good plates and the yellow bow tie napkins.

"You should warn Baba then," I said.

Baba, who had a lot of time on his hands now that he couldn't get to his office, insisted on airing out his soul-searching to anyone who cared to listen.

The Karantina Camp, a neighborhood northeast of Beirut that housed poor Lebanese, Palestinians, and Kurds, was under siege. The Christian party, convinced that the camp had been infiltrated by Palestinian guerillas, had cut off food, water, and medical supplies. In the evening, Baba and I would sit on the balcony and discuss the war.

I reported what the neighbors said about the camp occupants, that they had gold teeth, color television sets, money buried in the walls, and ammunitions packed in underground tunnels to kill the Christians.

"They're only poor," Baba said.

"So, it's propaganda?" I asked.

"What if there's a sliver of truth?" he asked, after a few moments of silence.

"You mean the few bad apples that spoil the barrel?" I was puzzled by his question, which was unlike anything I'd heard from him before.

"A few, many. Bad apples for one are political dissenters for another."

"The party leaders say we must hurry," I said. "We're running out of time. We must kill the terrorists before they kill us."

"War is always in a hurry," he said, "and she's a crafty talker."

"So kill them all just to be on the safe side?" I asked. "Surely that's monstrous."

"It is war, my little lamb. I'd look away and let them sacrifice the whole lot to keep the three of you safe. But that's the worst of a person. Fathers don't get a pass."

He avoided my eyes. That's how I knew this wasn't an empty exercise but a struggle against some darkness waging war on his soul. We fell into a heavy silence. "That could have been me," he added later, 'living stateless in a camp." But for the slimmest of odds."This Christian-Muslim strife didn't exist in Palestine. I didn't find it here—not in the heart of Beirut or in the mixed villages clustered on the mountains. But now it has become ingrained in our bones. Fear is detestable my little lamb," he continued. "It makes us act like monsters. Good guys, bad guys. *The fault, dear Brutus, is not in our stars, but in ourselves.*"

I had no idea who Brutus was, but I vaguely understood what he meant. Fear let the devils inside our heads out into the world.

Lunch went well. Baba and Seta's father discovered a common affection for London. Baba had visited the city in his youth to meet an old Italian flame he'd known at their university. It was wonderful to see him so happy, and he looked like himself again, confident and animated. Mama shot me a gloating look. See? Your father knows how to behave himself. No politics, no problem.

After lunch the adults retired to the living room, while the rest of us went to the bedroom to look at Rasha's new outfits. Claire discussed Montreal and its women, who she said were as skinny as teenage boys, and her intention to enhance the lives of Canadian men with her hourglass figure. Seta and I exchanged smiles across the room, pleased to see our big sisters getting along so well.

Just then there were gunshots. Mama explained from the other room that they were firing in the air.

"First you massacre the poor, then you celebrate," Claire said.

"Why do you say that?" I asked.

"Because it's the truth. It's only a matter of time before the camp falls."

My sister gave me a sidelong glance before pulling another dress from her closet, but we had lost interest.

All those years of my hot-cold friendship with Seta and my efforts to please her came to a head. Here they were, about to roll out of our lives into the safety of Canada, and Claire was pointing fingers.

The words hurled out. "Everyone has blood on their hands," I said. "I know people in the party. Someone's brother or cousin is always joining, and I just can't imagine. They don't kill at close range, in cold blood. They don't rape women."

I stood up.

I said, "Isn't it the duty of the party to keep us safe?"

"They call it purifying, cleansing," Claire said drily. "Cheap nylon slippers are stomping on valuable beachside real estate. The party will tear down the shacks and tenements and build something nice and flashy to show the world that we are still the Paris and Switzerland of the Middle East. What's the deal with the labels, anyway? Do they not understand how insulting they are?"

Was she aware how badly *she* was acting? Even though she sounded like Baba, I didn't budge. And although the words that came out of my mouth were the polite version of my thoughts, my intent was clear. Because you have no business telling those who stay behind how to live their lives as you are about to leave for the safety and comforts of Canada. You are already too far away to distinguish the real stories from the ones you like telling yourself. You don't think I want peace and justice in the world? To forget these stupid divisions? Muslim, Christian—are we still living in the Middle Ages? And those stupid seventeen-year-olds playing cowboys with the world's most expensive artillery. You don't believe they'd leave the battleground if someone offered them a job and some security? I'm here to tell you that everyone has blood on their hands. You're leaving, and I'm not.

She had an answer for everything, but nothing she said changed my mind. The more she spoke condescendingly, as if to a child, the more stubborn I became, until even Rasha took her side.

"I think you should stop now," my sister said crossly.

Seta didn't say anything, her silence a dagger to my heart.

After they left, I filled Mama in while we cleared the table.

"It's a good thing they're leaving," she said. "There's no telling how much trouble they'd have gotten themselves into with the party."

I didn't tell Baba. He might have found Claire's certainty appealing next to his confusion, and I wanted desperately to cling to my anger. I suspected that if Claire was already too far off from the true story, I was probably too close.

The next day, feeling down, I drew a chair to the balcony. Our neighborhood was strangely quiet, and the once bustling autostrade was deserted. There hadn't been any peddlers calling out their wares from the sidewalk in months. The Nawar had walked out on the candy factory. There were no pedestrians or construction workers around. The broken glass had been swept up. A heap of rubble and broken branches remained by the side of the road, waiting to be collected.

Despite the gray sky, it was hot, and the weather seemed as out of place as the rest of the world. I stood up, gripped the railing, and craned my neck to look over at the neighbors' balconies. The tables and chairs were put away, and the plants had withered in their pots. This was not unusual for this time of year, but the sight did little to lift my spirits.

I couldn't show my face at Seta's. I'd slept poorly all night after my outburst, tormented by shame while still clinging, if not to my words, then to the feelings of loss and anger that had compelled me to say them. I didn't know what to believe anymore.

I got up, put my chair back in the corridor, and wandered

aimlessly. From the kitchen my mother asked, "Why don't you go and visit Seta?"

I followed her advice, gathered my courage, and walked over to Seta's. Auntie Sylvie answered the door. She greeted me warmly and led me to the kitchen, where I found my friend sitting in front of a half-eaten chocolate cake. Her face brightened when she saw me, and she pulled a plate from the cupboard and offered me a piece. We spent the next few minutes praising the cake, and it was nice to see Auntie Sylvie's face light up with delight and regain some of its former beauty. Their original plan to fly to Montreal had fallen through, and they would instead stay at her aunt's house in Nice while waiting for their Canadian visas. I was happy with the news. Seta would remain close for a little while longer, and we would continue to share the same natural cycles and the gentle eddies of the Mediterranean against our shores.

Seta got two glasses of water, and I went with her to her room. Claire was reading in the bunk above. I gathered my courage and apologized.

"Don't worry about it," Claire said with a shrug. "And now be quiet. I want to sleep."

She dropped her book and turned away. A great burden was lifted. I sat next to Seta on the floor cushions, thumbing through old magazines, until Claire complained that she couldn't fall asleep with us in the room. We got up and went outside to the terrace. Seta's mother had done a wonderful job. Beautiful plants surrounded us, their healthy, gleaming leaves a bright and cheerful note in the surrounding grayness.

It was great to see my friend and spend the time we had together talking and laughing. How foolish of me to have stayed away all this time—her departure would come all too soon, and I'd have plenty of time to mourn her absence then. But my head was racing with questions. I could feel the weight of the unspoken between us, and it seemed fitting that I should ask the questions on my mind now, before our lives separated.

I wanted to know why she had never been a consistent and

reliable friend. But instead, I asked her what she thought about the war and the party. And when she didn't answer, I asked again. Finally, she turned to face me and said that she despised politics. What was going on was terrible, and she didn't want anything to do with it.

"But you must have an opinion!" I asked.

I insisted. It became critical to know where things stood, to define and delineate. So many hours I'd lain in the dark, my ears ringing from the blasts, wondering if I'd make it through this battle and the next one. How could it be possible not to take sides?

I wanted—needed—my friend to share her thoughts, not only for the clarity they might provide, but also because that's what friends did: they trusted each other with the truth. She had always kept parts of herself hidden from me, and I needed her to open up to me before she left for France.

Seta bent her head, and her hair tumbled across her face, obscuring her features.

"Say something," I pleaded.

"Please, let's change the subject," she replied. Her voice was filled with a plea that brought me to tears, and I felt remorseful and cruel.

Everything slowed. We sat in silence. The clouds gathered in the sky above us, and a gentle breeze blew in from the sea.

It was up to me, who had torn through our friendship, to start the mending. I met her gaze. But just as I was beginning to feel a reprieve come between us, she clamped down again, loosened herself from my gaze, then stood up and went inside. I followed her to her room. She lay on the floor paging through a magazine without looking at me, and I knew that my visit was over.

I returned two days later. Seta, generous, took me back. The days leading up to their departure were spent packing. Seta couldn't decide which magazines to take, so she gave me her entire collection. From Auntie Sylvie, we got a narcissus.

I visited regularly that week. Seta and I were warm with each other again. I gave her my flowered skirt. She looked so pleased, cocking her head and looking in the mirror. She gave me her teddy bear, Schtroumpf, who had been our plaything when we were younger, a pillow or ball we tossed back and forth, a baby we swung in our arms, or a pupil we tormented.

In late September the city was plunged again into bedlam. I stood on the balcony, watching as the city burned and black smoke rose against the horizon. There were a series of kidnappings. The snipers terrorized the population. Eighty-five unidentified cadavers were discovered in a mass grave.

The calm returned just in time for the airport to reopen. School started a few days before Seta was supposed to leave. It seemed cruel to be separated from her by classes just as she was about to leave my life. She did not have to attend. Her parents saw no point in extending a structure that was already unnecessary and belonged to the past. Every day after school I rushed home to see her. Their apartment was in shambles, with furniture dismantled and boxes stacked against the wall, awaiting shipment. I made myself small to avoid getting in the way. The rooms were filled with the sounds of echoing steps and doors swinging open, and as they rushed and whirled past me, I felt invisible and discarded, an expanse growing between us, and I looked for something to hold on to, to keep me steady amid the commotion.

On the eve of their departure I stayed in bed, my heart heavy with sadness. Seta had been leaving a little more each day, buoyed by anticipation, and I had to deal with the pain caused by her lightness. Although I had accepted the one-sided nature of our friendship, her joy was still hard to bear.

Yet she had warned me. Being Armenian meant that your birth country coexisted with another place that lived in your grandparents' memories. That, despite being fully assimilated, a small part of you still yearned to be in that place. Your kin scattered around the world were a call to come and see if being elsewhere brought you any closer to the original land. But the secret wasn't in being Armenian. In those final days, Seta could only shield herself with lightness. And if, as I stood back, mentally tracing the outlines of her face until the image burned itself into my eyes, her cheerfulness seemed to be a way of separating herself from her own heart, it also helped free me from any illusions. I finally knew, with a certainty that cut through any fantasies I might have carried, that she had slipped from my life and would never return.

Of course, there were angry moments. I told myself that I should have trusted my intuition. After saying their farewells, most people turned back for one final look, but Seta never did. Her goodbyes were always abrupt, and I was afraid I'd never see her again as she rushed away to her next destination. She would always be waiting for the school bus the next morning, and I would feel relieved, as if I had half-expected her to be gone. And now I understood I'd been right all along: she'd been preparing for the day she'd go for good, and she'd restrained herself from looking back for fear of not having the courage to follow through.

The next morning found me at her door. I knelt and placed my old copy of *Le Grand Meaulnes* on the welcome mat. It had all my annotations and the creases from my pauses. It was a book about those who leave, and I hoped that the pages, infused with my thoughts, would give her a sense of the longing of those who stayed behind.

But it was time to reckon with the present. I had loved her, and I knew I would miss her for a long time to come. But what remained of our friendship was mine, and I didn't need her to share it with me any longer. I returned home. With a sense of sadness mixed with relief, I looked forward to the day when she would be a hazy image, a wispy memory drifting beyond my reach, and I would finally be free of her.

11

Hisham

It was the week of cleanliness. They woke on Sunday to a thin layer of snow, a miracle.

Water on the streets, front steps, and storefronts, and water flushed down gutters with short-handled brooms. A small flood. Like being in the village on laundry day. He recalled water in large boiling pots on stoves, plastic bins and pails, and puddles in the busy square. There were never any men in the village on laundry days. But today the men were sweeping the sidewalks, scrubbing the store windows with newspaper, and spit-shining them. It was what their mothers had taught them, and it was what they continued to do: spit and shine and flash their broad grins.

Snow is a miracle. There was enough for footprints, snowballs, and happy children. The snow cleansed, germs died, and our monstrosities perished. What was buried would resurface later. What was buried seeped into the soil and returned to the grass blades and the air coiled around lungs.

The sun was the enemy of snow. It was never gone for long, and it always reappeared before you could miss it. Water was also the enemy of snow, running dark rivulets on white powder and melting large patches of the miracle. Perhaps there was enough snow to withstand the assault and afford the extravagance of this frenzy, all this water squandered on cleaning the street.

The traffic policeman danced in the middle of the street. He blew his whistle, stretched out his arms, and beckoned. *You go, and then you go, and now you.* He was dressed like a movie star, with sunglasses, a clean uniform, and a white kepi. Legs swung, hands spun. Light flowed from his fluttering fingers. The women adored him. They stood on the side of the road, squealing like teenagers and throwing flower petals, their laughter filling the chilly morning air. A sight for sore eyes, not just for those shimmying hips that sent shivers down their spines. A police officer waving you on your way, a relic from another era. It gave them great hope. They were also hopeful a few weeks earlier when they marched through the streets demanding an end to the killing. The muezzins sang and the church bells tolled. Rockets landed close. But there were 50,000 of them marching and that was reason for rejoicing. And hope gave birth to more hope.

Hisham was happy. He charged into the street, snorting with laughter. Gisele was at his side. She had walked in with sponges and pail, sloshing soapy water on the street. He took her in his arms. They were young. They danced to the music and the laughter of the crowd, the two of them clinging to life and life clinging to them in the softly falling flakes.

Rita

School, after all this time. We barely paid attention to the teachers. We had fallen out of the habit of school.

October the Terrible kept us behind locked doors. November was calmer. It passed by without incident. It was the month of snipers, kidnappings, and counter-kidnappings, and the month of flying checkpoints. There was dread that could not be seen, terror that came in the night, but no bombs.

November was wet. The wind groaned and rattled the windows. The sun disappeared behind the clouds. We crammed the covered schoolyard and the benches and stood at the railing like crows on a line, looking out at the gray sky.

I scanned the schoolyard, remembering those who had left for safer places, girls I knew well, others barely or not at all. Seta was gone. Loneliness welled up inside of me. I wanted to leave, but my family couldn't afford it. Tarawa was the farthest we got. Tarawa, where Fadi was maybe still living a sheltered life. My family could afford a school that packed enough learning into each cycle of hell, but we couldn't afford a life abroad.

We were serious-faced, subdued. We'd developed the habit of recoiling from the outside world, becoming less noticeable and less likely to leave our mark on the world.

Week 3: We found out that Amal was a secret Muslim.

Lovely, scatterbrained Amal with the smelly armpits and easy laugh?

Rumors swirled. Did the sisters know? Or had they been strung along like the rest of us? What went through her mind as she sat through catechism, attended Mass, and received Christ's body into her lying heart? What will happen next? Will she be taken to the party's headquarters, thrown in jail, expelled from Christian Beirut?

The girls were brought together by gossip. They stood in small groups, staring at Amal and whispering.

Amal, who didn't know that her secret was out, scratched at the wall erected to keep her out, every new day another devastating failure. Her face was a mask of emotions, shifting from bewilderment to cautious hope to grim acceptance. Whispers and expulsion were the girls' weapons, a slow siphoning of her right to belong. She kept her head bowed, her neck hunched into her shoulders, a walking apology for being alive.

A correction was issued: Amal's parents were Muslim, but she had been baptized for a promise. Her barren mother had pledged her unborn child to the Blessed Virgin in exchange for a new religion. Amal was a miracle, her birth almost holy, almost Jesus-like in crossing lines.

I was conflicted. I hated seeing her mistreated, but I was angered by the lie. We had grown closer since Seta's departure, and while Amal could never replace Seta, she had helped ease the pain of separation, and I sought her out to help anchor me in the present and quiet the tugs of the past.

But I wasn't sure what to make of the new Amal. Paralyzed by doubt, I stood by and watched without intervening.

When she looked scared, we knew that she knew.

The correction did not stop the rumors. Nothing could return to normal until we had sorted through the shocking news—who she was in our world, whether we sat on opposite sides or merely at a distance, like strangers sharing a park bench. Was it too far-fetched to speculate on the family's loyalties? Spies hiding in plain sight had been known to exist. How did they continue to live here without fear of retaliation? Did they secretly wish for the party's demise and actively work to undermine its victory? Religion defined political identification, and people seldom strayed.

The only way to defend Amal was to disprove the rumor. For one thing, the likelihood of cross-pollination between the faiths was small. It's true that Mary was venerated in Islam, and Amal was born before the war, when there was still a semblance of peace. But crossing over was a major transgression for two faiths that were always trying to outrank each other. Auntie Salma, if she took such a step at all, would not have done it lightly.

As usual, Rasha disagreed. Christmas was observed by many Muslims. Jesus was a prophet in the Qur'an. Auntie Salma's behavior wasn't as unusual as I made it seem.

If it wasn't a big deal, why was there a war?

"Why aren't you defending your friend?" my sister said. Her eyes expressed disapproval. I knew I was being a coward. There was a tight knot in my stomach that wouldn't release, and to untie it meant reckoning with the complicated strands running through my confusion, the guilt and cowardice and feelings of betrayal and, worst of all, the sectarianism that had infested my soul despite Baba's best efforts. In the end I had no choice but to believe a rumor that Amal herself had not refuted. I needed Baba's wisdom, but he looked frail, so I decided not to trouble him with my questions. Besides, I anticipated what he would say. Both Christian and Muslim. Think of the possibilities, my little lamb. She's our new world order.

Amal looked astonished to find herself the target of such hostility, while I did nothing to help her, she who loved to laugh and make people happy. I continued to avoid the gossip, but when she found me during recess, I didn't know what to say. She looked at me with pained eyes, her hands drawn under her armpits, as we sat in silence.

Then it was my turn to be the subject of sly looks and whispers. I was the Muslim lover who would bring Christendom to its knees. I remained steadfast on the outside, but the attacks didn't leave me cold.

Doubt seeped into my heart. What if she wasn't quite so innocent? She was a loyal friend. I didn't know what I had done to deserve her devotion, but I accepted it without question, savoring it when it suited me, and avoiding her when it got too much. But everything changed as a result of the new revelations, and her eagerness to please seemed suspicious, as I felt the girls' eyes on me, watching to see what I would do next.

I went up to her after dismissal. She smiled hopefully when she saw me, but when I questioned her directly about the rumors, her face darkened. I said, "Whether they are true or not doesn't matter; I want to know the truth, and honesty is a quality I value highly." I made a big deal out of the last sentence to make sure she knew I meant it, and I hoped for her sincerity in return.

For several minutes her lovely face locked onto mine, and she looked like the Amal I knew. I could see her mind racing to come up with an answer. She chuckled nervously and lowered her gaze. Frustrated by her silence, I pressed for an explanation until her cheeks grew red. She gave me a reproachful look, then straightened her shoulders and walked away. I didn't go after her, and I watched her walk toward the gate before I turned around and found my bus.

There was now no question in my mind that the story was true. Who was this Amal I thought I knew? She was Amal and not Amal. Loss waited around every corner.

Why did she lie? Of course, I knew why. What choice did she have?

Days passed. Her shoulders sagged and she wilted, but every now and then she tried charming her way back into the games and banter of the playground, as if the preceding days of meanness had been only a harmless prank. As a reward for her efforts, the girls allowed her to join their games as a lowly helper tasked with retrieving props and stray balls. She was obedient and docile, but it was obvious that she was devastated.

The watchful eyes remained vigilant. She was radioactive. I abandoned her to the wolves.

One day, shells landed near the school. It was a first, and we were terrified. The younger grades had already left for the day, and we were instructed to hide in the primary classrooms, which had windows that looked out onto the schoolyard. My group was to be under the supervision of Monsieur Bassil.

We repositioned the desks against the wall. Girls wept and trembled.

"I hope you're happy," someone said to Amal.

She started crying.

"Enough!" Monsieur Bassil ordered.

Amal continued to sob. My eyes welled up with tears, and I went to her and put my arm around her shoulder. When my eyes met Monsieur Bassil's, I could see by his expression that my kindness had arrived too late.

She did not return to school the following day. Weeks later, she was still missing. I walked over to her apartment. The windows were shut, and the spot where her father's white car used to stand was empty. I returned a few more times. The wilted potted plants were still in their spots, and the laundry pegs were arranged on the line just as they had been the previous time. My eyes had memorized every detail in order to alert me to any changes that might indicate the family's return. But they didn't come back. The curtains were drawn quickly and decisively on Amal and her family.

The passive was false. We were the ones who had pulled the curtains shut. We had slammed and locked the door, breaking a sweet young girl's heart. My hopes of seeing her again were dashed. Her absence sat alongside the weight in my chest and memories of Amal bending to retrieve the ball and handing it to me with a big smile, asking, *What will it be now? What will we do next to amuse ourselves?*

Hisham

His fingers skimmed the book spines, pausing when a title caught his eye. He didn't have a specific list in mind, but he had formed general boundaries of what was appropriate to lend a student for summer reading. There should be no overt sex references (his litmus test being *Madame Bovary* and *The Red and the Black*, both of which were taught in the upper classes; what was good for the French was also good for the lowly Arabic teacher) and no Palestinian writers. In the absence of clear indications of the student's and her family's politics, throwing Palestinians into the mix would unnecessarily complicate his mission.

He tilted his head to read the titles and pondered whether the books under consideration could ignite a spirit of empathy and independence, his two prerequisites for a sound education, without the parents accusing him of corrupting the youth. On his desk was a stack of books by Khalil Gibran and May Ziadeh, Ghada Al-Samman and Tawfiq al-Hakim. The last two, published shortly before the war, were eerily prophetic. He added Taha Hussein for his storytelling.

He'd decided to take on Rita's education after seeing her join the rest in shunning poor Amal, who turned out to be either Muslim or Christian from a Muslim family, he couldn't tell. His prized student displayed a mean streak. He'd believed from reading her writing that there was a girl who could think for herself, but she had joined the others in humiliating the unfortunate Amal. Had he taught them nothing? Had Rita succumbed to the ugliness of the times?

The girls acted as if Amal were a criminal. He'd take on the entire grade's education if he could, but he was too tired. He was surprised he had the energy to do this, to care enough about Rita to try to steer her back, even though it would require little effort on his part. He wouldn't have to write a synopsis for each book or explain in great detail why he chose them, and no paper was due at the start of classes in the fall that he would then have to grade. After handing her the books, he would tell her that he hoped she would learn from them about being open and kind and spread the word, the young being our best hope for a country that had been spiraling into horrific cruelty.

He divided the stack in half, creating two piles around him, and leaned into the tunnel between them, with his elbows resting on the desk and his gaze fixed on the calendar hanging on the wall. He decided to give Rita the books the next morning before the siege of the Karantina Camp spiraled into a full-on confrontation.

Books like a fortress against disaster. A pair of shoes in his car's trunk. Something about him tending to these girls with items he thought would keep them safe. Unlike Jumana's shoes, the books would reach their destination.

Jumana's memory lingered, heightened by her absence. Although the chances of delivering the shoes were slim, he had not given up hope. Why else would he not have thrown them away?

With Rita he was more cautious, careful not to place too much emphasis on that interaction and see, as he was prone to do, in the gift he had chosen, a way to make and keep a bond. He had guessed in himself a vague and awkward desire to send something out into the world in the form of kindness or meeting a need, or whatever inarticulate instinct had driven him to cling to something he should have long despaired of giving. Perhaps it was his teacher's need to give and guide, and even though his desire to teach had waned in the months before he decided that Rita needed to be enlightened, it had still been sending out tendrils and hanging on threadlike but strong.

Perhaps it was something more sinister, some selfishness and arrogance about wanting to leave his mark on the world and forge a bond of gratitude and admiration. But why continue with these internal monologues? They were useless. Despite the scrutiny, a large part of the self remained opaque and slippery, and it was just as well.

Books were what held the three of them together—Jumana bent over hers in the lobby, deaf to the rest of the world, and He and Rita were always reading. When he remembered that simple fact, the questions about his true motivations evaporated.

Hisham paid frequent visits to his sister-in-law in her parents' village. He arrived with arms full of sweets and toys. It both thrilled him and broke his heart to see the dear children: Karim, tall and lanky, confined by a small village; and Layla, who'd lost her liveliness despite scraping some up for him when he came by. She took his hand as she sat next to him and drew fanciful figures on his palm.

During one of his visits Grace's parents criticized Fuad for ignoring his obligations. Grace cut them off and brought him to the terrace, where she apologized and burst into tears. The children were suffering.

Once again he invited her to move in with them. They'd find a good school for Layla and Karim, and she'd stay for as long as it took to sort things out. She seemed to like the idea and agreed to start looking for work.

He was in a better mood after his visit. Gisele agreed to his plan. Grace interviewed at a nearby school and was hired in the office. The pay was low, but the children could attend school for free. Hisham began preparing for their arrival. Then Grace had a change of heart. Layla was having nightmares and throwing tantrums, refusing to return to Beirut. Hisham's spirits plummeted. He had hoped to help. Now they were back where they had started.

He continued to visit any time he could. Their lives were governed by the status of the roads broadcast hourly on the radio, which ones were safe, and which ones should be avoided at all costs.

War was many things: animal terror, loss of control, and obsessive attention to daily details. The lines separating the divided city were safe one day and minefields the next, and the erratic shifts drove him to a breaking point. Books offered stability. He never had to fumble around in the dark while reading, and whenever he was baffled and wondered about a character's actions, he did so with delight, as if piecing together an intricate puzzle, with no aggravation more than was necessary for the effort. Even when he lived vicariously through the characters, the line was always clear, and whatever occurred remained on the page and never directly affected him, and in that there was both freedom and safety.

No matter what happened, there would always be the last page and an ending. Books allayed his deepest fears. They would do well by Rita, he thought, slipping the stack in his bag.

Rita

The shops were empty. The cats had taken over the street. They were happy. They screamed and played in the trash and with one another. They sat on their haunches and rotated their heads to survey the landscape. They trawled beneath my window on quiet nights, upsetting trash cans and leaping from balconies. They didn't have much to eat, and they were skinny but boisterous, as if food had become secondary in their newfound freedom. They yowled and scratched at the metal curtains that covered the shops. They were scary. They multiplied, while we died by the thousands.

We took offense at their happiness. They liked to show off how well they were getting on without us. They had figured out a way around the war, which was to ignore it by pursuing life.

We lacked their quickness. The violence lingered in us, continuing to reverberate long after the guns had gone silent. Our world got smaller. It had the circumference of fear.

I listened to music. The Beatles, Fairuz, Pavarotti. I no longer danced.

On the rare nights when we had electricity, Baba drank tea in front of the television set. He looked terrible, his eyes dark with exhaustion. In the glare of the screen, I saw his chipped toenails and the folds of loose skin where his fat used to be. I tried to remember how happy I was when we used to watch television together before the war. But all I could think about now was which of the two would wreck our little distraction, a power outage or the explosives.

You could hear the war sharpening its teeth on quiet nights. When that happened, everything else fell silent—the cats, the lapping waves, and the street vendors.

During the lulls we lifted a corner of the curtain and watched the cats. They stalked, unafraid in the dark, then looked up at the moon and made loud bleating sounds. A mysterious thrill overtook us as we threw our heads back and stared silently at the moon. The cries of the cats sent shivers up our spines. The howling and mewling rose to the heavens, and we were alive and brave.

But the moment quickly passed. We dropped the curtain and walked away. The spell was gone, and our brief happiness ended. It was too late to undo the damage. We were too filled with our own destruction. Let the cats have at it.

Hisham

He gave the books to Rita. She returned the Taha Hussein to him a week later during the lunch break. If he had another by the same author, she'd like to read it. She was intrigued by the Gibran and Ziadeh correspondence and said she wanted to know about that as well, how it was possible to maintain a correspondence for two decades without ever setting eyes on each other.

Her gaze wandered around the room. He had a feeling there was something else she wanted to tell him but didn't know where to start. To put her at ease, he motioned for her to sit and pointed to a chair. He asked, "Have you eaten?" When she shook her head, he took an apple and half a sandwich from his bag and placed them on the desk in front of her. She blushed and declined. Her mother had packed her lunch, but she wasn't hungry.

He asked how she had fared during the long periods when school was out. She said it was hard. She would leave the country one day because there was nothing to keep her here. His chest tightened. He thought of his absent brother, and those who had left or were about to leave. He told her this without mentioning his brother and asked her what would happen if everyone suddenly abandoned the country to its fate, and she said his words reminded her of her mother, who spoke of Lebanon as if it were an orphaned child. She went on to say that she felt a deep tenderness for her beleaguered country, but she was only a child and didn't know what to do except seek her own survival.

He was struck by the thought she had put into it, but he suspected there was something else on her mind. He shared a few butter cookies with her. Those she ate after thanking him with a smile, and they sat for a few moments in silence, eating the cookies.

After a while, she asked if he had heard that Seta Arslanian had left the country. He said he had received a notice from the office. So many people had left, either to go abroad or for the mountains. "Amal too," she added, blushing, and all the Muslim students. The entire world was either leaving or waiting to leave, she said.

He'd always seen her as a rough outline, a girl in uniform with dark hair down to her chin. He enjoyed her writing and that was enough for him. Now, as he examined her closely, he noticed how her eyes wandered when she spoke, and her face became animated. She picked at the cookie crumbs, piling them in a clump, spreading them, her hands moving continuously. It seemed to be her way of bridging the uncomfortable silences between them.

She claimed to have said some stupid things and had a lot of regrets, and that the war had changed her into someone she didn't like. She spoke about how cruel she had been to Amal. She paused for a moment before adding that she was constantly afraid, always preparing for disaster. Even after the fighting stopped, she was still in the line of fire.

"It'll happen again," she stammered.

Her expression changed as she spoke, and despite her youth he could see the lines the war had already left on her face. Fear had wedged itself in her soul. She kept her eyes downcast, and he could tell she was having an internal monologue and was using him as a sounding board.

Then she told him about her dream. She was in a vehicle that was larger than a car but had no doors, like a trolley. She was sitting on the side where the road dropped, unable to change seats or exit. The trolley came to a halt at the entrance of a dark tunnel. On the other side she could see houses and roads brimming with people, but in order to get there she had to go through the tunnel first. She was terrified, but there was no other way. Her face became solemn as she told him how, just before entering the tunnel, she looked down and discovered that she was completely covered with dust.

Her words made him uneasy, and he said it was natural for her to feel this way after everything they had gone through. Then he rose and promised to look for the books and bring her one or two by Taha Hussein the next day.

Before she could respond, the others entered. She rose quietly and walked to her desk.

He wrote their assignment on the board, then took a book from his bag and began reading. He felt bad about his abruptness and shot brief looks at Rita, who was hard at work at her desk.

He had hurt her feelings. He hadn't anticipated her unexpected visit. As her confessor, he had sat there. He was already exhausted after a dispute with Gisele, and hearing Rita's suffering made him feel even more depleted. He and Gisele had been arguing more frequently, and he struggled to resist an overwhelming sense of loneliness. He had encouraged Rita to confide in him, and when she did, he recoiled.

He approached her before the bell the next morning and asked her to meet him during recess. She returned at lunchtime, this time with a sandwich. He took the promised Taha Hussein as well as Gibran's love letters to May Ziadeh from his bag and added Najib Mahfūz and Yusuf Idris.

She expressed her renewed interest in the platonic correspondence between Ziadeh and Khalil Gibran and asked him why it had survived despite the great distance. He replied that there were two kinds of absence: one that caused the heart to wither and one that allowed the imagination to flourish. The two authors' intellectual and emotional bond appeared to have satisfied their need for connection, making meeting in person secondary, if not undesirable. They seemed to bring out the best in each other. If he was right, she claimed, the correspondence was narcissistic because neither party truly knew the other. Wasn't their love a figment of their imagination? The only proof of love, it seemed to her, was a clear-eyed devotion to the other.

"We make each other up then. I wouldn't like it," she said.

Then she admitted to him that there were moments when she thought she had reached her breaking point. Then something unusual began to happen. When she felt the walls closing in on her, she would hear a voice in her brain telling her how to keep going. She didn't know whose voice it was, but it sounded like it might belong to an elderly woman, because it was kind and knowing and seemed to genuinely care about her. She said she missed her grandmother and wished she could see her more often, but her father didn't like driving to the mountains.

He told her she needed to write everything down because the voice was her inner knowledge teaching her the road to survival. The similarities in their experiences took him by surprise. The writing hadn't gone very far on his end. He'd given up soon after the first attempts, and aside from a few pieces that didn't make him feel any better, he hadn't written anything significant. Rita's revelation gave him hope. Writing was not going to save them. But the fellowship was a comfort.

This is nice, he thought, as they ate and talked until the others arrived.

RITA

I followed Monsieur Bassil's advice and tried to write. I took out my pen, opened a new page in my notebook, and tried to conjure the voice that occasionally spoke to me during the worst battles. But she seemed to come into my thoughts only when I was under the bombs. I scribbled down a few sentences that I recalled, trying to represent both her soothing voice and the sterner one she used when I was in distress. The memories were still vivid, so transcribing them wasn't difficult, but the writing felt lifeless, and after a few minutes I gave up and went out on the balcony.

It was a beautiful November day. The rain had stopped, and Baba had suggested we should go out for dinner, which made me very happy. I was also looking forward to Christmas. Although it was still weeks away, I'd removed the boxes of trimmings from the closet and had been pulling out a few ornaments each day, trying to make the fun last. For years we'd used the same brown paper to cover the manger and the area outside where the Magi waited to bring their gifts to the newborn Jesus. The paper had faded but was still nice and sturdy, so I crumpled up a few sheets into boulders to line the Magi's path.

I'd been eating roasted pumpkin seeds and putting the shells in a plastic bag on my lap, all the while rocking my chair back and forth on its hind legs to close the balcony door that kept opening behind me. I must have been creating quite a noise, with the chair thudding down as it landed on its front and the door creaking back and forth on its hinges. This was too much for Baba, who appeared from behind me and seized my chair just as it was about to fall on all four legs again, and asked me, quite harshly, I thought, to stop making all that noise because Mama was trying to nap.

This naturally lowered my mood. I put the pumpkin seeds away, sat still in my chair, and left the door alone. In normal circumstances, the din of the traffic would have drowned out my sounds, but it was a peaceful Sunday afternoon. I wondered about the slow traffic, which was often a bad omen, but I didn't want to listen to the news, which would almost certainly be bad and ruin the day. The "voice" had encouraged me to hold on to my happy memories. I remembered telling Monsieur Bassil in class, a few weeks before the start of the war, that averting our gaze was a form of cowardice. I was still convinced that it was, but there were times when the forces of evil were too strong to apprehend, and you had to hold on to some beauty in the world, even if it was a figment of your imagination or a long-lost memory; otherwise you were done for. I went to my room and wrote a few lines in my notebook, and by the time I was finished I had forgotten about Baba's harshness, and I was looking forward to our outing and Christmas again, and I thought that maybe things would get better, at least for a short while, which would still be a pretty good thing.

12

Hisham

It was the day after, and the press had already come up with a name. Black Saturday was a fitting label for a city in mourning.

Four Christian militants discovered shot in their car led to hundreds of civilians slain at checkpoints by rival militias. The roads emptied out. The city became silent while the carnage unfolded. The leaders fought and bickered, blaming each other for fueling the fires of vengeance.

The next day he was still reading all the newspapers he could get his hands on. They were full of death tales that twisted and coiled around him. He imagined the victims crying and pleading for their lives. He could feel the hatred and blood-lust of their killers. Each murderous spree was followed by complete silence. The silence was a welcome relief after the imploring screams in the stench of terror. When they finished killing, their heartbeats slowed. The veil that had engulfed the world lifted, and everything, the pavement and the curbstone, and the small plants sprouting between the rocks, seemed like themselves again.

He hated being invaded by these monsters, but his imagination was raging, and the images unspooled their stories and anguish in him. He thought of Fuad, who was not a monster but still killed from a distance, without considering the human cost of his actions. Hisham could partially understand the motivations of these beings he imagined, but he couldn't understand his brother. But Fuad was family, and so was ungraspable beneath all the knots of denial and pain. It was easier to make up stories about an invented other.

He wrote:

This is not right, I say.

It's a quiet Saturday morning where I live, but down the street, a massacre is taking place. The road to the harbor is littered with corpses. We've gathered on the hill to watch the city cannibalize itself.

An eye for an eye. Who will make it stop?

But my companions shrug dismissively. If the shoe were on the other foot, you'd be calling for blood, they tell me. Four young men slain. Let there be bloodshed in retaliation.

I say, trying to convince them: Imagine. A masked man reaches in, pulls you out of the car, and grabs your ID. He kicks you to the ground and you fall to your knees. You try to run, but he kicks you again and you roll on your back. The sky is blue, and the sunlight blinds you. You put your hands out and plead.

All you wanted this morning was some labneh and za'atar for your breakfast. My food is in the car, you cry. I have never hurt anyone, you cry. I don't own a gun. I know nothing about politics. I work and go home, I swear. You cry and plead, and you have no shame. Warm piss trickles down your legs. You have no shame. You try everything. I have a mother, sisters, a fiancée. Have pity, you say.

But the masked man has eyes only for your religion. Muslim, Masihi—Which one are you?

Are these your last minutes on earth? You kiss his boot. He strikes you with the butt of his rifle, hits your face, your stomach, your groin, and you curl up in pain. You don't know why he hates you. Who are you, that he hates you this much? Of course, you know. You are your religion on your ID card.

You are the man who loves labneh and za'atar and who's engaged to the prettiest girl in the neighborhood. You are the man who's gone about his business although you should have long ago moved out of the neighborhood—are you crazy for staying in this neighborhood with this religion on your ID? You are the man who might have been this crazy masked man had the shoe been on the other foot.

Pinned under this corner of sky.

These can't be your last moments on earth. Otherwise, it would have been over by now, right?

The people I say this to, the people on the hill, shrug. You can't show compassion, they say. None would be shown to you if the shoe were on the other foot.

Those four men, shot and dumped on the side of the road. What about them, eh? That father lost two sons in less than three months. What about him? Do you have any compassion for him? We weren't the ones who started it.

Revenge calls.

I try to build a repulsive vision of revenge for my companions. Imagine a man possessed by the need for vengeance. His hair protrudes from his head like flames, and his clothes are stained with the blood of his victims. His killing spree has no end; as soon as one victim dies at his hands, he moves on to the next.

Four men shot and dumped on the side of the road. Multiply them into a bloodbath.

This is not right, I say again.

I say my bit and fall silent. It is enough for one day. Asking them to imagine doesn't do any good. Their imagination has been hijacked by hatred. Besides, I am not in the habit of sticking my neck out. Here is where I draw the line. Here is my box. I will not step outside. I am of the right religion in the right place. The masked men will not go after me. I belong here and I am safe.

But you. The sky is so blue, and you pray for a miracle, even though his boot has pinned you to the ground and the mouth of the gun is in your mouth.

You will never eat your breakfast of labneh and za'atar.

For you, this is the end.

Hisham

A truce on Christmas Eve. Their spindly tree stood in the living room, the tip of the angel's head rubbing against the rain-beaded glass door. Gisele roasted a turkey stuffed with rice and chestnuts and lit candles and oil lamps. They looked at the lilting shadows on the wall, recalling past Christmases when they'd have ice cream in long fluted glasses in Bab Idriss, then walk along the seafront or ride the Ferris wheel at Luna Park.

A week later, it was 1976. He took an envelope from the bookshelf that held his writing and set it on his desk. What a relief it was to throw out that review and let go of the arrogant notion that he could offer an authoritative judgment on someone else's writing. He extracted a few sheets from the envelope. The war engulfs and dwarfs everything. You vanish. Even if you don't die, you vanish in the barrage of bombs, he had scrawled on a piece of paper.

He heard Gisele's key in the lock and hid the envelope in a drawer. He followed her into the living room, where she removed her shoes and sat on the couch, pillows propping up her tired feet. She asked about his day. He made up a story about how he had prepared for school all day. He inquired about her new job. She didn't like the clothes, and the pay was lower. But at least it was in a convenient location. What else was she going to do? She could no longer go to Hamra. "What's for dinner?" she asked. She got angry when he stared at her blankly, having completely forgotten that it was his turn to cook. "You've been here all day and haven't made anything to eat," she said, then got up and marched into the bedroom, slamming the door behind her.

He had been forgetting to eat and had lost weight. Vartkes, the street cobbler, punched new holes in his belt every few weeks. Vartkes inquired about Fuad, who used to stop by for a chat during his visits. Hisham was evasive. He couldn't tell the truth, but he also didn't want to tell a lie. Hisham pictured Fuad standing where he stood—the shop was small and filled with objects, so this seemed likely—and questioning Vartkes about his family and life. Fuad was always interested in other people.

A week into January, they were back in school. Rita's desk was empty. When she was still absent two days later, he asked the secretary and learned that her father had died.

She returned the following week, dressed in black under her uniform and with dark circles around her eyes. To his surprise, she came at lunchtime.

He offered his condolences, and she nodded in thanks. To fill the awkward silence, he gave her a book by Mahmoud Darwish. She said her father had grown up in Palestine. She didn't know much about his upbringing, and now it was too late.

"Do you have relatives you can ask?" he inquired.

"Maybe," she said, shrugging.

He knew she wasn't waffling. For these relatives, the difficult past was over. Why would they want to bring it back now, of all times?

13

Baba is Dead

16 January 1976

By Rita Sfeir

My father died alone. When the fighting intensified, we fled to our mountain home in Tarawa. But Baba hated the countryside and wanted to get back to the city. At Mama's insistence, he agreed to stay with my uncle at his apartment in Jounieh. This way he wouldn't be alone, and the town was outside the line of fire. It was a good compromise, as good as one could hope for with my stubborn father. It took a toll on Mama, though, all that back and forth between Jounieh and Tarawa, attending to an ailing husband and my little brother.

I was wrenched from sleep by the bloodcurdling screams. I leaped out of bed and raced down the stairs. My uncle had gone out to fetch the paper and returned to find Baba's body lifeless on the living room floor. "He fell like a tree," my uncle said, sobbing.

It was shattering. I moved as though in the grip of a dream. In the living room, the words burst through the wailing. "Baba died" cut like a blade into me. It would be like this forever, before and after. Between them a millennium.

"Tell me he's still alive and I will pray, and he will recover," my mother pleaded with my uncle. My uncle took pity and said, "Yes, he's still with us," and then saw the cruelty of that lie and gently tendered a truth crueler still. "No, my sister, he's gone."

I stepped outside and sat on the ledge of the big church, weeping. It was a cold day in December, but the sun blazed, and the sky was spotless. Snow blanketed the ground and the mountaintops glistened. The street heaved with familiar noises. But the life I knew was gone.

My hands slid up and down my thighs. I doubled over and threw up. A neighbor came. Crying, she took my arm and brought me back inside the house. I let her lead me. I wanted to curl up in her lap for all time.

People swirled around me. The neighbors had rushed in to help. He had been expected that same day. In the trash went the lunch of stuffed tripe he had requested and a bottle of his favorite arak.

We drove to my uncle's apartment in Jounieh. Seeing the sea after weeks of absence brought no warm feelings. I hated the city with all my heart.

Baba lay in bed dressed in his blue suit. Rasha and Mama wept by his side. I turned away from him and buried my face in the curtain.

Later, the hearse came and took him to Tarawa. I rode in the car behind, my eyes never leaving his coffin. In Tarawa, men stood on the sides of the road with their rifles pointed skyward. When the first burst of gunfire rang out, silent screams rose in my throat. Yes. Shoot at the sky and rip it open. Burn up the world. My father is dead.

A week after his death, he came to me in a dream. I was asleep in the middle of a large field. I felt a light touch on my hair, a kiss. I opened my eyes and there he was, beaming. *Hello, my little lamb*, he said. Such happiness flooded me at the sight of him. I woke up, feeling his spirit in the room. I went back to sleep, feeling a flicker of that bygone peace returning.

Our world dissolved. My mother, a widow, and we, fatherless. My mother withered overnight, took on another twenty years to her forty-two. Rasha swore his spirit had brushed past her on the night of his death. She had been seized by giggles a few minutes before she felt him, shudders after. Tony cried alone behind closed doors. As for me, I obsessed over his features, panicked that I might forget him. I organized our photo albums and looked in vain for recordings of his voice.

Time will pass, people said in consolation, and heal our wound.

But there are worlds from which you return a stranger to yourself.

And me: I don't know who I am without Baba.

Hisham

He writes:

January 18, 1976: Karantina has fallen. The camp was bulldozed. The militants are jubilant. Their leaders say the shantytown was built on private land. The country is in desperate need of land, and now the plot has been freed and it can be developed.

I'm not Palestinian, he says.

Do you hear my accent? See, right here on my ID. It says I grew up in Akkar. Do you know Akkar? You should go in the spring when the almond trees are in bloom. In my village, I worked my orchard. Why did I have to leave? I had nothing. Nothing then, nothing now. But the city feeds you dreams. Clean the municipal buildings long enough, and I can leave this slum. I'm not Palestinian. I am Lebanese and poor as dirt.

Please, please, he cries.

You're a dog, I say and shoot him.

The ground runs red with blood. It is soft and marshy. A trail of cardboard squares has been blown over from the windows. I leap from one to the next to stay clear of the blood-soaked ground.

It is getting dark. The bodies are starting to rot. You can cut the stench with a knife. I pull my bandanna over my face and clutch my rifle, finger on the trigger, searching. I look for my comrades, who must be celebrating. Somewhere in the city the bombs are raining down. But this is my quarter tonight, this slum teeming with Muslims, corpses most of them. I chuckle. I feel no pity for them, least of all for my countrymen, who sided with the foreigners.

Fires are burning in the bombed-out buildings and hollowed-out cars. Burned to a crisp. It'll be good to see that for a change. I'm sick of staring at the bloated corpses. The junk they owned! I'd strike a match to the piles if I had one, burn the whole thing to ashes and then sweep it into the sea.

A bulldozer stands surrounded by smashed concrete, with its bucket full of broken pieces. Someone left to celebrate before the job was completed. There's so much to do, a fire is just the beginning. Bring a giant sledgehammer and atomize the whole area.

When I look back, I see my footprints in the twilight. I fire a round in the air. A short burst of gunfire answers me. I walk toward the sound.

Outside the slum, traffic thunders as if everything is normal. It's our job to keep the city clean, purged of undesirable elements. Everything is neat and on time, as much as you can expect in our part of the world where we march to our own drum. But you get the idea. It's no coincidence that our founder was inspired by Hitler's youth movement. But he liked only the discipline, not the Nazi horrors that they keep trying to stick him with. The truth is that our forces are being trained by Israelis across the border. How about that for irony? I laugh again.

There's not a peep. If there are survivors, they have gone into hiding. The silence of the dead is heavy, but that's because the blood is still new. We'll forget everything once we've razed the camp to the ground and replaced it with something new and nice, like a shopping center or a nightclub.

The night has come. The moon starts to leak. The streetlights are turned on. I'm laughing. It's odd that tonight of all nights there should be power. But the light is insufficient. The world around me darkens. I light a joint. And as I'm standing there smoking, she appears out of nowhere, waving a white flag and begging me not to shoot.

Now this one here is a Palestinian. It's in her accent and all over her face. I can smell her stench despite the rotting corpses. Her fleshy chin quivers every time she opens her mouth. I burst out laughing. This shuts her up. She looks at me with pleading eyes. But all I see is a woman who might have given birth to the man who killed my brother, and I aim. She whimpers, patting her skirt down as if smoothing it for her maker. Her face wrinkles, and tears stream down her cheeks. She is speaking, but all I hear are gargled sounds. Pity and a desire for revenge wage a war inside me, but not for long. When I shoot, she collapses on her back in one swift motion, and then it's all over.

That's when I notice the little girl. She's small and pale with fear. She squats next to the corpse. She is filthy. Everything about her, from her matted hair down to her knobby knees and mud-covered boots, disgusts me.

When I run, my boots make a sucking sound. At last I see my comrades gathered around their jeeps, drinking champagne straight from the bottles while music blasts from the radio. There are girls in combat fatigues looking sexy, passing joints and swearing like sailors.

We are the winners, and to us belong the spoils. Give me my prize, my sweet, ravishing stupor, my blue liquid peace. Let me pass out on your breast and cover my face with your palms until I vanish.

A few days later, he is back at his desk. This time he's in school. In retaliation for Karantina, the forces of the leftist alliance destroyed Damour, a Christian village south of Beirut.

He imagines a young girl. She has dark hair and a mole on her cheek. She's the oldest of five children. She likes feeding the birds that visit the garden behind her house. She collects bread crumbs in a small plastic bag for them. She likes the singer Fairuz and has made up her mind to become a singer.

The killing went on for several days. They dug up our graves and left our coffins on the grass. The dogs howled nonstop. We hid in an old silk factory. We fled to the slope one night and stood there, gathering our courage, staring at the bridge behind the banana plantation and the sea in the distance. We ran down the slope and crossed the bridge when the moon was hidden behind the clouds, then waited on the riverbank for the boat that would take us across the river and into the sea to Jounieh.

But no boat arrived. Our father told us to swim to the other side while he waited for the boat with Mama, who couldn't swim. But we declined. We could tell he was feeling guilty. We should have heeded the warning and evacuated before the Muslims and their allies arrived. The party dispatched many boats at that time. But we were careless, and we loved our home too much and our garden in the back, and the orange trees were heavy with fruit. We were deaf to the warnings, the fear that gripped the village, and the bells that tolled as each boat left with more people. When we saw our neighbors marching with their belongings toward the river, we turned away. We sat on the grass, eating bananas and reading magazines under the sun, which in January is perfect, strong enough to keep us warm in the brisk wind. We want to stay, we told our father as we drew near. The clouds had moved on, and the moon spilled across the river. We knew there would be no boat.

The image of a young man materializes in his thoughts. He is slender and small, with a mass of black hair and a bald scar streaking across the stubble on his chin. He has just stepped out of the jeep that transported him from Beirut. He's been in many battles before. Every time he thinks he's about to die, he escapes by a hair. He's convinced his mother is watching out for him. She died in the Karantina Camp. He does not remember his father, who was Kurdish and died when he was a child. His Palestinian mother told him about Palestine. Her homeland was a few raveled pictures, an old key, and an aching.

He writes:

She said to me, "Yes, I wear a cross around my neck, but it doesn't have to divide us." I looked into her brown eyes and shot her in the heart. I did not rape her. I should have. No pity for infidels, enemies of the revolution, Israeli collaborators, Zionists, capitalists, or baby killers.

She was pretty. She was dressed in a navy dress with small pink flowers. I imagined her small breasts pushing against her dress. Even after she died, I yearned to touch them. But I did not. I'd shot her in the heart. Her chest had a hole the size of my fist. A pity. Such a pretty girl. She would have made someone a good wife, nice to cuddle with at night, feel the warmth between her legs. I moan.

She peed herself when I aimed at her heart. We both looked down at the puddle on the ground, and when our eyes met, I shot her. I wanted to remember her slim hips and the way she extended her neck and thrust her chest at me to show me the cross that wasn't meant to separate us. In the end she died because of that cross. It was stupid of her to keep it on when she knew we were coming. But hiding it would not have saved her. We knew this was a Christian village. The Christians are self-hating Arabs. They would side with anyone—Israel, France, the Americans—except their own people. We came to avenge Karantina and all the Karantinas before and after, and our God-forsaken lives and tin roofs, and our barefoot children who know nothing but violence and the world's disdain. We don't shoot to calm the beast within. We are the beast, we sprang from your head, from your filthy back-alley dealings and power-mongering alliances, from your blindness and cold, cruel bigotry, from the hatred in your eyes when you look at our filthy rags and bad teeth and blame us for everything you have sown.

An eye for an eye will make the whole world blind. I say an eye for an eye is like the chicken-and-egg riddle. What came first? But this is the least of your worries when you hear stories of their savagery and seethe with hatred. When you see your dead mother lying beneath the ruins, her dress lifted for all to see her nakedness. Her face is so twisted that you recognize her only by her dress, which she patched together from the discarded scraps of fabric she had found in trash cans. Later, you remember it as the day you stopped crying.

14

2 February 1976

My dear brother Hisham,

I've been meaning to write to you for a long time. It's easier than talking face to face, where your disappointment binds my tongue and brings me to the brink of tears. I understand that my decision to enter the armed conflict has upset you. I know that I have let you and everyone else down.

Knowing me, you can probably guess that joining the armed forces was not a decision I made lightly. I'd like to explain the scope of my commitment in this letter. Before all of this, I was a fighter who used words instead of machine guns. But I felt compelled to change, for reasons that I will try to explain.

When we were boys, I was sensitive to every injustice I observed. As you know, I read the papers religiously and I had strong feelings about everything. I recognized early on that unless we banded together and took action to oppose the powerful, they would always triumph. Seeing the state of our village's crumbling roads and meager resources and the negligence of the government, as well as our father's struggle to make ends meet, was a lesson that deeply shaped me and that I'll never forget. You and I worked; there was no shame in what we did, and despite your long face and all the breaks you took to read under a tree while I covered for you, I was glad to have you there. It showed me the importance of working hard to earn our place in the sun, as well as working wisely and understanding the contours of power. This was the reason I left the village, even though I disliked the city and wished more than anything to wake up in my own bed in our village. I was closer to the seat of power in the capital, and I saw with my own eyes our government's corruption and its devastating effects on the most vulnerable people in our country.

I refused to be defined by my surname or my upbringing, and I wanted a country in which all citizens were protected regardless of class or religion. People insist on labeling the conflict as religious. I strongly disagree with that assessment and am deeply embarrassed by it.

You will recall that after a fight with Baba, I would always leave the house and disappear for a while. I'd go to Akkar or Tripoli, sometimes all the way to Beirut or the South. The poverty I witnessed made our family seem privileged in comparison—children hustling the streets for money, and slums full of rural migrants and refugees bolstering the wealth of the few with their cheap labor. The rich's callous indifference convinced me that nothing would change unless we acted. But I also found my crowd on these streets. Student and laborer groups of many creeds and classes fought side by side for justice. The babel of languages and accents was a reminder of our flawed but persistent coexistence, which in our tiny village we did our best to ignore. The sectarian violence that erupted during the war was a symptom, not the root cause of our affliction. This was a war on the poor. I joined the armed struggle. I wasn't the only Christian who did so.

It felt necessary for me to fight. I did not come to this conclusion carelessly. On the one hand, there was the pull and push of the pacifist impulse, which is as strong in me as it is in you, and on the other, there was the here and now as well as the bigger picture of where we wanted to go.

I think up to this point you sympathize with my thinking. It is the killing you cannot abide. You also think I'm a bad husband and father. I miss Karim and Layla terribly. But I'm fighting for both them and the country. They have a right to a better world.

You must recall the difficulties of our early days, our fear of waking up the next day without food on the table, the constant feeling of being defenseless against the world's assaults. Despite this, we had a house and a small garden in the back that met our basic needs, a family that sent us gifts of food, and a standing chance to make something of ourselves. But many of our citizens live in such deplorable poverty that it is impossible for them to rise from the ground without significant help from the government. And instead of doing its job, our government has largely ignored and worsened their plight by promoting policies that bolstered the interests of the rich.

The government has been waging a war on the poor since independence. There is nowhere to hide the poor in a small country. And yet, in our willful desire to live in selfish greed and pleasure, we have lost sight of them, and blame them for their predicament. The system is designed to keep us from seeing. But violence unseen is not the absence of violence.

That violence has now erupted on a national scale for all of us to witness. We can no longer avert our eyes. I am part of the problem, but we have turned the tables and now we all know what it's like to wake up every day with a gun to our head, which is what it's like to live with the oppression and apathy of the ruling class and our indifferent countrymen. If handing up our guns means going back to a time when violence was exclusively used against the poor, I'd rather stay on my current path. It is the only way to mobilize the masses to effect change on behalf of the voiceless. We seek medical attention only when we are in pain. Something heinous is living within us and rotting our souls, and it must be extinguished with force. Sitting back and watching the conflict play out without intervening would have been a cowardly act.

If I had believed that this was a religious war, as so many have claimed, I would never have taken up arms. I've never accepted the religious divide, and fortunately, neither have my comrades. This is not to say that I haven't seen my fair share of bigotry in the ranks. But I never bowed down, even at personal risk. I want you to know that I spoke out as loudly as you knew I could.

It's hardly surprising that the conflict seems sectarian. We have a crazy system, my brother, and the poisonous seed of sectarianism has been ground into our government's scaffolding. Assigning government positions based on religious affiliations has widened our schisms and pitted us in rival camps. By defending Christian minority rights and national sovereignty against Palestinians, the Christian party is effectively maintaining its political and financial dominance and forging ties with Israel and the West that harm our people. And when Muslims oppose them, it is because they want to seize that power for themselves. I have staked my place outside these differences, which are a distraction from the real problem of economic injustice.

The powerful will go to any length to stifle rebellion. They prey on the public, manipulating their emotions and spreading lies. They use religion as a ploy to arouse our baser instincts and divide us. The divide-and-conquer strategy is so old that mentioning it seems unnecessary. It has been extremely successful. When power needs a diversion, the most vulnerable are blamed for the ills of society. I never blamed civilians even when I disagreed with their ideas. I was only sorry that the victims were the weakest link in the chain, but the powerful had used them as fuel while taking cover in their mansions and hideouts in the West, and I had no choice but to push back. I was always glad to hear about the assassination of such and such a leader, and I even attempted to enter the rings where I could perform such assassinations myself, but I never made it. That would have been my true calling.

I recognize that greater forces have a vested interest in keeping the war going. With that realization, and because of my own conflict about violence, as well as recent internal strife and bickering within my group, I was on the verge of dropping my weapons. But for the time being I'm fighting, because quitting seems worse than continuing. I bring up my concerns about the use of force not to elicit sympathy, but to inform you of the current state of my soul and the tortuous path I have taken to reach this point. Despite what you may be thinking, I have not become hardened to the killing. I know that when I launch a rocket, someone dies on the other side. I can't think like that when I'm on the battleground. I must focus entirely on the acts of war. Sometimes war cannot be avoided. I have nightmares about you and Gisele being struck by one of my missiles.

I know that this isn't what you wanted to read, but I hope it sheds some light on my thinking so that you can understand, if not condone, my actions. I have always valued your opinion of me, and I hope that my explanations have helped to alleviate some of your disappointment.

I'll be sending this letter with a driver I know who can travel between our divided city. I'm looking forward to hearing from you. If you choose to respond, please use the same driver. I trust him. He can be found at the Tripoli taxi stand, where we used to take a shared taxi to the village before I bought my first car. I'll understand if you don't want to write. But don't expect me to explain my reasoning in person. I can only explain my conflicting emotions in writing.

I hope the war ends soon and that we can all be reunited under one roof. I miss your sulky nature and long pauses before answering any question. This is not to say you can't be funny. Your Shushu impersonation is hilarious.

Your loving brother, Fuad

15

Hisham

One clear morning in March, almost a year after the start of the war, Hisham drove up the road from his apartment and found himself in a village he didn't remember seeing before. Aside from a few stone houses and a stream running alongside the road, the village appeared to be mostly made up of forested mountains, with houses here and there standing over cliffs or looking toward the ravine.

It was a lovely spring day. The sound of cicadas and rustling leaves filled the hills. He parked the car and began walking down a dirt path that wound between houses with balconies overlooking garden plots and orchards. The houses were accessed through narrow stone steps leading up to terraces shaded by grapevine canopies. There were big luxurious hydrangeas and cascades of bougainvillea in purples and pinks and lavender.

The path became narrower as the plants encroached, leaving thorns in his skin. But the thorns came off easily with a light pressure of his fingers. In a clearing he saw the entire sky, green hills, and a waterfall in the distance. But after a turn, he came face to face with a high mound of earth with a tunnel dug through it. The only way to get to the other side was to crawl through the tunnel. He decided against it and turned around.

Two birds took off with a rustle of wings when he came to a small wooden bridge. The bridge was a bit rickety, with rotted pieces and holes chewed out by small animals, and it crossed a stream. He had no recollection of crossing it and concluded that he must have taken a different route. He couldn't keep track of where he was going because the path kept forking in different directions. After a while all the trees looked the same.

He was halfway down the valley when he noticed a gate with the words *Private Property*. He retraced his steps and turned right at a fork in the road. The sound of an electric saw came from the houses above. Two older women, each with a small child, were walking in his direction. He asked where he could find water for his bottle, and they directed him to a source farther ahead. He thanked them and walked away. A bench next to a yellow house was a few meters ahead. He sat in the sunlight, holding the sandwich he had packed before leaving. A woman walked out of the house with two small dogs on leashes and stopped to chat. One of the dogs was blind. It walked slowly but confidently. The woman said that last night was cold, but today the weather was splendid. He concurred. He was surprised to see the dogs—so few people had pets—but he said nothing. She said goodbye with a nod and walked away, flanked by her short-legged dogs.

He got up and went to the water source to fill his bottle. The water was cold, with a floral sweetness to it. Across the street an elderly woman was weeding her garden. "It's a lot of work," he said. "Yes, but the garden is so much cleaner this way," she replied. She wiped her brow with her sleeve, smiling. Farther out, a brown dog with white legs sprawled out on its side lifted its head when Hisham appeared and ambled ahead, slowly enough for Hisham to keep pace. He was surprised once more. These villagers seemed to have an unusual fondness for animals. The dog frequently stopped to sniff the ground. Hisham was pleased with the company. He wished he knew the dog's name, but there was no one around to ask.

Every few feet the dog sprinted ahead, then returned, slowing down to allow Hisham to catch up. Hisham was relieved that the dog wasn't cloying and overly affectionate. It had a cat-like demeanor, aloof and wary of intruding. Hisham was uneasy around animals.

The woman with the blind dog had finished her walk and was returning home. One of the dogs began barking at Hisham's dog. The little hound sounded agitated, and Hisham, who knew nothing about dogs, wondered if these two had a long feud. But Hisham's dog kept jogging, unfazed by the furious barking, sniffing the ground and marking its territory, and looking back to make sure Hisham was following.

He wondered where the dog was taking him. He imagined it was the incarnation of a loving ancestor guiding him to a special place or making sure he didn't get lost in this maze of trails. It made him feel good to think that someone was looking out for him. Discovering the strange village had turned him to mysticism and seeing signs meant only for him.

When they came to a stream, the dog broke into a run and leaped in the water, and Hisham's theory fell apart. He grinned as he watched the dog splash and paddle across the stream, then climb on a rock and shake itself dry. Why it did that was a mystery, because it jumped right back into the stream after drying off.

After a few minutes Hisham turned around to leave. He heard the click of paws behind him, and then the dog zoomed by, coat gleaming, spraying a mist in its wake.

The path uphill split into several leafy trails. After a time, Hisham chose a trail where the leaves formed a high arch. He had always loved archways. He parted the branches and entered an enclosed space where he had to stoop until the trail opened onto a large field covered in tall grass and trees, with a ring of mountains in the distance. Several walking paths had been cleared. He spotted a field of yellow flowers on the right and walked toward it, but the path veered away from the field, forcing him to return to the beginning and try again. He was more successful the next time, and the flowers came into sight, huddled together in an exquisite explosion of yellow. He was captivated by their beauty. But he had to leave because the trees were blocking the mountain, which he wanted to see as he ate his apple.

He cut across the field, heading for a large tree at the grass's edge. In the shade, two women were having a picnic. "Let's remember this tree when we come back," the older woman advised her younger companion. He made his way through the grass-lined path. The path slanted downward. He moved slowly. Around him the grass bent with the wind. He looked for a spot with a long view of the field and the mountains, but eventually he gave up and spread his blanket in a random spot.

From here he could see the mountain peaks and a cloudless sky. Around him a tangle of weeds rose, some with flowers, others desiccated and brown, with spiky crowns and milky tufts. A small plane was roaring overhead, and birds were chirping. This was not the ideal spot, but he was afraid to leave for fear of not finding a better one. Besides, he was content here, eating his apple and forgetting about the rest of the world.

A large black butterfly with yellow-trimmed wings landed on a purple thistle. A smaller one, in phosphorescent yellow, flew by and suckled on a flower. The two butterflies took off together, fluttering back and forth a few times. Each butterfly seemed to have a favorite flower to which it returned time and again. A closer examination uncovered thin black lines on the yellow butterflies, like veins on a paper-thin leaf. A yellow-breasted bird twittered as it flew by. Such a preponderance of yellow!

A second yellow butterfly, identical to the first, joined its twin on a nearby flower. The black butterfly suddenly swooped down from the thistles, followed by a double. Following a brief chase, the two spiraled upward into the blue light in a black-and-yellow frenzy. He craned his neck to look up, beyond the treetops. A plane emerged, flying low and leaving two identical white lines in its wake, as he sat staring at the spot where the dancing couple had vanished.

All these pairings! Envy rose within him. His eyes roved and settled on a bee hovering around a clump of weeds at his feet, a fickle and modest traveler going around the same cluster for quick sips before hopping on to the next flower.

Sadness welled up inside him. He looked around at the scenery, which had absorbed him completely only a minute before but now seemed far away. Nature was throwing its lovers and joys in his face and leaving him with the familiar feeling of being left out, yearning for something he couldn't have.

He and Gisele had grown further apart. He hadn't spoken to his brother in weeks.

Gisele told him she was pregnant as he was leaving that morning. She cupped her stomach. In her eyes, a question. Now what?

They had no desire for a child. But his heart leaped in his chest, and he stared at the circle inside the parentheses of her hands, feeling the faint flutter of a beating heart beneath the skin, the luminous translucence. It was a new life born of loss. As stupid as that. And it made him weep.

Because the flesh of his flesh had come too late, and he felt broken. The thought of someone new to love terrified him.

But how the butterflies danced! Circling upward in an ecstatic whirl of mirrored selves, weightless.

Basic biology had taught him that nature was always reproducing itself in an infinite stream of repeating selves, introducing minor variations to confuse disease and advance the species. Yet he was taken aback by the butterflies' uncanny resemblance. He might have noticed differences if he had looked closer. Change may have happened slowly in the insect world. At the human level, seismic shifts rocked the world every second, splintering reality into a million pieces and shattering the heart.

The sun was setting. He was compelled to keep going, to wander until he found what he was looking for.

He sat in the same spot on the outskirts of an unknown village, surrounded by waves of yellowing grass.

A church bell chimed, his signal to leave. After a loop, he was back in his car. He leaned forward. The light shivered across the green hills before dimming. Two rows of tall cypress trees, their tops touching, surrounded the entrance of the village, a tunnel he drove through on his way out.

Then it was the evening, and he was on the beach. At the horizon, the sky turned orange. He was the only one there, rocks digging into his soles, his shoes soaked. In the brilliant light the sky was clear and pure.

He was holding the plastic bag. Inside the bag there were more bags to protect Jumana's shoes from the elements.

On the other side of the sea, where the lights twinkled, lay the city he had loved and lost. He squatted near the water's edge and released the bag. A cold feeling crept into him, and his hands grasped, then let go. Unburdening was like a fresh wound.

The bag bobbed in the surf. It would find its way to Jumana or someone else. Someone discovering it on the beach he remembered, in the city he couldn't get to, where the brother he hadn't seen in a long time still lived and fought. Despite the stories he made up to explain the world around him, Hisham didn't understand his brother.

It was a silly and arrogant gift, but it was all he could do. Jumana didn't need shoes. He was the one who needed to reach across a chasm, despite the risks and blunders and the failure of the eyes to see clearly.

He imagined Jumana leaping into the waves when she saw the bag. She sat on the sand, her feet tucked beneath her. Her fingers flew around, untying the knots. When she saw the shoes, she squealed.

He saw his wife's hands cradling her stomach, and suddenly a pure feeling of happiness spread through him.

That accursed hope.

15 April 1976

Dearest Hisham,

I have just learned that the letter I wrote you in February was never delivered because the driver I entrusted it to was killed while crossing the bridge to your side of town. I don't know the specifics of his death, but the news has shaken me because he was a good, kind man who doubled as an emissary, bringing people news and safely transporting them from one side to the other thanks to his many connections. I was also upset to realize that the peace I'd felt after sending that letter to you was an illusion, since it never reached you. I've been feeling disconnected since learning of that poor man's death, which has been very difficult to bear.

As you can see, I did not leave you or my roots behind. I think about my family daily, and I hope that you're handling the situation as well as can be expected. None of this is pleasant. For every gain and certainty, there are numerous doubts and losses.

I'm hoping to find another emissary soon. Otherwise, attempting to stay connected across lines of violence will be a futile exercise. I'm hoping we can still find a way.

Your loving brother, Fuad

Hisham

He writes:

It Was Us

We were at the site of the explosion. We looked up and saw the mouth of the bomb barreling down on us. Not us, not us, we cried. We knew and did not know.

There was a huge flash of light, and a savage roar came from the earth. We were tossed up to the blackened sky, then fell into a river of blood. The flames burned. Oh! How they burned! Pain tore through every nerve. We scooped up our scattered parts and clutched them to us, but nothing we did worked. We slid off bone and spilled, and every drop was like a fingerprint lost to the haze of time.

We were inconsolable. We wailed—we did not know how long. When we got tired, we resisted the pull of sleep, afraid it might be our last. Then we gave in and fell into a deep slumber. When we awakened, we were in a dark hole, sunk beneath layers that felt like earth and had the same color. It was very cold, and we trembled, but we were pinned down and could not go in search of warmth.

When morning came, the earth lifted, and we started the search. Every time we found a limb we wept. We called on our beloveds who dwelled in the yellow light, choked with grief. The children cried for their parents. We scratched at the screen that separated us from the light, but nothing worked. Not a single hole opened to let us through. We were as soundless as fish in deep waters, our lips moving without sound.

After a while the flies stopped buzzing. Slowly we drifted away. We were the plundered. We carried our limbs on our backs and walked on.

The American Embassy

April 18, 1983

We watch the horror from the rooftop.
Wails of terror burst from our throats.
The barbarians have taken Beirut.

—From "The Siege of West Beirut"
by Hisham Bassil, 13 June 1982

Hisham

He was among the first in line. A guard escorted him to the steps in front of the embassy and pressed the intercom. There was a heavy buzz, and the door clicked open. Hisham walked into a well-lit room with a picture of Reagan beaming overhead. There were cameras pointing in every direction. A middle-aged man standing behind a glass window waved him over. He checked Hisham's passport, then pulled out papers from the file in front of him and proceeded to read them. His eyes ran quickly down the pages. Every now and again he would stop, as if something had caught his attention or was confusing, and Hisham could feel his heart beating faster. To distract himself he tried peering around the man so he could describe the room to Gisele later, but he could see only the white wall with pictures of the American and Lebanese presidents staring across the room at each other. He knew he was being taped and was careful to keep his expression blank.

Satisfied, the man stamped the document and told Hisham to wait in the lobby. He found a chair in a quiet corner and took a seat. Around him people were walking hurriedly, and phones rang. The entire façade above the lobby was made of glass. All that glass made him nervous. He fiddled with the strap of the satchel Gisele had given him to keep the file where she had stored the papers for the interview.

"You know how it is," she'd told him that morning. "You'd lose your head if it weren't…" She let the words trail off. He hated the expression. Plus, it wasn't entirely true. He lost things, but no more than others.

She amended. "What you need is containment, to put things inside things. Otherwise, you get lost in your excesses. And remember everything so you can tell me later."

She was lying down in bed, with the morning light breaking through the window. Salim was fast asleep against her. He had been having nightmares and had woken up early and run to them in tears. Gisele kept one hand on the boy's shoulder while the other rested on her belly.

Round with child, she looked beautiful. She'd been following doctor's orders and keeping to her bed. But she missed the world. When he came home she would ask him to describe everything he had done and seen. Of course, on the days when they were caught in the bombing, he had nothing to offer that she didn't already know. And the war had gone on, longer than they ever imagined possible, and would continue the length of their lives, they felt, into forever. And he had continued to teach, with longer stretches of interruption when the battles raged, his heart only half in it by now.

He bent down and gave her a kiss, then laid his cheek on her belly. No movement—his girl must be sleeping. For it was a girl, he had decided. A father knew. He even had a name: Liliane, Lily after the flower.

Another surprise, his Lily. After a difficult first pregnancy and harrowing labor—Salim, who was making small heaving sounds on his mother's chest, his cheeks streaked with dried-up tears, was born under the bombs—they had sworn off having more children. With Lily, they let the shock and fear take their course, then delight flooded them. It had gone well the first time, after the first major hurdles. Why not again?

This was nice, his familial cocoon. He would have liked to give in to the tug of sleep. But he had somewhere he needed to be. He ruffled his son's hair—named Salim after Hisham's father, who lived long enough to watch his grandchild take his first wobbly steps. Then Hisham's mother passed away, a few months after her husband.

After making sure Gisele had what she needed, he left the apartment.

A young woman called his name from the doorway. He

followed her and was ushered into a room with a round table and two chairs. He pulled his file out of the satchel and placed it on the table, then took a seat. More chairs were stacked in a corner. More pictures of the two presidents on the white walls. The thin gray light coming from the window was boosted by neon lights.

He was here pleading for an asylum he could purchase, thanks to the rich relative on his mother's side who had dropped out of the sky and offered him a job at his construction company in Houston, Texas, where his Arabic would come in handy with the Arabian Gulf clients bloated with oil wealth.

The surprise existence of this relative and his willingness to help was a stroke of luck. Without a penny to his name, Hisham would never have been able to step inside the embassy. He now had to convince the Americans that letting him in with his family wouldn't drive the country to ruin.

The consular officer came in and sat in the chair opposite. His name was John Samuels. He had red hair, and his pale skin was as smooth as a child's. His eyes were a light color Hisham could not pinpoint, between green and hazel.

"Start with a non-immigrant work visa," the relative said when he phoned. "A good lawyer will take care of the rest."

After skimming the pages, Mr. Samuels put down the documents, flipped his pad to a clean page, and picked up a pen. He wanted to know where Hisham and his family would be staying in Texas, why he was leaving a good job to start from scratch, and why he had chosen the US. Hisham gave his answers patiently, in the English he had practiced in a book borrowed from the English teacher at his school. Mr. Samuels wrote in his pad. He kept a closed look, without emotion or facial expressions Hisham could interpret.

Houston, Texas, Hisham said. He thought he saw a slight change steal into the American's expression, and he wondered whether Houston alone would have sufficed. The famous need no surnames. Perhaps Texas was overkill. Like this suit. Across the table from him Mr. Samuels was dressed casually in short sleeves and gabardine pants. He felt the assault of a thousand needles on his pride. The morning dragged on.

"Your wife is pregnant," Mr. Samuels remarked.

The tone was neutral, but what Hisham heard was this: If she were to deliver on American soil, your child would be an American citizen, and we would never be rid of you.

What Hisham would have liked to say, if his English had allowed, was this: My skills are many, but what interests you is how I will contribute to your society and whether I pose a risk. I understand your desire to get your money's worth. I guarantee that I will be a net gain. My taxes will help fill your coffers. My wife and children are my legal dependents, so don't worry about them if I'm struck by lightning. My relative has agreed to sponsor me as additional insurance. In addition, I am also a peaceful man, a respected teacher, a husband, and a father. As you can see, I am very desirable.

He wanted to say: no one does this out of choice.

Instead he answered, "Yes, in her seventh month."

The next item on Mr. Samuels' agenda was Fuad. From his questions it quickly became clear that much was known about his brother, whose tale Hisham was asked to reveal in specifics already familiar to the American, making the interrogation a test of Hisham's truthfulness rather than a query into Fuad's life. He described how, five years earlier, he drove to the hospital where his brother had been admitted after his legs were blown off. Shrapnel wedged in the back of his neck had caused paralysis from the waist down, so that even if he had kept his legs, they would have been useless. The shrapnel interrupted the blood flow to Fuad's brain long enough to leave damage.

What the American did not know was that his brother, who had been living in the village, was a great father and uncle. He could make the children laugh—Karim and Layla, adolescents now, indulged him with the consideration of well-raised offspring, but Salim nearly fell off his chair laughing. He could play cards and a watered-down game of chess, and his laughter rang out in the clear mornings. In the evenings, he would remember the bomb and cry out, and his hands would frantically stroke the nonexistent legs. Hisham put these scenes in a secret chamber of his brain to save them from the American's inspection, and he placed the old Fuad there, too, when a wave of longing suddenly came over him for the brother he had, in the end, lost. There was no undoing the damage. There was only the remembering, the slow and meticulous reconstruction of the past.

Where did it all land Fuad? His ideology, his desire to see wrongs righted and figure a way out of the dark levies of history. He lost everything while the war wrecked and gutted, tore limb from bone and snatched all hope from the spirit.

"My brother's decision to take up arms broke my heart," Hisham told Mr. Samuels. "There was nothing I could do to change his mind. But I am a peaceful man looking out for my family."

On his tongue, a bitter taste of betrayal.

"My wife is carrying a girl," he added. "She will be beautiful and smart. Her name is Liliane." The words leaped out. He was overrun by a sense of failure. Pawning his daughter for a visa. He would lose his soul before this was over.

Silence greeted him. Hisham was tired of the man's probing stare.

Mr. Samuels closed the passport and excused himself. Hisham felt small. His feet tapped the mottled floor in nervous anticipation.

When he had told people of his upcoming interview, someone taught him to embroider his English, say *thank you ever so much* and *I beg your pardon*. The circumlocutions showed style, put him above the fray, and signaled his readiness to learn and evolve beyond the basics.

Mr. Samuels returned with a slip of paper where he had scribbled a list of additional documents he needed before he could reach a decision. Another appointment was scheduled.

"Thank you ever so much."

He had no choice. Everyone who could was leaving. The American gave a quick nod and left the room.

He exited the embassy and stood on the covered patio shuffling papers. He slid the papers into a file and the file back inside the satchel.

The clouds had moved in. He threw his head back and looked up at the overcast sky, then looked down ahead of him. The low rumble of cars reached him from the street. There was the sea a little way ahead. It was the same color as the sky, gray and glassy, covered with the haze of a day that had yet to see the sun and have the heaviness lifted off it and flung away like a needless blanket. He could see his car parked by the water's edge, away from the embassy as a security measure, the front end scraped up when he'd pulled up sharply against the curb in his hurry that morning to get to his appointment on time.

A guard yelled at him to keep walking. Although Hisham wanted to get away as quickly as possible from this place, this additional wound to his pride propelled him to take his time coming down the steps, then saunter toward the heavy gate manned by a young Marine. He felt the guard's eyes boring through his back as he exited the embassy grounds.

He crossed the street, resisting the temptation to toss the file in the garbage.

He saw Salim shaking with sobs when explosions ripped the air around them. He heard Liliane laughing when he laid his hand on Gisele's belly and his daughter rippled under his touch, a flutter that painted the sky blue and the days ahead with scenes he imagined late at night—Liliane walking, Liliane talking, Liliane calling him Baba. Once a reluctant father, now struck dumb with love. He had the sense that the world was opening up, and over there was the sea with all its prospects, and there was the sky, where he and his family would travel on the plane carrying them to the new country where they would no longer be afraid, out of this city where they felt like prisoners waiting out their sentence.

Eight years and five days since the start of the war. You could get accustomed to anything.

He would get them the documents. He would get them whatever they wanted.

One day people like him, forced into exile by war and suffering, would be automatically given entrance.

He heard the sharp blast of a horn and looked behind him. A pickup truck was speeding down the street toward the embassy. Instinctively he clutched the satchel to his chest and turned his back to the street. He slipped a hand in his pocket, then the next. No keys. They might have slipped out of his pocket when he was dawdling through the embassy grounds, showing the uppity guard he was no dog jumping to the sound of his master's whistle. Behind him now was the sound of something hurtling toward disaster, shouting, the cracks of rifles. He marched steadily across the boardwalk, gripping the metal railing. The waves gathered and broke against the rocks; the seagulls wailed. He stood, frozen, neck hunched into his shoulders, terror mounting in him. He still had to buy a present for Salim's birthday, drive Gisele to her doctor's appointment, meet his unborn daughter. He said Liliane's name to the breeze, birthed her to the water and the grass, to the birds singing atop the branches and the gulls swooping down with outstretched wings.

A gap in the clouds, there, a gleam. The weather was about to turn.

For a second there was a hush. He ran. Then an ear-splitting roar, and the sky rained fire.

Massachusetts 2019

Rita

I keep a shoebox full of pictures from my time in Lebanon on a shelf in my closet. I'm in a restaurant with my family in one of the photos. Tony and I are watching the ducks from the railing next to our table. I'm thirteen, and Tony is three. My hand is extended behind me to take a large piece of bread from my mother. My father, who is sitting next to my mother, is leaning on the table with both elbows and looking at Rasha, who can be seen in profile opposite him. The photo, which is in black and white and bears the restaurant's logo at the top, was given to us as a souvenir at the end of our lunch.

The day has stayed sharp in my mind after all these years. The restaurant formed a rectangle that wrapped around the river. Trees bowed and dropped their leaves in the water, and vines grew from the stones and along the rocks below the railing. The river rushed down toward the edge, where it fell in loud, vaporous waves. A small bridge connected one side of the restaurant to the other.

I tore up the bread my mother had given me and divided it with Tony to throw at the ducks. The current was strong, and the water rushed toward the fall. But the ducks flocked to us, quacking and paddling quickly to stay in the middle of the river.

Tony clutched the bread with his small hands, releasing all of it at once. I gave him some of my pieces and showed him how to pace himself and watch for the ducks who paddled at the edges and were too timid to fight their way to the middle. Then I taught him to toss the bread in different directions to give all the ducks, not just the most aggressive ones, a chance to eat.

Tony and I were the only ones at the railing with our shower of bread and the ducks sometimes catching a piece in flight, then dunking it in water and swallowing it whole. Behind us our parents and Rasha sat at the table with plates of food laid out before them. Music blared from the loudspeakers. The silverware sparkled and white folded napkins bloomed from tall glasses. In the aisles, waiters in black suits rushed back and forth with trays of food.

In the photo, my brother and I are partly in shadow and partly in full sun, the part that was reaching out to the ducks. I remember tossing the bread in grand, studied gestures, arms sweeping wide, the bread making an arc before reaching the water. When we ran out of bread, we extended our hands for more. We did not turn to look at our mother as she passed the bread. We feared we might lose sight of the ducks if we took our eyes off for even a few seconds.

The entire transaction was conducted in silence. We had no need for words. We had been going to the same restaurant for years, standing in the same place to feed the ducks. Until recently, Rasha had joined us. But she was seventeen and had more pressing things on her mind. Behind us, she traded news and college plans with our father.

The sun glinted off certain areas in the water, blinding me. I saw only movement where the ducks clustered, quacking and pecking, their orange feet swirling the water. I squinted my eyes but could only distinguish outlines of the ducks with their white flutter and commotion. But the real story was happening behind me, in the conversation between my sister and my father, her voice trembling with excitement, his calm, and my mother's reverent silence.

One day it would be my turn to be seated at the table while Tony stood at the railing and fed the ducks. I would be the one telling my father about my future plans, while he nodded and guided and my mother sat across from us, offering her silent approval. I saw all of it with great anticipation: I was to set sail, their voices in my ear holding me up, nudging, *Go, go, you can always come back.*

Instead, the ducks moved on with the current, the restaurant of our Sunday outings closed with the war, and my father died.

Eight years into the war, I left my country for the United States. Despite the passing decades, the day of my departure is still remarkably vivid in my mind: my uncle driving us to the airport at dawn, the sky a pale blue, the sun a promise in the horizon. I drink in the Mediterranean: its dear array of colors, light's playthings, its ancient song.

My city at this early hour is still free of dust and noise, in the pre-dawn listlessness of another summer day. We eye the sky for signs of violence, but we are too drowsy after a sleepless night to marshal more than vague worries. The car speeds ahead on the empty autostrade. We hope the lull in the fighting will last until we have said our farewells and my family is safely back in our apartment.

Here we are at the airport, holding on to each other tearfully. I am leaving my family behind in the middle of a war. They are sending me off, a new bride, to the unknown. My husband is American by birth, Lebanese by descent. I like his accented Arabic. I can't say that I love him. He is giving me a lifeboat, and I am grateful. I have not met his immigrant parents, who live in Vermont. I hope we like each other. I hope that my own family will be able to follow shortly.

When our flight is announced, I let go of my mother and walk away with my new husband. On the plane I tip my head to the window and watch the tarmac rush past. The events of our last night together play in my head: Rasha helping me pack, Tony watching silently from the doorway, refusing to look me in the eye, angry with me for leaving. My mother, coming and going, busy in the kitchen, although at what at this late hour? She brings burning incense and gives me her final blessings.

The plane surges forward, piercing the air. And even though I am being lifted to better prospects, I feel the world grow dark around me.

Today I teach high school French in a small town in Massachusetts. Where I took my first steps and my present existence are worlds apart. But the past is never far. A particular smell, a small alley lined with trees brings a sharp longing. Most of all, I miss the sea.

I have been gone more than three decades. For the first few years, my husband and I would fly every year in July and spend the month with our families. The war was still raging, and when Beirut was under the bombs, we'd divide our time between Tarawa and Samir's ancestral home in the Bekaa valley.

Teta died five years after my departure. Mama, Rasha, and Tony immigrated to Canada, which had opened its doors to the Lebanese fleeing the war. Suddenly I had fewer reasons to visit Lebanon. My marriage was failing, and I stopped accompanying my husband when he flew home.

It was a while before I stopped jumping at loud noises and waking up in the middle of the night soaked in sweat. But the war stalks me. I move through life with caution, burdened with a constant sense of foreboding as close to me as my own skin. Any moment, everything I have might be taken away.

So, why dredge up the past?

Let it come, I say. The war, that bully that claims center stage—pay it the attention it craves. It must be fed before it lies still, replete with its own importance. The truth is, I have no choice—all I have from that time is linked to the war.

Sometimes the memories sweep over me like a wave. The outside world shrinks to a pulse, a flickering light, and all that remains is the grip of the water, and this aching lightness that says, in a moment it will all come to you like a flood if you don't resist. It's a dangerous seduction. I crave the memories, even as they repel me. I am nothing without them.

And so, I say: Let it come. I am tired of the dullness of an old grief.

Before Baba's death, Seta's leaving was the first acute loss I experienced. She left with her family first to Nice, where they awaited their Canadian papers, then to Montreal, where they have lived since. She sent me letters from Nice and pictures of her standing in front of an apartment building next to a bed of flowers, looking happy and tan. She seemed out of reach and safe, while for us the war raged on, and the sight of her, bathed in the glow of the flowers, filled me with envy, as though she knew good fortune that would never be mine. The ringing blue sky we shared, mine as pure as the one that appeared in her picture, seemed to envelop her with a sense of well-being it withheld from me, and as I gazed at her dear happy face, I felt a keen sense of deprivation and loss.

I visited her in Montreal when we were both in our thirties and I still wore a wedding band on my finger even though the marriage had already gone to seed. She was now a psychiatrist. We sat across the table from each other at a coffee shop on Sainte-Catherine. She had ordered a bottle of mineral water while waiting for my arrival and looked happy and fit, efficient in a new short haircut that made her face look narrower than I remembered. There was still a lot of affection between us, but there was also a little unease, as if we'd grown out of the habit of being together and were now half-strangers, affable but with a dim memory of what had once bound us.

After coffee, she took me to a restaurant in the old Montreal, and there, with a pitcher of red wine between us, something of our earlier ease returned. I told her that Schtroumpf sat on my bookshelves for years until it got lost in one of my moves, and the narcissus Auntie Sylvie gave my mother bloomed on our balcony. She told me about the last two decades, how school had been difficult at first, the Canadian French something of a puzzle, the informal interactions between students and teachers confusing. Then she spoke of her sister, Claire, who had married a renowned architect and settled happily into her roles of wife and mother.

I was a little disappointed by the news, as though a cherished figure had toppled from a pedestal. That I had expected Claire herself to become a famous architect, or something akin to that, was entirely based on my memory of her, and I suppose the letdown I experienced was the first recognition that there could never be a revival of the past. If I gleaned a sense of lost potential, I realized that the perception was something I myself, in my infatuation with Claire, had imposed on her. The future rarely mirrored the past, it seemed, as though our histories were spun from inconsistent thread. There was Seta, sitting across the table from me, as beautiful as I remembered her, yet also profoundly changed. Only the lived present was real, and then barely.

Seta dropped me off at the metro station. We embraced and promised to keep in touch, which we did regularly for a while, until our thinning threads broke again.

It was years before I saw her again. We bumped into each other in the Mont-Royal Park, where I had been sitting on a bench reading in the warm July sun. She was on her way to the store. She said she had been thinking about me lately, wondering why we never managed to keep in touch despite the short distance between us. In the years since we had seen each other, she had gotten married and had two children, a boy and a girl, both at university. I withheld from her my failed marriage. She was dressed casually in loose pants and an oversized shirt. Her face had lost none of its beauty. In our youth I had been so much in thrall to her, and the thought made me smile, as I gazed at her with affection, happy to see her still so lively and beautiful despite the passage of time. I wondered vaguely what she saw when she looked at me. When I gazed at myself in the mirror, I still saw an attractive woman, but I no longer trusted my perceptions. I led a lonely life, with few friends and fleeting romantic attachments, and I feared that my solitude might have given me a slanted view of the world.

We said goodbye at the subway entrance, vowing to stay in touch.

I was staying with my mother in her apartment on the Côte-des-Neiges Street. Rasha lived half an hour outside Montreal. She was married to a Canadian and had two boys I adored. Tony had moved to Brussels for graduate school and had settled there, marrying a Belgian woman.

I found it difficult to sleep that night. My mother had been diagnosed with Alzheimer's disease a year earlier, and the previous night I had woken to the sound of her feet as she roamed the apartment in a confused state. I worried that we were approaching the time when we would have to make difficult decisions on her behalf.

I lay awake on the living room futon, my attention straying to Seta, and eventually Claire. I remembered the argument Claire and I had all those years ago when they came over for lunch. It was much later, when I had been in the US a few years, that I finally realized my foolishness. But I was so young then, and knew so little of the world outside my immediate circle. With the war, my world had gotten smaller. We closed ranks. And as the number of deaths soared and the horrors multiplied, our hearts hardened. We were evil, as war is evil. And I recognized, in the same breath I had recognized the absurdity of my comments, that despite all the wickedness we ascribed to our enemy, we were brothers and sisters under that same dazzling sun.

A year after my second meeting with Seta, my mother lay dying in Montreal. In her Alzheimer's fog, she was back in her apartment in Beirut, her children young, her husband alive. Habibi, she said. My love. The regression might have given her some happiness, except for the excruciating pain that offered her no peace. She had been living a long time in the twilight, her brain gradually cutting its connections and forgetting the rudiments of what had made her whole. During the war we would sometimes lose track of time, and seeing her years later haunted by her disease, I thought of terror and illness as two instances where time collapsed. In the shelter, the hours had tumbled by unmarked, and without the bounds of time, we were disappearing. In the grip of her illness, my mother had, in many ways, already disappeared.

I sat by her hospital bed staring at her for long hours, trying to inscribe her traits into my memory just as I had done with Baba. She was still beautiful despite old age and the ravages of Alzheimer's that contorted her expression, once so sweet, into a permanent scowl of pain and rage. With the terrible ordeal of her lingering consciousness, she prayed for death, hollered and cursed, stomping the foot of her bed. We watched, shocked by so much anger, terrified by her new tyranny and grunginess, when she had once been so fastidious, and all the matter her body could still exude despite its fading. After a lifetime of repression, her body now wanted revenge, and the eruptive force of its final protest devastated us. At the end of her life, my mother forgot herself, and I regretted for her sake that she hadn't done so earlier, when she was still young enough to find some happiness in her recklessness.

She died on New Year's Eve, eighty-four years old to my father's forty-eight. What were the odds of such reversal? It felt like the completion of a cycle. There was nothing left of her—not her polished toes, the birthmark on her lower lip, her Dr. Scholl's sandals, or her palette of joyless colors. She was in me, that's all. I wore her watch on my wrist. In the months that followed her death I would sometimes lie motionless in bed, imagining her last days and trying to feel what she felt, pinned down by the same excruciating pain, her mind a tangle of thorns hurting and wild.

Tony and his family flew in from Brussels for the funeral. How handsome he had become, how poised and confident! He had studied astronomy and spent his days researching the stars at a university outside Brussels. It was a miracle Baba's death had not broken him, that somehow he had found the strength to outgrow the crushing loss of a father and a war that wouldn't let up. His wife was pregnant with their third child; the other two, a girl and a boy, ran around the lawn of the church where we had gathered, shrieking with happiness. They, along with Rasha's boys, who stood somberly to the side, bereaved by the death of a grandmother they had adored, filled my heart with tenderness. All that young life, just when my mother had died! I cut a strange figure next to their abundant lives. I was childless and alone, and despite my youthful appearance, I felt parched and old.

After Mama was lowered into the ground, we gathered at

Rasha's house. We were orphans. Baba's loss had forever shaken our sense of safety in the world. Our mother's death gutted us. For the first time I understood the depth of Mama's sadness after she returned from burying her own mother in Lebanon. Teta had died in the car, on her way home from the hospital. Expired like a candle. If only Mama had been this lucky.

I never dreamed of Mama after she died. I was disappointed and angry, as if she had deliberately avoided me. I needed to know that at least in death she had recovered, that her gentle soul would return to erase the terrible ordeal of the previous months, when my mother was hijacked by a monstrous illness.

But she didn't come, and following my habit of bringing up whatever I could from the past to soothe my present, I went looking for her, for all of them.

If I close my eyes I am almost there, bumping along on the mountain road in the hot July sun with the bitter taste of Dramamine in my throat. In front, I can see my father's hands on the wheel. His handkerchief lies on the console. Every now and then he passes it over his face and the back of his neck. There's my mother in the next seat, sitting with her knees angled toward him. Her hands rest on her lap, her fingers manicured and elegant.

The summer in question—the war had been raging for a year. It was Baba's final summer before his death in December.

We had been at Teta's in Tarawa, my father leaving, then returning on the weekends as was his habit. Rasha, Teta, and I would sit in the living room, laughing as the bedroom floor above us creaked with our parents' lovemaking.

I remember my first crush, Fadi. That day during the Assumption Feast I was in front, setting the pace. We had left the festivities behind, expecting to find something better ahead. We forgot the war. I stopped to tie my shoe. I did not look up, and he did not offer to help me. He waited silently for me to finish, and when I stood up and turned to smile, there he was, awash in the fading light.

Today the memory makes me smile—I love that girl and her young body, her future winding like a river, and she, in thrall, smiling, taking her first confident steps.

It was on a clear October morning, while visiting a farmer's market in a town near my home in Massachusetts, that I spotted Amal. I had recently bought a new house because it had come at a good price. I was planning to retire in a few years and downsizing seemed to be a sensible option. But although I liked many features of the house, I hated its small windows. I craved natural light, and there was little of it in my new home. As a result, I found myself spending a lot more time outdoors, seeking the sunlight with an increasing sense of urgency as the cold months loomed ahead. The prospect of throwing all caution to the wind, putting the house on the market, and finding something more to my liking, grew more appealing with every passing day.

I was heading toward the flower stand, lured by the stalks of sunflowers sticking up from a bucket and imagining them already on my kitchen table, when my gaze fell on a woman standing a few feet away at the adjoining stand. She was pointing to a pile of sweet potatoes and asking the farmer for two pounds in a thickly accented English. He said something, and when she laughed, I felt a sudden rush of giddiness and shock that made me reach for a nearby table to keep myself steady.

I could have recognized that laugh anywhere. I stared in disbelief as she opened the top of a folding dolly cart that stood at her side and put the potatoes inside. Once again she laughed as she held a big cabbage and shook it as though it might rattle, then slid it into the cart and paid.

Yet I hesitated to approach her. After all these years, I was still ashamed of the pain I had caused her. Finally, I called her name. When she turned and looked at me, her face at first puzzled, then flushed with the shock of recognition before it lit up with a wide grin, it was all I could do not to burst into tears.

We rushed into each other's arms, laughing and talking over

each other, shocked to find ourselves in a small New England town after decades of being apart. As Amal dragged the cart behind her, she slid her arm through mine and led us both to a nearby coffee shop.

I ordered coffee while she had a soda. Since it was almost noon, we decided to have lunch. Time had been kind to her, and I could still see the fourteen-year-old girl I remembered. I'd noticed it in my sister, then in Seta when I met her in Montreal, and of course in myself, how a sliver of youth would suddenly flash and animate our features, and our childhood selves would flicker through the layers of age. Yet our faces looked different, the musculature and skeletal structure altered, and although we were still middle-aged, I knew there would come a time when we seemed dramatically other than who we had once been. We were all being led toward a common ending, our bodies transformed in preparation. I remembered seeing death on my mother's face even before she took her last breath, having seen it on my father before. Both appeared alien and unattainable, half-gone.

These were morbid thoughts, yet I couldn't help reflecting about time passing, especially as I was fast approaching sixty.

I told Amal how great she looked. Her face was still lovely. Her blond hair, which had been short in youth, now fell to her shoulders. She asked if I colored my hair, and when I said yes, she teased me and said no dye had ever touched hers. I said that she was lucky because the gray, which she most certainly had in abundance, blended with her naturally light hair, and that she would have been a regular at the hair salon if she had been born with my dark mane.

She was living in a small town in New Jersey. She and her American husband had met at the American Embassy in Beirut, where she had worked after college. They left shortly before the embassy was bombed, and after a long stint in the Arabian Gulf, they returned to her husband's native New Jersey with their three children, who were now scattered along the West Coast. After telling me that she was visiting her sister-in-law who lived a few miles away, she struck her forehead and said how foolish she was not to have invited me over for a proper meal instead of the two sorry chicken salads we had ordered.

She talked as fast as I remembered, breathlessly, as though she were being chased and she had to deliver her speech before she got caught. She asked whether I had any children, and I told her I'd had two miscarriages before my husband and I decided to stop trying. I said nothing about my failed marriage. Only Rasha and Tony knew of our separation. Even after all these years I still felt the shackles of convention, and it was easier to pretend that I was still married. Technically, I was.

We fell to a few moments of silence as we picked through our salads. I put down my fork and apologized for my behavior in school. She looked genuinely surprised. She thought I had behaved far better than most. She could tell I had been thrown by the news of her unconventional family and had struggled to make sense of it. It was normal, she added, under the circumstances.

I told her that after graduating from high school I enrolled in a French literature program, but classes were frequently disrupted because of the fighting. It was here, at the local university, that I completed my degree, then obtained my teaching credentials and began teaching French at the high school. Then I asked where she had gone with her family following their disappearance. Laughing, she responded that *disappearance* was a strong word; it made her think of spy movies in which people went underground. They had simply decided to live in their native village, where she attended a boring and mediocre school and learned practically nothing. It was a wonder she went to college in Beirut after graduation, and after that to law school. "You're a lawyer!" I exclaimed. "Yes," she responded proudly. She had worked at a successful firm in Beirut but retired after coming to the US. The prospect of taking classes and starting from scratch as a junior lawyer was daunting.

I told her I stuck with Sacré Coeur until graduation. She asked about Seta, and this naturally led to Monsieur Sami. The memory of Seta screaming out her adolescent love at our math teacher must have been burned in the memory of every girl who attended the retreat that year. She asked if Monsieur Sami ever came back. I said he did, a year before my graduation, when he visited the school with his new wife. I wondered about the impact our teasing had had on him. His wife was beautiful and appeared kind. She seemed to give him something of her own poise and confidence, and we agreed that it was a good thing, and that we had been terrible to him and felt genuinely sorry about all the teasing we had inflicted.

We talked until the waiter asked if we were ready for the check. A line had formed at the door. We paid and left. Amal asked if I had any more time to chat, and when I said yes, she led me to her car, where she dropped off her groceries. I smiled to see she had an Audi, a popular make in Lebanon. Despite her American husband, she maintained her Lebanese manners, as evidenced by the numerous pieces of jewelry she wore. Every inch of her was meticulously cared for, and next to her I felt messy and plain.

There was a park across the street. We found a bench near a small pond with a family of ducks paddling through. With the golden light growing warmer as the afternoon wore on, and the piles of red and orange leaves strewn along the edge of the water and under the trees, we fell to quiet, our mood now pensive. Suddenly Amal said she had struggled with the strange circumstances of her family's religions. When the war broke out she was in agony, feeling constantly afraid of being found out. So when the news broke, she wasn't surprised, but in her fear she thought something terrible would happen to her. When I asked what she was afraid of, she said she would lie awake at night picturing Christian militants barging through their door and kidnapping her parents.

In college she fell in love with a Muslim man. He lived in West Beirut and the two would meet at the crossing line between the two halves of the city, a no-man's-land overtaken by rubble and wild vegetation. Oddly, she felt most at peace there. In the warm months, the plants sprouting from the wreckage grew thick and tangled, giving the place its second name, the Green Line. Despite their dangerous meeting spot, she felt more alive there, with the man she loved and who loved her back, than she did when she lived on her side of the city, attending classes and hiding in shelters. When I asked what happened to him, she waved her hand to say it ended a long time ago, and added, laughing, that when she met her American husband there was no turning back.

She then mentioned Monsieur Bassil. I explained I hadn't seen him since graduation. "You had a crush on him, didn't you?" she asked, narrowing her eyes.

"Of course not!" I exclaimed. "Why would you say that?" I wasn't lying. It had been more than just a crush. He was my guide and mentor during a difficult time.

I told her about our lunches, how kindly he would listen as I told him about my sadness and confusion. I said we lost touch after I graduated, but I assumed he continued to teach until retirement. He might have been in his thirties back then, I said, although I couldn't be sure.

"You did not hear?" she asked.

Something in her expression scared me. I shook my head.

"He was at the American embassy when it exploded," she said. "No part of his body was ever found. They looked for him for months. Every day they would search the body bags and make inquiries, but he could not be found. It was immensely sad to see his pregnant wife and young child at the funeral. Sometime later, his wife found several pieces of his writing hidden in his closet and sent them to a publisher. The book came out on the first anniversary of his disappearance."

The tears pricked my eyes. I was surprised to learn he was a father. To me he had never been anything but my Arabic teacher, without family attachments. Over the years it didn't occur to me to look him up on the internet. In the early years, marriage and separation from my immediate family kept me tethered to the past. But once my marriage ended and my family relocated to Canada, I strived to break ties with my birth country, preferring to live in my memories.

I remembered our lunch sessions with extreme fondness. I had kept the letter he wrote in response to my essay about the war. To be seen and acknowledged was a turning point. In a time of crisis, in all the years where I felt lost in a new country, I would reach back for the memories, and he would be there, talking to me in that calm way he possessed, and his image would warm my spirit.

"Write your address here," she said, handing me a small notebook. "I will send you a copy of his book."

I did as she asked, my eyes welling up with tears.

"I was at the embassy in June of 1983 getting my own visa," I said, handing her back the paper. "To think that he was there in April of that same year!"

I recalled waiting in line in the hot sun while jumpy American soldiers yelled at us in an English we barely understood. The realization that he had died violently on the same grounds just a few months before broke my heart. Amal placed a hand on my arm. I finally cried.

After a while, she said she was expected and rose to her feet. By then I had calmed down. We said goodbye next to her car. I walked slowly to mine. Despite my assurances, my heart was still heavy.

When I got home, I ran to the attic and looked in the suitcase where I kept my mementos. I retrieved a reading journal full of meticulous notes about the books I was reading. Leafing through the pages, I found my notes about Monsieur Bassil's books. Then there was the piece I wrote when the war was closing its jaws around my throat and life seemed extremely bleak. A voice sprang into my head, and every time I felt hopeless, this voice talked to me. I remembered how much relief it gave me to write it down the way Monsieur Bassil had directed me, so that it would be there for me to come back to again and again, like a prayer that helped me get through those difficult times. He was right—it was my own voice, drawn from a power

I didn't know I possessed, showing me the path to resilience. I never heard it again, but it may have blended wonderfully with my own voice, and looking back, I had acquired that resilience of the spirit that I had attributed to that guiding voice.

My connection with Monsieur Bassil lasted a short while after my father's death, then petered out after the tenth grade. My classes were on the top floor, and I had different Arabic teachers. Occasionally we would bump into each other on the stairs and stop for a chat. After graduation, I lost sight of him altogether.

"We are the trodden, Rita," I heard his voice saying.

At the bottom of the page, these words I had scribbled in capital letters: ESCAPE, MADEMOISELLE SFEIR, OR SURVIVAL??

Amal was true to her word—the book arrived in the mail a week after our encounter. It was a slim volume that bore the title of its final piece, *A Guide to Surviving War*. In a corner of the cover, there was a picture of red roses in bloom, and across the page, more roses were outlined in dark strokes, slithering upward like snakes. In the distance, a field of flowers rose in a constellation of red and purple, and in the middle, at the bottom of the page, lay a dark and shapeless mass from which protruded what appeared to be gun barrels.

I put the book on my nightstand without opening it. A week would elapse before I picked it up and ran my fingers across the soft cover and the title, then down to his name etched in white letters. And as I did, all the anguish of those years rose in me, as did the power that had drawn me to his words. I felt the pull of his mind and his profound kindness. My adolescent mind had seen in him a window to a world my parents alone could not have provided. And as I got to know him better during our lunch encounters, I recognized in him, despite the years between us, a kindred spirit who, like me, saw in books not simply inspiration and the aesthetic pleasure of good and solid writing, but also a moral guide that lit our way in those dark times.

I opened the book. A brief foreword described how the manuscript came to be discovered. I read it all in one long sitting, pausing to breathe and give free rein to the tears. The horror flashed through my mind, and the same fear I'd known returned as if it had never left. Yet I also saw and heard him in the words, this time through the eyes of a grown woman, and my fondness for him grew. In my own teaching I had long stuck to the safety of academics, my demeanor toward my students full of encouragement and honest praise and yet fundamentally distant. But every now and again a student would strike me with her unusual potential, or something of our common humanity would shine in her face, and I would reach out and experience the satisfaction of a connection Monsieur Bassil had practiced daily.

Around the middle of the book was this short paragraph:

You will rise from the terrible wreckage. War cannot break the dance of life, which has no bounds. You will be in the flicker of light and the sighs of the waves, in the words that freeze time, in my memory as I am in yours, in the unbreakable bond of our atoms and the threaded sprinkles of our breath upon the tumbling years.

Tears streamed down my cheeks as I read it over and over. And he was here with me, helping me in a land I had still not made my own, despite all the years of living here, waking to a light that fell softly upon my lids without awakening my senses. His words gave me back my past. There it was again—all that I had lost. I thanked him and wished him peace.

For the first time in two decades, I am back in Lebanon. I return to my grandmother's house in Tarawa. I go down the stone steps that lead to the garden, stand at the bottom, and take stock: to my left is a short stone wall that borders what used to be the herb and vegetable patch. Rows of parsley, basil, and thyme preceded the tomatoes and cucumbers. Sometimes my grandmother planted green beans and zucchini along with various kinds of lettuce. The mint went rampant. Today nothing has remained except the stained concrete and scattered debris swept up by the wind.

Turn and face the house. Above the garden there's the kitchen and a ledge jutting out over the garden and leading to the bathroom. When my sister was two, she fell and landed in the garden. Panicked, my mother ran to jump after her, but my uncle caught her in time and led her down the steps, and by that time my sister was already up, brushing herself off.

Look straight ahead, right next to the herb garden. There are the two long flower beds, my grandmother's pride and joy. They are empty except for a few clumps of desiccated dirt.

Next to the steps is a room without a door. Many years ago, it was the root cellar. Later, it stored wood planks and big rolls of plastic and scraps of metal for my uncle's various building projects. I go in. The floor is covered with broken concrete. A bucket filled with dried mortar sits in the corner, latticed by cobwebs.

I turn away and stand in the doorway, facing the empty wall where my uncle's cot once stood. I remember lying down under the grapevine trellis, with the sun filtering through the leaves and clusters of green grapes. At night, the moon shone on the leaves. I would sit with my uncle listening to the cicadas. How wonderful it would be to sleep under the stars! I thought. But I didn't dare because of the bees. The trellis is gone, as is the Spanish fountain that stood in the middle. After my uncle died, the house remained shuttered for years until my aunt, the only surviving member of the family, hired an old housekeeper who came once a week and did some light upkeep.

I climb the stairs and enter through the kitchen. There's the same big stone sink, the white refrigerator and the stove under the window. A hanging pantry in the corner used to keep the food safe from the ants. In the corner stood a giant stone mortar and pestle, where my grandmother pounded goat meat for kibbeh.

Next to the kitchen is the room where my grandmother slept. In the winter, the room became the center of the house. My uncle installed a wood stove, and that's where he and my grandmother spent most of their time because the rest of the house was freezing. After Baba died, we spent a lot of time in Tarawa while the battles raged in Beirut, and I experienced the harsh winters of the mountain and my first snowstorm. My grandmother loved roasting chestnuts and potato slices on the stove. I'd huddle next to her on the sofa eating whatever she offered, my throat scratchy from the smoke.

The living room has a few straw chairs strewn against the walls, a worn rug with complicated patterns in the center. The yellow and plum sofas and the wall rug with the deer are still there, faded with age, and the window where I stood for hours hoping to catch a glimpse of Fadi is grimy with neglect.

The bedrooms are on the second floor. I pause in the doorway. It was there where I learned of my father's death on that beautiful December morning. The details of that sad day are still seared in my memory. I enter my uncle's bedroom and find his bed still in the corner, the bookshelf stacked with books. I loved the room and would sleep there whenever he was away. There were always things to read, and from the small window I could follow the comings and goings in the back alley and watch the sunset farther to the west.

It was in Tarawa where my parents fell in love, and my father courted my mother in the house I still call my grandmother's house, with its creaky floor and thick stone walls and red-tiled roof, with its garden fountain and buzzing bees. Even though it is only the house of my summer vacations and my escape from the war, when I return to my past it is the first thing I seek, the primary object of my longing.

I spend the last week of my stay in Beirut in a small apartment by the sea. After all this time the city is unrecognizable, with so many new highways and cars. There is no place to walk in this transformed city. Our apartment building looks ugly and neglected, the paint peeled and stained with mildew. I go to the city center, to what we used to call West Beirut. No one uses the term anymore, but the lines still exist, obscured by a new will to move on. I recognize very little: the Domtex building where my mother bought linens; the long walk down the hill to the sea; the corniche where we walked on Sundays with cotton-candy cones in our hands. After that, I get back in my car and drive to my school. I stand outside without going in. There's the green gate. I imagine the buses lined up before dismissal, the girls sleepy at their desks, impatient for the bell. But it is July, and the school is empty. I push on.

I walk the streets whose names became famous during the war. The buildings still wear their scars. I walk for long hours. One day, strolling through the streets of old Jounieh, I go down a small alley and come face to face with the water. I stand on the shore, the Mediterranean only a few feet away with nothing between us, and I can feel its breath on my face.

Hello, old friend, I say, and burst into tears.

I was a girl once. We lived on a small pinch of land by the sea before our world came to a halt.

I brought my dead back, the memories flicking like prayer beads.

Rita, Mama trills, her voice rising in the song of dawn.

My little lamb, Baba says softly, his lips on my head.

There's an expanse of sea, an undulation of mountains.

ACKNOWLEDGMENTS

Thank you:

To the most generous friends and readers I could have asked for: Sabine Charton-Long, Justine Dymond, Rana Knio, Elizabeth Porto, Julie Rivera, Kamila Shamsie, and Pam Thompson.

To Liza Birnbaum, Anne Horowitz, and Shana Kelly, for your excellent comments.

To Will Barnes, Nadine Karel, Gunter Löffler, Vera Mark, and Meg Soyers Van Hauen for your inspiring company along the way.

To Jaynie Royal and everyone at Regal House Publishing for your confidence and support.

To my sister and brother, in remembrance of our parents.

To Martin, for all the good conversations and endless encouragement, and for dancing with me.

And to James and Nicholas, my habibis.

Book Club Questions

1. What is the significance of the title?
2. How has the war affected Hisham and Rita? How does it change them?
3. Have you read other books about Lebanon? How much did you know about the events that led up to the civil war before reading *We Walked On*? Did the novel bring you a new perspective on any events you were already familiar with?
4. Hisham and Rita take turns narrating their stories. What effect did this have on your reading of the novel?
5. Hisham writes to deal with the violence and gain a better understanding of the war from various perspectives. He advises Rita to do the same. How did their writings affect your reading of the novel?